STRANGE CONFLICT

The Admiral paused for a moment, then went on with quiet grimness . . .

'Like a drowning man I'm prepared to clutch at any straw, and there's something about you which somehow gives me the wild hope that instead of a straw you may prove a life saving raft.' He stood up and held out his hand. 'For God's sake do your damn'dest.'

'I will,' said the Duke, and he added a phrase of which he alone knew the true significance. 'I'll get to the bottom of this even if I have to go to Hell to do it.'

Dennis Wheatley

STRANGE
CONFLICT

ARROW BOOKS

Arrow Books Limited
3 Fitzroy Square, London W1

An imprint of the Hutchinson Publishing Group

London Melbourne Sydney Auckland
Wellington Johannesburg and agencies
throughout the world

First published by
Hutchinson & Co (Publishers) Ltd 1941
Arrow edition 1959
Second impression 1961
Third impression 1965
Fifth impression 1969
This new edition 1969
Second impression 1969
Third impression 1970
Fourth impression 1971
Fifth impression 1973
Sixth impression 1974
Seventh impression 1974
Eighth impression 1975
Ninth impression 1978

Made and printed in Great Britain
by The Anchor Press Ltd
Tiptree, Essex

ISBN 0 09 908900 9

1

A Fantastic Theory

The Duke de Richleau and Sir Pellinore Gwaine-Cust had gone into dinner at eight o'clock, but coffee was not served till after ten.

The war had been in progress for many months and the bombing of London for some weeks. A small shower of incendiary bombs having fallen in Curzon Street, just outside the Duke's flat, had caused an interruption of the meal while they went down to lend a hand in extinguishing them, but both were by now so hardened to the blitzkrieg that after a wash they returned to the table as though nothing very out-of-the-ordinary had happened.

The Duke and his guest had much in common. Both had been blessed with an ancient name, good looks, brains and charm, which had made them outstanding figures in the European society of their day. That day was passing, but they had made the most of it and regretted nothing of their tempestuous early years when they had fought and loved to the limit of their capacity, or the quiet period that had followed, during which they had dabbled most successfully in high finance and played a hand in many of the secret moves behind the diplomatic scene. That a better world might emerge with the passing of the privileged caste that they represented they both hoped, but rather doubted, and as each was unshakably convinced that it would not do so if the Nazis were not utterly destroyed it is doubtful if Hitler had two more inveterate enemies.

These men had lived their lives, and it meant very little to them now if they lost them. They had no jobs to lose, no favours to seek, no ambition which was not already satisfied, and neither acknowledged any master except the King of England; so they said what they thought, often with brutal frankness, and used every ounce of power and prestige that they possessed, through their many contacts in high places, to force the pace of the war regardless of all considerations except that of Victory.

Although they had so much in common, they were very different in appearance. Sir Pellinore, who was considerably the older of the two, stood six feet two in his socks. He had a head of fine white hair, bright blue eyes, a great sweeping cavalry moustache, a booming voice and an abrupt, forthright way of speaking. The Duke was a slim, delicate-looking man, somewhat above middle height, with slender, fragile hands and greying hair but with no trace of weakness in his fine, distinguished face. His aquiline nose, broad forehead and grey 'devil's' eyebrows might well have replaced those of the Cavalier in the Van Dyck that gazed down from the wall opposite his chair.

It would have been utterly against the principles of either to allow the war to interfere with their custom of changing for dinner, but instead of the conventional black the Duke wore a claret-coloured vicuna smoking-suit with silk lapels and braided fastenings. This touch of colour increased his likeness to the portrait.

During dinner they had talked of the war, but when coffee was served there fell a short silence as Max, the Duke's man, produced the long Hoyo de Monterrey cigars which were his master's especial pride, and the Duke was thinking: 'Now I shall learn what old Gwaine-Cust really wanted to see me about. I'll bet a monkey that he didn't propose himself for dinner here just to discuss the general situation.

As Max left the quiet, candle-lit room the anti-aircraft guns in Hyde Park came into action, shattering the silence. Sir Pellinore looked across, and said a little thoughtfully:

'Wonder you stay here with this damn'd racket goin' on night after night.'

De Richleau shrugged. 'I don't find the bombing particularly terrifying. Perhaps that's because London covers such a vast area. Anyhow, it's child's play compared to some of the bombardments which I have survived in other wars. I think that American journalist hit the nail on the head when he said that at this rate it would take the Nazis two thousand weeks to destroy London and he didn't think that Hitler had another forty years to live.'

'Damn' good!' guffawed Sir Pellinore. 'Damn' good! All the same, it makes things deuced uncomfortable. They've outed two of my clubs, and it's the devil's own job to get hold of one's friends on the telephone. As you've no job that ties you here I wonder you don't clear out to the country.'

'For that matter, my dear fellow, why don't you—since you're in the same category? Or has the Government had the wisdom to avail itself of your services?'

'Good Lord, no! They've no time for old fogeys like me, They're right, too. This is a young man's war. Still, it wouldn't be a good show if some of us didn't stick it when there are so many people who darned well have to.'

'Exactly,' replied the Duke smoothly. 'And that is the answer to your own question. I loathe discomfort and boredom, but no amount of either would induce me to leave London when there are such thousands of poor people who cannot afford to do so.'

There was another silence as de Richleau waited with inward amusement for Sir Pellinore to make a fresh opening, and after a moment the elderly Baronet said:

'Of course, by staying on one is able to keep in touch with things. The very fact of knowing a lot of people enables me to push the boat along here and there.'

A mocking little smile lit the Duke's grey eyes, which at times could flash with such piercing brilliance. 'Perhaps, then, you would like to tell me in which particular direction you are now contemplating pushing *my* canoe?'

'Ha!' Sir Pellinore brushed up his fine cavalry moustache. 'You're a shrewd feller—always were. I might have known you'd guess that I didn't ask myself here for the sake of your drink and cigars, superb as they are. I've hardly seen you alone for a moment, though, since the slaughter started; so d'you mind telling me what you've been up to so far? I'm damned certain you haven't been idle.'

The smile moved to de Richleau's strong, thin-lipped mouth. 'I have fought in many wars, but I am too old to become again a junior officer and far too young in temperament ever to become a Civil Servant; so, like yourself, I have not even the status of an unpaid A.R.P. Warden. In consequence, you will forgive me if I suggest that neither of us has any right to question the other.'

'You old fox! Cornered me, eh? All right. I'm close to the War Cabinet. *Why,* God knows! But some of the people there still seem to think I'm useful, although everybody knows that I've no brains. I've always had an eye for a horse or a pretty woman and an infinite capacity for vintage port; but no brains—no brains at all.'

'That,' murmured the Duke, 'accounts for the fact that after being compelled to leave the Army because of your debts, somewhere way back in the '90's, you managed to amass a fortune of a cool ten million. Am I to take it that you have been sent to see me?'

'No. But it amounts to the same thing. My powers are pretty wide. I can't get people shot, as I would like to, for criminal negligence, but I've been instrumental in getting some of our slower movers sacked, and most of my recommendations go through except where they come into direct conflict with government policy. Unofficially, too, I've been able to initiate various little matters which have given the Nazis a pain in the neck. We're all in this thing together, and when I saw you admiring the ducks in St. James's Park the other day I had a hunch that you might be the very man to help us in something that at the moment is giving the Government very grave concern. *Now* will you tell me what you've been up to?'

De Richleau swivelled the old brandy in the medium-sized ballon-shaped glass that he was holding, sniffed its ethers appreciatively and replied: 'Certainly. Before Britain declared war on Germany I flew with some friends of mine to Poland.'

Sir Pellinore gave him a sharp glance. 'The fellers who accompanied you on your Russian and Spanish exploits? I remember hearing about your adventures in the Forbidden Territory and later that fantastic story of the eight million pounds in gold that the four of you got out of Spain during the Civil War. One was the son of old Channock Van Ryn, the American banker, wasn't he? I've never met the other two, but I'd like to some time.'

'Rex Van Ryn is the one of whom you're thinking; the

8

other two are Richard Eaton and Simon Aron. All three of them were with me through the Polish Campaign. What we did there is far too long a story to tell now, but I'll give it to you some time. We got out by the skin of our teeth in a manner which was most inconvenient for certain persons; but, that, of course, was entirely their affair for trying to stop us. When we eventually arrived back in England no particular opening offered in which we could work together, so we decided to split up.'

'What happened to the others?'

'Rex, as you may know, is an ace airman, and although he's an American citizen he managed to wangle his way into the Royal Air Force. He did magnificent work in the battles of August and September and was awarded the D.F.C.; but early in October he ran into a flock of Nazis where the odds were six to one, and they got him. His left leg was badly smashed. He's well on the road to recovery now, but I'm afraid his wounds will prevent him from flying as a fighter-pilot any more.

'Simon Aron went back to his counting-house. He is a director of one of our big financial houses and he felt that he could give his best service to the country by helping the dollar position and in all the intricacies of foreign exchange that he understands so well.

'Richard Eaton is an airman, too, but he's over age for a fighter-pilot so they wouldn't take him—which made poor Richard very sick. But he has a big place down in Worcestershire, so he went in at once for intensive farming. However, he comes to London now and again to console himself for not being able to do anything more actively offensive in the war, by helping me in one or two little jobs that I've been fortunate enough to be able to take on.'

'What sort of jobs?' boomed Sir Pellinore.

'Details would only bore you but, like yourself, I have many friends and I also speak several languages with considerable fluency, so here and there I've been tipped off to keep my eyes open and I've been successful in putting a number of unpleasant people behind the bars. Incidentally, I made a secret trip to Czechoslovakia last spring and I've been in the Low Countries since the German occupation—in fact, I only got back last week. But of course I have no official position—no official position at all.'

9

Sir Pellinore's blue eyes twinkled. 'You certainly haven't let the grass grow under your feet. As a matter of fact, I had it through official channels that you had been making yourself pretty useful in a variety of ways, because I made inquiries before coming along to see you tonight, although I didn't press for details. What are you up to now?'

'Nothing of any great importance. Just keeping my eye on a few people who in any other country but this would have been put against a wall well over a year ago, and trying to trace various leakages of information which come from people who regard themselves as patriotic citizens but talk too much to the ladies of their acquaintance. There is nothing at all to prevent me from packing a bag and leaving for Kamchatka or Peru tomorrow morning if you feel that by so doing I could drive another nail into Hitler's coffin.'

'That's the sort of thing I like to hear,' roared Sir Pellinore. 'Wish to God some of the people in our government departments showed the same keenness to get these German swine under. But I don't think we'll have to call on you even to leave London—although one can never tell. It's the use of that fine brain of yours I want, and you mentioned the subject yourself only a moment ago when you spoke of leakage of information.'

De Richleau raised his slanting eyebrows. 'I shouldn't have thought there was any grave cause to worry about that. Even the smallest indiscretions should be jumped on, of course, but from all I've gathered very little important stuff has got through since all normal communications with the Continent was severed after the collapse of France.'

'In a way you're right.' Sir Pellinore nodded his white head. 'We ourselves were amazed in the difference that made. For example, when the first major air-attacks on this country started many of us were acutely anxious about the Air Force. We feared that by sheer weight of numbers the Germans would smash more planes on the ground than we could possibly afford to lose. As everybody knows now, we cleared all our airfields on the south and east coasts before the attack developed, so that there was nothing left for the Nazis to smash except the empty hangars and machine shops. Directly they had done that we expected them to start on our new bases, but they didn't; they kept on hammering day after day at the old ones when there was nothing left but burnt-out sheds for them to strike at; which proved quite definitely that they hadn't the faintest idea that we had ever shifted our planes at all. That's ancient history now, of course, but in all sorts of other ways the same thing has gone on in recent months, demonstrating beyond doubt that once the German agents here were cut off from the Continent their whole system of conveying information speedily to the enemy had broken down.'

'I don't understand, then, what you're worrying about.'

'The fact that it has not broken down in one particular direction. The biggest menace that we're up against at the moment is our shipping losses, and the extraordinary thing is that although the Nazis now seem to have only the vaguest idea of what is going on here in every other direction, they have our shipping arrangements absolutely taped. Naturally, every convoy that sails to or from America is sent by a different route. Sometimes they go right up into the Arctic, sometimes as far south as Madeira, and sometimes dead-straight across; but, whichever way we choose, the Nazis seem to know about it. They meet each convoy in mid-Atlantic after its escort has left it, just as though they were keeping a prearranged appointment.'

'That *is* pretty grim.'

'Yes. It's no laughing matter; and to be quite honest we're at our wits' end. The Navy is working night and day, and the Air Arm too; but the sea and sky are big places. Our Intelligence people have done their damn'dest—and they're pretty hot—whatever uninformed people may think about them—but just this one thing seems to have got them beaten.'

'Why should you imagine that I might succeed where the best brains in our Intelligence have failed?' asked the Duke mildly.

'Because I feel that our only chance now is to get an entirely fresh mind on the subject; someone who isn't fogged by knowing too much detail and having his nose too close to the charts, yet someone who has imagination and a great reservoir of general knowledge. The Nazis must be using some channel which is quite outside normal espionage methods—the sort of thing to which there is no clue but that anyone with a shrewd mind might happen on by chance.

11

That's why, when I saw you the other day, it occurred to me that it might be a good idea to put this damnable problem up to you.'

De Richleau stared at Sir Pellinore for a moment. 'You are absolutely certain that the Nazi Intelligence are not using any normal method of communication in this thing?'

'Absolutely. The fact that all sorts of other vital information does not get through proves it.'

'Then, if they are not using normal methods, they must be using subnormal—or rather, the supernatural.'

It was Sir Pellinore's turn to stare. 'What the blazes d'you mean?' he boomed abruptly.

The Duke leant forward and gently knocked the inch-long piece of ash from his cigar into the onyx ash-tray as he said: 'That they are using what for lack of a better term is called Black Magic.'

'You're joking!' gasped Sir Pellinore.

'On the contrary,' said the Duke quietly: 'I was never more serious in my life.'

2

Believe It or Not

A strange expression crept into Sir Pellinore's blue eyes. He had known the Duke for many years, but never intimately; only as one of that vast army of acquaintances who drifted across his path from time to time for a brief week-end at a country-house, in the smoking-room of a West End club or during the season at fashionable resorts such as Deauville. He had often heard de Richleau spoken of as a man of dauntless courage and infinite resource, but also as a person whom normal people might well regard as eccentric. The Duke had never been seen in a bowler-hat or wielding that emblem of English respectability, an umbrella. Instead, when he walked abroad he carried a beautiful Malacca cane. In peace-time he drove about London in a huge silver Hispano with a chauffeur and footman on the box, both dressed like Cossacks and wearing tall, grey, astrakhan *papenkas*. Some people considered that the most vulgar ostentation, while to the Duke himself it was only a deplorable substitute for the sixteen outriders who had habitually preceded his forebears in more spacious days. Sir Pellinore being a broad-minded man had put these little foibles down to the Duke's foreign ancestry, but it now occurred to him that in some respects de Richleau had probably always been slightly abnormal and that, although he appeared perfectly sane, a near miss from a Nazi bomb might recently have unhinged his brain.

'Black Magic, eh?' he said with unwonted gentleness. 'Most interesting theory. Well, if you—er—get any more ideas on the subject you must let me know.'

'I shall be delighted to do so,' replied the Duke with suave courtesy. 'And now I will tell you what has just been passing through your mind. You have been thinking: "I've drawn a blank here; this fellow's no good; he's got a screw loose; probably sustained concussion in an air-raid. Pity, as I was rather hoping that he might produce some practical suggestions for the Intelligence people to work on. As it is, I must remember to tell my secretary to put him off politely if he rings up—one can't waste time with fellows who've gone nuts, while there's a war on." '

'Damme!' Sir Pellinore thumped the table with his huge fist. 'You're right, Duke; I admit it. But you must agree that no sane person could take your suggestion seriously.'

'I wouldn't go as far as that, but I would agree that anyone who has no personal knowledge of the occult is quite entitled to disbelieve in it. I assume that you've never witnessed the materialisation of an astral force or, to put it into common parlance "seen a ghost" with your own eyes?'

'Never,' said Sir Pellinore emphatically.

'D'you know anything of hypnotism?'

'Yes. As a matter of fact, I'm gifted with slight hypnotic powers myself. When I was a young man I sometimes used to amuse my friends by giving mild demonstrations, and I've often found that I can make people do minor things, such as opening up on a particular subject, merely by willing them to do so.'

'Good. Then at least we're at one on the fact that certain forces can be called into play which the average person does not understand.'

'I suppose so, within limits.'

'Why "within limits"? Surely, fifty years ago you would have considered wireless to be utterly outside such limits if somebody had endeavoured to convince you that messages and even pictures could be transferred from one end of the world to the other upon ether waves.'

'Of course,' Sir Pellinore boomed. 'But wireless is different; and as for hypnotism, that's simply the power of the human will.'

'Ah, there you have it.' The Duke sat forward suddenly. *The will to good* and *the will to evil.* That is the whole matter in a nutshell. The human will is like a wireless set

14

and when properly adjusted can tune in with the invisible influences which are all about us.'

'Invisible influences, eh? No, I'm sorry, Duke, I just don't believe in such things.'

'Do you believe in the miracles performed by Jesus Christ?'

'Yes. I'm old-fashioned enough to have remained an unquestioning believer in the Christian faith, although God knows I've committed enough sins in my time.'

'You also believe, then, in the miracles performed by Christ's disciples and certain of the Saints?'

'I do. But they had some special powers granted to them.'

'Exactly. *Special powers.* But I suppose you would deny that Gautama Buddha and his disciples performed miracles of a similar nature?'

'Not a bit of it. I'm sufficiently broad-minded to believe that Buddha was a sort of Indian Christ, or at least a very holy man, and no doubt he, too, had some special power granted to him.'

'Then if you admit that miracles, as you call them—although you object to the word *Magic*—have been performed by two men of different faiths, living in different countries and in periods hundreds of years apart, you can't reasonably deny that other mystics have also performed similar acts in many portions of the globe and, therefore, that there is a power existing outside us which is *not peculiar to any religion* but can be utilised if one can get into communication with it.'

Sir Pellinore laughed. 'I've never looked at it that way before, but I suppose you're right.'

De Richleau poured another portion of the old brandy into his friend's glass as Sir Pellinore went on more slowly.

'All the same, it doesn't follow that because a number of good men have been granted supernatural powers there is anything in Black Magic.'

'Then you do not believe in witchcraft?'

'Nobody does these days.'

'Really? How long d'you think it is since the last trial for witchcraft took place?'

'Two hundred years.'

'No. It was in January 1926, at Melun, near Paris.'

'God bless my soul! D'you mean that?'

15

'I do,' de Richlaeau assured him solemnly. 'The records of the court are the proof of it; so, you see, you are hardly accurate when you say that *nobody* believes in witchcraft in these days; and many, many thousands still believe in a personal Devil.'

'Central European peasants, perhaps, but not educated people.'

'Yet every thinking man must admit that there is such a thing as the power of Evil.'

'Why?'

'My dear fellow, all qualities have their opposites, like love and hate, pleasure and pain, generosity and avarice. How could we recognise the goodness of Jesus Christ, Lao-Tze, Ashoka, Marcus Aurelius, Francis of Assisi, and thousands of others, if it were not for the evil lives of Herod, Cesare Borgia, Rasputin, Landru and the rest?'

'That's true.'

'Then, if an intensive cultivation of Good can beget strange powers, is there any reason why an intensive cultivation of Evil should not beget them also?'

'That sounds feasible.'

'I hope I'm not boring you; but just on the off-chance that there might be something in my suggestion that the Nazis are using occult forces to get information out of this country, I think it is really important that you should understand the theory of the occult, since you appear to know so little about it.'

'Go ahead, go ahead.' Sir Pellinore waved a large hand. 'Mind you, I don't say that I'm prepared to take for granted everything you may tell me, but you certainly won't bore me.'

De Richleau sat forward. 'Very well; I'll try and expound to you the simple rudiments of the Old Wisdom which has come down to us through the ages. You will have heard of the Persian myth of Ormuzd and Ahriman, the eternal powers of Light and Darkness, said to be co-equal and warring without cessation for the good or ill of mankind. All ancient Sun and Nature worship—Festivals of Spring and so on—were only an outward expression of that myth, for Light typifies Health and Wisdom, Growth and Life, while Darkness means Disease and Ignorance, Decay and Death.

'In its highest sense Light symbolises the growth of the spirit towards that perfection in which it becomes Light itself. But the road to perfection is long and arduous, too much to hope for in one short human life; hence the widespread belief in Reincarnation: that we are born again and again until we begin to transcend the pleasures of the flesh. This doctrine is so old that no man can trace its origin, yet it is the inner core of Truth common to all religions at their inception. Consider the teaching of Jesus Christ with that in mind and you will be amazed that you have not realised before the true purport of His message. Did He not say that the Kingdom of God was within us? And when he walked upon the waters he declared: "These things that I do ye shall do also, and greater things than these shall ye do, for I go unto my Father which is in Heaven"; meaning most certainly that he was nearing perfection but that others had the same power within each one of them to do likewise.'

De Richleau paused for a moment, then went on more slowly: 'Unfortunately the hours of the night are still equal to the hours of the day, so the power of Darkness is no less active than when the world was young, and no sooner does a fresh Master appear to reveal the Light than Ignorance, Greed and Lust for Power cloud the minds of his followers. The message becomes distorted and the simplicity of the Truth submerged and forgotten in the pomp of ceremonies and the meticulous performance of rituals which have lost their meaning. Yet the real Truth is never entirely lost, and through the centuries new Masters are continually arising either to proclaim it or, if the time is not propitious, to pass it on in secret to the chosen few.

'Apollonius of Tyana learned it in the East. The so-called heretics whom we know as the Albigenses preached it in the twelfth century throughout Southern France until they were exterminated. Christian Rosenkreutz had it in the Middle Ages; it was the innermost secret of the Order of the Templars, who were suppressed because of it by the Church of Rome; the alchemists, too, searched for and practised it. Only the ignorant take literally their struggle to find the Elixir of Life. Behind such phrases, designed to protect them from the persecution of their enemies, they sought Eternal Life, and their efforts to transmute basemetals into gold were only symbolical of their sublimation

17

of matter into Light. And still today, while the bombing of London goes on about us, there are mystics and adepts who are seeking the Way to Perfection in many corners of the earth.'

'You honestly believe that?' remarked Sir Pellinore with mild scepticism.

'I do.' De Richleau's answer held no trace of doubt.

'Granted that there are such mystics who follow this particular Faith which is outside all organised religions, I still don't see where Black Magic comes in.'

'Let's not talk of Black Magic, which is associated with the preposterous in our day, but of the Order of the Left-Hand Path. That, too, has its adepts, and just as the Reincarnationists scattered all over the world are the preservers of the Way of Light, the Way of Darkness is perpetuated in the horrible Voodoo cult which had its origin in Madagascar and has held Africa, the Dark Continent, in its grip for centuries and spread with the slave trade to the West Indies.'

A stick of bombs crumped dully in the distance and Sir Pellinore smiled. 'It's a pretty long cry from the mumbo-jumbo stuff practised by the Negroes of the Caribbean to the machinations of this damn'd feller Hitler.'

'Not so far as you might suppose. Most of the black man's Magic is crude stuff but that does not affect the fact that certain of these Voodoo priests have cultivated the power of Evil to a very high degree. Among whites, though, it is generally the wealthy and intellectual, who are avaricious for greater riches or power, to whom it appeals. In the Paris of Louis XIV, long after the Middle Ages were forgotten, the Black Art was particularly rampant. The poisoner, La Voisin, was proved to have procured over fifteen hundred children for the infamous Abbé Guibourg to sacrifice at Black Masses. He used to cut their throats, drain the blood into a chalice and then pour it over the naked body of the inquirer which lay stretched upon the altar. I speak of actual history, and you can read the records of the trial that followed, in which two hundred and forty-six men and women were indicted for these hellish practices.'

'Come, come; that's all a very long time ago.'

'If you need more modern evidence of its continuance

18

there is the well-authenticated case of Prince Borghese. He let his Venetian *palazzo* on a long lease, expiring as late as 1895. The tenants had not realised that the lease had run out until he notified them of his intention to resume possession. They protested, but Borghese's agents forced an entry. What d'you think they found?'

'Lord knows.'

'That the principal salon had been redecorated at enormous cost and converted into a Satanic Temple. The walls were hung from ceiling to floor with heavy curtains of scarlet-and-black silk damask to exclude the light. At the further end, dominating the whole room, there was stretched a large tapestry upon which was woven a colossal figure of Lucifer. Beneath it an altar had been built and amply furnished with the whole liturgy of Hell; black candles, vessels, rituals—nothing was lacking. Cushioned *prie-dieus* and luxurious chairs of crimson and-gold were set in order for the assistants and the chamber was lit with electricity fantastically arranged so that it should glare through an enormous human eye.

'If that's not enough I can give you even more modern instances of Satanic temples here in London; not so luxuriously furnished, perhaps, but having all the essentials for performing Black Masses. There was one in Earl's Court after the 1914–1918 War, there was another in St. John's Wood as recently as 1935, which I myself had occasion to visit, and less than three years ago there was one in Dover Street, where a woman was flogged to death during one of the ceremonies.'

De Richleau hammered the table with his clenched fist. 'These are facts that I'm giving you—things I can prove by eye-witnesses still living. Despite our electricity, our aeroplanes, our modern scepticism, the Power of Darkness is still a living force, worshipped by depraved human beings for their unholy ends in the great cities of Europe and America to this very day.'

Sir Pellinore shrugged his broad shoulders. 'I'm quite prepared to take your word for all this, and, of course, I have myself heard from time to time that such things go on, even to an occasional murder the motive for which remains undiscovered by the police. But, quite honestly,

I feel that you're putting an entirey wrong interpretation upon the facts. Such parties are simply an excuse for certain wealthy and very decadent people, of which a certain number exist in every great city, to indulge in deliberately planned orgies where they can give themselves up to the most revolting sexual practices. Such circles are, in fact, very exclusive vice-clubs, generally run by clever crooks who make an exceedingly good thing out of them. I don't for one moment doubt that you're right about the trimmings, but in my view the ceremonial part of it is simply a mental stimulant which serves to get these people into the right frame of mind for the abominable licence in which they intend to indulge later the same night when they've got their clothes off. I don't believe that these so-called Satanists could harm a rabbit by exercising supernatural powers in the manner that you suggest.'

'That is a pity,' replied the Duke; 'because this is no question of my endeavouring to convince you that I am right for the mere pleasure of triumphing in a purely academic argument. You came to me this evening with a problem which it is vital that we should solve if we are to get the better of the Nazis. I put up what I consider to be a possible solution to that problem. If you brush it aside as nonsense, yet it later proves that I am right, entirely through your reluctance to accept what may sound a fantastic solution we shall be in a fair way to lose the war, or at least it will be prolonged to a point where grave hardship will be inflicted upon our entire people. Either my theory is a possible one, or it is not. If it *is* possible, we can take steps to counter the menace. Therefore, whether you like it or not, you have laid it upon me as a national duty to convince you that Magic is an actual scientific force and may, therefore, be employed by our enemies.'

Sir Pellinore nodded gravely. 'I appreciate your point, Duke, and there can be no question whatever about the sincerity of your own belief or the honesty of your intentions, but if we sat here until the middle of next week you would never succeed in convincing me that anyone could use occult forces in a similar manner to that in which they could operate a wireless.'

'Oh, yes, I shall,' replied the Duke, and his grey eyes bored into Sir Pellinore's with a strange, hard light. 'You force me, in the interests of the nation, to do something that I do not like; but I know sufficient about this business to call certain supernatural forces to my aid, and when you leave this flat tonight you will never again be able to say that you do not believe in Magic.'

3

The Old Wisdom

Sir Pellinore looked a little startled, then his hearty laugh rang out. 'Not proposing to turn me into a donkey or anything, are you?'

'No,' de Richleau smiled. 'I rather doubt if my powers extend that far, but I might cause you to lose your memory for the best part of a week.'

'The devil! That would be deuced inconvenient.'

'Don't worry; I have no intention of doing so. I'm happy to say that I have never allowed myself to be tempted into practising anything but White Magic.'

'White Magic—White Magic,' repeated Sir Pellinore suspiciously. 'But that's only conjuring-tricks, isn't it?'

'Not at all.' The Duke's voice was a trifle acid. 'It only differs from Black Magic in that it is a ceremony performed without intent to bring harm to anyone or any personal gain to the practitioner. I propose to use such powers as I possess to bring it about that a certain wish which you have expressed tonight shall be granted. Let's go into the other room, shall we?'

Distinctly mystified and vaguely uneasy at this unusual proposal for his after-dinner entertainment, Sir Pellinore passed with the Duke into that room in the Curzon Street flat which was so memorable for those who had been privileged to visit it; not so much on account of its size and decorations as for the unique collection of rare and beautiful objects which it contained—a Tibetan Buddha seated upon the Lotus, bronze figurines from Ancient Greece, delicately chased rapiers of Toledo steel and Moorish pistols inlaid with turquoise and gold, ikons from Holy Russia set with semi-precious stones, and curiously carved ivories from the East—each a memento of some strange adventure which de Richleau had undertaken as a soldier of fortune or traveller in little-known lands. The walls were lined shoulder-high with richly bound books and the spaces above them were decorated with priceless historical documents, old colour-prints and maps.

Having settled his guest in a comfortable chair before the glowing fire, the Duke went over to a great carved-ivory chest, which he unlocked with a long, spindle-like key. On the front of it being lowered one hundred and one drawers were disclosed—deep and shallow, large and small. From one of the larger drawers he took a battered old iron tray, twenty-one inches long and seven inches broad, which had certain curious markings engraved upon it, and this he placed on top of the chest; from another drawer he took an incense burner and some cones of incense which he inserted in the burner then lit with a white taper.

When the incense was well alight he left the chest and went over to a handsome table-desk, where he sat down and, picking up a pen, drew a sheet of notepaper towards him. Having covered both sides of the sheet with neat writing he folded it, placed it in an envelope and, turning, handed it to Sir Pellinore, as he said:

'Slip that in your pocket. When the time is ripe I shall ask you to open it, and if my ceremony is successful it will prove to you that there has been no element of coincidence about this business.'

De Richleau next took from the ivory chest four little bronze bowls, each supported by three winged legs obviously fashioned after a portion of the male body. To the contents of one he applied the lighted taper, upon which the matter in it began to burn with a steady blue flame. Another of the bowls already had some dark substance in it, while the remaining two were empty. Taking one of them, he walked over to a tray of drinks that stood on a side-table and half-filled it from a bottle of Malvern water. As he replaced the bowl in a line with the three others he glanced across at the Baronet, who was watching him with faintly cynical disapproval, and remarked:

'Here we have the four Elements, Air, Earth, Fire, and

23

Water, all of which are necessary to the performance of any magical ceremony.'

The cones of incense were now giving off spirals of blue smoke which scented the air of the quiet room with a strong, musky perfume, and as the Duke selected three small pay-envelopes from a number of others, each marked with a name, that were arranged alphabetically in one of the drawers, he added:

'This doubtless seems a lot of tomfoolery to you, yet there is a sound reason for everything in these little-understood but very ancient practices. For example, the incense will prevent our noses being offended by the—to some—unpleasant odour of the things which I am about to dissolve by fire.'

'What are they?' Sir Pellinore inquired.

The Duke opened one of the little envelopes, tapped its contents into the palm of his hand and held it out. 'They are, as you see, the parings of human nails.'

'Good God!' Sir Pellinore turned away quickly. He was not at all happy about this business as his life-long disbelief in the occult had suddenly become tinged with a vague fear now that all against his wish he was being brought in direct contact with it. The fact that he had won a V.C. in the Boer War, and had performed many acts of bravery since, was not the least comfort to him. Bullets and bombs he understood; but not erudite gentlemen who proposed to bring about abnormal happenings by burning small portions of the human body.

De Richleau read his thoughts and smiled. Returning to the ivory chest, he took from it a silvery powder of which he made three little heaps on the old iron tray, and upon each heap he put a few pieces of the nail parings. He then made a sign which was neither that of the Cross nor the touching of the forehead that Mohammedans make when they mention the Prophet, lit one of the little heaps of powder and in a ringing voice, which startled Sir Pellinore, pronounced an incantation of eleven words from a long-dead language.

The powder flared up in a dazzling flame, the nail-parings were consumed in a little puff of acrid smoke and de Richleau repeated the sign which was neither that of

the Cross nor the touching of the forehead that Mohammedans make when they mention the Prophet.

Twice more the Duke went through the same motions
and the same words; then he put out the flame which was
burning in one bowl, emptied the water from another,
snuffed out the incense in the burner, and, putting all his
impedimenta back into the ivory chest, relocked it with the
spindle-like key.

'There,' he said, in the same inconsequent tone that he
might have used had he just finished demonstrating a new
type of carpet-sweeper. 'It will be a little time before the
logical results of the enchantment which I have effected
will become apparent, so what about a drink? Brandy,
Chartreuse, or a glass of wine—which do you prefer?'

'Brandy-and-soda, thanks,' replied Sir Pellinore, distinctly relieved that the queer antics of his friend were
over.

As he brought the drink and sat down before the fire the
Duke smiled genially. 'I'm so sorry to have made you uncomfortable—a great failing in any host towards his guest
—but you brought it on yourself, you know.'

'Good Lord, yes! You have every possible right to prove
your own statement if you can, and I'm delighted for you
to do so; although I must confess that this business gave
me a rather crèepy feeling—sort of thing I haven't experienced for years. D'you honestly believe, though, that the
Fuehrer monkeys about with incense and bowls of this and
that, and bits of human nail, as you have done tonight?'

'I haven't the least doubt that he does; everything that is
known about him indicates it. Witness his love of high
places, the fact that he shuts himself up in that secret room
of his at Berchtesgaden, sometimes for as much as twelve
hours at a stretch, when nobody is allowed to disturb him
however urgent their business; his so-called fits, and, above
all, his way of life: no women, no alcohol and a vegetarian
diet.'

'What on earth's that got to do with it?'

'To attain occult power it is generally essential to forgo
all joys of the flesh, often even to the point of carrying out
prolonged fasts, so as to purify the body. You will recall
that all the holy men who performed miracles were famed
for their asceticism, and it is just as necessary to deny one-

25

self every sort of self-indulgence if one wishes to practise the Black Art as for any other form of occultism.'

'That doesn't fit in with your own performance this evening. We enjoyed a darned good dinner and plenty of fine liquor before you set to work.'

'True. But then, as I told you, I only proposed to perform quite a small magic. I couldn't have attempted anything really difficult without having first got myself back into training.'

Sir Pellinore nodded. 'All the same, I find it impossible to believe that a man in Hitler's position would be able to give the time to a whole series of these—er—ceremonies day after day, week after week, to discover the route by which each of our convoys is sailing, when he must have such a mass of important things to attend to.'

'I shouldn't think so either. Doubtless there are many people round him to whom he could delegate such routine work, while reserving himself for special occasions on which he seeks power to bring about far greater Evils.'

'God bless my soul! Are you suggesting that all the Nazis are tarred with the same brush?'

'Not all of them, but a considerable number. I don't suppose it has ever occurred to you to wonder why they chose a left-handed Swastika as their symbol?'

'I've always thought that it was on account of their pro-Aryan policy. The Swastika is Aryan in origin, isn't it?'

'Yes. Long before the Cross was ever heard of the Swastika was the Aryan symbol for Light, and its history is so ancient that no man can trace it; but that was a right-handed Swastika, whereas the Nazi badge is left-handed and, being the direct opposite, was the symbol for Darkness.'

Sir Pellinore frowned. 'All this is absolutely new to me, and I find it very difficult to accept your theory.'

De Richleau laughed. 'If you had time to go into the whole matter you'd soon find that it's much more than a theory. D'you know anything about astrology?'

'Not a thing; though a feller did my horoscope once and I must confess he made a remarkably good job of it. That's many years ago now, but practically everything he predicted about me has since come true.'

'It always does if the astrologer really knows his job, is

provided with accurate data and spends enough time on it. The sort of horoscope that people get for half a guinea is rarely much good, because astrology is a little-understood but very exact science and it takes many hours of intricate calculation to work out the influence which each celestial body will have upon a child at the hour of birth. Even hard work and a sound knowledge of the science are not alone sufficient, as the astrologer must have had years of practice in assessing the manner in which the influence of one heavenly body will increase or detract from the influence of all the others that are above the horizon at the natal hour. But the labourer is worthy of his hire, and to pay ten or twenty guineas to have the job done by a man who really understands his stuff is worth it a hundredfold. One can make a really good horoscope the key to one's life by using the warnings it contains to remould tendencies and thus guard against many ills.'

'Really?' Sir Pellinore looked a little surprised. 'I was under the impression that these astrologer gentry all believed that what the stars foretold *must* come to pass. That's why I've never regarded my horoscope as anything but a curiosity. Nothing would induce me to believe that we're not the masters of our own fate.'

'We are,' the Duke replied mildly; 'but our paths are circumscribed. The Great Planners give to each child at its birth circumstances together with certain strengths and weaknesses of character which are exactly suited to it and are, in fact, the outcome of the sum of all its previous existence. On broad lines, the life of that child is laid out, because its parents and environment will automatically have a great influence upon its future and it is pre-ordained that from time to time during its life other persons will come into its orbit, exercising great influence for good or ill upon it. Temptations will be put in its path, but also chances for it to achieve advancement. These things are decreed by the Overseers in accordance with the vast plan into which everything fits perfectly; and that is why character, tendencies and periods of special stress or opportunity can be predicted from the stars prevailing at any birth. But free will remains, and that is why, although future events can be foreseen in a life with a great degree of probability, they cannot be foretold with absolute certainty; because the person concerned may suddenly evince some hidden weakness or great strength and thus depart from the apparent destiny.'

'Then a horoscope is by no means final?'

'Certainly not; yet it can be an invaluable guide to one's own shortcomings and potentialities, and the fact that we frequently go off the predestined track in one direction or another does not necessarily mean that we leave it for good. Surely you've noticed how people often fail in some direction through their own folly yet achieve their aims a little later by some quite unexpected avenue; and again, how, through what appear to be entirely fortuitous circumstances, a man's life is often completely changed so that his whole future is given an entirely different direction. That is not chance, because there is no such thing; it is merely that, having been faced with a certain test, and having reacted with unexpected strength or weakness to it, he is swung back, by powers over which he has no control, on to the path where other trials or opportunities have been laid out in advance for him.'

The anti-aircraft fire flared up again so that the glasses on the side-table jingled, then two bombs whined over the house and exploded somewhere behind it in the direction of Piccadilly. The whole place shuddered and the menacing hum of the enemy planes could be heard clearly overhead.

For a few moments they sat silent, then when the din had faded, Sir Pellinore said: 'Damn that house-painter feller! There soon won't be a window left in any of the clubs. But what were you going to say about him and astrology?'

'Simply that his every major move so far—with one exception—has been made at a time when his stars were in the ascendant. His march into the Rhine, his *Anschluss* with Austria, the rape of Czechoslovakia and a score of smaller but nevertheless important acts in his career all took place upon dates when the stars were particularly propitious to him. I don't ask you to accept my word for that—go to any reputable astrologer and he will substantiate what I say—but, to my mind, that is conclusive proof that Hitler either practises astrology himself or employs a first-class astrologer and definitely chooses the dates for each big move he makes in accordance with occult forces ruling at those times.'

28

'What was the exception?'

'September the 2nd, 1939. Evil persons can use occult forces for their own ends, but only within limits. The all-seeing powers of Light are ever watchful, and inevitably a time comes when they trap the Black occultist through his own acts. They trapped Hitler over Poland. I am sure he never thought for one moment that Great Britain would go to war on account of his marching into Danzig; therefore when he consulted the stars as to a propitious date for that adventure he was thinking only in terms of Poland. He chose a date upon which Poland's stars were bad and his stars were good; but he forgot or neglected to take into account the stars of Great Britain and her Empire on that date and the day following. We all know what happened to Poland; but the same thing has not happened to Britain yet—and will never happen. In the map of the heavens for September the 3rd, 1939, you will find that Britain's stars are more powerful than Hitler's. He thought that he was only going to launch a short, devastating attack on Poland on the 2nd, whereas, actually, he precipitated a second World War; and that is where this servant of Darkness has at last been trapped by the powers of Light.'

'Just supposing—*supposing*, mind—that you were right about this thing, how d'you think Hitler's people would go to work in passing on information by occult means?'

'Whoever secures the information about the sailings must either be capable of maintaining continuity of thought while awake and asleep or pass the information on to somebody else who can do that.'

'What the deuce are you talking about?'

De Richleau smiled as he took his friend's glass over to the side-table and refilled it. 'To explain what I mean I shall have to take you a little further along the path of the Old Wisdom. Since you're a Christian you already subscribe to the belief that when you die your spirit lives on and that what we call Death is really Life Eternal?'

'Certainly.'

'But there is much more to it than that. As I remarked some time ago, the basis of every great religion, without exception, is the belief in Reincarnation and that at intervals which vary considerably each one of us is born into the world again in a fresh body in order that we may gain further experience and a greater command over ourselves. Those periods are rather like short terms at school, since in them we are compelled to learn, whether we will or no, and we rarely manage to achieve happiness for any considerable length of time. The periods when we are free of a body, which are much longer, are the holidays in which we gain strength for new trials, enjoy the companionship of all the dear friends that we have made on our long journey through innumerable past lives and live in a far higher and more blissful state than is ever possible on Earth. That is the real Eternal Life; yet each time that we are born again in the flesh we do not entirely lose touch with that other spiritual plane where we live our true lives and know real happiness. Whenever we sleep our spirit leaves its body and is free to refortify itself for the trials of the morrow by visiting the astral sphere to meet and talk with others many of whose bodies are also sleeping on Earth.

'Some people dream a lot, others very little—or so they say; but what they actually mean is that they are incapable of remembering their dreams when they wake. The fact is that we all dream—or, if you prefer, leave our bodies— from the very moment we fall asleep. A dream, therefore, is really no more than a confused memory of our activities while the body is sleeping. By writing down everything one can remember of one's dreams, immediately upon waking, it is perfectly possible gradually to train oneself to recall what one's spirit did when it was absent from the body. It needs considerable strength of will to rouse oneself at once and the process of establishing a really clear memory requires a very great patience; but you may take my word for it that it can be done. If you doubt me, I could easily produce at least half a dozen other people living in England at the present time who have trained themselves to a degree in which they can recall, without the least difficulty, their nightly journeyings. And, of course, the spirit needs no training to remember what it has done in the body during the daytime. That's what I mean by continuity of thought when waking and sleeping.'

'I seldom dream,' announced Sir Pellinore, 'and if ever I do it's just an absurd, confused muddle.'

'That is the case with most people, but the explanation is quite simple. When you're out of your body, time, as we know it, ceases to exist, so in a single night you may journey great distances, meet many people and do an extraordinary variety of things. Therefore, when you awake, if you have any memory at all, it is only of the high spots in your night's adventures.'

'But they don't make sense. One thing doesn't even lead to another.'

'Of course not. But tell me about your normal waking life. Starting from Monday morning, what have you done this week?'

'Well, now, let me see. On Monday I had a meeting with Beaverbrook—very interesting. On Tuesday I lunched with the Admiral responsible for arranging our convoy routes—no, that was Wednesday—it was Tuesday I damn'd-near ricked my ankle—slid down the Duke of York's Steps. That morning, too, I had a letter from my nephew—hadn't heard from the young devil for months— he's with the Coldstream, in the Middle East. Wednesday I lost an important paper, got in a hell of a stew; quite unnecessary, as I had it in the lining of my hat-band all the time, but it gave me a devilish bad half-hour. Yesterday I met you and . . .'

'That's quite enough to illustrate my point,' interrupted the Duke. 'If those three days had been compressed into a one-night dream you would probably have wakened up with a muddled impression that you were walking in an aircraft factory with Lord Beaverbrook when you suddenly fell and nearly ricked your ankle, to pick yourself up and find that he had disappeared and that you were out with the Admiral on the cold waters of the Atlantic where we are losing so much of our shipping; then that you had the awful impression that you had lost something of the greatest importance, although you couldn't think what it was, and that you were hunting for it with your soldier-nephew in the sands of Libya, in an interval from chasing the Italians. That is what is called telescoping. None of these things would have had the least apparent connection any more than the events in real life which you gave to me; but it's quite natural that memory either of real life or of dream activities leaps to the matters which have made great impressions upon the mind. Things of less importance very soon become submerged in the general stream of the subconscious, and I'm willing to bet you a tenner that you could not now recall accurately what you ate at each meal during those three days, however hard you tried. It's just the same with the memory of a dream, except that by training one can bring oneself to fill in gaps and follow the whole sequence.'

'Yes; I get your line of argument. But how would this help a German spy to convey information to the enemy?'

'Once one is able to remember one's dreams clearly, the next step is to learn how to direct them, since that, too, can be done by practice. One can go to sleep having made up one's mind that one wishes to meet a certain friend on the astral and be quite certain of doing so. Such a state is not easy of achievement, but it is possible to anybody who has sufficient determination to go through the dreary training without losing heart, and it is no matter of education or secret ritual but simply a case of having enough will-power to force oneself into swift wakefulness each morning and concentrating one's entire strength of mind upon endeavouring to recall every possible detail about one's dreams. Once that has been successfully accomplished, one has only to go to sleep thinking of the person whom one wishes to meet on the astral plane, then one wakes in the morning with the full consciousness of having done so. It is a tragic fact that countless couples who have been separated by the war *do* meet each other every night in their spirit bodies, but, through never having trained themselves, by the time they are fully awake the next morning barely one out of ten thousand is conscious of the meeting. However, you will readily appreciate that if lovers can meet on the astral while the bodies they inhabit in the daytime are sleeping thousand of miles apart, there is nothing to prevent enemy agents also doing so.'

'God bless my soul!' Sir Pellinore suddenly sat forward. 'Are you suggesting that if a German agent in England had certain information he could go to sleep, report in a dream to some damn'd Gestapo feller who was asleep in Germany, and that if the Gestapo feller was a dream-rememberer he could wake up with the information in his head the following morning?'

'Exactly,' said the Duke quietly.

'But, man alive, that'd be a terrible thing! It's too

32

frightful to contemplate. No, no; I don't want to be rude or anything of that kind, and I'm quite sure you're not deliberately trying to make a fool of me, but honestly, my dear feller, I just don't believe it.'

De Richleau shrugged. 'There are plenty of people in London who will support my contention; and if I am not greatly mistaken, here comes one of them.'

As he was speaking there had been a soft rap on the door and his manservant, Max, now appeared, to murmur: 'Excellency, Mr. Simon Aron has called and wishes to know if you will receive him.'

'Ask him to come in, Max,' the Duke replied, and turned to Sir Pellinore with a smile. 'This is one of my old friends of whom we were speaking earlier in the evening.'

Max had thrown the door open and Simon stood upon the threshold, smiling a little diffidently. He was a thin, slightly built man of middle height, with black hair, a rather receding chin, a great beak of a nose and dark, restless, intelligent eyes. As he came forward the Duke introduced him to Sir Pellinore and the two shook hands.

'Delighted to meet you,' boomed Sir Pellinore. 'At one time or another I've heard quite a lot about you as one of the people who accompanied de Richleau on some of his famous exploits.'

Simon wriggled his bird-like head in a little nervous gesture and smiled. ' 'Fraid I can't claim much credit for that. The others did all the exciting stuff; I don't—er—really care much about adventures.' He glanced swiftly at the Duke, and went on: 'I do hope I'm not interrupting. Just thought I'd look in—make certain that you hadn't been bombed.'

'Thank you, Simon. That was most kind of you, but I didn't know that you were given to wandering about London at night while the blitzkrieg is in progress?'

'Ner.' Simon stooped his head towards his hand to cover a somewhat sheepish grin, as he uttered the curious negative that he sometimes used. 'As a matter of fact, I'm not —much too careful of myself; but it occurred to me about half an hour ago that I hadn't seen you for a week, so when I'd finished my rubber at bridge I jumped into a taxi and came along.'

'Good! Help yourself to a drink.' De Richleau motioned towards the side-table and, as Simon picked up the brandy decanter, went on: 'We were talking about occult matters and debating whether it was possible for a German agent in Britain to transmit intelligence to a colleague in Germany by a conversation on the astral plane while both of them were sleeping. What do you think?'

Simon jerked his head in assent. 'Um—I should say that it was perfectly possible.'

Sir Pellinore looked at him a little suspiciously. 'I take it, sir, that you're a believer in all this occult stuff?'

'Um,' Simon nodded again. 'If it hadn't been for the Duke I might have lost something more precious than my reason through monkeying with the occult some years ago.'

De Richleau smiled. 'Naturally you'll consider that Aron is prejudiced, but whatever beliefs he may hold about the occult, his record shows him to have an extraordinarily astute—in fact, I might say brilliant—brain, and I personally vouch for his integrity. You can speak in front of him with perfect confidence that nothing you say will go outside these four walls, and I think it would be an excellent idea if you put up to him the proposition that you put up to me just after dinner.'

'Very well,' Sir Pellinore agreed, and he gave Simon a brief outline of the grave position regarding Britain's shipping losses.

When he had done, Simon proceeded to embroider the subject in a quick spate of words during which he quoted accurate figures and cases in which convoys had suffered severely.

'Wait a moment, young feller,' Sir Pellinore exclaimed. 'How d'you know all this? It's supposed to be highly secret.'

Simon grinned. 'Of course. And I wouldn't dream of mentioning figures to an outsider, but it's partly my job to know these things. Got to, because they affect the markets and, er—the Government aren't the only people who have an Intelligence Service, you know. It's never occurred to me before, but the transmission of information by occult means is definitely possible. Shouldn't be a bit surprised if that's the explanation of the leakage. Anyhow, I think the Duke's idea ought to be investigated.'

Sir Pellinore glanced at the Duke. 'How would you set about such an investigation?'

'I should need to be put in touch with all the people at

the Admiralty who are in the secret as to the route each convoy is to take. Then I should go out at night to cover them when they leave their bodies in sleep, to see if I could find the person who is communicating with the enemy.'

'Are you seriously suggesting that your spirit could shadow theirs on the—er—astral plane?'

'That's the idea. I see no other way in which one could attempt to solve such a mystery. It would be a long job, too, if there are many people in the secret.'

'And damnably dangerous,' added Simon.

'Why?' Sir Pellinore inquired.

'Because whoever is giving the information away might find out what I was up to,' replied the Duke, 'and would then stick at nothing to stop me.'

'How?'

'When a spirit goes out from a body that is asleep, as long as life continues in the body the spirit is attached to it by a tenuously thin cord of silver light which is capable of stretching to any distance. The cord acts as a telephone wire, and that is how, if sudden danger threatens the body, it is able to recall the spirit to animate it. But if that silver cord is once severed the body dies—in fact, that is what has actually happened when people are said to have died in their sleep. If my intentions are discovered the Powers of Darkness will do their damn'dest to break the silver cord that links my spirit with my body, so that I can never get back to it and report the result of my investigations to you.'

The elderly Baronet had considerable difficulty in keeping open disbelief out of his voice as he grunted: 'So even the spirits go in for murder, eh?'

'Certainly. The eternal fight between Good and Evil rages just as fiercely on the astral plane as it does here; only the weapons used are much more terrible, and if one comes into conflict with one of the entities of the Outer Circle one's soul may sustain grievous harm which is infinitely worse than the mere loss of a body.'

Sir Pellinore glanced at the clock and stood up. 'Well,' he said, with his genial bluffness, 'it's been a most interesting evening—thoroughly enjoyed myself—but I must be getting along.'

'No, no,' said the Duke. 'I can see that you still think I'm talking nonsense, but in fairness to me you must await the outcome of my magical experiment.'

'What have you been up to?' Simon inquired with sudden interest, but the others ignored him, as Sir Pellinore replied:

'Of course I will, if you wish, but honestly, my dear fellow, I don't think anything you could do would really convince me. All this business about silver cords, spirits committing murder, and even one's immortal soul not being safe in God's keeping, is a bit too much for a man of my age to swallow.'

At that moment there was another knock on the door and Max stood there again. 'Excellency, Mr. Rex Van Ryn and Mr. Richard Eaton are here and wish to know if you will receive them.'

'Certainly,' said the Duke. 'Ask them to come in.'

Rex, tall, broad-shouldered, in the uniform of an R.A.F. flight-lieutenant but leaning heavily on a stick, was the first to enter, and Sir Pellinore greeted him with hearty congratulations on his D.F.C. Richard, much slighter in build, followed him and was duly introduced.

'Well, well,' laughed Sir Pellinore to his host, 'it seems that you're holding quite a reception tonight, and the four famous companions are now reunited.'

A broad smile lit Rex's ugly attractive face as he said to the Duke: 'Richard and I had just negotiated a spot of dinner together round the corner, at the Dorchester, when we had a hunch, almost simultaneously, that after we'd finished our magnum it'd be a great idea to drop along and take a brandy off you.'

De Richleau turned to Sir Pellinore. 'The note that I gave you—would you produce it now?'

Sir Pellinore fished in his pocket, brought out the envelope, ripped it open and read what the Duke had written half an hour before. It ran as follows:

'You will bear witness that since writing this note I have not left your presence, used the telephone, or communicated in any way with my servants. You expressed the wish, just after dinner, to meet my friends, Simon Aron, Rex Van Ryn, and Richard Eaton.

'If they are not in London the ceremony that I propose

36

to perform will not be successful, because they will not have time to reach here before you go home, but if, as I believe, they are, it is virtually certain that at least one of them will put in an appearance here before midnight.

'If any or all of them turn up I shall see to it that they testify, without prompting, that they have not called upon me by arrangement but have done so purely owing to a sudden idea that they would like to see me which came into their minds. That idea is no matter of mere chance but because *through a magical ceremony I have conveyed to them my will that they shall appear here.*

'If the ceremony is successful I trust that this will convince you that the Nazis may use magic for infinitely more nefarious purposes and that it is *our* duty to conduct an investigation in this matter with the least possible delay.'

Sir Pellinore lowered the note and glanced round the little circle. His blue eyes held a queer, puzzled look, as he exclaimed:

'By God, I'd never have believed it! You win, Duke, I've got to admit that. Mind you, that's not to say I'm prepared to swallow all the extraordinary things you've said this evening. Still, in a case like this we can't afford to neglect *any* avenue. Our Atlantic Life-line is our one weak spot and it may be—yes, it may be that in those slender hands of yours lies the Victory or Defeat of Britain.'

4

For Those in Peril on the Sea

'I shall need help,' said the Duke gravely.

'Anything in reason for which you care to ask shall be given to you,' Sir Pellinore replied at once.

'I meant *skilled* help—people who understand something of psychic lore—who can work with me and whom I can trust.' De Richleau glanced round at his friends. 'I take it that I can count upon you three?'

Simon nodded, and Richard said with a smile: 'Of course; but as Rex and I have only just turned up we haven't the faintest idea yet what all this is about.'

Sir Pellinore told them, upon which Rex said:

'All three of us were with the Duke in that ghastly Talisman of Set affair, so we're acquainted with the occult sufficiently to lend a hand under his direction, but right now I'm tied up with the Royal Air Force.'

'I could arrange for your leave to be indefinitely extended,' said Sir Pellinore.

'Good,' remarked the Duke. 'Richard is his own master; but how about you, Simon? Can you manage to get away from your office possibly for several weeks?'

'Um—don't want to a bit, but this is obviously more important.'

As the Duke spoke again his first words were almost drowned in the booming of the guns, but the others just caught them.

'If we're going to wage war on the astral plane we'll have to leave London. It's essential that we should be able to work in some place where we shall run as little risk as

38

possible of being disturbed by purely physical excitements.'

'You'd better all come down and stay at Cardinals Folly,' suggested Richard at once. 'We hardly even hear a plane go over down there in the depths of the country, and you know that Marie Lou would be delighted to have you.'

'No, Richard,' de Richleau shook his head. 'We brought quite enough trouble on Marie Lou last time we broke a lance against the Devil, and with Fleur in the house I wouldn't even consider it.'

'Fleur's not in the house; she's sharing a governess with another little girl, the daughter of friends of mine who live up in Scotland. And remember, as Marie Lou was involved last time she knows as much about this sort of thing as Simon, Rex or myself.'

De Richleau considered for a moment. He knew that Richard's beautiful little wife had an abundance of sound common sense as well as an extraordinarily strong will and that, as had often happened before, her counsel might be most useful to them. This was Total war, and while women everywhere were risking their lives to carry on the nation's work during the blitzkrieg there could be no case for exempting a woman from this very curious job of war work in which she could be just as effective as any man. At length he said:

'Thanks, then, Richard; we'll accept your offer. The next thing is for me to meet the man at the Admiralty who decides the routes that the convoys are to take.'

Sir Pellinore looked a little startled. 'I, er . . .' he began, 'I hardly feel that we can let the Admiral in on what you propose to do. You've made me feel that it's just possible that you've hit the nail on the head as to the manner in which this leakage of information is reaching Germany, but I'm afraid you'd find him a much more sticky proposition.'

'It's not necessary,' smiled the Duke. 'All I need is to meet him socially for an hour or two.'

'Well, that's easy. I've already arranged for him to lunch with me tomorrow because I felt pretty confident that I could interest you in this business tonight; and as no time must be lost in getting to work I was hoping that you would join us so that you could put up any questions you might have.'

'Splendid. A general discussion on the subject would, in any case, prove helpful, and of course it's still quite possible that my theory that the occult is being used is entirely wrong.' De Richleau looked round at the others. 'Then, if you're agreeable, we'll all go down to Cardinals Folly in the afternoon.'

They sat talking together for another half-hour, then there came a lull in the blitzkrieg so de Richleau's guests decided to set off for home before it flared up again.

On the following day the Duke lunched with the Admiral and a naval staff-captain, at Sir Pellinore's mansion in Carlton House Terrace. The Admiral was square-chinned, paunchy and bald; the Captain a merry-eyed man with sparse brown hair and a fine, broad forehead.

They held a long discussion, and afterwards examined a number of large-scale charts of the Western and North-Western Approaches which the naval officers had brought with them. The situation was considerably worse than de Richleau had imagined and he questioned the Admiral as to how many people actually had access to each route planned before it was handed to the officer commanding a convoy.

The Admiral jerked his pink, bald head towards the Captain. 'Nobody except Fennimere and myself. We plot the routes together, taking into consideration the latest information regarding enemy forces in each locality; then Fennimere writes the orders out by hand, so that there is no question of even a confidential typist being involved. The orders are sealed in a canvas-lined envelope which is weighted with lead so that it can be thrown into the sea and will sink immediately in the event of an emergency. It is then locked in a steel despatch-box which Fennimere personally takes to the port from which the convoy is proceeding. He hands it over to the officer commanding the escort, who in turn hands it to the officer commanding the convoy—but only when the convoy is already several hundred miles out and the escort is about to return to port. In this manner even the officer commanding the convoy cannot possibly know what route he is to take until he is actually at sea, since the sealed orders do not even pass into his possession until the escort is about to leave him.'

'That certainly narrows the field,' said the Duke, 'and I

don't see how you could possibly take any greater precautions.'

The Admiral shrugged wearily. 'Neither do I. The problem as to how they get their information defeats me utterly, and you'll be doing us an immense service if only you can put your finger upon the place where the leakage occurs.'

'You see,' added Fennimere, 'even if one of the officers commanding a convoy were a traitor and had a secret wireless apparatus by which he could inform the enemy of his approximate position twenty-four hours after the escort had left him, that does not solve the problem, because it postulates that every officer commanding a convoy is a traitor—which is manifestly absurd.'

'Yes, I appreciate that,' the Duke agreed. 'Therefore the leakage must occur in London, where the routes of all convoys are settled. May I have your private address?'

The Captain looked a little surprised, but the Admiral smiled. 'He's perfectly logical in assuming that it must be you or I, Fennimere, and since the Intelligence people have been shadowing both of us for weeks what does one more sleuth matter?—in fact the more the better. If only they would provide a couple of attractive young women to sleep with us each night our innocence would be proved conclusively.'

'Of course you're right, sir,' Fennimere laughed. 'I'm quite used to tripping over detectives wherever I go now, so if His Grace pops out of the bathroom cupboard one morning I shan't mind a bit.' He turned to de Richleau. 'I've taken a temporary lease of a flat, No. 43, North Gate Mansions, Regent's Park, and the Admiral has a house, No. 22, Orme Square, Bayswater.'

'If you'd care to look over the place any time,' the Admiral suggested, 'I'll leave word with my wife that you're to have the run of it for as long as you like.'

'The same goes for my flat,' added the Captain.

'Thank you, gent'emen, but I only asked for your private addresses in case I wanted to get in touch with you urgently,' lied the Duke smoothly.

An hour later he was with Rex, Simon and Richard in the latter's car running through the half-empty streets of bomb-torn London on the way to Worcestershire.

The last part of their journey had to be done in the

blackout, but Richard knew the way so well that when they left the great arterial road he had no difficulty in twisting through the narrow country lanes until he drove through the open park-gates and pulled up in front of his lovely country home.

The east wing of the rambling old house was very ancient and said to have been at one time part of a great abbey but centuries later these thick-walled remains had been built on to, while in recent years Richard and his lovely wife, the some-time Princess Marie Louise Héloïse Aphrodite Blankfort De Cantezane de Schulemoff, had spared neither pains nor money to make its interior both comfortable and beautiful. The heavy, oak, nail-studded door was no sooner opened by Malin, Richard's elderly butler, than Marie Lou herself came running forward to welcome them.

She was a tiny person with chestnut curls, a heart-shaped face and big, violet eyes which gave her a certain resemblance to a Persian kitten. In spite of her diminutive size and her slim feet, hands, wrists and ankles, she was plump in all the right places, so that de Richleau often said that she was the most exquisite creature that he had ever seen and many people nicknamed her 'Richard's Pocket Venus'. Their devotion to each other had remained absolute ever since the days when he had found her among the Siberian snows and brought her out of the Forbidden Territory to be his wife.

They embraced as though they had not met for months, and when at last he released her she said breathlessly: 'Darling, I only had your telegram an hour ago, although you send it off last night. None of the rooms are ready yet, but the maids are busy lighting the fires and putting bottles in the beds, and it's too lovely for words to have you all here again.' As she spoke she tiptoed from one to the other, giving each a swift kiss upon the cheek.

Malin had gone out to unload the car as the Duke smiled down at her. 'Perhaps it's just as well, Princess, because I have a somewhat unusual request to make. It is that I should be allowed to sleep in the library.'

'Greyeyes, darling!' she exclaimed. 'Surely you, of all people, aren't afraid of bombs! We haven't had one within miles of Cardinals Folly, so you'll be perfectly safe in your old room upstairs; but of course you can sleep in the library if you prefer.'

'No, it's not fear of bombs that has brought me out of London, my dear, but something much more desperate.'

Her gay face suddenly went serious and she nodded quickly. 'All right, then. But come inside. At least I've had time to mix the cocktails.'

Richard made a grimace as he followed her into the long, low drawing-room which in summer had such a lovely view through its french windows over the terraced garden. 'I'm afraid our luck's out, darling; we're all on the wagon.'

She stopped dead and her eyes grew rounder, showing just a trace of fear as she stared at de Richleau. 'The library—no drinks!—you—you don't mean that one of you is threatened again by something awful from the other side?'

'No,' the Duke reassured her, 'but it has fallen to us to break a lance against Hitler on the astral.'

'I don't like it,' she said suddenly, 'I don't like it.'

Richard put his arm round her shoulders. 'Darling, the Blacks are getting information into Germany by occult means—at least, that's what we believe—and someone's got to go out from Earth to try to stop them. As you know very well, one needs quiet and peaceful surroundings for work of that kind, so I felt sure that I was doing what you would have wished in telling Greyeyes that he must come and stay with us while he wages this strangest of all battles for Britain.'

She spread out her hands in a little foreign gesture. 'Of course you were right. I should never have forgiven him if I'd learnt afterwards that he had gone elsewhere. I only meant that anything to do with the occult is so damnably dangerous.'

'After the way you stuck it with your mobile canteen in Coventry all through the night that the Nazis turned the place into a living Hell, I'd come to the conclusion that you'd ceased to fear anything,' Richard said seriously.

She squeezed his hand. 'That was different, darling. What could any of us do but carry on? And at least we *knew* the worst that could happen—whereas on the other side there are some horrors that one can't even visualise. I'm frightened for you and Rex and Simon more than for myself, because out of my body I'm much stronger than most men.'

De Richleau took her free hand and kissed it. 'I knew I could count on you, Princess, and, if need be, now we're together we'll be able to form a cohort of five warriors of the Light.'

Rex had picked up the cocktail-shaker and was smelling its contents. 'What a lousy break!' he murmured. 'Pine-apple-juice and Bacardi rum, my favourite cocktail, yet I mustn't drink any.' He glanced at Marie Lou. 'I'll bet fifty bucks, too, that Greyeyes means to crack down hard on anything good you may have thought up for our dinner.'

'Oh dear!' she exclaimed ruefully. 'If I'd had the least warning of this I should have known that he'd want us all to become vegetarians for the time being. As it is, I've just been getting all sorts of lovely things out from my emergency war stores—foie gras, peaches in Benedictine, tinned cream ...'

'Now, stop making my mouth water, you little hoarder!' Rex waved her into silence with one of his huge hands.

'Hoarder—nothing!' laughed Richard. 'All our supplies were bought months before the war, when the seas were still open to replace them and the fact of buying extra stuff was good for trade. Why the Government didn't run a cam-paign urging everybody to buy all the tinned things they could, while the going was good, I can't imagine. Innumer-able little private stocks scattered in thousands of homes all over the country would have proved an absolute blessing now that the nation's on short rations.'

'One man I know did, in the spring of 1939,' said the Duke. 'He was at that time writing for the *Sunday Graphic* and his theory was that everybody who could possibly afford to lay in stocks, however small, should do so; be-cause then, if we had to go to war and a time of shortage came, richer people would be partially provided for and that would leave much more in the shops for the poorer people. But the only encouragement he got from the Min-istry of Home Security was a semi-official announcement that there was no *harm* in people laying in emergency stores. But I don't doubt that the people who took his tip are grateful to him this winter.'

'Well, we just mustn't think about all those nice things we were going to have for dinner,' said the practical Marie Lou. 'Instead, you'd better tell me what you'd like.'

'No meat, or soup with meat-juice in it,' said the Duke; 'a little fish, if you have it, and vegetables with fruit or nuts afterwards.'

Rex groaned, but Simon said jerkily with a grin at Marie Lou: 'Left a parcel with Malin—five Dover soles—knew what we were in for, so thought they might come in useful.'

'Simon, darling, you always were the most thoughtful person in the world, bless you. Except for tinned things there's not a scrap of fish in the house; but I can manage the fruit and nuts.' Marie Lou hurried away to give fresh orders for their dinner while Richard led the men upstairs to park their things and wash.

When they came down again Richard said to the Duke: 'Why do you want to sleep in the library? D'you mean to erect a pentacle there, as you did before?'

'Yes. I thought it would be easier for you to strip the library than one of the bedrooms upstairs and to keep it locked up so that the servants don't go into it in the daytime. I only wish that I'd had a chance to get into proper training for this business, but every day is precious, so I mean to start tonight.'

'That's taking a pretty big risk, isn't it?'

'I don't think so. As the Blacks can't possibly know yet that we intend to go out against them there's not the least likelihood of their attacking me on the astral or endeavouring to harm my body while I'm out of it. The trouble will start if I once get on to anything and they happen to notice me snooping about. After all, this is just the same as any other investigation except that it is to be carried out on a different plane. If we were dealing with enemy agents in their physical bodies I should probably get myself a job in the Admiral's house, and nobody operating there would take much interest in me until they noticed that I was following them or prying into matters which were no concern of mine. A really good detective is rarely spotted until he has his man in the bag, therefore I've good reason to hope that nobody will tumble to what I'm up to till I've found out what I want to know; and once I've done that we should be in a position to take counter-measures. Just as a safeguard I propose that you three should take turns to sit up and watch while I sleep, as all of you know enough to help me to get back to my body quickly if I run into any trouble, and, in addition, you'll be on hand in the unlikely event of my being abruptly awakened by a burglar or a bomb.'

'Right-oh,' said Richard. 'Directly we've dined we'll set about clearing the library.'

Thanks to the Dover soles which Simon had had the forethought to purchase before they left London that afternoon, their simple meal, washed down with water, was palatable beyond their expectations. When they had finished, Richard gave instructions to his butler that on no account were they to be disturbed and they all migrated to the big library.

The library, octagonal in shape and slightly sunken below ground level, was the principal room in the oldest part of the house. Comfortable sofas and large armchairs stood about the uneven polished oak of the floor, a pair of globes occupied two angles of the book-lined walls, and a great oval, mahogany writing-table of Chippendale design stood before the wide french window. Owing to its sunken position the lighting of the room was dim in daylight yet its atmosphere was by no means gloomy. A log-fire upon a twelve-inch pile of ashes was kept burning in the wide fireplace all through the year and at night when the curtains were drawn—as they now were—the room was lit with the soft radiance of concealed ceiling-lights which Richard had installed. It was a friendly, restful place, well suited for quiet work or idle conversation.

'We must strip the room of furniture, carpets—everything,' said the Duke, 'and I shall need brooms and a mop to polish the floor.'

The men then began moving the furniture out into the hall while Marie Lou fetched a selection of implements from the housemaid's cupboard. For a quarter of an hour they worked in silence, until nothing remained in the big library except the serried rows of gilt-tooled books.

'I would like the room to be gone over thoroughly,' the Duke smiled at Marie Lou, 'particularly the floor, since evil emanations can fasten on the least trace of dust to assist their materialisation, and I may, if I get into trouble, be chased back here.'

'Certainly, Greyeyes dear,' said Marie Lou, and with the help of the others she set about dusting, sweeping and polishing while de Richleau went out to collect a suit-case holding his ritual paraphernalia and a number of large parcels containing numerous items which he had purchased that morning. As the Duke unpacked them the others saw that they consisted of several pillows, rubber Li-Los, silk dressing-gowns, sets of pyjamas and bedroom slippers.

'Whatever have you brought all those things for?' asked Marie Lou.

'Surely you remember that nothing which is even slightly soiled must be within the pentacle,' he replied. 'Impurities are bound to linger in bedding and clothes even if they have only been used for a few hours, and it is just upon such things that elementals fasten most readily; but I'm relying on you to provide us with clean sheets, blankets and pillowcases.'

'Of course,' she said gravely. 'I'll go up and raid the linen-cupboard. How many sets do you want?'

'Only one for the moment as I am going out alone tonight. The others will be able to sleep in their own beds except during the few hours that each of them will be on watch here beside me.'

The floor was now so scrupulously clean that they could have eaten from it, and as Marie Lou went off to fetch the things for which the Duke had asked he opened his suit-case and took from it a piece of chalk, a length of string and a foot-rule. Marking a spot in the centre of the room he asked Richard to hold the end of the string to it, measured off exactly seven feet, and then, using him as a pivot, drew a large circle in chalk upon the floor.

Next the string was lengthened and an outer circle drawn, then the more complicated part of the operation began. A five-rayed star had to be made with its points touching the outer circle and its valleys resting upon the inner; but while such a defence can be highly potent if it is constructed with geometrical accuracy, should the angles vary more than a fraction the pentacle would prove not only useless but even dangerous.

For half an hour they measured and checked with string and rule and marking-chalk, but at last the broad chalk-lines were drawn to the Duke's satisfaction, forming the magical five-pointed star which would give him protection from any evil thing which might endeavour to molest him while he slept.

He then, with careful spacing, chalked in round the rim of the inner circle the following powerful exorcism: INRI ✠ ADAM ✠ TE ✠ DAGERAM ✠ AMRTET ✠ ALGAR ✠ ALGASTNA ✠ and after reference to an old book which he had brought with him drew certain curious and ancient symbols in the valleys and the mounts of the microcosmic star.

Simon, whose previous experiences had taught him something of pentacles, remembered certain of them as cabalistic signs taken from the Sephirotic Tree—*Kether, Binah, Gebirah, Hod, Malkulth* and the rest—and others, like the Eye of Horus, that were of Egyptian origin; but others, again, were in some ancient Aryan script which he did not understand.

When the skeleton of this astral fortress was completed the clean bedding was laid out in its centre. The Duke selected Richard to keep first watch so the two of them now went upstairs to change into new night-things while Marie Lou, Simon and Rex made up the bed and blew up one of the spare Li-Los for Richard to sit on.

They had not long finished when the other two returned, de Richleau carrying a glass jug of freshly drawn water. This he set down and charged with Power by placing the first and second fingers of his right hand in a line with his eye so that the invisible force which he was drawing down flowed from it, along his fingers into the water. After the operation, which took some moments, he unpacked further impedimenta from his case. Telling them all to watch his movements carefully, he sealed the windows and a door concealed in the bookshelves, which led to the room above, each at both sides and at the tops and the bottoms, with lengths of asafœtida grass and blue wax, making the sign of the Cross with the charged water over every seal as he completed it. He then produced five little silver cups which he filled two-thirds full with the water and placed one in each valley of the pentacle. Next he took five long, white, tapering candles and set them upright, one at each apex of the five-pointed star. Having charged five brand-new horseshoes he placed these in the rear of the candles with their horns pointing outwards, and beyond each vase of charged water he set bunches of certain strong-smelling herbs.

These complicated formulas for the erection of outward barriers being at last completed, the Duke turned his attention to his friends.

'Richard will remain with me until one o'clock,' he said, 'Simon will relieve him at that hour and remain on duty until four o'clock, Rex will take on then until I wake, which will probably be soon after seven, but he is not to rouse me unless danger threatens; which, of course, also applies to Richard and Simon. You understand that?'

Rex nodded, and the Duke went on: 'You have all seen how the sealing is done. When you others have left us, Richard will seal the door to the hall, but, naturally, Simon will have to break the seals when he comes in to start his watch, so he will re-seal the door when Richard has gone out and Rex will re-seal it again after he has relieved Simon.'

'Where do I come in?' asked Marie Lou.

'You don't, Princess, for the moment.' The Duke smiled. 'I purposely gave Richard first watch so that he would not disturb you after one o'clock; but I shall certainly need your help later on. We must now see to our personal protection.'

He moved over to his case again and produced some long wreaths of garlic flowers, Rosaries with little golden Crucifixes attached, medals of Saint Benedict, holding the Cross in his right hand and the Holy Rule in his left, and phials of salt and mercury. Having charged the crucifixes and medals he placed one set of this strange regalia about Richard's neck and another round his own while he gave instructions that Richard was to pass his set on to Simon, and Simon to Rex, as they relieved one another.

As the Duke closed his case Richard remarked: 'It's only just on ten o'clock, so isn't it a bit early to turn in?'

De Richleau shook his head. 'No. It's impossible to guess what time the Admiral will go to bed. If by chance he was working very late last night, it's quite on the cards that he might turn in early tonight and it's essential that I should be with him when he leaves his body, otherwise I might not be able to recognise him in his spirit form and the whole night would be wasted.'

'Right-oh, then; off you go, people.' Richard kissed Marie Lou fondly and smiled at the others. 'I'll be seeing you, Simon, around one o'clock, but if by chance you fall asleep I'll carry on till Rex puts in an appearance.' He flourished some clean sheets of paper and a brand-new pencil. 'This is just the opportunity I've been waiting for to write an article on substitute foods for poultry in war-time, and as I'm not much of an author it will keep me busy for hours.'

'You won't get more than three hours,' Simon smiled; 'I shall be here on the dot of one. You know I never go to bed before two, in any case.'

'You will tonight, Simon dear,' said Marie Lou firmly, 'because you must be fresh for your turn of duty, and even if you don't sleep you're to lie down and doze in the dark. I mean to provide both you and Rex with alarm clocks so that you'll wake in good time.'

When Marie Lou, Simon and Rex had left them Richard sealed the main door of the room and made up the fire while the Duke switched out all the lights and lit the five long white candles from an old-fashioned tinder-box. They then both entered the pentacle.

The Duke performed the ceremony of sealing the nine openings of his own body with certain mystic signs and said a short prayer asking for power, guidance and protection upon his astral journey, then got into bed while Richard settled himself on his Li-Lo.

They wished each other good night and the Duke turned over on his side. The silence was broken only by the gentle scratching of pencil on paper, as Richard began his article, and the faint hissing of the fire. De Richleau had said that in this first step there was little likelihood of his running into danger, but Richard was not so sure; the leprous, sack-like Thing, crepitating with horrid laughter, which he had seen in that room in very similar circumstances some years before, had left an indelible impression on his memory. He did not want to start imagining things or to fall asleep, and that was why he had decided to attempt a little article on the extremely prosaic matter of poultry-feeding; it should keep his mind on normal things without being of sufficient interest to distract him from his watch. After almost every sentence that he wrote he paused to give a swift glance round.

The steady ticking of a clock came faintly from somewhere in the depths of the house. Occasionally a log fell with a loud plop in the grate, then the little noises of the night were hushed and an immense silence, brooding and mysterious, seemed to have fallen upon them. In some strange way it did not seem as though the quiet, octagonal room was any longer a portion of the house. There was something a little unreal about the great chalked pentacle in the centre of which they reposed, with its vessels of charged water, bunches of herbs and horseshoes dotted here and there, but the five long, tapering candles burned with a steady flame so Richard knew that all was well.

The distant clock chimed the half-hour and Richard glanced at the Duke. His body was relaxed and he was breathing evenly. That dauntless spirit had left its mortal case of flesh and had gone out into the Great Beyond upon the strangest mission ever attempted in the Second World War.

5

The Admiral Goes Aloft

As he dropped off to sleep the Duke hovered for a little above his own body, looking down on to it and at Richard quietly writing beside the makeshift bed; then he felt the full strength of his spiritual being fill his astral body and a simple thought was enough to cause him to pass out of the house on his way to London.

In a matter of seconds he was poised above the great, sprawling city. An air-raid was in progress and he paused for a moment to view with interest London as it must appear to a Nazi airman. The broad, curving serpent of the Thames was clearly visible, and that alone was sufficient for him to identify various districts, but away from the river it was clear that the Nazi raiders could make only the vaguest guess as to when they were over their targets except on a night when the moon was particularly bright. The black-out was undoubtedly efficient, since although pin-points of light could be seen as far as the eye could reach in every direction they were no more than glimmers, so that it was impossible to detect any pattern in their dispositions which might have given away the situation of broad thoroughfares, railway-stations or big buildings.

The gunfire was sporadic, but in certain cases the flashes were so bright that for a second they lit the whole area in which the more powerful anti-aircraft batteries were situated. Two largish fires were burning, one in the neighbour-hood of Chelsea and another much further down the river, either in Bermondsey or near it, but neither was sufficiently large to give the German bombers much help and in both cases smoke partially obscured the red glow of the flames. Occasionally there was a bright flash as a bomb exploded on the ground or an anti-aircraft shell in the sky.

One of the latter seemed to tear the air asunder with a frightful ripping sound within a few feet of the Duke, and had he been poised there in his physical body, swinging from a parachute, he would have been blown to ribbons, but, as it was, he did not even feel the faintest shock. While he was still studying the scene a Nazi murder-plane hummed past him and he would have given a very great deal to have been able to strangle its pilot and bring it crashing to earth. He could easily have entered it, but to have done so would have been pointless, since in his spirit body he could not make himself either heard or felt, and to have upset the airman's mentality by bringing psychic force to bear would have been contrary to the Law which has created all things as they are.

At that moment the plane released a heavy bomb and de Richleau, deciding that he must not hang about up there but get on with his own business, dropped swiftly with it to within twenty feet of the dark roof-tops. The bomb struck a block of flats; brick, glass and cement were hurled high into the air and one corner of the block dissolved in flaming ruins. That it had killed several people the Duke knew, as he saw their spiritual bodies rise up from the smoking debris. One—evidently that of a person who in life had been conscious of the hidden truths—gave a shout of joy, which was perceptible to de Richleau, and made off at once, full of happy purpose. The others remained hovering there, forlorn, unhappy and bewildered, evidently not fully understanding yet what had happened to them and that they were dead; but they were not left in that state for long.

Even before the fire-fighters and rescue-squads came clattering into the street below to aid the still living, if there were any such pinned beneath the smoking heap of rubble, the spiritual rescue-squads appeared to aid those from whom life had been stricken. Some, as the Duke knew, were helpers who had no present incarnation, while others of them were just like himself—spirits whose Earthly bodies were sleeping; but there was no means to distinguish which was which. It was part of the duties of the enlightened to help the unenlightened over to the other side immediately after they had sustained the shock of death, and the Duke himself had often performed such work, leaving his body while he slept to travel in spirit to places where large numbers of people were being wiped out, without warning, through war or great disaster. He would have helped on this occasion had his own business not been urgent and had it not been apparent that ample helpers were already busy leading the bewildered newly dead away.

Although the jumble of dark roof-tops would have been incredibly confusing to the physical eye, the Duke knew not only that he was in Kensington, but his exact whereabouts. Flashing over the great, flattened dome of the Albert Hall he turned north across the Park and, coming down a little, arrived in Orme Square.

His method of travel never failed to give him a pleasurable exhilaration and it is one which most people have experienced from time to time in their dreams. He moved quite effortlessly, as though he was flying some feet above the pavement, with his head held forward and his legs stretched out behind him, but he was not conscious of their having any weight, and was able to direct himself to right or left without any motion at all but by the mere suggestion of his mind.

As he entered the Square he noted that the house on its north-west corner had already been demolished by a bomb; then he suddenly remembered that he did not know where No. 22 was situated and that it would be impossible for him to find it by normal means in the black-out, since he could not ask any policeman or air-raid warden who might be about. However, the matter presented no great difficulty, as by focusing his spiritual retina he could see perfectly clearly in the darkness, and he soon discovered No. 22.

Passing through a curtained window on the ground-floor, he found himself in an unlit dining-room where a number of naval prints decorated the walls. The hall was dimly lit and, adjusting his sight again, he saw that on the hall-stand were a few letters addressed to the Admiral, which satisfied him that he was definitely in the right house. He then drifted, silent and invisible, up the stairs.

The drawing-room was in darkness, so he travelled up

another flight to the best bedroom, which was above it, and there he found an elderly lady, whom he assumed to be the Admiral's wife, sitting up in bed reading. Apparently the Admiral had not yet got home, and after verifying this by a swift inspection of the other rooms, the Duke returned to the bedroom.

He did not sit down in a chair, as he would have done had he been in the flesh, because there was no necessity whatever to rest his limbs, and he remained effortlessly poised near the ceiling, perfectly content to await the Admiral's return. The grey-haired lady was, of course, entirely unaware that a strange presence had entered her bedroom and she continued quietly reading.

For three-quarters of an hour they both remained almost unmoving. Only once, when some bombs crumped in the near distance, the Admiral's wife gave a little wriggle of her shoulders. She was evidently a woman of that fine breed which refuses to admit fear and had decided that if she was to be killed in an air-raid she much preferred that it should be in her own bed rather than in the cold discomfort of the basement.

At the end of this lengthy wait there was a sound of feet upon the stairs. The door opened and the Admiral came in, carrying a satchel of papers. He flung the satchel on to a nearby chair and greeted his wife cheerfully, but he looked tired and harassed.

A tray with drinks and some sandwiches wrapped in a napkin had been left ready on a side-table for him, and for a little time, while he ate the sandwiches and drank a stiff whisky-and-soda, he walked about the room talking and unburdening himself of his anxieties. It was clear that he could not get his intense worry about Britain's shipping losses out of his mind, and his elderly wife listened with most sympathetic interest; but de Richleau noted that although he spoke of the gravity of the situation generally he did not disclose details or particulars of the most recent sinkings even to his wife, so evidently he was a man of real discretion.

In due course he undressed, got into bed, kissed his wife affectionately and put out the light. Ten minutes later he was in the process of drifting off to sleep.

The Duke, having adjusted his retina again, watched the

larger of the two forms under the bedclothes most intently as he speculated upon what form the Admiral's astral would take.

With the uninitiated the astral body is simply a replica of the mortal body, and until a spirit has reached a certain degree of advancement it often lacks the power to provide its astral form with clothes, or forgets to do so; which results in those dreams where, to their embarrassment, people find themselves quite naked in a mixed assembly. But once it has learnt the trick the spirit can clothe itself at will and, as its powers increase, alter its age, sex and form as desired; all of which things de Richleau could do.

Any other astral who had been present at that moment would have seen the Duke as a handsome fellow of about thirty-five, clad in a comfortable white flowing garment with a gold key-pattern hem. He had always considered it an interesting fact that astrals who had achieved power to alter their appearance rarely gave themselves back their first youth as young men and girls of about twenty. Instead, they selected the period at which they doubtless considered they had reached true maturity, which with the men was usually the middle thirties and with the women somewhere around twenty-eight.

The Admiral's wife was moving a little restlessly, not yet asleep, but the Admiral had dropped off, and while nothing at all would have been apparent to anyone awake had they been watching the bed, the Duke could now see a shimmering phosphorescence a little above the outline of the Admiral's body. After a moment it seemed to solidify and the Admiral's astral slowly sat up.

By what might be termed a flick of the will, de Richleau changed his face to that of a boy in his early teens, for although waking mortals cannot see astrals, except in comparatively rare circumstances, astrals can see one another, and he did not want the Admiral to recognise him; but, as there is no privacy on the astral plane unless special steps are taken to ensure it, he remained where he was, knowing that the Admiral would not consider it any more surprising to find a strange astral in his bedroom than, when awake, to pass a strange person in the street.

The Admiral rose to his full height, gave a friendly nod to the Duke and passed out of the room. He was obviously blissfully unaware that he was stark naked, but that fact immediatey informed de Richleau of one of the things he was anxious to know. The Admiral was a young soul and all but the minor mysteries of the Great Beyond still remained veiled to him.

This simplified matters considerably for the purpose of the investigation, as there are seven planes, or levels of consciousness, of which the Earth is the lowest and the normal sleep plane the next; but to ascend to each of those beyond requires ever greater degrees of power. De Richleau could achieve the fourth and had glimpsed the fifth on very rare occasions, but if the Admiral had been far advanced upon the great journey and had chosen to ascend into the realms of the greater Beatitudes, the Duke could not have followed him. The number of people living on this Earth who are capable of reaching the higher spheres is, however, extremely limited, and comparatively few ever get beyond the third plane in their nightly wanderings; while in the Admiral's case it was quite clear from his nudity that he was still held very near to Earth even when out of his body.

As the elderly lady was still turning restlessly, de Richleau compassionately made a sign above her which immediately sent her into peaceful sleep, but he did not wait to witness the materialisation of her astral and, leaving the room, floated gently after her husband.

The Admiral paused for a little above Orme Square to regard the blitzkrieg which was still in progress. Having muttered some profane things about the Nazis he shrugged his shoulders and turned east, moving at great speed. De Richleau followed with equal swiftness but keeping at some distance, and as they journeyed eastward through the night they passed many other astrals floating in the stratosphere. As their speed further increased these became only little blurs then faint streaks of light, until finally they made no impression at all on the surrounding darkness.

In less time than it takes to walk down the Haymarket they had left Earth behind, the darkness faded and the Duke saw that they were travelling in a country which he knew to be the astral equivalent of China. With the coming of full light the Admiral entered a rice field outside a town and began to walk along a path towards the nearest houses.

De Richleau followed, changing his costume and appearance as he did so to that of a middle-aged Chinaman.

There was nothing at all in the whole landscape to indicate that they were not actually in China. The ground was hard to the feet, a gentle wind was blowing and the leaves of a grove of bamboos were rustling in it. Only one thing indicated that they were, in fact, upon the astral plane, and this was that the Admiral, although stepping out with commendable vigour for one of his years, was still stark naked.

A hundred yards further on, a group of coolies were working among the bushes of a tea plantation. As the Admiral drew near they suddenly noticed him, stopped work, pointed and began to titter. Glancing down at himself he suddenly realised his plight and, evidently recalling the first trick which is learnt by a young spirit in its nightly wandering, exercised his will to good effect by clothing himself in the white tropical uniform of a British midshipman.

Soon afterwards he entered the Chinese city and the Duke followed him through numerous twisting byways until they reached a charming little house set apart in a garden. Secure from recognition in his disguise as a Chinaman, de Richleau had almost caught up with his quarry and could now see that although the Admiral's will had not proved strong enough to give him back his lost youth a good twenty years had fallen from him. He was more upright, less paunchy and appeared to be in the early forties, which, admittedly, was an advanced age for a midshipman but not too bad in view of his obvious intentions, for, having knocked upon the door of the little house, it had been opened to him by a smiling and most attractive young woman whose almond eyes and golden skin betrayed her oriental origin.

De Richleau sat down for a little while beneath a peach tree that was in blossom near the garden gate. It was reasonable to suppose that for one reason or another the Admiral now desired privacy and would therefore be putting up resistance to any other astral appearing to interrupt his *tête-à-tête*; yet it was necessary that the Duke should make quite certain that his quarry was not giving away information. He therefore left the astral plane, rising to the next highest level of consciousness, which is as far removed from the astral as the astral is from Earth. Invisible and soundless to the Admiral now, he drifted in through an open window. At once he observed with entirely detached interest certain not altogether unexpected, and by no means original, exercises which the Midshipman-Admiral, now once more unclothed, was performing with the willing assistance of the delightful almond-eyed lady. He then discreetly withdrew, having concluded that it was now about six to four against his discovering that willingly, or unwillingly, the Admiral spent any portion of his nights in communicating Britain's secrets to her enemies.

However, the Duke was a man who believed in always making dead certain of his facts, and it was still quite on the cards that after the Admiral had rendered the little yellow person what was obviously her due he might turn his attention to more serious matters. Clearly he must be kept under supervision until he returned to his body, so de Richleau elected to while away the time of waiting by summoning a friend. Back in the street he returned to his normal form, clothing himself as a European gentleman travelling in the Tropics, then he pronounced certain words very softly, several times, and waited for a few moments.

Shortly afterwards a plump, genial-faced Roman Catholic priest came walking down the street and he and de Richleau greeted each other with evident affection. The priest was not in a state of incarnation at this time so had no mortal body, but de Richleau had known him for many centuries and had often met him in various incarnations on Earth; at one time the two of them had been twin sisters and they were devoted to each other.

There was a tea-house near by, from the verandah of which the Duke could keep an eye upon the little house where the Admiral was disporting himself, so at his suggestion they went over and, sitting down at a table, ordered tea.

Although he was pleased to see the Duke the priest at once expressed considerable concern at being called from his duties. For years past the slaughter by violence in China had been positively appalling and he was one of the many who were helping over the unenlightened spirits that were

59

being divorced from their bodies in hundreds, day and night. De Richleau explained his own mission and asked for the counsel of his wise friend, who replied:

'I don't think there's any better line than the one you're taking at the moment. That your theory is correct I haven't the least doubt, as the Nazis are the strongest force for Evil which the Master of Evil has succeeded in introducing into the world for a very considerable time. Obviously many of their leaders must be well aware of that fact and must be utilising such powers as they possess to marshal the forces of Darkness to their aid. But I beg of you to be careful, my dear friend, since once you succeed in uncovering the mystic who is acting as their agent you'll almost certainly bring yourself into grave peril.'

'I know it,' nodded the Duke; 'but to fear anything is to open the road by which one may succumb to it.'

'True,' nodded the other. 'Fearlessness is our only armour; yet when the time comes the test may prove a terrible one.'

After that, while they sipped their tea, they talked casually of various acquaintances, just as though they had been on Earth. At length the door of the little house across the street opened and the middle-aged Midshipman stepped out of it to be waved away by his little Chinese girl-friend. De Richleau bade a hurried farewell to his companion and followed the Admiral at a distance.

When they had traversed a few hundred yards the Duke noticed that the scene about him was beginning to blur and grow indistinct, and having by certain means associated himself for the time being with the spirit of the Admiral, he realised that that worthy was about to leave the astral equivalent of China. They took the air almost at the same moment and again journeyed very fast through space until they reached a totally different scene. It was the quiet English countryside in summer, and soon the Duke was following the Admiral through the back gate of a garden, from the depths of which gay, laughing voices came to him.

They came, as he saw a few minutes later, from a tennis court about which a number of young people were assembled, and he paused to watch the scene while the Admiral went forward, now clothed in flannels and swinging a tennis-racket, to be greeted with shouts of delight from the little crowd that were evidently his friends.

There followed rather a boring time for the Duke as the Admiral, although not a particularly good performer, played six sets of tennis with considerable vigour. De Richleau meantime had again exercised those powers that were his as an old soul far advanced upon the great upward journey and removed himself to the third level of consciousness from which he could continue to observe while remaining unobserved himself.

He was considerably relieved when the scene began to fade once more and after further travel the Admiral entered a naval dockyard where, in the uniform of a lieutenant-commander, he went on board a destroyer. It was clear that he was revelling again in the joy of his first command, since the ship was of an almost obsolete pattern, having only the most primitive wireless and no anti-aircraft guns.

The Duke became even more bored with the destroyer than he had been with the tennis-party; moreover, he was now beginning to feel the strain of remaining on the third level. Just as one can only sleep for a certain time, so the period that one can remain on any of the higher levels is limited. His power to stay at such a spiritual altitude was waning, so his only course was to return to the astral and adopt a disguise. The most suitable seemed to be that of an inconspicuous member of the crew, so he became a young A.B. whose duties kept him in the neighbourhood of the bridge. Astrals are not affected by Earth conditions but are fully conscious of the climate in any astral scene in which they may happen to be, and the weather was both cold and wet, so de Richleau could cheerfully have murdered the Admiral when he decided to take the destroyer to sea. They put out of harbour with half a gale blowing and, to the Duke's fury, he was compelled to hang about the bridge of the heaving vessel for the equivalent of many hours in Earthly time while the Admiral, apparently filled with tireless energy and boundless delight, put her through endless evolutions.

It was, therefore, with a great sigh of thankfulness that the Duke observed the Admiral suddenly stagger, rock upon his feet and grab at the bridge-rail, as the scene once more dissolved. With incredible swiftness they returned to the bedroom in Orme Square and de Richleau saw, as he had guessed, that the Amdiral's wife had him by the shoulder and was gently shaking him, as she said:

'Wake up, darling, wake up; it's seven o'clock,'

Waiting for nothing more, de Richleau returned to Cardinals Folly, lay down in his Earthly body, remained still for a moment, then, opening his eyes, yawned and sat up.

'Well,' said Rex, who was seated beside him, 'how did it go?'

'Splendidly,' murmured the Duke sleepily. 'The Admiral is a dear, simple fellow and the leakage certainly does not come through him directly, although there's still just a chance that at times, all unknown to himself, he may be made the tool of some Evil force. Tomorrow night I shall spend with Captain Fennimere, but I do hope that he's not quite so keen on his job, as I positively loathe having to play the part of an Able Seaman in a gale.'

'What in heck do you mean?' asked the astonished Rex.

De Richleau smiled. 'I'm quite certain that Sir Pellinore would never believe me if I told him of my night's adventures; but you know the old saying: "There are stranger things in Heaven and Earth than are ever dreamt of in our philosophy".'

6

The Captain Goes Below

It was still early so the Duke and Rex decided to turn in for
an hour or two. Having carefully locked the door of the
library behind them and removed the key so that the servants should not see or interfere with the pentacle, they
went upstairs to their bedrooms.

In spite of his night's activities, de Richleau did not feel
the least bit tired; in fact he felt remarkably fresh, as his
sleep from half-past ten until seven o'clock was much longer than that which he usually enjoyed and his tranquillity
had not been disturbed by bombs or gunfire. Actually, he
had not exerted himself during his astral journey to anything like the same extent as the Admiral, and the only difference between them was that de Richleau had the power
to retain full and coherent memory of the things that he
had seen and done, whereas the Admiral would wake after
a good night's rest remembering nothing of his night's adventures or—at most—a muddled dream in which, perhaps,
he had played tennis on his first ship and disported himself
not altogether creditably with an oriental lady in the
middle of a tennis-court. In the meantime, while they had
been absent from their bodies their etheric bodies, which
are exact replicas of each person's physical form and remain with them always until death, had been recharged
with vitality just as a battery is recharged, since it is to give
opportunity for this absolutely essential operation that we
sleep each night.

As the Eatons, and any guests who were staying with
them, habitually breakfasted in bed, it was not until they

were all gathered in the long drawing-room before lunch that the Duke regaled the others with an amusing account of the Admiral's frolics of which he had been the unsuspected witness.

'How livid the old boy would be if he knew that you had been snooping on him!' laughed Marie Lou.

De Richleau smiled. 'He is a very young soul, so I'm quite certain that he wouldn't believe such a thing possible even if he were told about it.'

'Anyhow, I suppose we can take it that his innocence is fully established?' Richard remarked.

De Richleau shook his head. 'We are hardly justified in assuming that whoever is communicating with the enemy on the astral plane does so every time he goes to sleep; so if there's nothing suspicious in Captain Fennimere's actions when he is out of his body tonight I shall have to spend further nights checking up on both of them.'

The day was wet and dreary, so they did not go out but spent the afternoon reading and in the casual, amusing conversation of which they never tired when they were together. After dinner they repaired once more to the library and the Duke remade the pentacle. Watches were changed round, so that Simon was to take the first, Rex the second and Richard the third. The same performance was gone through as on the previous evening and by ten o'clock de Richleau, with Simon beside him to keep watch, was tucked up in bed all ready to set out on his astral journey.

He reached London about half-past ten and observed at once that there was a lull in the blitzkrieg. After the previous nights the quiet of the great city seemed a little sinister, as in view of the fact that comparatively few of London's millions could yet be asleep the silence was unnatural.

Although the night was dark and rainy the Duke had no difficulty in identifying the lake in Regent's Park and, coming down near it, he glided northwards, across the canal to the great dark block of North Gate Mansions. There were several doors to the solid, well-built flats but he soon found the hallway that served No. 43 and sailing up the lift-shaft he passed through the door of Captain Fennimere's flat to find that the Captain was off duty and had been entertaining a decidedly attractive young woman to dinner.

From their conversation it was soon clear to the Duke

that she was neither the Captain's wife nor his fiancé; but that their relations had reached a degree of no uncertain intimacy was soon manifest. A little before eleven a mid-servant came in to inquire if there was anything more that the Captain required and having been answered in the negative went off to bed. The Captain then experienced no difficulty in persuading his charming guest to remove her dress, lest it should become creased, and they settled down together very happily on a large sofa which they had drawn up in front of the fire.

The Duke viewed these proceedings with considerable regret; not because he was in any way a Puritan and would willingly have deprived either party of the recreation upon which they were bent, but because he foresaw a long and, for him, tiresome wait before there was any hope of the Captain's going to sleep.

It was hardly likely that these two obviously healthy people would have concluded their somewhat spasmodic and entirely uninteresting conversation for another hour or two, and then it was a foregone conclusion that the sailor would see the lady home; so it was quite on the cards that his astral might not emerge from its mortal frame before two or three o'clock in the morning.

However, as the conversation progressed, the Duke became aware that the couple, although obviously enamoured of each other, were not in the first hectic flush of an amour which might well have led to their remaining embraced until the early hours of the morning. He would have been prepared to wager that the affair had reached a more or less routine stage where enjoyment was had by all, but parting could be borne without heart-ache after reasonable indulgence. He therefore decided to leave them to it and return in half an hour, meanwhile occupying himself with any good work which he could find to do in the big block of mansions.

Several of the flats he visited had been evacuated by their occupants, and others provided a quiet domestic scene which failed to give him the sort of opportunity that he was seeking.

After visiting several he entered a bedroom in which a little girl was tossing sleeplessly, tortured with ear-ache. A few passes over her were sufficient to relieve the pain and send her to sleep, upon which her astral rose from her body in the form of a middle-aged man with distinguished features; who proved at once to be 'aware', as before moving off to attend to his own affairs he thanked the Duke most courteously for his kindness.

In another flat de Richleau found an elderly woman with a nasty wound in her shoulder which had been caused by the splinter of an anti-aircraft shell. He sent her to sleep also, but her astral proved to be a dull, almost sightless replica of herself which stood naked and ugly, peering at him suspiciously; upon which he promptly left her and returned to see how Captain Fennimere was getting on.

It proved that the Duke had judged his time well, as the Captain's charming guest was in the process of dressing and the Captain, who was not in the room, returned shortly afterwards with a mirror which he held for her while she tidied her hair. After she had put herself to rights they had a whisky-and-soda and a cigarette apiece, ate some biscuits and embraced with care so that the lady's make-up should not suffer in the process. De Richleau observed with some surprise that as the Captain saw her to the hall door he did not put on his cap and coat but let the girl pass out and stood there smiling 'good-night' as she went down in the lift.

'This is strangely ungallant conduct in a naval man,' thought the Duke, 'and he certainly does not deserve his good fortune.' A moment later, however, he realised that he had misjudged the Captain most unfairly, as the lift did not descend to the ground-floor but stopped two floors below, and the girl got out. Prompted by idle curiosity, de Rich'eau slid down after her and followed her through the door of a flat which was obviously her home. In the drawing-room an elderly man was sitting reading, and the Duke was considerably amused to hear the Captain's girl-friend say brightly as she came in:

'Hullo, Daddy! I do hope you weren't anxious about me but my taxi took simply ages getting across London in the black-out. Anyhow, Muriel and I spent hours practising on each other with those beastly bandages so I think we've both got a good chance of passing our First-Aid exam. tomorrow.'

'First-Aid,' murmured the Duke inaudibly. 'First-Aid,

indeed—you little minx!' Then he left the lovely liar to pass through the ceiling and the flat above into Captain Fennimere's abode.

The Captain was partially undressed and splashing about at the fixed wash-basin in his bathroom. Five minutes later he was in bed and, apparently untroubled by any pangs of conscience over his illicit affair with his neighbour's daughter or by anxieties over Britain's shipping losses, he was very soon asleep.

As he began to snore gently, his astral rose through the bedclothes and de Richleau saw at once that the Captain had reached a much more advanced state than the Admiral. Fennimere's astral immediately took the form of an extremely good-looking woman with a broad forehead and well-modelled chin which denoted intelligence and determination. She was dressed in flowing garments not unlike those that de Richleau himself was wearing and her dark hair was done high on her head in hundreds of small curls, as was the fashion in Roman times.

The Duke turned his face away so that he should not be recognised, but after one swift glance in his direction the Captain's astral made a swift and purposeful exit. From what followed, the Duke knew that they were journeying back in time. When the mist cleared, the lady with the flowing robes was walking in the garden of a Roman villa surrounded by tall cypresses and above a rocky beach which was gently lapped by the blue waters of the Mediterranean. De Richleau instantly lifted himself to a higher level of consciousness so that he would be invisible but remained in the vicinity of the moss-patched balustrade that ran along the terrace, while he kept an eye upon his quarry.

Evidently the Captain's Roman incarnation had been a particularly happy one so he returned to it as the woman he had then been, to renew his mental strength and tranquility of mind; but the Duke felt certain that he would not stay there for very long, as there is always work waiting for those who have knowledge, and such spirits are not apt to be self-indulgent.

His guess proved correct. After sauntering a little among the ilex and sweet-smelling flowering shrubs, while she gazed out with a thoughtful look across the lovely bay, the

Roman lady shook herself slightly, the whole scene disappeared and they came back through time to a very different one.

The crump of bombs and the crashing of anti-aircraft guns suddenly rent the silence and the Duke found that they were above a large city. It was not London, and for the moment he had no means of identifying it, but he assumed that it was somewhere in the Provinces. The Captain's astral went, without hesitation, to a spot where a land-mine had just exploded, and with others who were moving from the upper sphere in that direction he began to help in the work of assisting the newly-dead to find their bearings.

De Richleau saw that the Captain had now taken the form of a hospital nurse, so evidently he liked himself best as a female, but the form he had chosen was admirably suited to his present activities, as for some time after they have been struck down those who have just died nearly always fail to realise that they are dead. Unless they are possessed of the Old Wisdom they know nothing except that they seem to have sustained a severe shock and are very cold, so they lend themselves to the ministrations of a nurse more readily than to any other person and gladly accept the hot soup and warm garments which are provided for them, without having the faintest idea that these are just as much of an astral nature as they themselves.

Judging that as the Captain was obviously a practised helper he would spend the best part of his night at this work of mercy, the Duke decided that the best thing he could do was to employ himself in a similar manner, so he clothed himself in the white garments of a surgeon and set about the business.

It was near dawn when the nurse whom de Richleau was keeping under observation ceased her labours. With other helpers they had gone from one bombed building to another during the night, and for hours after the bombing ceased had busied themselves with the mortally-wounded who passed from Earth life in First-Aid Posts and hospitals.

At last the martyred provincial city faded and the Duke was aware that Captain Fennimere was once more going back in time. When he caught up with him it was to find the Captain, now in male form and dressed with the richness of a wealthy merchant of the eighteenth century, entering a long music-room in a big, well-furnished house. It then became apparent that in one of his incarnations— and probably the last—the Captain had been a most accomplished musician, or possibly even a composer. He sat down at a piano and without hesitation began to play certain soothing and delightful pieces, evidently with the intention of restoring calm to his spirit after the horrors it had witnessed during the night.

Having played for about half an hour, Captain Fennimere stopped abruptly and returned with lightning speed to his mortal body. De Richleau followed, entering the flat at North Gate just in time to see the maid set down the Captain's morning-tea at his bedside as he raised himself sleepily on one elbow. Two minutes later the Duke was back at Cardinals Folly and waking by his own will to tell Richard that all was well with him but that his night's journey had again proved fruitless.

Unlike the previous morning, de Richleau felt unrefreshed by his sleep, as is always the case after a night which one's astral has been working instead of merely amusing itself. On reaching his room, therefore, he turned in and slept for another couple of hours, this time renewing his strength by idling in those pleasant places which he could reach at will.

Later that day, after the Duke had recounted his night's adventures to the others, Richard remarked: 'How queer it is that the Admiral, who appears to be such a devoted husband in this world, should promptly rush off in his astral for fun and games with a little bit of Chinese nonsense, while the Captain, who is evidently a gay lad here, devotes himself to good works when he's on the other side.'

'There's nothing particularly strange in that,' replied the Duke. 'A person may be in a comparatively low state of spiritual development yet through energy and singleness of purpose achieve a position of considerable authority during one of his lives on Earth, just as the Admiral has done. On the other hand, however advanced people may be in their true selves, each time they are born again their knowledge is obscured by the flesh; so until their consciousness about the eternal truths is awakened through some fresh contact they may behave as though they were still in the lowest form—sometimes they even die without apparently having achieved any further progress.'

'That sounds an awful waste of time,' protested Rex.

'Oh, no, it's not; because in every life one pays off certain debts and learns something. I once knew an old ploughman who could not even read or write, yet he was in his last Earthly incarnation and due to ascend to the Buddhaic sphere. He had no idea of that at all while in his body, but I knew it because I used to seek guidance from him on the astral. He had only one lesson left to learn—that of humility—and of his own free will he had deliberately elected to be born as a poor peasant to whom all knowledge of the Old Wisdom should be denied during his last life on Earth.'

'Didn't realise one could choose the state one would like to be born in,' Simon commented.

'You cannot until you're nearing the end of your Earthly lives and have very little left to learn. It is then granted to you to select such incarnations as will enable you to master those last lessons most rapidly—just as an advanced student at a university is allowed considerable latitude in the choice of the subjects he wishes to take and his hours of work. Our Lord, for example, took the extreme step of electing to bear the pains and penalties of his last three lives in one incarnation. In the short space of thirty years he paid off every remaining debt that he had incurred during his many lives on this, the material plane, and with an unsurpassed display of fortitude supported all the resulting suffering so that he might free himself from the flesh for ever.'

'He obviously had true memory, though,' remarked Marie Lou. 'Any number of his sayings bear witness to it.'

'Certainly. Most people who are well on the upward path are reawakened some time in each Earthly incarnation. The *chance* of acquiring knowledge comes to many, either through someone they meet or through a book. Those who are not ready refuse to accept it, but those who *are* ready instinctively realise at once that all other faiths contain only a portion of the truth, because every single one of them embodies inconsistencies which cannot be got over; whereas the true wisdom is absolutely logical and completely just. No-one who has knowledge ever endeavours to force it on anyone else, because to do so is sheer waste of time; but whenever anyone is ready to receive it, steps are taken to ensure that he shall do so.'

'I wonder if I was really ready when, some years ago, you first brought it to us?' said Richard. 'I believed all right, because everything you'd ever told us fitted in, and the law of Karma, by which one reaps exactly what one sows, not an atom more nor an atom less, is so obviously fair. It does away once and for all with the hopelessly unsatisfactory teaching that after one short life—a life of only a few years for those who die in childhood—a soul is either given entry to Heaven or damned to rot in Hell for all eternity. No thinking person can possibly subscribe to a belief which is based on such an absurd travesty of justice. But except on very rare occasions I've never succeeded in remembering my dreams and at one time both Marie Lou and I tried very hard indeed. She succeeded comparatively easily, whereas I could make no headway at all.'

'That, Richard, is because Marie Lou had trained herself in past lives and at one time she was what is called a "looker" in a temple, so it was easy for her to pick up again. You, on the other hand, although you probably don't realise it, are a "healer", as for a long time past you have steadily been cultivating your powers in that direction.'

'That's interesting,' Richard smiled. 'If Marie Lou gets a headache I can certainly take it away by just a few minutes' massage.'

De Richleau nodded. 'If you started to train again you could probably do quite a lot in the way of taking pain from people who had toothache, rheumatism, and so on, as well. In any case, it is only by pure chance that Marie Lou happens to be more advanced than you are, and the fact that she remembers her dreams with unusual clarity has nothing whatever to do with it.'

'Where do I come in?' asked Simon. 'I can remember bits of my dreams every morning—that is if I concentrate when I wake up—but I've never been able to achieve continuity.'

'You're fairly well on the road, as in past lives you trained as a neophyte.'

'And me?' Rex inquired.

'You, Rex, are much the youngest soul among us and that, perhaps, is why you're so successful with all modern things on the material plane, such as handling racing-cars and aeroplanes. You have only just reached the stage at which it was time for you to be given your first opportunity to achieve wisdom. That, undoubtedly, is the reason why it was decreed that you and I should become friends.'

There was a little silence, then Simon said: 'Er—getting back to the business in hand—it seems that you're stymied with both the Admiral and the Captain, so what's the drill now?'

'I shan't bother any more with the Captain,' replied the Duke. 'From his performance last night it's clear that he is a regular helper and quite definitely one of us. I don't suppose he remembers his dreams—unless at some time he has trained himself to do so—but on the astral he obviously has full consciousness of his past lives and is well set upon the upward path. It's quite unthinkable that anyone so advanced would be led into betraying his country unconsciously, and I'm sure that he could put up sufficient resistance on his own account to prevent any evil entity forcing him into anything that he didn't wish to do. I'll have to give the Admiral a little more supervision, though, as his astral life definitely still lacks continuity, and there may be periods when he is got hold of by our enemies without his understanding what is happening to him.'

In consequence, for the next seven nights de Richleau again accompanied the Admiral upon what were undoubtedly unplanned journeys to a great variety of places. The old boy was trying very hard to master the art of regaining his lost youth but as yet he evidently had only the most rudimentary notions as to how this could be done. Once he succeeded too well and de Richleau was amused to find him enthusiastically bowling a hoop in Kensington Gardens, while on another occasion, although apparently well advanced in years, he appeared in a sloe-eyed Spanish dancer's bedroom dressed in an Eton suit. But in spite of these slight misadventures he brought all the vigour of his indestructible true personality to the full enjoyment of his nights. His lady-friends were many and varied. Innumerable sets of tennis were played with one group of acquaintances or another, he took frequent occasion to swim, with a great spluttering, and appeared to find particular delight— which the Duke by no means shared—in going to sea in the various ships that he had commanded, preferably in the roughest possible weather.

After a week of nights in the Admiral's company, during which nothing that could be regarded as in the least suspicious had occurred, the Duke formed the definte opinion that his hardy sailor could not be the unconscious means through which the Nazis were getting their information, so he decided that he must adopt a different line of investigation and went up to London to see Sir Pellinore.

He did not describe to the elderly Baronet the astral doings of the Admiral or the Captain, as he felt quite convinced that if he did Sir Pellinore's original scepticism would immediately return; it would have been asking too much of him to accept such apparently fantastic happenings, however natural they might be on the astral plane. Instead, the Duke gave a dry, business-like almost scientific report to the effect that during the past ten days he had utilised his powers to examine the subconscious of the two naval officers while they slept and had formed the opinion that neither was in any way responsible for the leakage.

'Then, if they're not, who the devil is?' grunted Sir Pellinore.

'Goodness knows,' replied the Duke. 'We are now up against exactly the same problem as we were when you originally vouched for the integrity of these two officers. They are the only people who know *all* the routes given to various convoys, and it is outside all reason to suppose that the captain of each convoy which goes out is a traitor who has means of communicating with the enemy when he js already several hundred miles from his port of departure.'

'Perhaps your theory is entirely wrong, then, and there is in the Admiralty, all unsuspected, a Nazi agent who has some means of photographing Fennimere's instructions to convoys after they're written out?'

De Richleau shrugged. 'But the Admiral himself told us that immediately the writing of them is finished Fennimere seals them up in their weighted envelopes and locks them away in his steel despatch-box. In addition, we have Fennimere's word for it that the despatch-boxes are never unlocked again before he hands them over to the various captains commanding convoy escorts, and I am quite prepared to take his word as to that.'

Sir Pellinore's blue eyes narrowed. 'I meant that the convoy instructions might be photographed by some new X-ray process through Fennimere's despatch-box, either while they are still at the Admiralty or while he is en route for one of the ports.'

'No,' de Richleau shook his head. 'Even if an X-ray apparatus has been invented which would photograph through steel, it's quite certain that the handwritten instructions are folded up before they are inserted into their envelopes; therefore the writing on them would come out in the photograph as an oblong of incredibly confused strokes owing to several lines of writing being photographed one on top of the other. I feel convinced that it would be quite impossible to decipher such a document—or at least, sufficient of it to make sense.'

'Damme!' exclaimed Sir Pellinore, 'you're right there. But we *must* get to the bottom of this business somehow. It's frightful—utterly shattering! We lost another hundred thousand tons last week. Britain's shipping losses in the Atlantic have become the crux of the whole war. If we can defeat the Nazis there everything else will take care of itself in due course; but if not, we'll never be able to build up an Air Force big enough to smash the enemy, we'll be faced with starvation and—and God knows what unthinkable fate may overtake us all.'

He rose a little wearily to indicate that the interview was over, as he added more slowly: 'It's good of you to have done what you have in an attempt to help us, but since you've failed we must try to think up other lines of investigation. I'm sure you'll forgive me now. Got a number of urgent things to which I must give my immediate attention.'

'One moment, 'said the Duke quietly. 'My own theory may be wrong, but I haven't the least intention of throwing in my hand. Since you did me the honour of calling me in, whether the leakage is on the astral or the physical plane I mean to find it.'

'That's decent of you, but I don't see what more you can do.'

'Having failed this end, I can try the other; if you're

74

prepared to get me particulars as to when the next convoy sails and the route it will take.'

'I see. You propose to try working back from an actual sinking?'

'That's the idea. But I must know approximately where the ships will be in order to find them in the great wastes of the Atlantic at night, as I make no pretence that my powers are omnipotent.'

Sir Pellinore nodded slowly. 'Well, it's a pretty stiff request—in fact, one which will have to be referred to the First Lord—but in such exceptional circumstances I've no doubt that I can fix it. Naturally, though, I wouldn't dare mention the most unusual line that your investigations are taking. And that's a nasty fence to get over, as I'm certain to be asked what use you propose to make of the information.'

'I don't think that need worry you,' replied the Duke. 'Tell them that I have a theory which I am not at the moment prepared to disclose but which concerns the interception of directional wireless, and that if I'm to check up on the messages sent out by any convoy it's essential that I should be informed of its approximate position.'

'That sounds all right on the face of it, but it won't wash in practice. I should have thought you would have realised that none of our ships use wireless once their escort has left them; to do so would give away their position to the enemy.'

'Of course,' de Richleau smiled, 'but the line I am suggesting is that, unknown to the Admiralty, somebody may use a new type of portable sending apparatus, and that I am endeavouring to find out if that is so.'

'Umph,' grunted the Baronet; 'that's pretty good. You're a shrewd feller, Duke. Very well; I'll see the people concerned tonight, and I may be able to give you the information you want tomorrow morning.'

Early next morning Sir Pellinore rang de Richleau up to tell him that he had made an appointment for him at the Admiralty, at eleven o'clock. On presenting himself there the Duke duly signed his name in the book and was taken straight up to the Admiral's room.

For a little time they discussed the theory of spies smuggling portable wireless transmitters on to one of the ships in each convoy, and the Admiral tried hard to pump his visitor about this line of investigation. But the Duke was a wily man, and although he actually knew very little about beam wireless he inferred that he was in touch with a civil radio expert who had certain original ideas on the subject and official access to B.B.C. apparatus which would enable him to make the necessary tests.

'You'll have to give this fellow particulars of the route, then,' said the Admiral glumly.

'No. That is not necessary,' de Richleau quickly reassured him; 'I can keep that part of it to myself.'

'Thank God,' the Admiral grunted. 'This business is getting us all down, but the fewer people who know how badly we're up against it the better, and I've already told you of the extreme care with which we guard the secret of each route from the moment it is decided. For that reason I must ask you to carry in your head the information which I shall give you. On no account must you write it down or make any notes about it afterwards, in case they fall into wrong hands.'

'Fortunately I have an excellent memory,' smiled the Duke.

'Very well, then. This is the situation. Our convoys are made up in various ports, mainly on the west coast and the north-east coast of Scotland. A convoy leaves every two or three days and the next one to sail is due to weigh anchor in the Mersey at eleven-fifteen tonight. It will proceed at a speed of approximately nine knots, the pace of the slowest ship, north-west by west to a point south of the Isle of Man. It will then pass through the North Channel between Ulster and Scotland until it has Malin Head, North Ireland, upon its beam, when it will set a course north-west by north to a point 58 degrees north and 12 degrees west. At that point its escort will leave it and it will turn west by south, continuing on that course until it reaches the twentieth meridian west, upon which it will turn south-west. I need not bother you with particulars regarding the latter half of its journey, since during that the convoy will have passed out of the danger area.'

Richleau repeated the particulars several times, then he said: 'I take it, then, that the sinkings all occur within two or three days of each convoy having been left by its escort?'

'Not all; but certainly eighty-five per cent of them take place within forty-eight hours of the escort's having turned for home.'

'Wouldn't it be possible, then, for the escorts to continue with convoys for an additional two days?'

The Admiral sadly shook his head. 'That is the obvious solution, but it just can't be done. Owing to our commitments in the Mediterranean, and the necessity for maintaining a strong fleet constantly in Home waters to repel any attempt at invasion, we simply have not enough destroyers to go round. Last spring we had virtually got the submarine menace under, but the collapse of France altered all that. The Italians would never have dared to come in if France hadn't cracked, and however much we may despise the cowardice of the Italian Navy it cannot possibly be ignored as long as it has warships which are capable of putting to sea and bringing their guns to bear upon either our shipping in the Mediterreanean or the coast towns of our Allies and ourselves.'

Turning in his swivel chair he pointed to a large wall map and went on: 'As you can see at a glance, the coasts of Italy, Sicily, Sardinia, Libya, the Dodecanese, Eritrea and Italian Somaliland together stretch for literally thousands of miles. They require a deal of watching to prevent Italian units skulking from port to port and massing somewhere so that they might suddenly emerge and take small portions of our Mediterranean Fleet by surprise. But that's not the end of the story. As Italy came in, throwing this huge additional task upon our shoulders, France went out. A number of her lighter ships came over to Britain with General de Gaulle, but the great bulk of the French Fleet was lost to us. In consequence, the Navy has ever since been faced with the positively Herculean labour of maintaining the freedom of the seas against two still considerable enemy Navies and the enemies' powerful long-range bombers, entirely on its own.'

De Richleau lit one of his long, fat Turkish cigarettes. 'Yes. I've never had any illusions as to what the collapse of France really meant for Britain. I was born a Frenchman myself, but I should be the very first to urge that when the war is over men of Bordeaux and Vichy should be dealt with without mercy. It's not only the crook politicians like Laval who are responsible; without adequate support they could not have done what they have done. I should say that if one includes high officers of the Navy, Army and Air Force, politicians and bureaucrats, there are at least two thousand Frenchmen who should be shot for the part they have played in disgracing the fair name of France and jeopardising the freedom of the world.'

'You're right there, and I only hope that our leaders will not show any stupid sentimental weakness once we're in a position to call these fellows to account. But the devil of it is that, although I would never admit it outside these four walls, our Victory still remains horribly uncertain. I tell you, Duke sometimes at night during the past few weeks I've wakened up in a cold sweat. The treachery of France is only now beginning to have its full effect through these terrible shipping losses which we're sustaining in the Western Atlantic. When I think of our ships going down night after night with hundred of decent sailormen and all those cargoes, the safe arrival of which alone can give us the power to break the Nazis, I could cheerfully cut the throat of every Frenchman indiscriminately.'

The Admiral paused for a moment, then went on with quiet grimness. 'Still, it's no good jobbing backwards; the foul deed of betrayal is history now, and it's left for people like you and me to try to counter the appalling results. I'm hanged if I can see why you should be able to do anything about it which we can't do here, and I don't get this beam wireless idea of yours at all. However, like a drowning man I'm prepared to clutch at any straw, and there's something about you which somehow gives me the wild hope that instead of a straw you may prove a solid wooden spar.' He stood up and held out his hand. 'For *God's* sake do your damn'dest.'

'I will,' said the Duke, and he added a phrase of which he alone knew the true significance. 'I'll get to the bottom of this even if I have to go to Hell to do it.'

7

Ghosts Over the Atlantic

As de Richleau sped back to Worcestershire that afternoon it caused him considerable amusement to speculate on what the Admiral's reactions would have been had he remarked on parting: 'I am not experimenting with beam wireless at all, but with something very different; the sort of thing which enables me to tell you, without ever having seen you undressed in the flesh, that you have a large red mole on the left side of your behind.'

But he knew that any such mischievous impulse would have been exceedingly ill-timed and that it was very much better that with the exception of Sir Pellinore the authorities should continue to believe him to be no more than an amateur in counter-espionage who had been called on the off-chance that he might produce an original idea which would furnish a key to the problem that was driving them all nearly insane with worry.

When he reached Cardinals Folly he asked Marie Lou to provide him with a light, early dinner so that he would be able to settle down in the pentacle for the night by nine o'clock. He had long since acquired the power to sleep at will and it was his intention to make an early start that night so that he could witness the departure of the convoy. By quarter-past nine, with Rex beside him as guardian for the first watch, he dropped off into an easy sleep and a few seconds later he was above Liverpool.

He did not know the whereabouts of Admiralty Headquarters there, but the impulse to reach it carried him to a big building down near the docks.

Soundless and invisible, he entered the building and made a tour of the first-floor rooms. It was there that he expected to find the office of the Admiral commanding the station and he was reasonably confident that it was in the Admiral's office that the sealed orders would be handed over to the O.C. convoy escort. For some moments he searched fruit-lessly. It then occurred to him that in view of the air-raids which Liverpool was sustaining it was probable that the Admiral's quarters had been transferred to the basement, where there would be considerably less risk of any import-ant papers, to which he and his immediate staff alone had access, being destroyed by fire or explosion.

Dropping down, he found that the whole basement had been strengthened with girders and was air-conditioned. The upper rooms—which were now evidently used only for routine work—were three-parts empty, but in spite of the lateness of the hour the basement was a hive of activity. Steel and gas-proof doors shut each compartment off from the other, and with the naval officers hurrying to and fron the place had a definite similarity to a scene below-decks on a warship.

After visiting a number of the cell-like offices he found the Admiral's room and, to his satisfaction, that both the Admiral and Captain Fennimere were in it. The Admiral was a shrewd-looking man with thin, dark hair brushed straight back, and de Richleau noticed that the handker-chief with which he was blowing his nose had, instead of a monogram, a small black crab embroidered in one corner. Fennimere was sitting opposite him clasping his steel des-patch-case on his knees though his life depended upon his not putting it down even for one moment. Two other senior officers were present, one of whom wore the ribbon of the V.C., and from the conversation that followed it transpired that he was O.C. anti-submarine devices for the Western Approaches.

Then a short, grizzle-haired Captain joined them and it soon became clear that he was the officer commanding the escort. One of the staff-officers gave him a sealed packet containing his own orders—which he was not to open until both convoy and escort were clear of the Mersey—and Fennimore handed over the steel despatch-box which would be passed to the O.C. convoy, according to the

Duke's reckoning, three nights hence when the escort was about to turn for home. The Admiral said a few words about some new special precautions which had just been instituted, and wished the grizzle-haired man luck; upon which he saluted and took his departure.

De Richleau followed him upstairs to the hall, where he was met by a lieutenant of Marines and two privates with fixed bayonets, who had evidently been detailed to act as his escort. All four of them got into a car and drove slowly through the black-out, down to the dockside. There they transferred to a naval pinnace and were taken out to the flotilla leader. The Captain went straight up to his bridge and locked the despatch box in a safe. Half an hour after he had come on board the big destroyer put to sea.

For the best part of an hour de Richleau moved over the dark waters, visiting first one ship of the convoy and then another, until he had had a look at the captains of all eighteen ships included in it. About the two other destroyers that formed the remainder of the escort he did not bother, as he felt satisfied that none of their personnel could be responsible for any leakage; it must lie somewhere between the captain of the escort and the officer commanding the convoy. Therefore, when he had completed his tour, which was through by half-past twelve, he returned to Cardinals Folly, woke himself up, and after a short chat with Simon, who was on duty, they both went upstairs to spend the remainder of the night in their comfortable beds.

On the following night de Richleau went to sleep within the pentacle at his usual hour and at once proceeded in search of the convoy. He found it emerging from the North Channel and no great distance from Malin Head. A choppy sea was running and the cargo-steamers wallowed through it while the destroyers slowly circled round their charge. Having counted the ships de Richleau found that so far none of them was missing; so he went aboard the flotilla leader and entered the Captain's bridge cabin. The grizzle-haired sailor was lying dozing on his bunk, but fully dressed even to his sea-boots so that in the event of an alarm he could jump up, run out on to the bridge and take immediate control.

After glancing at him de Richleau moved towards the safe and—just as he could pass through walls or floors in his astral state—the steel safe presented no barrier to his superhuman sight. He saw at once that the despatch-box was lying there, on the second shelf, in the exact position which the Captain had left it the night before and that the document inside had not been tampered with. Satisfied on this point, there was nothing else that he could do, so he returned home, woke himself up and went upstairs to bed.

On the second night of the convoy's voyage he followed exactly the same procedure, and with the same results. The despatch-box had not been opened or even moved. He had not thought it likely that it wou!d be, but the journey took him little time and he considered it well worth while to make absolutely certain of his facts at each stage of the investigation.

According to his estimate, based on the speed of nine knots, at which average the convoy was travelling, he anticipated that it would reach the spot where its escort was to leave it at about five o'clock in the morning on the third night out, but it might do so earlier if conditions proved unexpectedly favourable or be several hours late if it met with bad weather. He assumed that at whatever time it reached the spot the sealed orders would be handed over and opened and it now seemed clear that it was from that moment that treachery was to be expected.

As it was unthinkable that the captains commanding convoys were all traitors the probability was that in each convoy leader the Germans planted somebody who was able to get access to the route instructions once they had been opened. So far there had been no indication of any kind that the Nazis were using the occult as a means of communication, and the Duke felt that it was quite on the cards that it might, after all, transpire that Nazi agents were smuggling aboard some new type of small but powerful wireless transmitter by which they could give the convoy's position once they had discovered it.

In either case, whether they were communicating by the occult or by radio, it was hardly likely that they would be able to get sight of the secret orders immediately the O.C. convoy opened them. Hours, or even a day and a night, might elapse before they were able to do so. In consequence, to discover the spy would necessitate the captain of the convoy leader, and his orders, being kept under close observation from the very moment that he received them, possibly for twenty consecutive hours or more, and here arose the snag that there were limits to the length of time that de Richleau could remain asleep.

Normally he rarely went to bed before two and woke about eight o'clock, and although he had to a certain degree mastered the art of prolonging his periods of sleep by will, during the past ten days he had to utilise this power to such an extent that he could see the 'red light' ahead. Since the beginning of his investigation he had on average been sleeping for three hours longer each night than was his normal custom, so altogether he had put in about thirty hours' extra sleep while at Cardinals Folly, and this was beginning seriously to upset the laws of Nature by which humans are bound, whatever may be the occult powers which they have acquired for use on special occasions.

To be on the safe side he thought that he ought to be aboard the flotilla leader again by two o'clock in the morning, but it was unlikely that the sealed orders would be handed over until hours later; and even then the spy might have no opportunity to get to work until late in the following day.

Consequently the Duke foresaw the danger that if it proved necessary for him to remain asleep for more than twelve hours during the coming night—and that he estimated to be about his limit—he might find himself absolutely compelled to wake up just at the critical moment, or before the Nazi agent started to get busy. It would be at least six hours before he could hope to sleep again even for a short period, and if the job were done during that interval all his previous investigations would be entirely wasted. He decided, therefore, that from this point on he must have help upon the astral.

That evening he consulted with his friends and explained the situation to them. Although only Marie Lou could recall her dreams perfectly, and Simon imperfectly, any of them could relieve de Richleau in his watch on the convoy while in their astrals and report to him when he came on duty again before returning to their bodies, and all four of them immediately volunteered to do so. It then became a suggestion as to which of them was the most suited to undertake the business.

Simon grinned broadly at the others. 'My job. None of you can deny that I know more about the occult than the rest of you. Never thought the day might come when I'd have cause to be glad about those months when I studied under that swine Mocata, but I learnt a lot from him before the Duke succeeded in chaining him and sending him down to Hell.'

'Nothing doing,' said Rex. 'I figure that the fact that you once darned-nearly became a Black Magician rules you right out of this. I was the first to be roped in as the Duke's helper on that other party so I claim that right again this time.'

Richard tapped the table thoughtfully. 'I entirely support Rex in his contention that this is no job for Simon.'

'Good man,' exclaimed Rex.

'But on the other hand,' Richard continued amiably, 'I don't think that it is any job for you, because you are the youngest soul amongst the five of us and therefore the least experienced. If we *do* run into the Black that we believe to be operating for the Nazis this may prove a highly dangerous business. It so happens that you're all in my house, and I couldn't think of letting any guest of mine run a risk when I'm in a position to take it myself; so it's quite obvious that I should be the one to go.'

'Ner,' Simon shook his head. 'The fact that I once very nearly became a Black was all washed out by the Lord of Light who appeared to us in that old Greek monastery; he gave me a free pardon for my idiocy. But you're right about the possible danger, and it's experience that counts in these things, Richard.'

'O.K., we'll grant you that,' Rex grinned; 'but if you're right we'll certainly need you for the big show-down later on, so you'd best let me handle this easy stuff at the beginning of the check-up. After all, it's not yet even certain that the Nazis *are* using the occult for their dirty business.'

'If you've all quite done,' said Marie Lou sweetly, 'the three of you can go quietly away into the garden while Greyeyes gives me my instructions.'

She waved away the chorus of protest and went on: 'My claim is quite incontestable, because except for dear

84

Greyeyes I am by far the most advanced among you, and although in my present earthly incarnation I may not understand as much of the theory of the occult as Simon does, I'm far more powerful than any of you on the astral; and while Richard's argument about being your host is a perfectly sound it one it applies equally to me since I happen to be your hostess. Am I right, Greyeyes?'

De Richleau nodded. 'You win, Princess. But I think that, on this first journey at least, it would be wise for you to have a companion, and in my view Simon is the best qualified to go with you.'

Marie Lou hummed a little song of triumph while Simon sat back and grinned at the ceiling. Richard and Rex both put up a show of protest, but it was only a show, as they knew from experience that the Duke once having made a decision could not be turned from it. He was already speaking again.

'This is what I propose. I shall go to sleep later than usual tonight and join the convoy at about two o'clock. Exactly *when* the documents will be handed over it is impossible to say, but I should think they will almost certainly reach the spot where it's to be done some time before dawn. I don't know yet which is the convoy leader, but it is probably the largest ship. In any case, I shall follow to whichever ship the sealed orders are taken and keep both them and its captain under observation. As I may have to go out again the following night I don't think that I had better strain myself by attempting to sleep for more than eight hours, which will bring us round to ten o'clock tomorrow morning.

'Marie Lou and Simon will then come out to relieve me and I shall be able to tell them if any treachery has yet occurred. If it has not, it'll be up to them during the daytime to keep watch on the captain commanding the convoy and on the sealed orders, which by then will almost certainly have been opened. It is important that one of them should keep very close to the captain in order that they may know if he reveals to any of his officers or others on the ship, the contents of the orders, because, should he do so, anyone he tells will have to be kept under observation too, as that may be the person who is communicating with the enemy. It's more probable, though, that once the orders have been opened some member of the crew will endeavour to get a sight of them while the captain is asleep or out of the way and then go off to perform his nefarious task. Should either of you discover that any act of treachery is about to be performed you will instantly call upon me and I shall join you.'

'If that happened only an hour or so after you'd got back you would hardly be able to go to sleep again so quickly,' remarked Richard.

'No,' agreed the Duke; 'but I could put myself into a self-induced trance. I don't wish to do that if I can avoid it, as it would prove an additional strain, but it's essential that I should be there if anything is going on, so I may have to.' He glanced at Marie Lou. 'How many hours' sleep do you think you could manage?'

'It all depends upon how tired we are when we go to bed,' said Marie Lou sensibly.

Simon nodded. 'I shall stay up all night.'

'That's the idea,' she agreed, 'and if we don't sleep until ten o'clock tomorrow morning we shall have been awake for twenty-six hours before we start off, so we ought easily to be able to manage ten hours.'

'In that case, if nothing has happened, I will relieve you again at seven o'clock in the evening,' said the Duke. 'That is only nine hours, but we mustn't risk any hiatus between spells. Now, about watchers. Simon and Marie Lou had better sit up with me all night, then they can keep each other awake. Richard and Rex will go to bed as usual and get a full night's sleep, and at nine they had better come downstairs and bed down the others beside me in the pentacle so that they drop off to sleep well before ten o'clock— but, naturally, I shall remain on duty until they turn up. Is that all quite clear?'

His question was answered by a chorus of agreement and Marie Lou left them to get out clean linen to make up beds for herself and Simon beside the Duke's in the pentacle.

After dinner that night they enjoyed a mild game of *Vingt-et-Un*. At one o'clock Richard and Rex went up to bed while the other three began their preparations in the library. Marie Lou had produced some new packs of cards so that she and Simon could play bezique and double patience as a variation to quiet conversation during their long vigil. By a quarter to two the Duke had settled down and by two o'clock he was asleep.

As he sped out over the cold, night-darkened waters of the North Atlantic he thought once again of the giant task with which the British Navy is faced in time of war. On any map the patches of blue look so relatively small that one gets the idea that a warship dotted here and there is ample to keep a great area under observation, but when actually at sea one realised the immensities of the oceans and the very considerable spaces of even what are termed 'the narrow waters'.

Below him lay a vast, desolate waste of gently-heaving, greenish sea, stretching unbroken from Northern Ireland to Iceland, and while passing over it he saw only two little dark shapes of patrolling naval vessels before he caught up with the convoy. It was still heading on the same course. Descending to it, he entered the bridge cabin of the flotilla leader and, hovering there without any sense of tiredness, patiently awaited events.

At four o'clock the Captain went out on to the bridge and through his conversation with the officer on watch the Duke learnt that the convoy had made good going and would reach the point where the escort should turn for home in about half an hour, but that the Captain had no intention of leaving his charge until daylight as he would then have the opportunity of making quite certain that the convoy had a clear horizon ahead.

Dawn came, grey, faint, uncertain, a little after seven, but it was not until eight o'clock that the officers on the flotilla-leader's bridge showed any unusual activity. An order was then given, a flag signal run up and the destroyer brought down to half speed.

As de Richleau watched he saw that the largest ship in the convoy—a liner of some 12,000 tons with six-inch guns mounted fore and aft—was about to lower a boat. It seemed a tricky proposition as a fierce sea was running, but evidently the seamen knew their business, for soon afterwards the boat cast off and headed for the flotilla leader. At periods it entirely disappeared in the trough of the waves but it was a broad-beamed motor-lifeboat and it made steady progress. The destroyer, meanwhile, further decreased her speed and manœuvred skilfully to enable it to come alongside. Lines were cast out, a safety-belt was buckled on to an oilskinned figure in the stern of the boat and a rope-ladder was lowered by which he came aboard.

Owing to the oilskins he wore the Duke could not ascertain his rank but he heard him addressed as Carruthers by the Captain of the escort, who at once led him up to his cabin, where they had a whisky-and-soda together while the safe was unlocked and the despatch-box handed over. They then shook hands, wished each other the best of luck and the man in the oilskins returned to his boat to be carried back to his own ship. De Richleau, silent and unseen, accompanied him to the liner, which they reached a quarter of an hour later. The destroyer flew another signal, all the ships in the convoy sounded their sirens by way of farewell and the warships, making a great circle, turned south-east by east, increased their speed until great sheets of spray were flying from their bows, and headed back towards England.

The Duke had followed Carruthers up the ladder to his own bridge cabin, where he removed his oilskins and revealed himself to be a naval officer of captain's rank. Taking a key from his pocket, he opened the despatch-box and the envelope it contained, ran his eyes swiftly over the secret instructions, replaced them in the box, locked it and then locked the box up in his safe; after which he went out on to the bridge and gave orders for a new course to be set.

The half-flotilla of destroyers had disappeared over the horizon and as a signal fluttered out from the halliards of the liner the whole convoy wheeled round. De Richleau saw that it had now turned west by south. This manœuvre was, he guessed, evidently a deliberate policy on the part of the Admiralty to ensure that no one who had been in the escort ship should be able to give away the direction in which the convoy was moving after they had left it.

The Duke kept Captain Carruthers constantly in view as he knew that the critical point of his investigation must now be approaching. He had established, beyond any question of doubt, that the leakage did not take place in London or while the sealed orders were in the care of the captain commanding the escort, but now that they had been opened there was an immediate possibility that Carruthers might mention their contents to one of his officers and that he, in turn, might spread through the ship particulars of the route which they had been ordered to take. If that occurred, the silent, invisible watcher knew that he would need all the vigilance he could command, as he might have to keep his eye upon a number of people at the same time; but he felt reasonably confident that he would be able to do so, even if they were dispersed in different parts of the ship, owing to his power of rapid movement from one place to another.

Having given the order for the change of course, however, Carruthers spoke to no one. He was a red-faced, tight-lipped man and the Duke soon formed the impression that he was not the type to give anything away by casual talk. It looked as if the Nazi spy—if there was one on board —gained his information by securing access to the orders when the Captain was not about, and any such attempt might not take place for several hours.

It was now getting on for ten o'clock and de Richleau began to look about for signs of Marie Lou or Simon. He was already conscious of an urge to get back to his own body and he hoped that they would not be late, as the strain of resisting the drag might become considerable.

It was just after ten when Marie Lou silently appeared beside him. She had purposely retained in her astral form the features which de Richleau knew in Earth life so that he should have no difficulty in recognising her, but she was considerably taller than her mortal self and under the yachting-cap which she was wearing he noted that she had given herself golden hair instead of her chestnut curls.

Both were naturally invisible and soundless to the men on the bridge near them but their astrals could speak to each other in their normal voices.

He smiled at her and said: 'Why the increase in height, Princess, when you are quite perfect in your mortal body? I don't like it at all.'

She looked slightly piqued. 'That's the first time I've ever had the reverse of a compliment from you, Greyeyes dear. I've always wanted to be taller; I'm such a silly little person when I'm on Earth and height gives me dignity.'

'You foolish child,' he laughed. 'Who would ever wish

you to be dignified? And, in any case, if it's your whim to
be taller you should certainly consult a cheval-glass when
composing your astral. Don't you see that although those
lovely long legs you have given yourself are remarkably
beautiful, as legs they are entirely out of proportion to your
body?'

Somewhat abashed, Marie Lou looked down and proceeded to adjust herself a little. 'How about my hair,
though?' she asked, removing her cap. 'Do you like me as
a blonde?'

He considered her carefully for a moment. 'Yes. Not
better, but as well; and you would be totally enchanting
whatever colour hair you had.'

'Thank you. Sometimes I make it powder-blue, but I
thought that was hardly suited to this occasion.'

'No,' the Duke agreed; 'a little too exotic. But I can
imagine situations in which it would prove immensely
attractive.'

'I suppose nothing's happened yet, or you wouldn't be
so concerned with my appearance?'

'No, nothing. Carruthers is the name of the man commanding the convoy; he's that rather red-faced fellow over
there standing on his own at the port side of the bridge,
staring out across the water. Directly he got back on board
with his orders he opened them up, read them and put
them in the safe, which is near the head of his bunk inside
his bridge cabin. Except to give the officer of the watch a
new course he hasn't spoken to a soul yet, so up to the
moment he remains the only person in the whole convoy
who knows the route that it has been ordered to take.'

At that moment Simon, who had been a little longer in
getting off to sleep than Marie Lou, joined them. They both
recognised him at once as he, too, had retained his earthly
features, but in all other respects his astral was very different
from his mortal body. Instead of the narrow-shouldered,
stooping fellow that they knew, Simon appeared as a
splendidly-set-up man of about thirty with dark, flashing
eyes and his head beautifully set on a pair of broad shoulders. He was dressed in a warm, leather ski-ing suit, a type
of garment that he never wore on Earth, and from the
vigour of his movements no one would have doubted that

90

he could have got his Cresta colours if that had been his wish.

'Well, how're things?' he asked in a rich, strong voice as he came towards them.

'I've just been telling Marie Lou,' said the Duke. 'The orders are in the safe and no one has yet seen them except the Captain, and he hasn't passed them on to anyone else, so for the time being your job is a very straightforward one: all you have to do is to watch the safe and the Captain.'

'Right,' said Simon. 'We'll take over, then, and you'd better get back. We'll expect to see you again at about seven o'clock this evening.'

'That's it,' agreed the Duke; 'but if you see anyone about to start any funny business you're both to summon me at once with all the force of your wills, and I shall join you as quickly as I can.'

As he finished speaking his astral faded and they knew that he had returned to his mortal body at Cardinals Folly.

The day was grey and dreary. Spread out over several miles the eighteen ships were slowly ploughing their way through the icy green seas of the North Atlantic. In each a sharp watch for enemy submarines was being kept by warmly-clad look-outs in the crow's-nests, while other members of the crew fore and aft stood near the anti-aircraft guns, scanning the skies, through binoculars, for Nazi planes. Otherwise there was little activity in any of the ships and the crews were going about their dangerous but monotonous routine duties.

At half-past ten Captain Carruthers went forward and carried out an inspection of a portion of the crew's quarters, after which he talked for a little with his second-in-command; but Simon, who was standing within a few feet of them, noted that the Captain made no mention of the route that the convoy had been ordered to take.

By half-past eleven the sun had come out so the navigating officer was able to get his midday observation without any difficulty. When he had worked out the ship's position he reported to Carruthers, who ordered a slight change of course which turned the convoy a few degrees further to southward. At one o'clock the Captain lunched in solitary state and immediately afterwards, fully dressed, he lay down on his bunk to sleep.

Shortly after three, a ship, half a mile away on the starboard quarter of the convoy leader, suddenly blazed off with one of its guns. Instantly every ship leapt into activity, put on its maximum speed and, altering course, began to zigzag from side to side.

Carruthers came running out on to the bridge with a pair of binoculars and swift signals from one ship to another fluttered up and down. But there was no more firing; very soon everything returned to normal and Carruthers went back to his bunk. One of the look-outs on the ship that had fired the gun had thought that he had sighted the periscope of an enemy submarine, but it had turned out to be a piece of driftwood which was bobbing up and down some distance away.

As the afternoon wore on Simon and Marie Lou became thoroughly bored with their job but they did not relax their vigilance. At five o'clock a steward roused the Captain and brought him tea, after which he went out on to the bridge again. Dusk was now closing in upon the troubled waters and the other ships were only just visible. In all the long day they had not sighted another vessel, and had seen only one British patrolling aeroplane, but at about half-past five they heard the drone of powerful engines and the sailors immediately rushed to anti-aircraft stations.

However, it proved that the planes were a flight of new bombers being flown across from Canada to Britain. As their leader sighted the convoy on the darkening sea he dipped in salute, bringing the great plane down quite low so that for a moment it looked as though it must graze the mast-heads, while the sailors, who had all run up on deck, gave the airmen a rousing cheer.

Just before six the second-in-command entered the bridge cabin and made a report to Carruthers about a seaman who had met with an accident the previous day. Apparently the doctor had feared that he would die, but the man had now taken a turn for the better. The two officers had a pink-gin together and talked for a little time about routine matters, then they listened to the six-o'clock news on the wireless.

By this time Simon was getting restless, as normally he needed little sleep and nine hours was an unusually long spell for him, although he had thought that he would manage it quite easily after having been up all the previous night. Marie Lou told him that he could go home if he wished, as she was quite capable of staying on duty for another couple of hours if necessary, and the Duke was due to put in an appearance long before that; but Simon said that he was determined to stick it out and subdue his urge to return to his body until de Richleau relieved him.

De Richleau arrived at seven o'clock to the moment, as the ship's bell was still clanging, and they told him that they had nothing to report. Night had now fallen and all three of them were standing out in the black darkness of the bridge. The Duke was just about to tell the others that they could return home when he suddenly shivered and looked about him quickly.

Astral bodies are not affected by the weather conditions of Earth, so the clothing that the three were wearing was a mental concession to the scene about them and in no sense because such garments were necessary to protect them from the wind and flying spray; but astral forms *do* feel the cold or heat natural to any astral phenomena which may be in their vicinity—hence the discomfort that the Duke had suffered when he had had to take the form of an Able Seaman on the first night that he had gone out to watch the Admiral and the Admiral had sailed an astral sea in on astral ship.

'Do either of you feel anything unusual?' the Duke asked sharply.

As astrals present in an Earth scene, neither of the others had, up to that moment, been conscious of the temperature at all, but as de Richleau spoke Marie Lou said:

'Yes. It seems to be getting awfully cold.'

Simon turned at the same moment and glanced over his shoulder. 'There's quite a wind blowing from somewhere, and it can't be an Earth wind; there must be something pretty nasty passing near us at the moment.'

De Richleau nodded. 'It may be passing; but somehow I don't think so. For the time being you two had better remain with me.'

The cold had increased to a deadly chill and he knew that abominable wind to be a certain indication of the presence of disembodied Evil. With a sudden absolute conviction that his theory was right—the Nazis *were* using the occult—he turned towards the cabin.

'Come on!' he cried. 'Quick! This is the thing for which we have been waiting.'

8

A Nightmare that was Lived

Now that the presence of the unknown Evil could be so
definitely felt, de Richleau knew that the astral which was
working for the Nazis might appear at any moment. If
they remained as they were the astral would see them and,
if it realised that they were spying on it, would either make
off or give battle, according to its power. In either case they
would be robbed of the opportunity of seeing how it did
its work, so as they passed into the Captain's cabin de
Richleau, knowing that his companions could not raise
themselves to a higher level of consciousness, swiftly told
them to change their forms. As he spoke, he became a fly
and they immediately followed suit.

So far no strange astral form was visible and there was
nothing whatever to indicate the presence of Evil except
that grim, unnatural cold which they could feel but which,
apparently, the Captain could not, for his cabin was warmly
heated and he was not wearing his fleece-lined oilskins or
sou'-wester.

Carruthers was now seated at a wall desk with a ledger
opened up in front of him. For some little time nothing
happened. Then Marie Lou, her sense of the mischievous
getting the better of her uneasiness about the source of the
cold, decided to amuse herse'f by tickling the taciturn sailor
and alighted with her six feet spread well out, on the tip of
his nose.

Contrary to her expectations, he did not draw back and
make an ineffective grab at her, but sat there unheeding, as
he continued to examine his accounts regarding the bottom

of his glass. She performed a little dance to rouse him, but almost at once de Richleau's voice reached her.

'This is no time for playing the fool,' he said with unusual sharpness, 'and you ought to have the sense to realise that he can neither feel nor see you, because whatever form you take you're still on the astral. I ordered the change only to make us less conspicuous to any evil entity that may appear.'

With a word of contrition, Marie Lou gave up her sport and flew off to one of the white-painted girders above the Captain's head. Just as she had settled there his steward came in to lay the table for dinner.

In due course dinner was served but the Captain did not seem to have much of an appetite and only toyed with his food. He sat there for some time over each course and appeared deep in thought; a "thriller" lay open on the table beside him but he did not attempt to read it.

Having finished his dinner Carruthers went over and lay down on his bunk, while the table was cleared and the cabin tidied. For the best part of an hour the intense cold had continued unabated, and Simon was now having to struggle hard to keep himself asleep, but no manifestation of any kind other than the cold was perceptible to the astral senses of the watchers.

It was well past eight when the Captain rolled off his bunk and, crossing the cabin to the safe, began to fumble for his keys.

De Richleau signed to his two companion flies to come near him so that all three of them by standing with their legs just touching could increase their resistance should the evil Entity actually appear now that the critical moment was come.

Carruthers got the safe open, pulled out the despatch-box, unlocked it and took out the convoy route order. Carrying it over to his bunk, he sat down with the instructions in his hand and began to re-read them.

The cold had now become positively icy and Simon felt himself absolutely drooping with desire to fall awake, but at a slight pressure from the Duke he roused and saw that something was moving just above the Captain's head.

Next minute the 'Thing' was plain to all three of them. It was a thick-lipped negroid face behind which a high-domed head and powerful shoulders began to materialise.

Instantly they realised that this was the enemy astral and that he was now memorising the convoy route as the Captain held it open in his hand.

Within a split second de Richleau had changed himself into a great blue dragon-fly of the highly-poisonous variety that is found in the forests of the Amazon. Almost as quickly Marie Lou converted herself into a fat black-and-yellow queen wasp. Together they launched themselves upon the Negro, while Simon, whose processes on the astral were much slower, was still struggling to equip himself suitably for participation in such a battle.

Although they streaked at him from behind, the negroid astral must have sensed the presence of an enemy. He suddenly changed form, becoming a huge black flying beetle which zoomed up to the roof of the cabin so that the dragon-fly and queen wasp shot past underneath him. Dropping like a plummet, he would have severed Marie Lou's pointed tail with his powerful pincers had not Simon, in the guise of a hornet, come hurtling towards him at that instant.

For the space of an aircraft dog-fight the four winged astrals circled about one another with amazing speed, the three bright champions of Light endeavouring to pierce the beetle's guard and bury their stings in his body. But his back was armoured, so they could not get at him from above, and each time they darted at him he drove them off with swift slashes of his formidable knife-like claws.

Suddenly the beetle changed, swelling in size and assuming the appearance of a large black bird with a vulture-like beak. One snap of that beak would have cut any of his three enemies clean in half, and his movements were so swift that Marie Lou and Simon had to zip with lightning speed to sanctuary in corners among the white-painted girders where the great bird could not get at them.

While they were both striving to formulate in their minds a more suitable astral the Duke had already changed to a golden eagle and one slash of his strong claws tore half a dozen feathers out of the black vulture's tail. The bird screeched with rage and next second was gone from the cabin with the eagle sailing swiftly in pursuit.

Both Simon and Marie Lou knew that they were leaving

Earth to continue this astral battle in other spheres and, converting themselves into powerful feathered creatures, they made off in the track of the two birds. As she left the cabin Marie Lou caught a last glimpse of Captain Carruthers. He had not seen or heard the faintest indication of that strange fight which had raged within a few feet of his head, and he was still sitting there holding the open order, evidently conscientiously committing its contents to memory.

The Evil entity led them to a dark country on the astral plane which has no replica on Earth. It was a place of black mountains and great gorges; yet it had a tropical richness of strange verdure in its valleys. Many of the plants were forms of cactus; others were like huge toadstools. Instead of grass the ground was covered with poison-ivy and fly-eating plants and the whole of this thick vegetation swarmed with poisonous insects and reptiles.

As yet the enemy had not thrown off his disguise and still appeared as a black vulture that flew screaming through the dark valleys which were lit only by a faint, uncanny, moon-like radiance. De Richleau, too, had continued his semblance of an eagle.

Suddenly the vulture dropped like a stone and disappeared among the leprous-looking foliage. De Richleau plunged after it and was lost to sight. The other two then knew that unless they were to lose their quarry they must assume forms which would enable them to follow through the seemingly impenetrable tangle of hideous undergrowth.

Marie Lou again became a queen wasp and Simon, with a great effort of his tired will, changed back into a hornet. Swiftly they flew between the needle-like cactus spines and darted in and out among the giant funguses until they reached a small, stony clearing where a terrible conflict was raging.

A whirl of claws, sharp teeth, fur, legs and tails made it impossible to distinguish at first which of the two animals was the Duke and the Evil astral; and the difficulty was increased by the fact that the two beasts changed their forms a dozen times in sixty seconds.

After an agonised snarl one beast detached itself from the other, and, whipping away, slithered swiftly along the rock in the form of a king cobra, by which the two watchers at once knew that this must be the enemy; but in an instant de Richleau had changed into a mongoose and was after the snake like a flash of light.

The cobra reared up, hissed and stabbed with its heavy, bespeckled head, but missed. The mongoose got its teeth into the snake's scaly body; the victim's tail began to thresh but it drew in, changed form and became one of the many great hairy legs of a huge tarantula.

In an instant the mongoose had become an armadillo, whose thick armour protected it from the tarantula's poisonous bite. Suddenly the tarantula seemed to disappear, but the armadillo routed furiously among the loose stones and narrowly escaped being stung in the boot by a baby scorpion. With a swift flick the armadillo half-crushed the scorpion beneath a stone but it changed into a crab that increased in size with extraordinary rapidity, forcing the stone upwards with its great back of solid shell and at the same time seizing the armadillo's long snout between one pair of its powerful pincers.

The Armadillo gave a screaming grunt, but Simon shot forward like a golden bullet and buried his hornet's sting in the soft part of the crab's great body. It made no sound, but its bulbous eyes on their long stalks jerked upward and it released its grip as the armadillo turned back into an eagle, having prevented its snout from being severed by this swift transformance of it into a steely beak.

For a moment the eagle circled above the crab and then swooped to attack its eyes, but the crab had changed into a great black panther which bounded into the air to meet the eagle's onrush. At that, Marie Lou saw her chance and took the form of a lion. As she sprang all three of them went down in a whirling ball of fur and feathers, while Simon, unable to change himself so easily as the others, gyrated above them in frantic circles.

The panther, bested by his two powerful antagonists, the King of Beasts and the King of Birds, saved itself by shrinking and a quick transformation into a deadly little black-widow spider. Both the lion and the eagle jerked away from it. Next second it was a hare, which bounded from them with such speed that they were compelled to disintegrate their astrals again into dragon-fly and queen wasp in order to keep up with it.

The effort of the new chase proved too much for Simon. He had now utterly exhausted all his powers of sleep. Although he fought with all his will to continue the pace, he found himself dropping behind and that the scene of those grim valleys was fading. Next moment he shuddered and was awake.

De Richleau outdistanced the hare, resumed the form of an eagle and suddenly pounced upon it, but the hare swerved, evaded the striking beak and raced on. Next moment it had gone under ground.

Marie Lou knew now what was ahead of them, and it was one of the tests which she loathed and dreaded more than anything else on the astral plane. They would have to follow through some long, narrow tunnel far below the soil, with the awful feeling that at any moment the tunnel would cave in upon them and that they would be buried alive. She knew perfectly well that in her astral form that could not occur, but it was a fear which she had carried over with her from her dreads as a mortal and had not yet conquered, so it was none the less real. Steeling herself to the ordeal she followed the Duke's example, changed herself into a ferret, and disappeared after him down the hole.

The tunnel was only just large enough for them to wriggle along it and it was useless for them to reduce their size because each time they did so the Evil thing ahead caused the walls of the tunnel to close in round them. It was abominably hot and stuffy and the darkness was impenetrable even to their astral eyes because they were surrounded by what—for lack of a better term—may be called astral matter, through which it was beyond their powers to see; and down in that foul warren the air was poisonous with the stench of decaying bodies.

The chase seemed interminable and hardly a minute passed without both the pursuers having the impressions that they were stuck underground and could go no further; only the extreme exercise of their will-power enabled them to do so.

Suddenly Marie Lou caught a muffled shout of warning from the Duke, and almost instantly he was swept back upon her as a strong current of water rushed against them and submerged them both.

They gasped and for a moment knew the first horror of drowning in an underground cavern, until they turned themselves into fish and determinedly struck forward against the current. As they darted along, Marie Lou caught a thought that de Richleau sent out to encourage her, 'We're wearing him down—he must be tiring or he would never have used that trick,' and a little further on the tunnel broadened until it grew in width to a great cleft which came out under water in a cave faintly lit by daylight.

The second they debouched into it the slimy tentacles of a huge octopus seized them, but both had the same inspriation and changed themselves before they could be crushed into electric eels. The giant squid released them as swiftly as it had seized upon them and disappeared in a cloud of inky fluid which it shot out to cover its retreat; but de Richleau was after it in the form of a swordfish, while Marie Lou quickly turned herself into a shark.

As they darted towards the entrance of the cavern they could see, by the full daylight which now percolated through the greenish waters, the red coral fans and the brilliant-coloured fish beneath them. During a few anxious moments they lost the octopus, but just in time Morie Lou saw it shrink into a tiny shrimp and, darting forward, snapped at it with her huge jaws. For a second the shrimp was actually in her mouth, but before she could crush it between her seven rows of teeth it slipped out again and began to swell to giant proportions, assuming the form of a vast hammer-head whale.

The great beast had only a tiny gullet so could not attack either opponent successfully with its mouth, but by threshing wildly it sought to smash them with its tail.

Marie Lou buried her sharp teeth in one of its fins, but de Richleau again sent out a mental message to her, calling her off with the words: 'Keep away from him and he can't harm us. Now that he's on the defensive we've got him beaten, but we must stick to him until we find out where he goes.'

While the whale plunged in and out of the waves like some gargantuan porpoise, churning the waters into foam, they drew off a little, then the Black astral, apparently realising that he could not overcome them, suddenly left the water to take his human form.

As the seascape dissolved they saw him far above them; a brawny Negro clad in white, with a row of human skulls tied about his girdle and several necklaces of shark's teeth about his neck. They had no means of knowing if this was the earthly form of their antagonist or just another disguise which his astral had adopted, but they instantly changed themselves into humans equipped for battle on the astral plane, and gave chase.

With incredible swiftness another scene opened up before them and they knew that this was no astral creation but that they had returned to some portion of Earth. Far below them, set in a gently moving sea, was a great promontory of land.

The towns were widely scattered and the villages few and far between; inland there were rugged mountains in the higher parts and the beaches appeared long and desolate. So much they could see with their astral sight but they knew that in fact this land was still shrouded in the darkness of night.

As they raced on they came over a great bay which in shape was not unlike a widely-opened lobster claw. It was then, high above the deserted beach, that their enemy suddenly turned and charged at them.

De Richleau met the shock and momentarily went down under it, his will failing him to resist the power of his dark adversary; but Marie Lou had not encountered evil entities on her previous astral journeys during many centuries without learning something about them. She knew that except in very rare cases they have the lusts of humans. In consequence, with one swift thought she changed herself from a warrior of the Light to her own earthly form and appeared there, dazzlingly beautiful and stark naked.

The big Negro's eyes glinted redly. He half released the Duke and stretched out a great hand to grab her, but she slipped away and the second's respite was enough for de Richleau to recover.

Another second and Marie Lou was back again in her form of a young warrior, and at the same instant she and the Duke flung themselves upon the Adversary. He gave back in desperate fear as they seized upon him to bind him and hurl him into Hell. In his extremity he used the only remedy left to him and called aloud in an ancient tongue upon his Satanic Master.

As his scream for help rent the air it seemed as though a dark cloud was forming and rising up from the land below, and de Richleau knew that all the followers of the Left-Hand Path in that place were hurrying to the assistance of their hard-pressed confrère.

Against such odds he and Marie Lou were utterly power-less. Too late he realised that having driven the evil entity into a corner they had been guilty of the most frightful rashness, and as the hosts of Satan rushed upon them he was terribly aware that it might now be beyond their powers to save themselves.

9

Trouble at Cardinals Folly

Even on Earth thought processes can be incredibly rapid, so that the human brain is capable of covering an enormous amount of ground in the space of a few seconds, yet this is slow compared with the speed with which an intelligence on the astral, being entirely free of matter, can carry out it's mental functions. In a split second de Richleau was conscious of many things.

The acquisition of occult power requires study, training, and regular practice, like any other art, and no art can be mastered to a considerable degree in one short lifetime. It takes many incarnations of devotion to any subject to achieve the status of genius in it, and that is why it is by no means unusual for very young children to astonish their parents by showing an extraordinary aptitude for music, drawing or certain languages. In their last incarnations they have already reached an outstanding proficiency in these particular things and so when born again appear as child prodigies in them. Then, having in that incarnation gone as far in their special subject as is possible for any human, in their next incarnation they take up some other subject for a number of Earth lives until they have mastered that; so that over a period of many milleniums we each graduate in every art and acquire all knowledge in our true selves, of which we are conscious only when we are either dead or sleeping.

As the occult is the one art which extends beyond Earth only the fringe of it can be studied while a spirit is still going through the process of earthly incarnations; yet even here the knowledge acquired in life after life gradually piles up, so that once an individual has been an adept, although the mysteries may be obscured from him for whole incarnations, each time the spark is rekindled the re-acquisition of the previous knowledge he has gained is an infinitely easier process. No one while in the physical body can hope to become fully conscious of his true astral life without having spent many previous incarnations in training to accomplish that end; yet Earth is now so old that there are few of us who have not done so at one period or another, which makes the re-acquisition of this knowledge by no means impossible providing that we work for it with real determination.

But it must not be forgotten that the whole vast scheme of things is planned like some great university. If a man having spent six terms studying history at Oxford then decided to go in for 'maths' and spent a further two years immersed in the study of higher mathematics, should he at the end of that time suddenly be called upon to do a paper on history it would not be surprising if his history proved distinctly rusty. The same applies in the cosmic university where each life on Earth is no more than a term and life itself in its true, astral sense is everlasting.

It was many incarnations since de Richleau had devoted several Earth lives in succession to the serious study of the occult, finally achieving almost to the limits of such occult knowledge as is ever permitted to humans. In more recent Earth lives he had turned his attention to various other paths of progress, although during a number of them and the present he had retained a knowledge of the great truths and the power to follow his unbroken astral existence. Consequently, although he could still perform minor feats of Magic, it was many centuries since he had practised as a powerful White Magician and he had temporarily forgotten much that he had originally learnt in connection with the higher mysteries.

He now realised that the present was literally a case of having rushed in where angels fear to tread. His belief that the Nazis were using the occult was proved beyond all shadow of doubt; but he had visualised them as employing an occultist with only limited powers such as his own or working through a trance medium; whereas it was now clear that they had in their service some great Master of the Left-Hand Path. He blamed himself most bitterly for not having foreseen such a possibility, as he knew that he should have done, in view of the fact that Hitler himself took care to plan each of his moves when the stars were propitious and that the very symbol of the Nazi Party showed them to be fundamentally allied to the powers of Darkness. With a nation of eighty million Germans, all the Black elements in which would automatically be in sympathy with the Nazis, it was only natural that they should employ a number of adepts of the first rank.

As the Satanic host rose up from the dark, sea-washed shore the Duke knew that to summon such a force his opponent must be a *Magister Templi* at the very least, and he marvelled now that with only Marie Lou and Simon to aid him he should have been able to drive back, harry and almost overcome such a mighty adversary. He knew, too, that only their instant determination to give battle, and the force with which they had pressed home their attack, had enabled them to do so.

Their astral action had, in fact, been a perfect parallel to that of the light cruisers *Ajax* and *Exeter*, outgunned and under-armoured, going in against the infinitely more powerful *Graf Spee*. But if, instead of seeking refuge in Montevideo harbour, the *Graf Spee* had been able to retire on Kiel and emerge again with a score of light cruisers and half a hundred destroyers, *Ajax* and *Exeter* would have stood no earthly chance against the hell of fire that could then have been brought to bear upon them; and that was the present case as regards Marie Lou and himself; their slender chance of saving themselves lay in instant flight.

'Back to your body!' he called to her with all his will, and turning together they fled with every ounce of speed of which they were capable.

A great roar of triumph went up from the emissaries of Hell as they streaked through the middle-air in furious pursuit, and the seconds that followed seemed years of nightmare battling to the pursued. The forces of Evil brought all their powers to bear, seeking to strike them down with astral missiles, striving to drag them back by the exertion of malignant will and casting up in front of

106

them every form of astral barrier which might terrify and check them.

Instead of the effortless flight to which they were accustomed they felt as though their astral bodies were weighted with lead. A frightful storm arose in which they were tossed about like thistledown in a gale. Forked lightning streaked the sky while incessant peals of thunder vibrated through the air like an intensive bombardment.

Both the fugitives knew that these were only manifestations which could not harm them providing they remained unafraid and kept their faith and purpose. Yet the great jagged streaks of lightning which were directed at them would have daunted the most fearless, and as they fled they instinctively swerved from side to side in an endeavour to evade them.

Suddenly the whole scene changed and instead of swirling black clouds pierced by the terrifying flashes they were faced by a great wall of fire which had neither top nor bottom. The wall was not composed of flames alone; it was like the interior of a furnace and one vast mass of solid, white-hot matter which glowed, bubbled and hissed, giving out a blinding light and a heat so intense that it seemed to shrivel up their astral bodies.

With a wail of fear Marie Lou faltered and stopped, but de Richleau knew that if they did not succeed in getting back to their bodies they would die in their sleep. That was part of the price they would have to pay for having gone out against Evil powers stronger than themselves. By their own rash act they would have brought their present incarnations to an untimely end—in fact, they would have committed a form of suicide—and that would mean for both of them a setback on the great journey—a setback of perhaps several lives.

Seizing her by the arm he dragged her with him straight into the glowing mass. For a second the pain was practically unendurable, then the fiery wall dissolved; the roaring of the flames gave place to a quietness which could almost be felt. Gasping with relief they both threw back the bedclothes and sat up to find Richard, Rex and Simon kneeling beside them in the pentacle with their heads bowed in prayer.

At the sound of their waking Richard opened his eyes and

grabbed Marie Lou to him. 'Thank God,' he murmured, 'thank God you're back. Simon told us, and I've been half crazy with fear for you ever since he woke up.'

Simon looked shamefacedly at the Duke. 'I'll never forgive myself for having had to leave you in a muddle, but—well, I just couldn't keep asleep.'

De Richleau mopped his perspiring face then laid a hand on Simon's arm. 'My dear fellow, don't be absurd; I thought you put up a marvellous performance in sticking it so long. I'll wager you can't remember when you last managed to sleep for eleven and a half hours in one stretch; and you saved me from that brute when in the form of a crab he had me by the nose.'

'By Jove!' Simon exclaimed, 'I remember now; I had the luck to get in under his guard and sting him in the belly.'

'It wasn't luck, Simon; it was sheer courage. You always say that you're a coward, but when it comes to a pinch you're the bravest of us all. With one swipe of its free claw that filthy beast could have damaged your astral so badly that you could never have returned to your body.'

'What happened?' asked Rex. 'When Simon got back he told us that he'd had to run out on you while you were mixed up in some sort of set-to with a wooglie but he couldn't recall the details, and there was just nothing that we could do but pray.'

'You couldn't have done anything better,' the Duke replied, 'and it's quite certain that your prayers must have helped us to win through. But next time you pray you should stand up to do it—as the Ancients did—and hold your hands out to the Infinite. The kneeling position is one of false humility, which was only introduced by the Christians, and since each one of us carries God within ourselves, it is not fitting that we should stoop before anything in Earth or Heaven.'

Richard had put a little bed-jacket about Marie Lou's shoulders, but in spite of that and the warmth of the room, in which a bright fire was still burning, she shivered slightly as she said:

'Although we've just come through the fiery furnace I'm still desperately cold.'

'We'll soon remedy that,' smiled the Duke. 'What we both want is a good meal; and we're going to have it.'

'Holy snakes!' ejaculated Rex. 'I've gotten so used to living on steamed fish and rabbit's food that I hardly remember how it feels to eat like a Christian. But surely you're not chucking your hand in?'

'No, I'm not doing that,' de Richleau said soberly, 'but I'm not going out again until I've had a chance to re-learn certain of the more powerful methods of protection. In the meantime it will do us all good to live like normal human beings for a spell.'

'D'you mean we'll be able to have civilised drinks?' asked Richard.

De Richleau nodded. 'Yes—in moderation.'

'Oh boy!' Rex laughed. 'What a cocktail I'll shake for you all this evening!'

'I've still got some pretty good hocks in London,' Simon murmured, 'Steinberg Cabinets and Schloss Johannesburgs of the rarer vintages; I must get some down. But tell us what happened to you after I had to quit.'

'What's the time?' asked the Duke.

'Just after midnight,' replied Richard.

De Richleau glanced at Marie Lou. 'The servants will be in bed, then, but I'm sure you won't mind, Princess, if we raid your larder and cook ourselves some supper.'

'Of course not, Greyeyes darling. The servants came to the conclusion that we'd all gone mad within twenty-four hours of your arrival. Our sudden change to a vegetarian diet, the banning of all drinks and the way in which this room's always kept locked, while some of us spend hours at a stretch in it, soon convinced them that we ought all to be put in the loony bin, so it won't make the least difference if we hold an orgy in their quarters.'

'Cook positively loathes anyone going into her kitchen,' said Richard dubiously.

But de Richleau laughed. 'I don't doubt a word from me in the morning will put matters right. Cook and I have always been on the most friendly terms. From the day I showed her how to produce poached eggs which had not gone hard in the middle of a cheese soufflé she recognised me as a fellow artist.'

'A word from you means a pound-note,' said Marie Lou quickly, 'and you over-tip the servants as it is. It's not the least necessary, Greyeyes. I am the mistress of this house, and I shall do what I like in my own kitchen.'

'Hurrah!' shouted Rex. 'That's the spirit! Come on, now; let's think of all the good things that we can possibly manage to eat one on top of the other.'

When they reached the kitchen, however, they all discovered that it was not the delicacies in Marie Lou's store-cupboard that they really wanted. Their recent abstinence from rich food had simplified their tastes, and as they were in the fortunate position of having plentiful supplies from the Home Farm they unanimously agreed that the best of all meals at the moment would be an unlimited supply of ham and eggs, to be followed by pancakes.

While Rex and Simon laid the kitchen table, Marie Lou cooked the ham and eggs, de Richleau prepared the batter for the pancakes, which he proposed to make himself, and Richard disappeared down to the cellar to return a few minutes later with a couple of magnums of champagne.

'Krug '26,' muttered Simon appreciatively as he saw the dusty labels. 'By Jove, it's a while since I saw any of that!'

Richard grinned. 'I thought at the time it came out that it was one of the wines of the century so I laid down quite a bit of it, and I reckon we'll still be able to knock off a magnum or two together long after Hitler's drunk his last glass of orange-juice.'

'Talking of which,' cut in Rex, 'we're all mighty anxious to hear the latest from the astral front.'

'Marie Lou shall tell you all about it when we've eaten,' said the Duke, and three-quarters of an hour later she gave them a graphic account of the desperate encounter which she and de Richleau had had with the enemy.

'What's the drill now?' Rex asked when she had done.

'My theory that the Nazis are using the occult having proved correct,' said the Duke, 'our next problem is to find in the flesh the Black occultist who is working for them. We must then kill him.'

'How d'you propose to set about the job of finding him?' asked Richard.

'We know that he's a Negro—a black Witch Doctor—and there can't be a great many people of that kind in Germany,' said Marie Lou.

'Maybe,' Rex cut in. 'And you can travel to Germany in

your astrals, but as long as you're on the astral plane yourselves you can't kill a human. So what's the big idea? D'you figure on our trying to get into Germany in the flesh?'

'It looks as if we may have to,' replied the Duke, 'and with Sir Pellinore's assistance I don't doubt that some of us could get through. I think, though, that Marie Lou is wrong in assuming that the person we are after is necessarily a Negro. The probability is that he only assumed that form when we saw him; it's much more likely that in the flesh he is a fair-haired, blue-eyed Hun.'

'That makes the proposition more tricky than ever,' said Richard glumly, 'since in Germany fair-haired, blue-eyed Huns are two a penny. Besides, for all you know, he might be a dark-haired Rhinelander or even a red-headed woman —in fact, it seems to me that up to date you've got no evidence at all to go upon.'

'Oh, yes, we have,' countered the Duke. 'There's one thing we know quite definitely: he comes from an island in which part of the coast is shaped rather like a lobster's claw with blunt ends. That was unquestionably a portion of this Earth and if I saw it again, or even the outline of it on a map, I should recognise it.'

'Are you quite sure that it was an island?' asked Marie Lou.

'I wouldn't swear to it, as the place covered a very considerable area and the further distances were indistinct, merging into the sea and sky; but that was the impression I got.'

'I didn't,' she shook her head. 'It seemed to me that we were just over the coast-line of a great peninsula, but I agree that it would be easy to recognise that bit of coast on seeing it again.'

'You're probably right about its having been a peninsula. It couldn't have been one of the Frisian Islands; they're too small and flat; yet it's almost certain to be a portion of the Continent of Europe. Still, as the Germans now control Denmark and Norway our enemy may quite well be operating from one of the islands in the Baltic or on the Norwegian coast.'

'That's it!' exclaimed Marie Lou. 'I remember that away from the shore the country was very mountainous, so it was probably a great cape jutting out between two of the Norwegian fjords.'

When they had finished their meal they went back to the library and, getting out Richard's *Times* atlas, began to study very carefully the coast-line of Northern Europe, but they could see no stretch of coast tallying with that over which their astrals had been poised earlier in the night.

'This atlas is the best of its kind in existence,' remarked the Duke, 'but to find what we want we really need a set of large-scale maps, so tomorrow I'll go up to the Admiralty. In any case I want to visit the British Museum to read up certain old key works on Magic, which they are bound to have there, in order to renew my knowledge of protection.'

It was now well past four in the morning so they decided to go up to bed, Richard and Rex to sleep, the others to lie down, but the Duke warned Marie Lou and Simon that if they fell asleep again, in spite of the long hours that they had slept during the day, they were to remain very close to their bodies because now that the adversary had seen them and, having followed them back to Cardinals Folly, knew where they lived he might still be lurking in the neighbourhood, waiting for a chance to attack them immediately they returned to the astral plane.

When they met again the following morning Simon reported that he had only dozed and had had no trouble, but Marie Lou came down the stairs looking pale and ill. She said that she had dropped off to sleep at about five o'clock and—certainly not through any exercise of her own will—had suddenly found herself in a maze like that at Hampton Court, except that the whole place positively reeked of evil, and, strive as she would, she could not find her way out. It had seemed to her that for hours on end she had fled in uncontrollable terror up and down countless paths flanked by tall box-hedges without being able to discover the exit, and all the time she was horribly aware that something intensely evil was stalking her from corridor to corridor of the maze, though it never actually got round each corner until she had put another one between herself and it.

She had been utterly dead-beat and was beginning to despair when Richard, in the uniform of a park-keeper, had

112

suddenly appeared on the stand in the centre of the maze, from which he could look down into all the paths and so direct her out of it; upon which she had wakened up still sweating with cold fear.

De Richleau regarded her gravely. 'I'm so sorry, Princess. This is my fault, and if I hadn't been so shaken after what occurred last night I should have realised it sooner. From now on none of you must sleep anywhere, even for an hour, except within the pentacle; and when you're asleep your astrals must not go outside it. Only so will you be safe from similar and perhaps even more terrible experiences.'

'Did you not experience anything?' she asked.

He shook his head. 'No. I was entirely unmolested. That may have been because I am the most powerful amongst us, and they would naturally seek to wear down and destroy the weaker of us two first; or it may be because you were still thinking of this business when you went to sleep, which would enable them to reach you more easily, whereas I took the precaution of cleansing my mind of the whole matter before I slept. I blame myself a lot for having forgotten to suggest these things to you.'

She shrugged a little wearily. 'It doesn't matter, Greyeyes dear, as long as the pentacle will give us adequate protection tonight.'

'It will, if you construct it correctly. I shall be in London and I can look after myself, but you've seen me make it so frequently in the past fortnight that you should be able to do it for yourself without any mistakes. Do you think you can?'

'Yes. In any case the others will be here to help me and see that I don't slip up in any of the details. It's rather surprising, though, that nothing happened to Simon—don't you think?'

'No. Apparently he only dozed; and, anyhow, our adversary only saw him as a hornet, whereas he saw you and me face to face. But now that the battle is on I shouldn't be surprised if the astral of everybody in this house is attacked systematically—even those of the servants.'

'Oh heavens!' Marie Lou made a face. 'What can we do to protect them?'

De Richleau laughed rather mirthlessly. 'Nothing, I'm

afraid; unless we make them all sleep in pentacles. But, quite frankly, I rather shrink from the task of endeavouring to explain warfare on the astral plane, and its possible consequences, to Malin and your maids; it would only confirm them in their view that we're off our heads and they would probably give notice in a body.'

'It looks as though they may do that anyhow,' said Richard glumly, 'but the main point is—can any harm come to them? If so, it's only right that I should send them away at once.'

'That's hardly necessary,' de Richleau replied. 'The forces against us will very soon discover which of the people in this house is giving active assistance to Marie Lou and myself. In consequence they'll concentrate their malice against them and leave the servants alone after giving them a few exceptionally unpleasant nightmares.'

'Nightmares don't actually hurt anyone, so if that's the case we're justified in saying nothing to them,' Richard declared, 'but while you're away the rest of us will definitely stick to the pentacle.'

'Definitely,' de Richleau agreed. 'This is a much more desperate business than I bargained for, but without asking I feel certain that you're all game to see it through.'

A murmur of assent went up and he continued. 'I shall probably be away for three or four days, reading up this stuff in the Museum. While I am absent for goodness' sake don't try anything on your own; as far as you can manage it you had better take turns to sleep two at a time. You'll each then have a companion while you're out of your bodies and two guardians who're awake to watch that no attempt is made by the forces of Evil to disturb or break the defences of the pentacle while the other two are sleeping. By the time I return I hope to be much better equipped to face the enemy than I was when I so rashly undertook this incredible campaign.'

After lunch the Duke left them to motor to London, and he dined that night with Sir Pellinore. In the simplest language that he could formulate, and omitting all those details which made the whole affair seem so preposterously unreal, he told the elderly Baronet what had happened and asked for arrangements to be made at the Admiralty so that he

114

could examine the large-scale charts of the coast of Northern Europe.

Sir Pellinore now treated the question with the utmost gravity. Having had some time to think over what de Richleau had told him of the occult, and having since taken the opportunity to hold several long conversations with other people who were interested in the subject, he had formed the conclusion that de Richleau's theory was by no means as wildly improbable as it had at first sounded. The more he went into the matter the more logical it became, as although he had asked question after question of an old friend of his who was a convinced believer in reincarnation, every question had been satisfactorily answered, leaving no loose ends, and while Sir Pellinore always declared that he had no brain at all, he certainly possessed an extraordinarily fine sense of logic. It was, in fact, this extraordinary facility for directness in thought, and complete confidence in his own judgments, that had given him his immense success in life. De Richleau therefore found him very much more subdued, interested and willing to consider further possible developments than he had expected, and the visit to the Admiralty was arranged for the following morning without any trouble.

Next day the Duke spent over three hours with a lieutenant-commander, who was a map expert, in one of the chart rooms at the Admiralty, but although he surveyed the coast of Norway from the Arctic to the Kattegat, a good part of the Baltic, the whole of Denmark, and the coasts of Germany, Holland, Belgium and France, he could not discover any island or promontory which had the same coastal formation as that which he and Marie Lou had seen in their hour of peril.

Having exhausted this avenue he obtained permission from one of the curators of the British Museum, who was a friend of his, to study certain priceless old manuscripts; which were removed, specially for him, from the vaults in which they had been placed to protect them from destruction in air-raids. For the best part of three days he devoted himself to these ancient screeds, making copious notes from them. He then paid a visit to Culpeper House, in Bruton Street, and purchased a strange assortment of items from the famous herbalists. On the fourth day he lunched with Sir Pellinore.

When he had reported his lack of success at the Admiralty the Baronet asked him what he intended to do.

'I must go out again,' replied the Duke, 'and utilise every means in my power to discover the identity of this person who is acting for the Nazis on the astral plane. Whoever he is, and wherever he is, we've got to find him and kill him.'

Sir Pellinore nodded. 'You're setting yourself no small task, and I imagine that the danger you'll have to run is considerable. I wish I could thank you officially, on behalf of the Government, but, quite honestly, they'd think that I'd gone off my rocker if I attempted to tell them of the extraordinary work you're doing. However, I'm sure it will be a great satisfaction to you to know that I heard this morning that the convoy, the start of which you witnessed, has so far remained immune from attack and is now outside the danger area.'

De Richleau smiled. 'Then we've done something at least. We evidently succeeded in disturbing the astral agent before he could memorise the full particulars of the route. But I must tell you frankly that the battle is only just beginning and I'm pretty anxious as to what may have happened at Cardinals Folly in my absence.'

'What do you fear?'

'I don't quite know, but it's hardly to be expected that the enemy will leave my friends alone having once located the spot from which we're working. It was a great misfortune that they were able to follow Mrs. Eaton and myself back that night. There's another thing, too. Since they can use the astral to communicate it will have been known in Berlin for some days now that we're on to what they're up to. In consequence, the Gestapo will almost certainly instruct their agents here to attack us on the physical plane, and a little matter like murder has never stopped the Nazis yet.'

'Good God! D'you mean to say you think that they'll send some of their people in this country gunning for you?'

'Yes. Just as my objective is to kill the occultist who is communicating, their objective will now be to kill myself and my friends so that we cannot operate further against them.'

Sir Pellinore let out a long whistle and quickly poured himself out another ration of old brandy before he said: 'I think I'd better secure police protection for you.'

De Richleau shook his head. 'That would require all sorts of difficult explanations, and the fewer of us that are involved in this business the better. It will take some time for Berlin to communicate with their agents here and set them on to us, so I don't fear anything of that kind for some days yet and I'd rather that you didn't get police protection for us unless it becomes absolutely necessary. At the moment my anxieties for my friends are confined to some form of astral attack that may be launched against them.'

When the Duke got back to Cardinals Folly that night he found that he had real reason for his anxiety. His four friends were seated in glum silence in the drawing-room, but immediately he entered it they all started to talk at once.

From the night of his departure to London the house had been rendered almost untenable by what Richard described as a whole company of poltergeists. They smashed china, tore the curtains, threw water upon the beds, slammed doors until the sound had driven nearly everybody crazy, and performed innumerable other acts of mischief each night while darkness lasted. On the second day the servants had left in a body, with the exception of Richard's faithful butler-valet, Malin, who had refused to be scared and, with his usual smiling urbanity, had just let the Duke into the house.

'I was afraid of something of this sort,' confessed de Richleau, and he looked at Marie Lou contritely. 'I can't say how sorry I am to have brought such trouble to your house, Princess.'

She gave him a forlorn smile. 'Don't worry, Greyeyes dear. At least it gives us the feeling that we're doing our bit. It's a little frightening at times and the inconvenience is absolutely infuriating, but it's nothing to the *flak* that our airmen must go through when they bomb Germany, or what our sailors have to put up with.'

'That's true,' the Duke nodded. 'I take it they haven't started on the physical plane? None of you have been attacked while walking in the grounds or seen any suspicious-looking strangers about, eh?'

'There were a couple of men this morning . . .' Richard began, but he left his sentence unfinished.

At that instant there was a sound of crashing glass as something hurtled through the window. Next second there rolled from underneath the curtains a large, round, black object. One glance at it was enough; with a horrid sinking feeling they all recognised it to be a high-explosive bomb.

10

The Bomb

The attack was so unexpected, yet synchronised so perfectly with de Richleau's question about suspicious persons loitering in the grounds, that none of them had the least doubt as to what the black object was. Quite clearly, their adversary on the astral had communicated with enemy agents in England who had now had time to reach Cardinals Folly and attempt their destruction.

From the fact that the attack had taken place within a few minutes of the Duke's arrival at the house, it looked as though their physical enemies had purposely waited for his return in order that an attempt might be made to blot all five of them out in one murderous stroke.

The bomb was a large pineapple grenade. De Richleau knew instantly that it was big enough to wreck the room and kill or mutilate them all. At any second it would disintegrate with a blinding flash into a hundred flying splinters of jagged steel.

Had the curtains not been drawn he would have grabbed it up and hurled it back through the window, praying that he might be in time to get it out of the house before it went off. But the curtains *were* drawn, so it would bounce off them into the middle of the floor. It seemed that the only thing he could do was to throw himself full-length upon it and endeavour to save his friends by deliberately sacrificing himself.

Just as he flung himself forward, Simon, who was nearer the bomb, jerked out his foot and kicked it away from them. With a frantic effort the Duke recovered his balance, swerved, and, grabbing an armchair, swung it round against a bookcase underneath which the bomb had rolled.

Marie Lou had been sitting in an armchair by the fire. She half rose from it then gave a stifled cry as she was knocked backwards into it again by Richard, who had thrown himself on top of her to protect her from the deadly splinters.

Next second there was a deafening roar. The whole house shook. For an instant the outlines of everything in the room seemed to quiver in a livid spurt of light, then all was plunged in darkness.

The Duke and Simon were hurled off their feet. The armchair in which Marie Lou was lying, with Richard spread-eagled on top of her, was thrown over sideways and they both rolled across the floor.

After a moment the darkness lightened. The bulk of the fire was still glowing although some of the burning logs had been blown out of the grate on to the hearth and a few embers had fallen on the Persian rugs. There was a strong smell of burning.

'Darling! Darling, are you all right?' Richard's voice came, frantic with anxiety, as he groped for Marie Lou.

'Yes,' she panted. 'But you—are you hurt?'

'No,' he gasped, scrambling to his feet. 'Simon—Greyeyes —where are you?'

'Here,' Simon replied, picking himself up from the other side of the fireplace. 'Anybody got a light?'

But from the Duke there was no reply.

A moment later they heard Malin calling from the door-way, 'Mr. Richard—sir—madam! What's happened? Are you hurt?'

'No, Malin, no. But I'm afraid His Grace is,' Richard called back. 'Quick! Get a light—some candles!'

As Malin hurried off, Marie Lou began piling the burning logs back into the grate so that they would give more light, while the two men groped about in the semi-darkness for de Richleau's body. From the little they could see it seemed that the whole bookcase had been flung on top of the Duke and that he must lie crushed beneath it. With frantic fingers they tore at the splintered wood.

'Where's Rex?' Richard cried suddenly. 'We need his strength to get this thing up. Rex! Where the hell are you?'

It was Marie Lou who answered. 'He's not here—he was standing near the door and I saw him spring through it into the hall just before the bomb exploded.'

Malin returned at that moment, carrying some lighted candles, and for the first time they were able to see the extent of the damage. The bomb had blown the whole of the lower portion of the bookcase to smithereens, and its top part, together with the books which had cascaded from it, lay in the centre of the room, a scattered heap, with the armchair overturned beneath it. There was a gaping hole in the lower part of the wall against which the bookcase had stood, several large lumps of plaster had fallen from the ceiling, the fireplace was full of soot, every ornament in the room was broken, and practically every piece of furniture was either scarred or torn.

As Malin held the lighted candles above his head they saw that the Duke was lying pinned beneath the armchair and half buried under the pile of books. Now that they could see properly they were soon able to get to work and within a few moments had dragged him clear.

At first they feared that he was dead, but they soon found that he was breathing, and although he had been badly cut about the face by flying glass from the bookcase they could find only one other wound upon him, which was in his right foot. Evidently in a last desperate effort to protect his friends as much as possible he had thrown himself, kneeling, into the armchair, facing towards the bookcase in an endeavour to keep it and the chair in position by his own weight. The explosion had thrown the whole lot over but the padding of the chair had saved him from the bomb fragments, except for the piece in his foot, which must have been dangling down.

'We'd better take him to the library,' said Richard, 'and put him in the pentacle; otherwise some of these swine may get him on the astral while he's unconscious.'

Malin helped them to carry the Duke, and it was the first time that he had been in the library since they had taken possession of it. Richard caught him eyeing with ill-concealed disapproval all the paraphernalia of the pentacle, so he said quietly:

'I expect you think we've been monkeying with spiritualism, Malin, and that it's our own fault that we've had all this trouble in the house these last few days, but I give you my word that we haven't been doing this for our own amusement.'

'It's not for me to criticise, Mr. Richard, sir,' replied the elderly retainer gravely, 'but I've always held that spiritualism never brought any good to anyone.'

'I heartily agree,' responded Richard feelingly, as they laid the Duke down on his bed. 'Still, that explosion just now had nothing to do with spirits; it was caused by a handgrenade hurled through the window by a Nazi spy.'

'Good gracious me, sir! We seem to have got ourselves right in the front line, then, in a manner of speaking.'

'That's just what it is, Malin, and—though this is hardly the time to explain things to you—all this paraphernalia here and the trouble we've been having is part of the same business. I'm most touched by the way you've stayed on, but I think now that the enemy has started in to try and murder us you had better, for your own safety, follow the example of the rest of the staff.'

'I shouldn't dream of doing so, sir, as long as you have any use for me. It's quite enough for me to know that His Grace and the rest of you are up against the Nazis. But I must say that I miss my sleep; the banging of the doors at night is something chronic. With your permission I was thinking of occupying a room in Mr. MacPherson's cottage for the time being and coming up to the house each day.'

MacPherson was Richard's head gardener, and he thought the plan an excellent one so he suggested that Malin should pack a bag and take up his quarters in the cottage that very evening.

Marie Lou came hurrying in with a basin of hot water, towels and bandages. She sponged the blood from the cuts on de Richleau's face and soon afterwards he came round, to heave a sigh of relief when he found that except for scratches and bruises the others were uninjured.

On removing his right shoe and sock they found that a tiny fragment of the bomb had torn its way through the flesh at the side of his foot. The wound was painful but it did not appear that any of the tendons were cut, so they considered that they had all come off very lightly.

By now they were wondering what in the world could have happened to Rex; but when Marie Lou was half way through bandaging the injured foot the mystery of his disappearance was solved.

There was a sound of trampling feet in the hall and Rex's voice shouting directions, then a little man staggered into the library, bowed almost double under the weight of a taller man whom he was carrying slung across his shoulders. Rex entered triumphantly behind them.

'Thank the Lord you're all all right!' he gasped, after a swift glance round; then with his mighty hand he gave the man in front of him a swift push which sent the fellow and his burden sprawling to the floor.

Suddenly he laughed. 'I got 'em—got both the devils. They were standing around waiting to come in after the pineapple went off—to make certain that they'd rubbed us out.'

'Well done, Rex—well done!' cried Marie Lou, and all eyes were turned upon the woebegone-looking prisoners.

The one whom Rex had forced to become a beast of burden was a short, wiry-looking little Japanese; the other, who was still unconscious, was a tall, thin, sallow-faced European. To have taken both of them captive was no small feat of work—but then, Rex was no ordinary man. His great height gave him a huge stride which few people could outdistance, and woe betide anybody who angered him once he was near enough to exert his giant strength agaisst the culprit.

He related quite casually that he had caught the Jap first and, picking him up by the neck, had used him as a missile to bring the other fellow down. The European had tried to knife him as he came up, but he had hit the man one sledge-hammer blow which had rendered him unconscious. In the meantime the Jap had attempted to make off again but had very soon been brought back and booted round in a circle until he had submitted to orders.

They all agreed that it was a grand piece of work and de Richleau, who had recovered a little, sat up to question the prisoners. He soon found, however, that in his still groggy state the job was too much for him, so Marie Lou insisted that he should lie down and leave it to the others.

The European prisoner was now groaning and soon came round sufficiently for them to heave him to his feet. It was then decided that both of them should be locked up in one of the numerous cellars which lay under the older wing of Cardinals Folly. Richard led the way out while Rex shepherded his charges along with ungentle prods and Simon went off with Marie Lou to help her to prepare dinner.

To have eaten in the pentacle would have destroyed its occult protection, so three-quarters of an hour later de Richleau was helped along to the dining-room where they gathered for their evening meal. Malin had departed for the gardener's cottage so they waited on themselves. Full night had come and with it the poltergeists had resumed their irritating activities, announcing their arrival by the violent banging of a door somewhere in the servants' quarters soon after the friends had sat down to table. They endeavoured to ignore the sound as they discussed the new situation.

Considering that one of the best rooms in his house had been totally wrecked, Richard was in good spirits, as he felt confident that they ought to be able to screw all sorts of useful information out of their two captives, but the Duke was by no means so optimistic.

'I doubt if they know anything about the astral side of the business,' he said. 'Our real adversary will have communicated with the head of the Nazi spy system in Britain and asked that we should be eliminated. These two thugs were detailed to do the job; but I should think it most unlikely that they have the least idea as to *why* they were ordered to murder us.'

'Still,' remarked Simon, 'if we hand them over to the police, Military Intelligence might be able to get out of them the name of the man from whom they received their instructions. Trouble is, though, that no one in this country dare handle spies without velvet gloves unless they're willing to risk the sack.'

'That's true,' Richard muttered bitterly. 'They've shot one or two recently, but we had to be at war for fifteen months and get a new Home Secretary before they even had the guts to do that. I'll bet anything that the Government hasn't given permission for our Intelligence people to third degree the swine yet. Lots of people still don't seem to have got it into their heads that Hitler is waging *Total* war against us, and that if we want to win we've got to wage *Total* war against him.'

'As I see it, what the counter-espionage people are allowed to do, or are not allowed to do, doesn't cut any ice with us,' commented Rex. 'We've got these two palookas in the can, so why not a little private session? I just hate hurting people, but I wouldn't lose any sleep at all on account of giving these hoodlums another beating-up.'

'You can try your hand, if you like, and see what you can get out of them,' de Richleau agreed. 'I'm feeling distinctly shaky still, so I'm going straight back to bed. I shan't try anything tonight on the astral but will concentrate on recouping my strength instead. All the same, I should be grateful if one of you would watch beside me until the rest turn in.'

'Um,' Simon nodded. 'Since you went to London and the trouble started here we've made it a rule to go about in couples after dark and for two of us to sleep by turns in the pentacle while the other two watch. Never have liked rough houses myself, so I'm game to leave our visitors to the tender care of Rex and Richard.'

'I'll sit with you as well,' said Marie Lou. 'Hark at that damn'd door! It's enough to drive anyone crazy.'

As they listened they could hear a door slamming somewhere in the west wing. It kept on banging rhythmically about every thirty seconds, as though someone was constantly opening it, pulling it back and then crashing it to.

'Let's make a move,' said the Duke abruptly. 'Tomorrow, when I'm feeling stronger, I'll perform a banishing ritual and try to get rid of these things for you. They're not dangerous in themselves and are quite a low form of elemental sent by our enemy to annoy us, so I don't think there should be any great difficulty in driving them away.'

As he limped off to the library with Marie Lou and Simon, to prepare the great pentacle for the night, Richard and Rex lit candles and together descended into the cellars of the house. They were centuries old, having thick stone walls and heavy doors so that they differed little from actual mediaeval dungeons and quite possibly had been used for that purpose in the bad old days when the Lord Abbots held temporal as well as spiritual sway over the lands adjacent to Cardinals Folly.

One of them was now used as a wine-cellar and two others for lumber of various kinds, but a fourth was empty and it was into this that Richard had locked the two enemy agents. Taking a huge key from its nail beside the door, he unlocked it, and holding their candles aloft they went in.

The Japanese was sitting cross-legged in the middle of the floor, and the other man was lying propped-up in a corner. They blinked a little from having been in total darkness for over two hours, and Rex said:

'Now then, you two, you'd better get this straight. We're not standing any nonsense. You tried to rub us out, and unless you answer the questions I'm going to put to you we're going to rub *you* out. Got that?'

'No understand Engleesh,' said the Jap.

'Oh yes, you do,' boomed Rex. 'And what's more, you're going to talk it, unless you want both your ears torn off.'

'No understand Engleesh,' repeated the Jap impassively.

Rex looked over at the other man. 'How about you, comrade? Are you going to talk a little Engleesh or do I knock your teeth down your throat?'

The man had scrambled slowly to his feet but he just stood there and dumbly shook his head.

'These guys are asking for trouble,' Rex remarked to Richard, 'and in a minute they're going to get it.'

Richard laid a hand on his arm. 'Before you start in on them, let me have a go. I'll bet they understand all right. With a war on, they couldn't keep out of the clutches of the police for twenty-four hours unless they could talk enough English to make themselves understood while getting about the country. But the Jap looks as though he could take a lot of punishment without squealing, so I think we stand a better chance of getting what we want by exerting mental pressure.'

'Play it your way if you like,' Rex shrugged. 'I don't want to soil my hands on the dirty little yellow rat.'

Richard then addressed the prisoners, speaking very slowly and clearly in a hard, cold voice. 'Listen, both of you. This is my house. There are no servants here and no one will come down to these cellars whatever happens. You can shout until you have no voices left, but nobody will hear you, and if you persist in forgetting how to talk I mean to forget that I have ever set eyes on either of you. This cellar, as you see, is absolutely empty; there is no food and no water in it, and not even a bed on which to lie down.

What is more, the stone floor is damp and cold. If you persist in refusing to answer my questions my friend and I will leave you here and we shall *not—come—back*. No food and no water will be brought to you, so in the course of a day or two you will die of thirst—and a very unpleasant form of death you will find it. *Now*, are you going to be sensible or do you prefer to die here?'

Both the prisoners maintained a sullen silence, so after waiting a little, Rex said: 'That line's no good, Richard—at least, it won't get us anywhere at the moment. They'd probably stick it for twenty-four hours anyhow before they decided to spill the beans. We'll have to try something else if we want quick results.'

It was very cold down in the cellar, and very quiet. The only sound that disturbed the stillness was the faint but persistent banging of the door upstairs in the west wing. It was the cold chill of the place which gave Richard a new inspiration.

'I know how we can hasten matters,' he said grimly. 'Whatever we get out of them, we shan't be able to make use of it until tomorrow morning, and in any case we ought to search their clothes to see if they have anything of interest on them. Let's strip them both and leave them here in the cold all night. I bet they'll be ready enough to talk by the time we've had our breakfast.'

'Yep,' Rex nodded. 'Good stunt, that; and if they die of pneumonia afterwards—what the hell! Better folk than they are dying as we stand here, as a result of the Nazi air-raids. Let's do as you say. For the sake of a blanket and a cup of hot soup apiece tomorrow morning they'll be ready to give their own mothers away.'

Carefully setting their candles down on the floor, near the door, they advanced upon the Jap. Having felt that they were more than a match for the two prisoners neither of them had thought it necessary to bring down a gun, and seeing that they were unarmed the Jap stood up, apparently prepared to defend himself. The European slithered sideways a little, as though about to make a dash for the door. Rex was watching him out of the corner of his eye and let him cover a few feet. Then, just as he was on the point of dashing forward, Rex suddenly swung round and struck him behind the ear. With a gasp he stumbled against the wall and slid to the floor.

The Japanese took advantage of the diversion to leap at Richard. They went down with a mighty crash that nearly drove the breath out of Richard's body. He was underneath, and he knew at once, from the way in which his arms were seized and twisted giving him a moment's excruciating pain, that the wiry little devil on top of him was a Judo expert.

But no amount of ju-jutsu could prevail against Rex's Herculean strength; his great hands closed about the Jap's collar and the seat of his pants. With one violent jerk he tore him from on top of Richard then flung him sideways against the stone wall of the cellar.

As Richard struggled, panting, to his feet, Rex dived after the Jap and, picking him up again, shook him as a terrier shakes a rat.

'Come on, Richard,' he cried; 'I've got the little swine; just tear his clothes off him for me, will you?'

In vain the Jap squirmed and kicked. Between them they ripped off every shred of his clothes and flung him, gasping, in a corner.

'Now for the other feller,' said Rex, kicking the Jap's clothes toward the door. Together they advanced upon the European, who, apparently only semi-conscious, lay moaning on the floor. Rex sat him up and Richard pulled off his coat. It was at that moment that over Rex's shoulder Richard caught sight of something which made his blood turn to water in his veins.

11

The Horror in the Cellars

The thing that Richard saw was not alarming in itself. Had
he been down in that cellar a month or so before and seen
it he would just have stood there wondering what on earth
it could be, since it was no more than a tiny blob of
purplish-red light, about as big as a firefly, hovering near
the ceiling. He would probably have thought then that it
was some form of phosphorescent beetle, but now he knew
instantly that it must be something infinitely more dangerous.

Ever since the Duke had started his operations on the
astral Richard had known that they might be subject to
attacks from Evil entities, and during the past few days they
had had ample evidence that the war was now being carried
into their own camp. This little glimmer of red light might
be only a low form of Elemental, like the poltergeists which
had been causing them so much annoyance but were comparatively harmless. On the other hand, it might be some
terrible Saatii manifestation from the Outer Circle which
had come on the scene to protect the two thugs who were
pawns in its physical game. If so, in the next few moments
both he and Rex, unprotected as they were by astral
barriers, stood a good chance of losing their reason.

With a strangled shout of 'Rex! Quick! Get out!' Richard
sprang away from the man whose clothes he had been
removing.

Rex instantly swung round and saw the Thing behind
him. Even in that brief space of time the reddish glow had
increased from the size of a peanut to that of a golf ball,

The radiance it gave off was much brighter, lighting the whole corner of the cellar and glinting redly upon the naked body of the Jap which lay below it. In the same glance Rex saw that the two candles which they had set up near the door were flickering wildly, though there was not even a breath of draught in the musty cellar. Simultaneously both of them flung themselves at the door and wrenched it open.

As they did so the candles fluttered out; yet the cellar was not plunged in darkness. The lurid red glow now lit the whole place and the manifestation had swollen to the size of a cricket ball. Sweating with terror they threw themselves out into the passage and started to run along it, but they both had the awful sensation that something was pulling them back.

To lift each foot meant a colossal effort. It was as though they were trying to run under water, and the dark passage stretched out before them seeming to be a hundred yards in length instead of the bare twenty that it actually measured. Utilising every ounce of their will-power they fought their way forward until, when they were half way along the passage, Rex gave a moaning cry, stumbled and fell.

Time seemed to be standing still in that awful moment, as Richard stooped and, grabbing Rex by the arm, endeavoured to heave him to his feet. As he pulled at the weighty, seemingly inert form of his friend he was striving with all his might to remember the words of certain abjurations against evil things which he had heard de Richleau utter years before; but his brain seemed to be clogged and sluggish, so that in spite of all his efforts he could not recall even the first words of the Latin exorcism that he was seeking.

Instinctively he muttered the simple plea, 'Lord, protect us; O Lord, protect us,' and his call was answered.

He remembered de Richleau telling him that one of the best protections against evil was the blue vibration: that one should think of oneself as entirely surrounded by an oval aura of blue light and as actually wearing on one's forehead a crucifix set in an up-ended horseshoe, both of which symbols were glowing there in brilliant blue, a few inches above one's eyes.

As he 'thought blue' new strength seemed to come to him.

Somehow he managed to jerk Rex back onto his feet while whispering hoarsely: 'The blue aura, Rex—the horseshoe and the Cross—think of them in blue.'

'Yes,' gasped Rex, 'yes.' And together they again stumbled along the passage. Yet the Thing behind them refused to give up its prey. Although they dared not look over their shoulders they knew that it had emerged from the cellar and was following with silent stealth, exerting all its force to drag them back.

For a few moments they can both see the Blue Light that was surrounding them, but gradually it dimmed, and by the time they reached the foot of the stairs the baleful Magenta Light from behind them had overcome it. The stairs appeared to stretch up and up into infinity and their feet were so weighted that it seemed impossible that either would ever be able to mount to the floor above. A terrible load now pressed upon their shoulders so that they could no longer stand upright. They were bent almost double, so that only the first few stairs came within the range of their vision.

'O Lord, protect us—O Lord, protect us,' Richard whispered again, and with a fresh effort they mounted the first three stairs only to collapse side by side upon the fourth.

A wave of reddish light seemed to pass over them, blinding them to all else. They were submerged in it, breathless, gasping. The beating of their hearts was laboured, slowing down, so that the redness before their eyes darkened to a purple-tinted blackness. Both felt that the end was upon them when suddenly Simon's voice cut into their dulled consciousness. He was calling from the top of the stairs.

'Richard! Rex!'

His shout was followed by a gasp of dismay as he saw them lying there huddled together. Then, in a ringing voice, he cried aloud the words that Richard had been unable to remember. *'Fundamenta ejus in montibus sanctis!'*

Immediately the Magenta Light faded, their limbs were free of the awful weight which held them down, and next moment Simon, who had rushed down towards them, was dragging them both helter-skelter up the stairs. Breathless, shaking, and still chilled with the terror of the Evil which had been upon them, they stumbled across the hall and into the library.

De Richleau was already asleep within the pentacle and Marie Lou, dressed for bed, was sitting beside him. As they burst into the room she made an angry gesture for silence, fearing that they would wake the Duke; then she caught sight of their white, scared faces.

'What's happened?' she asked sharply.

It was Simon who answered after swiftly shutting the door and making the sign of the Cross over it.

'I'd just been upstairs getting ready for the night,' he panted; 'suddenly struck me that Richard and Rex had been down in that cellar a long time; wondered if anything had gone wrong, so I—er—went down to see—found them in a shocking muddle.'

Richard was mopping the perspiration from his forehead but Simon's old expression for any sort of trouble brought a faint smile to his lips, and he took up the tale:

'The prisoners wouldn't talk, so Rex and I decided to leave them without clothes down in that damp, cold cellar for the night. We'd stripped the Jap and were just about to start on the other feller when the Big Black that we're up against must have tumbled to what was on. Either he arrived in person or sent something pretty nasty to get us. I've never been more utterly afraid in all my life.'

'That goes for me too.' A shudder ran through Rex's mighty frame. 'God knows what would have happened to us if good old Simon hadn't come down into the filthy purple mist and pulled us out.'

'Oh, bless you, Simon,' Marie Lou exclaimed; then, after a moment, she sighed. 'I can't tell you how I'm hating this business. It's the thought that we might all be driven mad if we're caught off our guard for a single second that is so terrifying, I think. Still, there can be no going back; we've got to go through with it.'

'Sure,' Rex agreed. 'And this was our own darned fault. In the midst of a show like this we were just clean crackers to go down to the cellars at all; I reckon it'd be dangerous even in daylight—let alone at night. We'll have to keep a sharper watch on ourselves for the future.'

Simon nodded his bird-like head and his dark eyes flickered from one to the other of them. 'That's it; mustn't take any chances at all from now on. You two had better undress here; I'll dash up and fetch your pyjamas then we'll all get into the safety of the pentacle.'

But they would not allow him to leave the room alone, so the three men crossed the hall and sped up the stairs together, visiting first Rex's room and then Richard's. It was only as Richard was about to snatch up the clean pyjamas which were laid out for him each night that he realised that all this time he had been clutching in his right hand the coat that he had dragged from the back of their European prisoner.

Flinging it on the bed, he swiftly ran through the pockets to find that, while the side-pockets were empty, the breast pocket contained a small sheaf of papers. Gripping these with one hand, and his pyjamas with the other, he turned to the door and, with his friends beside him, dashed downstairs back to the library.

Simon and Marie Lou had already remade the pentacle for the night, before de Richleau had dropped off to sleep, so nothing remained to be done but to seal the doors and windows of the room; and this Simon did while the other two were undressing. With a sigh of thankfulness they all crawled into their makeshift beds, which were arranged like a five-pointed star, with their heads to the centre and their feet to the rim of the pentacle.

Richard had brought with him the papers that he had found in the prisoner's pocket, and in whispers, so as not to arouse the sleeping Duke, they began to examine and discuss them.

The papers consisted of a passport issued to one Alfonse Rodin, as a member of the Free French Forces, and a number of letters written to him. There was also the sum of four-pounds-ten in British treasury notes. Marie Lou, whose French was much more perfect than that of any of her companions, read the letters through carefully. They were from three different women and all of them were a queer mixture of love and business which at first she could not understand; but when she had translated them Richard said:

'I think I can guess this particular riddle. They are from three French prostitutes who are plying their trade in the West End of London. This fellow is evidently one of the brutes who protect such women, but take most of their

133

money off them after providing them with flats and clothes. The poor wretches have to try and kid themselves that there's some romance in their lives else they'd go insane, so they usually pin their affections on their so-called protector while they sell themselves for his benefit. Hence the love passages which appear in the letters all mixed up with accounts of daily payments into the bank.'

'Um; that's about it,' Simon nodded. 'One of them even mentions a fine of thirty bob, though she doesn't say what it was for—evidently she was pinched for accosting and run in by the police.'

'The filthy swine!' muttered Rex. 'If I'd been wise to his business I'd have made such a mess of his face that not even the oldest tart in Marseilles would ever have worked for him again. But it doesn't seem that those letters get us any place.'

'No.' Marie Lou shook her curls. 'But I wonder what this white-slaver was doing in General de Gaulle's Free Force?'

'Cover, probably,' replied Richard. 'He may have been operating in London for years, but every Frenchman's done his term of military service, and this chap may have thought that the authorities would sling him out after the collapse of France unless he wangled his way into de Gaulle's legion.'

'That's about the size of it,' Rex agreed. 'De Gaulle seems a grand guy and many of his people are splendid fellows, but it must be mighty difficult for them to know whom they dare trust in these days. It wasn't only the politicians who went bad on us last summer. The Nazis' rot got right into the nation, and it's my view that even now the bulk of the French upper classes are playing for a draw.'

Marie Lou nodded quickly: 'And, of course, they'll come sneaking in again on our side to save their faces when we've as good as won the war off our own bat. But at the moment we're up against something infinitely worse than German bullies, Italian gangsters or French crooks, and I think we ought to try to get some sleep. Who's going to take first watch?'

'I will,' volunteered Rex and Simon together.

'Let Simon take it, Rex,' said Marie Lou. 'You and Richard ought to have a good long sleep after your nasty experience tonight. If Simon watches till one, I'll take on

[*Richard Eaton's views on the French collapse were rather strong, so Mr. Wheatley decided that as a matter of courtesy to the Free French Forces they should be deleted.*]

from one till three, which will give both of you the best part of five hours before your turn of duty. Then you can take three till five, and Richard five till seven.'

So it was settled, and with the exception of Simon they snuggled down under their covers.

During most of his watch Simon played a very complicated form of patience with a new pack of cards which he had brought into the pentacle; but every few minutes he looked up from his game to glance round the quiet room. In the distance the monotonous but petulant banging of the door continued, and once he caught the faint crash of china from the kitchen, where another poltergeist was evidently at work, but otherwise his watch proved uneventful, and at one o'clock he woke Marie Lou.

She wished him happy dreams, carefully snuffed the candles, examined the little vases of charged water, the horseshoes and the bunches of herbs to see that they were all in place, then settled down to read a brand-new book which Richard had bought for her from a shop in the village that afternoon.

Like many women who have particularly large and beautiful eyes, her sight was not very strong, so she always wore spectacles for reading, and to her annoyance she found that she had forgotten to bring hers downstairs when she had gone up to get ready for the night. As the print of the book was fairly large she was able to read for some time without them, but after a while she began to feel the strain and had to put the book down.

Without anything at all to occupy her she found watching to be a dreary business and she half-decided to play a game of patience with Simon's cards but abandoned the idea because to get at them she would have had to crawl across his body and might have wakened him.

The door had at last cease to bang, and an utter silence had descended upon the old house, so that even the normal little noises of the night did not seem to disturb it any more. The big fire was still burning in the wide hearth and the candle flames were dead steady. The room was warm and cosy. No breath of that cold, repellent Evil intruded to trouble her mind and it seemed that the five of them within their strong occult defences were absolutely safe from all harm. She knew that although their bodies were still sleeping all four of her friends were still very near her, because, as things were, even their astrals would not venture outside the pentacle that night.

For over an hour she sat there doing nothing but ruminate quietly upon this extraordinary weaponless fight in which they were involved against Hitler and wondering what would be its end. The strain of reading had tired her eyes a little and for a few moments she allowed the heavy lids to sink down over them.

When she opened them again all was still well, so she closed them once more; and for how long she remained with her eyes shut she never knew. Sitting there with her hands clasped round her knees and her head sunk forward on her chest, she was almost asleep—but not quite. She was just wondering how much longer there was to go before she could rouse Rex for his turn at watching, when she suddenly became conscious that in the last few moments the temperature of the room had changed; from a pleasant warmth it had fallen to a comfortless chill that seemed to be creeping up all her limbs.

Instantly she was fully awake and staring anxiously about her. To her alarm and dismay she saw that the fire was out and that each of the five candle-flames had shrunk to a bare glimmer, so that the whole room was practically in darkness.

Jerking round, she thrust out her hands to rouse the others but from sheer terror her cry of warning was stifled in her throat. Crouching upon de Richleau's breast was a huge and horrid black thing. As her eyes swiftly became accustomed to the dim light she saw that it was a great vampire bat, as big as a large dog; a phosphorescent glow which came from the brute's eyes showed that its teeth were buried in the Duke's throat.

Her temporary paralysis passed. She let out a piercing scream. Richard, Rex and Simon threw off their bedclothes and sprang up, but de Richleau only moaned loudly and seemed to struggle in his sleep.

None of them had any weapon, but Rex grabbed at the foul creature with his bare hands. It was forced to withdraw its teeth from the Duke's throat but slithered through Rex's hands, spread its powerful wings and came rushing straight at Marie Lou's face.

She screamed again and jerked backwards. Richard struck out at it, hitting it full in the breast and knocking it to the floor. For a second it lay there squirming, then suddenly changed its form into that of a great serpent with seven heads.

Simon had grabbed the Duke under the armpits and was dragging him from his bed across the floor. 'Out of the pentacle, all of you!' he yelled. 'Get out of the pentacle!'

Coiled on its tail, the great snake hissed and its seven heads struck out in all directions at once. Marie Lou rolled over and over away from it, Rex leapt aside but Richard slipped and fell. The snake reared above him and for a moment he lay there, wondering in horror which of its heads would strike him first.

'O Lord,' he prayed, 'deliver me.' And at that second he found that one of his outflung hands was touching one of the little silver vases that contained charged water. Dipping his fingers into it, with a frantic jerk of his hand he flicked a few drops in the direction of the snake. Some of them hit it and sizzled as though they had fallen upon white-hot metal. The snake recoiled with incredible swiftness as Richard rolled away from under it.

All five of them were now outside the pentacle. Rex, Richard and Marie Lou, staring at the Monster, were still jittering with fear, but Simon, who had once so nearly become a Black Magician, knew that for the time being they were safe. The pentacle was a barrier of immense power which worked both ways. It could keep any evil thing from entering it, but at the same time it could prevent the escape of any Evil thing which was inside it. The ab-human threshed violently from side to side, striking with its seven heads at the empty air above the line of the candles and the charged-water vases; but it was caged and could not pursue them.

De Richleau had struggled into wakefulness directly Simon had succeeded in getting him outside the pentacle. One glance was enough to show him the terrible peril they had just escaped. Staggering to his feet, he limped over to his suitcase which stood in a corner of the room. Wrenching from it a full bottle of charged water, that he had kept in reserve, he began to sprinkle it by flicking the bottle-top so that the water fell into the centre of the circle, while he pronounced aloud a Latin abjuration.

For fifty heart-beats the Monster continued to glide and dart from side to side in an endeavour to evade the scalding drops; then it gave up the struggle and with an angry hissing disappeared in a little cloud of evil green vapour.

It was many minutes before any of them could breathe evenly, but at last, in a stifled voice, de Richleau asked what had happened, and Marie Lou said:

'The brute was a huge bat, and when I first saw it its fangs were buried in your throat.'

'Um,' nodded Simon. 'Look, there are the marks, two little round punctures near your jugular vein.'

De Richleau touched the spot. 'Yes; I can feel them. In a minute I must do a purifying rite to cleanse the place, but fortunately it could have had its fangs in me only for a few seconds otherwise I should feel much weaker than I do. The thing that worries me, though, is the fact that a Satanic force managed to get inside the pentacle. You must have made some slip when you were erecting our astral defences last night.'

Marie Lou shook her head. 'It wasn't that. Simon and I made the pentacle together while you were getting ready to go to sleep, and we checked each other's every move.'

'Then one of you must have brought something unclean into the pentacle with you,' said the Duke.

'That's it!' exclaimed Richard. 'And it's entirely my fault. There were some letters and a passport; papers that I got out of the pocket of one of the prisoners. Rex and I had a pretty nasty turn last night down in the cellars. If I'd been my normal self I should never have done such a thing, but as it was, I brought the stuff with me when we came to bed and we were looking through it before going to sleep. I can't say how desperately sorry I am.'

De Richleau nodded. 'Anything of that kind would be quite sufficient to enable an Evil Entity to materialise. Well, that explains the matter.'

'It was just as much my fault,' said Marie Lou quickly; 'I forgot to bring down my "specs" so I couldn't read for long, and I very nearly went to sleep—at least, I shut my eyes for a little and that gave the Thing time to materialise before I could warn you. I feel absolutely frightful about it.'

'There's no need for you and Richard to blame yourselves unduly,' the Duke smiled, 'as the fault really lies with me. I said that I wasn't going out tonight. I ought to have stuck to that and remained in the pentacle near my body; then I should have seen at once what was happening, and could have slipped back into it before the brute had gained sufficient solidity to attack me. As it was, soon after I'd gone to sleep I decided that, after all, there couldn't be any great danger in my going off to see if I could get some information that I am most anxious to obtain.'

'That was pretty rash,' said Simon.

'I know; and if Marie Lou hadn't roused up in time I might have paid for it in no uncertain manner. But I've discovered the thing for which I went to search the records, and I've got something extraordinarily interesting to tell you all—I now know the earthly base from which our enemy is operating.'

A murmur of quick interest interrupted him for a moment, then he went on: 'I was right about the lobster-claw piece of coast that Marie Lou and I saw—it *is* a portion of an island—and I believe that the Nazis have got hold of a High Priest of Voodoo to work for them on the astral. The island is the Negro Republic of Haiti, in the West Indies, and if we're to stop this menace to British shipping we'll have to go there.'

12

Crime Does Not Pay

'What a break!' Rex exclaimed. 'Out there in the West Indies we'll be able to forget this filthy war for a bit. Think of it—sunshine, bathing, dancing, big game, fishing, lots of good things to eat and drink—all the fun we used to have in those old peace-time days when we packed our grips for the sunny South.'

Richard sighed. 'Those lovely winter holidays in the sunshine are what Marie Lou and I have missed most. We've so often said what heaven it would be to go cruising with you all on the yacht again. Yet somehow it doesn't seem right to leave England while there's a war on, and I'll bet that when we really got down to trying to enjoy ourselves we just wouldn't be able to, because all the time we'd be thinking of what's going on here.'

Marie Lou slipped her hand through his arm. 'You silly darling; it isn't a question of enjoying ourselves and you know quite well that not one of us would dream of quitting for our own sakes; but this is different.'

'Of course,' added the Duke. 'Far from running away from danger, we shall be going further into it, and this is a fight for Britain which only we can wage.'

'I suppose you're right,' Richard agreed, still a shade reluctantly. 'Anyhow, you've always been our leader and what you say goes.'

'Thanks, Richard,' de Richleau smiled. 'We'll set about our preparations tomorrow morning. In the meantime we've quite a lot to do after the narrow escape we had tonight; then some of us at least should get a little more sleep.'

For the next hour they employed themselves in banishing all traces of the evil manifestation which had attacked them. The whole floor had to be thoroughly cleaned while the Duke performed certain exorcisms and the pentacle was re-made. The French prisoner's papers were taken outside to the hall, the Duke attended to the marks on his throat, the door was re-sealed, and they settled down again, with Richard and Rex to watch while the other three slept.

When they awoke Richard, Rex and Simon, still wearing their wreaths of garlic flowers and crucifixes for protection, went down into the cellars to find out if the two prisoners were still there; but in the previous night's panic the door had been left open and, as they had expected, both the Frenchman and the Jap had escaped, leaving no trace behind them.

In the meantime Marie Lou helped the Duke upstairs to his bedroom and set about attending to his injured foot. As she dressed the gash he remarked:

'Don't put on too thick a bandage, because I must get a shoe over it. I'm going up to London to see Pellinore.'

'No, Greyeyes, you're not,' she contradicted him promptly. 'You put up a splendid front last night but that explosion shook you much more than you'd have us believe, and you can't possibly expect this place in your foot to heal unless you keep your leg up. You're not moving out of this house today and you're going to spend it resting.'

De Richleau was one of the most determined people in the world, but he had come up against Marie Lou before, and knew that she could be extraordinarily pig-headed. He glanced up at her uneasily as she went on:

'Richard can quite well go up to London for you. All you have to do is to tell him what you want done. He will see Sir Pellinore and make all arrangements for our journey. You know as well as I do that he's extraordinarily competent at that sort of thing.'

'Of course he is,' agreed the Duke, 'but it's essential that I should see Pellinore myself.'

'Then it's a case of Mohammed and the Mountain,' she countered. 'Since I will not allow you to go up to see him he must come down here to see you.'

142

'Impossible; he's much too busy,' said the Duke a trifle curtly.

Upon which, somewhat to his surprise, Marie Lou replied: 'Well, if he really is too busy to come down I suppose I'll have to let you go, but I insist on your staying in bed for breakfast.'

'That's settled, then,' de Richleau smiled. Yet he remained vaguely suspicious about her sudden surrender; and, as it proved, with good reason. An hour or so later, just as he was finishing his breakfast, she returned to his room and said with a mischievous smile:

'You needn't bother to get up, after all. I was lucky enough to get a personal call through to London with comparatively little delay, and I've spoken to Sir Pellinore. He says that no business is as important at the moment as the business which we are engaged on, and that as you're laid up he'll motor down to join us for luncheon.'

The Duke laughed as he took her small hand and kissed it. 'I might have known that you'd get the best of me—and, frankly, I'm not sorry. That bomb shook me up pretty badly and it's rather a relief to be able to take things easy.'

Soon after one Sir Pellinore was with them. When he was shown Marie Lou's devastated sitting-room he expressed real concern and insisted that now that this strange war within the war had been carried on to the physical plane they must have a police guard to protect them from further attempts upon their lives.

De Richleau laughingly protested that it was quite useless to have police officers in the house, as instead of their being able to *give* protection after dark they would themselves require it and would only add to his own burdens; but Sir Pellinore persisted that, in any case, police could patrol the grounds to prevent strangers from getting near the house, and he forthwith put through a priority call to the Special Branch at Scotland Yard to arrange matters, at the same time giving particulars of the two enemy agents who had thrown the bomb and afterwards escaped.

At the Duke's special request he added that the officer in charge was not to call at the house or institute any inquiry but to confine his activities to seeing that no stranger was allowed to approach within two hundred yards of the house or its outbuildings.

Over luncheon the Duke announced his discovery that the enemy was operating from Haiti and that it would be necessary for them to go there.

'Why?' asked Sir Pellinore bluntly. 'From what I've gathered of this extraordinary business, you people seem to be able to travel anywhere, with perfect ease, in your sleep, so what's to be gained by your all sailing off to the West Indies in the flesh?'

'There is only one way in which we can stop this thing,' said the Duke promptly. 'The Adept of the Left-Hand Path whose astral gets on board each convoy-leader secure particulars of the route planned for it. He must then communicate with a Nazi occultist in Germany. The Nazi then wakes up and gives particulars to the German Admiralty, who issue code instructions to their submarines which are patrolling the Atlantic or dispatch dive-bombers from the French coast to attack the convoy; but each morning the Adept, however powerful he is, has to wake up in his body *in Haiti*, and he is the fellow we want to get at.'

'One thing I don't understand.' Simon gave a little nervous wriggle of his head. 'If an Adept in Haiti can get the information, why can't the Nazi occultist to whom it is passed on get it for himself?'

De Richleau shrugged. 'That's more than I can say for the moment; but I believe it's a question of relative power. You must remember that when I started to operate I had definite facts to work upon. I knew the time and place from which the convoy was sailing and the route that it was to take. Therefore, each time I went out I knew, within a relatively small area, where to look for it. Our enemy, on the other hand, has no such information, and to search for a group of ships in the vast spaces of the Atlantic, without any guide at all as to where they are to be found, would be like looking for a needle in a haystack. And, mark you, they must be located within twenty-four hours of their escort having left them, otherwise they would be getting to the limit of the belt in which the enemy can operate. If I were given such a job it's almost certain that I should miss nine out of ten of the convoys, and probably the German occultist would be no more successful.'

'Whereas the fellow we're up against manages to locate

every convoy in the limited time at his disposal,' cut in Richard.

'Exactly. How he does so I don't pretend to know, but he is evidently an Adept of very great power, and that, I think, is why the Germans have to work through him instead of doing the job for themselves.'

'Sounds feasible,' boomed Sir Pellinore; 'that is, as far as any of this stuff can be said to make sense at all. But I still don't see why you've got to go all the way to Haiti to deal with the feller—I mean, since this battle is being fought on the—er—astral plane.'

'Because,' said the Duke patiently, 'the only way in which we can stop this thing is by killing the Haitian Adept, and only in our physical bodies can we do that.'

'Sure. That adds up about having to go there if we want to rub him out,' said Rex. 'But how's killing him going to prevent his astral from carrying on the dirty work and continuing to turn over the information that they want to his Nazi friends while they're asleep?'

'A very shrewd question, Rex,' the Duke smiled, 'and the answer lies in the law of the Timeless Ones who have created all things as they are. As I explained to Pellinore some time ago, and as all of you are aware, when we have achieved a certain state of advancement through many lives we have complete continuity of consciousness—that is to say, when we are asleep our astral knows everything there is to know about the physical body to which it is temporarily attached, and when we are awake we are able, through long practice, to remember all that we do on the astral plane. More: when we achieve true memory we are able to look back and recall all that we did in our innumerable past lives on Earth. Therefore, the genuine Adept, whether of the Right or the Left-Hand Path, can view his existence, either in the flesh or out of it, as one continuous whole.'

Simon nodded. 'That's what makes it so difficult to trap a really powerful Black. Having continuity of consciousness enables him to be perpetually on guard, so it's practically impossible to take him by surprise; whether he's in his body or out of it, he's always on the look-out to foil any attempt which may be made to get at him.'

'True,' de Richleau agreed. 'But the Wise Ones foresaw

that and provided for it. However powerful an individual may become, there is always one moment, which occurs every two or three hundred years, when he is completely helpless. That moment is at the end of each Earth life. It doesn't in the least matter if people die in bed of so-called old age, or, at the height of their strength, through violence. As each incarnation finishes, there is a brief space of time in which the individual suffers a complete black-out, and it is then, in the case of a Black Magician, that the warriors of Light can rush in and chain him.'

Sir Pellinore passed a large hand over his fine head of white hair. 'Dear me, this is all very—well, I won't say that it's beyond me—but a bit outside the compass of an ordinary feller like myself. Still, I've no doubt that you know what you're talking about, and it all seems to fit in. I take it, then, that you propose to kill the chap who's making all the trouble and collar his—er—soul I suppose you'd call it —while the going's good. What happens to him then? Not that I care what you do to the feller, but just as a matter of interest. Is it possible to kill his soul too?'

'No,' smiled the Duke; 'but we can cast it into prison. No individual is wholly bad, and Black Magicians are only people who have gone astray throughout a number of incarnations. It's quite a reasonable analogy to compare them with men who have become habitual criminals in this life. Most crooks start their criminal careers as youngsters who through bad example, or a sudden impulse, pick a pocket or rob a till and get away with it. They know perfectly well that they're running a risk and that sooner or later they will be caught and punished, but they're tempted through laziness or ambition, and, more often still, by false pride which flatters them into thinking how clever they are to continue obtaining money by illicit means instead of working for it. Sometimes the shock of being caught and put on probation or given a light prison sentence is enough to bring them to their senses and they mend their ways. In other cases they have to be given sentence after sentence before they finally decide that *crime does not pay*.'

'Oh, come!' protested Sir Pellinore. 'What about the old lags? The really hardened crooks never give up their profession however often they're jailed.'

'One moment. I grant you that the average Earth life of

seventy years is not long enough to cure the worst cases. But if men lived for seven thousand years, instead of for seventy, I think you'll agree that the most hardened crook that ever lived would get a little tired of prison after he had done about two thousand years inside and each new sentence was getting longer and longer.'

'Ha!' Sir Pellinore guffawed. 'That's good. Yes, you're right there, Duke; I see your point.'

'Well, that's what happens on the astral. There's not one of us who hasn't dabbled in Black Magic at some time or other during our many lives, and at one time I could do as neat a job of sorcery as most people myself; but the majority of us give it up after being hauled up and cautioned, while the hardened cases go on for maybe a dozen lives or more, until they're caught out and sentenced to a really long spell. If that's not enough they get an even heavier sentence next time they're caught; and, of course, each prison sentence sets them back on the upward journey which we all have to accomplish sooner or later whether we like it or not.'

'How d'you mean?'

'Simply that if a spirit is cast into prison for having taken the Left-Hand Path it is automatically debarred from any chance of reincarnation during the term of its imprisonment. Prison sentences are much longer on the astral than they are on Earth, so a bad Black might easily get a thousand years. That would set him back three or four lives and the long intervening periods in which we are not in incarnation; and as he has to live those lives some time before he can possibly pass on to a higher sphere all that lost time later proves a heavy handicap. However, as you've got to get back to London we mustn't wander too far from the matter in hand. I take it that you can arrange passages to Haiti for us?'

'Certainly,' said Sir Pellinore quickly. 'I'll have you flown over to Lisbon and will see that seats are reserved for you on the *Clipper* to New York. From there, Pan-American Airways would take you down to Cuba and you could go on by sea. Wait a minute, though: if you did that you might be held up for a week or more in Cuba; trade with the Negro Republic is practically non-existent, so sailings to it from Havana are probably infrequent. It would be better for you to fly from New York to Miami and hire a plane there to take you on to your destination. Money, of course, is no object, but speed is of the first importance.'

'Situation's still pretty bad, then,' hazarded Simon.

'Bad!' echoed Sir Pellinore, lifting his blue eyes heavenwards. 'My God, if you only knew! The Intelligence people are going grey with worry over it, and even the "silent" service has been forced to admit that it's at its wits' end. Up to the moment the P.M. has been most sympathetic with the difficulties of all concerned, but I can see the point coming when *his* patience will be exhausted; and when that happens I'd rather have to face Hitler.'

'Our losses in tonnage were considerably down last week, though,' Richard remarked.

'Yes; thanks to brilliant handling of their ships by our seamen—plus, apparently, the fact that de Richleau put a spoke in the Nazis' wheel and enabled one convoy to get through without being attacked. However, the menace is still there. Britain entered the war with twenty-one million tons of shipping, but that is dispersed all over the world, and since September we've lost hundreds of thousands of tons every month in Atlantic waters. We can't go on that way. It's not only the ships—it's hundreds of fine seamen who can't be replaced—the very salt of our island race— many of them young men who've not lived long enough yet to beget sons and so pass on the blood that for centuries has given England the mastery of the seas and of the narrow waters. Then there's the cargoes; loss of exports means loss in dollars, and, more important still, it's temporarily halved our imports in such vital commodities as food, tommy-guns and the planes from America which we're counting upon to enable us to beat the Germans in 1941.'

'Well, you can rely upon us to do our damn'dest,' said the Duke soberly.

'I know. But I cannot too heavily stress the absolutely vital issues which are at stake. All our splendid naval successes in the Mediterranean, and the magnificent work in the Libyan Desert by which the Army has regained the confidence of the nation, will go for nothing unless this mass destruction of our shipping can be checked. The Western Approaches have now become the focal point of the whole war, and as the spring advances Hitler will unquestionably intensify his attacks. I don't pretend to understand what you're up to, but you seem to have got a line on this thing and you're the only people in Britain who have, so I beg of you not to spare yourselves. If you're victorious we shall never be able to tell the public how the Nazi counter-blockade was broken, but you yourselves will have the satisfaction of knowing that you five have gained as great a triumph for Britain as any military commander, with the whole of our new Armies, could do in the field.'

Simon tittered into his hand. 'That ranks us as equal to about ten divisions apiece; pretty good going, eh?'

'I mean it,' insisted Sir Pellinore. 'Now, when can you start?'

'I think I can say for all of us that we're ready to leave as soon as you can complete arrangements for our journey,' said the Duke, looking round at the others, who all nodded silent agreement.

'Good. That will be the day after tomorrow, then. The *Clipper* leaves Lisbon on Friday, and there's no sense in your kicking your heels there for twenty-four hours which you could doubtless better employ here.'

'Would you be able to get us places at such short notice?' Rex asked. 'I gather the *Clipper's* pretty crowded these days.'

Sir Pellinore waved the question aside with one of his large hands. 'Your countrymen are in this thing with us now, Van Ryn, praise be to God. I have only to ask one of the officials of the War Cabinet to get on to the American Embassy and—whoever has to be turned off—they'll see to it for us that you have places on the plane.'

Shortly afterwards, having earnestly wished them God's blessing on their strange mission, Sir Pellinore left for London. The Duke then told the others that he intended to set about purging the house of the poltergeists.

Marie Lou remonstrated with him because she wanted him to lie down again and rest his injured foot, but he pointed out to her that as there would be quite a number of things to do in London before setting out on their journey they would have to leave Cardinals Folly very early the following morning, and he was anxious that the house should be made habitable so that the servants could return to it before they left.

Seeing the sense of that she gave way but asked him a question that had been puzzling her for some days.

'Why is it that, while *we* can't make ourselves either felt or heard when we're out of our bodies, a poltergeist can perform all sorts of physical acts?'

'It's because they are not individuals, but elementals,' he replied. 'They differ from living spirits in the same way as a poisonous jelly-fish differs from a human being. Both these low forms are unpleasant and malignant but they are blind and lack all intelligence. Both can make themselves felt in a way that we cannot, but can easily be destroyed by us.'

They spent the next two hours accompanying the Duke as he moved from room to room with bell and book and water sprinkler. In each room he remained standing and read an exorcism, while they stood on either side of him murmuring the responses to his prompting. He then sprinkled the four corners of the room, the doorway and the hearth, while reciting certain powerful abjurations which from time immemorial have been known to drive away evil spirits.

In room after room as each ceremony was completed there was temporarily a disgusting stench until they had flung wide the windows and let in the cold winter air. At one place in the west wing the horrible smell of rotting meat was so bad that Marie Lou was on the point of vomiting, until de Richleau told her that if she were in her 'astral she would laugh to see the fun. The poltergeists were little 'blacks' like round balloons about the size of footballs, and each time the holy water hit one it burst, disintegrating in a puff of astral smoke which gave off the beastly smell of the earthly filth from the essence of which it derived its strength.

That night they again slept in the pentacle, taking turns to watch, while the astrals of those who slept never left it. In consequence they passed an untroubled night and beyond the library door silence reigned all through the dark hours, showing that the purification of the house which had been carried out that afternoon had proved entirely successful.

They were up very early the following morning. As soon as they had dressed they packed their bags, and while

Marie Lou did Richard's packing he had a talk with Malin, giving the butler a number of post-dated cheques with which to run the house while its master and mistress were absent. Malin also undertook to reassure such members of the staff as were willing to return that they would not be troubled by any further curious happenings. At nine o'clock he deferentially shook hands with them all and wished them good luck as they got into Richard's car and set off for London.

All five of them spent a busy day. At the Duke's request, Simon telephoned to Sir Pellinore and arranged for the issue of a special treasury-permit enabling them to transfer ample funds to a bank in Port-au-Prince, the capital of Haiti. Marie Lou did a hectic afternoon's shopping, acquiring the sort of lovely, light, gay clothes for tropical sunshine which she had never hoped to wear again until the war was over. Rex reported to Air Force Headquarters and ascertained that his indefinite extension of leave was all in order. De Richleau purchased an additional supply of rare herbs from Culpeper House while Richard, the ever-practical, saw that the armaments of the whole party were in proper order. They all possessed automatics from their past adventures, with permits to retain them, but none of the weapons had been used for several years and for two of the guns he had to obtain a new supply of ammunition.

At cocktail-time they met at the Duke's flat, as it had been decided that after rendezvousing there for drinks they would dine at the Dorchester and make a holiday of this their last night for none of them knew how long in dear, bomb-torn London.

They had just satisfied themselves that all their arrangements had been completed, and were about to move off for the Dorchester, when the telephone bell rang. De Richleau picked up the receiver and Sir Pellinore's deep voice boomed along the line.

'That you, de Richleau? Listen, I've got a favour to ask of you.'

'Certainly. What is it?' replied the Duke.

'There's a young woman—daughter of a man I know—her name's Philippa Ricardi—he's very anxious to get her out of England and he has an estate in Jamaica—grows sugar or something of the kind, and the place is run for him by his sister. He's already made arrangements to send the girl there by the *Clipper* leaving on Friday, so her permits and passport are all in order. She's travelling alone, though, and I was wondering if Mrs. Eaton would be good enough to chaperone her as far as Miami. It would be a great kindness if she would.'

'Hold on one moment.' De Richleau turned and repeated the request to Marie Lou.

'Of course I will,' she said at once, and the Duke told Sir Pellinore that it would be quite all right.

'Splendid,' boomed the Baronet. 'Please convey my most grateful thanks to Mrs. Eaton. Miss Ricardi will meet you at Waterloo tomorrow morning. Oh, by the by, I forgot to tell you, and I can't stay to explain further, because I'm wanted on another line, but the poor girl's a mute—you know, deaf-and-dumb.'

13

The Beautiful Mute

It was still half dark when they drove through London the
following morning. A gentle drizzle was falling and the chill
half-light disclosed a scene which could hardly have been
more depressing. Only about a third of London's pre-war
traffic was now on the streets. Hardly one out of every hundred houses that they passed had actually been destroyed
by a bomb but many appeared to have been shut and abandoned by their owners and in the vicinity of each wrecked
house a dozen others near it had patched or boarded
windows as a result of the explosion. Yet London was
carrying on with grim determination, as could be seen from
the little crowds of men and girls getting off buses and
coming out of tube-stations on their way to work.

At Waterloo they were conducted to a Pullman which
had been reserved for passengers travelling on the Lisbon
plane, and among the little group of people on the platform
they at once picked out Philippa Ricardi. The only other
woman there was an elderly lady, so they felt certain that
the girl standing a little apart, with a tall, grey-haired man,
must be their charge. As they approached the man stepped
forward and raised his hat to Marie Lou.

'I'm sure you must be Mrs. Eaton,' he said, and as she
smiled he went on: 'It's most kind of you to take charge of
my daughter. As she's unable to talk it would be terribly
difficult for her to make the journey alone, and we're both
awfully grateful to you.'

'*Please,*' Marie Lou protested, 'I'm delighted to think we

shall be able to make things easier for her.' She turned quickly to the girl and held out her hand.

There was nothing at all about Philippa to indicate her terrible affliction. She was of medium height, with black hair which curled under a smart little hat, and she was dressed in neat, expensive travelling tweeds. Her eyes were large, dark and intelligent, her mouth full-lipped and generous. Her skin, which was particularly good, had a warm, faintly dusky hue and was the only thing about her which betrayed the fact that she had a dash of black blood in her veins. She looked about twenty-three but might have been younger, and if they had not known of her connections with Jamaica they would hardly have suspected that she was an octoroon.

It is not the easiest of situations to find oneself suddenly confronted with a deaf-mute but Marie Lou had already made up her mind that the best policy was to ignore the poor girl's affliction as far as possible, so she proceeded to introduce the others just as though Philippa could hear what she was saying, and the girl bowed to each of them in turn.

Shortly afterwards an official asked them to take their places so Philippa took an affectionate leave of her father and they all got into the train. Two minutes later the whistle blew and it slowly steamed out of the station.

As Philippa sat back from the window they saw that her large dark eyes were half-filled with tears and that she was having great difficulty in controlling her emotions, so for a few moments they looked away from her and busied themselves with their rugs and papers. Then Simon produced from his pocket one of those magic slates consisting of a sheet of celluloid under which, if it is scrawled upon with anything pointed, writing appears but can be wiped out again by pulling the small attachment at the bottom of the pad, which leaves the slate perfectly clean.

On it he wrote: 'Cheer up! We're all going to the sunshine.'

Marie Lou, watching him, felt how typical of the gentle, thoughtful Simon it was to have foreseen that although the girl could not talk or hear they would be able to communicate with her in writing, and by some strange means, prob-

154

ably involving considerable trouble, to have procured over-night such an admirable vehicle for the purpose.

Producing a similar magic slate from her bag, Philippa wrote on it: 'Yes. But I hate leaving London.'

Simon wrote: 'Why?'

Philippa replied: 'It seems like running away,' and added: 'Why are you writing things down? I can hear perfectly well.'

Simon gave her a startled glance and said: 'I thought you were—er—deaf and dumb.'

She shook her head and wrote on her pad: 'Only dumb!'

The others, who had been following this interchange with the greatest interest, could hardly conceal their relief at this good news which would make things so much easier, and they all began to talk at once, telling Philippa how much they hoped that she would enjoy the trip out to the West Indies with them.

Before the train was clear of the murky London suburbs they received another surprise. When Philippa learnt that Rex was a fighter-pilot on indefinite convalescent leave on account of a bad wound in his leg, she wrote: 'As a V.A.D. I nursed a number of airmen and I specialised in massage so I'll be able to give your leg treatment.'

De Richleau expressed surprise that, being unable to talk, she had succeeded in qualifying as a V.A.D., upon which it transpired that her affliction was not a natural one. Her hospital had been bombed the previous September and it was only after the rescue squad had dragged her from under the wreckage that she or they realised that she had been struck dumb by the frightful shock of the explosion. Ever since, she had been treated by doctor after doctor, but none of them had been able to restore her speech; the last had suggested that, although her case seemed hopeless, speech might come back to her if she were sent abroad to a place where there was no chance of her hearing further bombs or explosions for many months to come.

It was still raining when they arrived at the south-coast port which, as the secret war-time terminus of the flying-boats making the daily run to and from Lisbon, must remain nameless. As is usual with air travel, owing to the comparatively small number of passengers, the formalities with the customs and emigration authorities were got

155

through quickly, and half an hour later a fast launch took them out to the big Empire flying-boat which was rocking gently at its moorings in the grey-green, choppy waters.

They were no sooner safely installed on board than the launch backed away, the moorings were cast off and the engines began to turn over. The flying-boat taxied for about a mile and a half across the bay, turned right round into the wind, and suddenly rushed forward. The passengers could hear the spray sheeting up past the cabin windows but they could not see it, as the windows were blacked out. Abruptly it ceased and the engines eased down as though the plane was about to stop; but they suddenly realised that they had left the water and were soaring up into the air.

De Richleau knew that even if they met enemy planes there was little likelihood of their being attacked, since the Lisbon plane carries all the English papers upon which the enemy rely for a considerable portion of their intelligence. On arrival in Portugal there are immediately dispatched to Germany and Italy; while the returning plane carries back from Lisbon to England copies of all the German and Italian papers for British Intelligence. The outward journey is, therefore, always a reasonably safe one as the Nazis are anxious not to interrupt the flow of information through this neutral channel.

The windows having been blacked out to prevent travellers learning military secrets, the journey was a dull one. As the weather was good none of them were air-sick. They read or dozed most of the way until at half past four the plane banked steeply and two minutes later came down with a splash in the mouth of the Tagus.

On leaving the seaplane for a launch they were all struck by the difference in the climate, and it seemed quite miraculous that such a change could be brought about by a five-hour journey. Instead of the grey, wintry skies of England, the Portuguese capital lay basking in the sunshine, and after half-empty London the bustle of Lisbon streets, teeming with traffic, filled them with a strange exhilaration. They drove past the crowded cafés facing on to the famous Rolling Stone Square and pulled up at a big luxury hotel, the Aviz, in the Avenida, where rooms had been reserved for passengers in the *Clipper*.

As they had all heard, Lisbon was packed with war

escapists. Great numbers of wealthy French people had fled there after the collapse of France. There were also many Jewish refugees from Germany and Italy and a certain number of English, most of whom—to their shame— were skulking there after having been driven from their safe retreats in the South of France.

In Lisbon the only evidence of the war, apart from the unusual fullness of the great hotels and cafés, was a serious shortage of food, as Portugal, although a neutral and not officially blockaded by either of the belligerents, was feeling the pinch through the Nazis' ruthless sinking of shipping.

Having rested after their journey they came downstairs to get as good a dinner as could be procured, and then went out to see what for them, after nearly a year and a half of black-out, was an incredibly gay sight—a great city in all the glory of its lights and sky-signs.

After they had walked through the crowded main streets for a while de Richleau, who knew Lisbon well, took them to the Metropole, the star night-club, and his friends were amazed at its palatial dimensions.

The great tiled entrance-hall was built like a Moorish colonnade. Under each archway was a separate shop; flowers, chocolates, scent, handbags, fans, jewellery, and so on, could all be purchased on the spot by the male patrons of the place who felt generously disposed towards their fair companions. Upstairs there were gaming rooms on one side and on the other a restaurant with a big dance-floor, where they later witnessed a most elaborate cabaret.

To Rex's fury, he found that his leg still pained him too much to dance; and the Duke—even if the wound in his foot, which was now healing well, had not still to be treated with care—never danced. But Richard, Marie Lou, Philippa and Simon all thoroughly enjoyed themselves and for a time forgot the war as they mingled with the crowd on the dance-floor.

Leaving them to it after the cabaret, the Duke and Rex made for the tables. Laughing, wisecracking and grumbling to his neighbours, Rex dropped quite a packet at Roulette; but de Richleau, playing Baccarat with the impassivity of a professional, managed to pick up over fifty pounds in a couple of hours.

They had set out with the intention of getting back to their hotel soon after midnight, as they had to be up by half past four in the morning, but they all enjoyed themselves so much that they stayed on at the Metropole until three, having decided that they would only go back to the hotel for a hot bath and breakfast before starting out to the *Clipper*.

Dawn found them, tired but happy, installed on board the giant American seaplane in the Cabo Ruiva airport, and as the first red streaks coloured the eastern sky over the lines of Torres Vedras, where long ago Wellington had held Napoleon's armies at bay, the great flying-boat took off on its long journey across the Atlantic.

The weather was good, and, having adjusted to an almost prone position the comfortable 'dentist's chairs' with which the plane was fitted, lulled by the steady hum of the engines they soon dropped off to sleep. However, when they had been in the air for some three hours the weather changed for the worse. They were wakened by the plane bumping badly, and Marie Lou and Simon were both air-sick.

For what seemed a long time they flew on through rough weather and they were all heartily glad when at last the plane circled and came down in the harbour of Horta, the capital of the Azores.

The navigator told them that the weather was too bad to attempt a further 'hop' that day, so they were taken ashore to an hotel, and as they had had only a few hours' sleep since leaving England they all went to bed for the afternoon.

When they met again for dinner they found that the shortage of food caused by the Nazis' massacre of shipping was having its effect far beyond war-torn Europe. After a somewhat meagre meal they went into the lounge for liqueurs and coffee, and Philippa, who had already learnt that the others were going to Haiti, wrote a question on her tablet asking if they knew anything about the Black Republic.

It was de Richleau who replied. 'I know only the rough outline of its troubled history. It was, of course, one of the first islands to be colonised by the Spaniards under Columbus, but the French turned the Spaniards out, and for the best part of two hundred years it was rich and prosperous

158

Then, inspired by the French Revolution, the population rose and, having butchered the wealthy planters, succeeded in getting some sort of independent constitution for themselves from the National Assembly in Paris.

'The French aristocrats who had escaped the massacre called in the English to their assistance but a slave named Toussaint l'Ouverture led another revolt in which most of the Whites were murdered. Napoleon made a half-hearted attempt to bring the island back under French rule and l'Ouverture was arrested and taken to France; but I suppose the Emperor was too busy in Europe to bother much about his West Indian possessions, and the Revolution had already played the devil with all law and order in the island. Anyhow, in 1804 the slaves rose again and the Europeans were finally slaughtered or driven out. Ever since it has been a Negro Republic.'

'I had no idea that the slaves had had their freedom there for so long,' remarked Richard. 'It'll be interesting to see what a coloured race has done for itself in the best part of a hundred and fifty years of self-government.'

Rex grinned. 'If you're looking for innovations you'll be mighty disappointed. As the Duke says, when the French had it that island was one of the richest in the Indies, and it's still got all its natural capacities for producing wealth, but the Blacks have just let the place go to rack and ruin.'

'Have you ever been there?' asked Marie Lou.

'No. But a friend of mine in our Marines was stationed there for some years and he told me a heap about it. Their Negro presidents made our crook politicians look like kindergarten kids at the graft game. Not one of them held down his office for a four-year term, and with every buckaroo who elected himself with a knife gang it was a race as to whether he could grab enough dough in six months to get out to Jamaica or if he got his throat cut by a would-be successor first. That's why the States took it over for a while and put in the Marines.'

'And what were we doing to let you?' inquired Richard with a smile. 'I thought it was Britain's exclusive privilege to do that sort of thing. I'm afraid the old country must be losing its grip after all.'

Rex laughed. 'It so happens that you had a war on your hands; it was in 1915 that we went into Haiti; but, in

159

any case, you land-grabbing Britons wouldn't have been allowed to muscle in there. Maybe you've heard of the Monroe Doctrine? And, as a matter of fact, you were glad enough for us to intervene. For years past the Germans had been lending these Black four-flushers money in the hope of getting a grip on the island and being able to play bailiff one day, but the United States scotched that idea and gave British interests a fair deal—which is a darned-sight more than the Germans would have done. For nineteen years we kept the peace among our poor black brothers, then we handed them back self-government and sailed away.'

'It was only quite recently you cleared out, then?'

'Yep. During Roosevelt's first administration, as a part of his good-neighbour policy. The Blacks wanted their island back and said they'd be good children, so we let 'em have it. But, ever since, all but the politicians have been mighty sick that they asked us to quit. They miss the dollars that our boys used to spend around the towns. Those coloured bums have just no powers of organisation at all and it's like one big tropical slum. If it weren't for the climate and the masses of fruit that can be had just for the plucking the whole darned lot of them would have starved to death long ago.'

Marie Lou made a face. 'You don't draw a very attractive picture of our destination. I thought it would be something like Cuba; not as grand as Havana, of course, but decent hotels run by half-castes; whereas it sounds as though we'll have to pig it in some bug-ridden boarding-house.'

He nodded. 'That's about all we'll find there. The niggers live in little more than tents made from tying a few banana palms together, and in the towns most of the houses are falling down. To compare it with Havana is like putting up a hick town in the Middle-West against New York.'

'Naturally, Havana is very different,' cut in the Duke. 'It's a great city, where we could live as comfortably as we could in peace-time in the South of France, but I had no idea that Haiti was quite as primitive as Rex suggests. Still, no doubt property and labour are very cheap, so, if necessary, we'll take a house and have the place scrubbed from top to bottom by a dozen native women.'

Philippa had written something on her tablet and showed

160

it to Simon, who read out her question: 'Do any of you speak Creole?'

The others looked hopefully at the Duke, who was a linguist of quite exceptional powers, but he shook his head.

'No. I'm afraid Creole is beyond me; it's a kind of bastard French; but I imagine there must be plenty of people in the island who speak proper French or English.'

Philippa wrote another sentence, 'Very few. Only a year or two before the Americans took over they had a President who couldn't even read or write.'

'Dear me,' murmured de Richleau, 'what a bore; but I've no doubt we'll be able to hire a French-speaking Mulatto as our interpreter.'

They went to bed early that night as, if the weather improved, the *Clipper* would be making an early start again the following morning. As they went upstairs Marie Lou asked the Duke if they ought to take any precautions against being attacked on the astral while they slept, but he shook his head.

'No. As I told you in London, since we left Cardinals Folly in daylight it is a million to one that the enemy has lost track of us. Doubtless he's wondering where we've got to and he may by now have traced us as far as my flat; but there's nothing there which would give him any clue as to our intentions so he might roam the world for a hundred thousand nights and still be no nearer finding us. We should continue wearing our charged amulets, but I'm confident that we haven't the least cause to worry.'

They were called at half past four so knew that their journey was to be resumed, and soon after dawn they were on their way once more. Hours later they came down at Bermuda, where they were glad of the opportunity of stretching their legs for half an hour while they went ashore to have their passports examined and the usual formalities seen to. That evening without any untoward incident they arrived safely in New York harbour.

Rex had cabled his father from Lisbon to expect them, and when they were still two hundred yards from the dock they could easily make out the huge, white-haired figure of old Channock Van Ryn towering head and shoulders above the rest of the little group who were waiting to meet passengers from the *Clipper*. He and the Duke were friends of many years' standing and they greeted each other with the enthusiasm of long-lost brothers. Rex introduced the rest of the party to his father, then the banker drove them all off to his great mansion on Riverside Drive.

When Rex broke the news that they were only passing through New York on a mission connected with the war and would have to leave on the next day's plane for Miami, the old man's face fell. He told them that he had arranged a big party for the following night to celebrate Rex's having been awarded the D.F.C. for his gallantry in the Royal Air Force; but de Richleau explained that, sorry as he was, their visit could only be a flying one; it was of the utmost importance that they got down to the West Indies without an hour's unavoidable delay.

With that immediate resilience to circumstances for which the Americans are justly famous, the old man said at once: 'All right, then; seems we'll have to hold the party tonight,' and directly they arrived at his house he got his two secretaries and his butler busy on the telephones ringing up all his friends to gather in as many of them as possible for an informal occasion after dinner.

Rex tried to stop him. He pleaded that he would only feel an embarrassed fool if he were lionised, and that it was the very last thing he wanted. But the huge old man, who was even taller than his giant son, turned round and said in a voice which had made Secretaries of State quail:

'Listen, son; no nonsense. I know that no decent man wants to talk about what he's done; but in this case you've darned-well got to. It's no matter of showing off, but aid for Britain. By half past ten we'll have half a hundred really influential folk here, most of 'em as pro-British as we are, but some who're waverers. You can do more tonight than shooting down half a dozen Messerschmitts if you'll just tell these people in your own simple way, without any frills, what's happening on the other side: how you've seen it all, been right in the thick of it, and know how those splendid English folk are carrying on—and *mean* to carry on whatever hellish tricks those darned Nazis bring against them. Maybe you noticed the Statue of Liberty standing up there out of the water, south of Manhattan, as you flew over Ellis Island an hour ago. Forget it, son. That statue doesn't stand there any longer; it stands today in the Straits of Dover;

162

and it's up to you to bring that home to our friends in a way that only a man who's been fighting for Liberty on the other side can do.'

Rex squeezed his father's arm. 'Sure, Dad; I get the idea and I'll do just as you say.'

Since she had been stricken dumb Philippa had naturally avoided even such parties as were going in wartime London, and after they had dined she asked to be excused. But Simon pleaded with her to reconsider her decision.

'Look here,' he said earnestly, having got her to himself in a corner; 'I think you're being wonderfully brave about what's happened to you. You must feel it like hell, but you never complain; and if there's really no way in which you can get your speech back you'll have to try to be even braver. I mean—you thoroughly enjoyed yourself with us the other night at the Metropole in Lisbon—didn't you? So what's it matter if there are a few more people? Surely you don't mean to cut all parties for the rest of your life? You'll have to face a crowd some time—why not start now?'

She wrote on her tablet: 'With friends who know about me I'm all right, but I couldn't bear to be stared at and pitied by a crowd; I might break down.'

'Ner,' he shook his head violently. 'You'll be all right. And this is work for Britain. You said you hated running away from England while there was a war on. Now you can prove it, if you want to. The old man asked Rex to do some propaganda for us by telling the people who're coming what the Nazis have done to London, but you can do much more by staying with us and not saying a word. I hate to be seeming to use the awful thing that's happened to you, but if only you can stand up to their stares, think what an effect it will have on these Americans! The word will go round: "That beautiful girl over there is English. She was a nurse in a hospital which the Nazis bombed, and when they dug her out of the ruins it was found that she had been struck dumb. That's what these swine do to women, and they'd be doing it here in New York if they had the chance." See what I mean?'

Philippa went a shade paler, then she smiled and wrote on her tablet: 'Thanks for the "beautiful". I shall hate it but I'm game if you promise not to leave me.'

'Grand.' Simon suddenly took her hand and squeezed it.

'And of course I won't leave you. Never meant to—not for a second.'

The party proved a huge success. With the Duke's encouragement Rex soon got over his embarrassment at having to talk about his exploits, and the fact that he was an American made every one of his father's guests feel something of reflected glory in the thought that one of their own people had shared in that epic defence of Britain and had been decorated for gallantry by England's King. But Philippa's presence, as Simon had so shrewdly foreseen, carried even greater weight. He had tipped off Marie Lou, Richard and the Duke so that all three of them told Philippa's story to the people they met when they were out of her hearing; and what Channock Van Ryn's guests said they would like to do to Goering's murder-pilots in consequence was just nobody's business!

On the following morning their host motored them out to the New York airport, and having taken an affectionate leave of the old man they set out on their journey South in a big American air-liner. The trip was much more interesting than those of the previous days; the plane was not blacked out and for the major portion of the time they were flying over the coastline and could watch the changing scenery through Maryland, Virginia and North and South Carolina, until they crossed the great bay east of Florida and came down at Miami.

Rex had suggested that since they had no idea how long they would have to stay in Haiti it would be better to charter a plane, without a pilot, as he would fly them over and they could then retain the plane there so that they could return in it at any time they wished, and Channock Van Ryn had that morning promised that he would make arrangements for an aircraft at Miami to be placed at their disposal for that purpose.

His father's agent was waiting to meet them on the airfield and took them at once to inspect a six-seater aircraft that he had hired, on instructions, for the trip to Haiti. Rex spent twenty minutes looking over the engine to make certain that it was in good order and, having satisfied himself on that point, told the mechanic to have it fuelled to capacity and ready for them at nine-thirty the following morning.

After thanking the agent they secured a taxi, and Rex, who knew the American pleasure-coast from end to end, took them all off to the Pancoast Hotel, which lies some way from the town, right out beyond the swamps, among its own palm groves and gardens, on the edge of the beach where the Atlantic rollers are for ever creaming.

It was here, for the first time, that they felt that they had at last passed beyond the limits of the vast territories affected by the war. As usual, in winter, the luxury hotel was crowded with wealthy holiday-making Americans. There was no dearth of food or drink and everyone was concerned only with the pleasure of the moment. Strong-limbed young men and lovely girls in summer raiment or smart beach attire were driving about in high-powered cars unhampered by any petrol ration, canoeing on the lake near the hotel or sun-bathing on the beach under brightly-coloured umbrellas.

For them the war was only a thing of pictures in the illustrated papers that they flicked over with idle fingers. To the Duke and his friends, having come fresh from the stark realities of the Battle for Britain, this pleasure-beach scene of pre-war colour, idleness and gaiety seemed as unreal as a stage-set in a musical comedy. But when they had registered, and seen their rooms, they sat for a little in the sun-baked garden, relaxing and trying to realise that this was in fact the same world as that in which during the past eighteen months literally millions of previously free men and women on the Continent of Europe had been enslaved, beaten, imprisoned, tortured, starved, frozen, shot, and burnt or blasted by bombs, through the hideous ferocity and ungovernable lust for conquest of the fanatical Nazi hordes.

After refreshing themselves with iced drinks they decided that it would be a good idea to have a bathe, so they unpacked their swim-suits and spent a jolly hour or more racing one another and romping in the invigorating surf, then they lounged about in the lovely sunshine until cocktail-time.

Simon had found out for Philippa that the weekly packet-boat by which she was to sail for Kingston, Jamaica, left Miami two days hence; but the rest of them would be departing for Haiti first thing the following morning so her time with them was drawing to a close, which made them a little subdued at dinner that night. Although they had known her for only four days they had spent the whole of each of those days with her and had therefore got to know her quite well, in spite of the handicap which she suffered in having to write everything that she wished to say to them. They all admired her cheerful, uncomplaining courage under her wretched affliction, and Simon was so unusually silent that evening that when Marie Lou was dancing with him she teased him with having fallen in love with their beautiful speechless companion.

He wriggled his neck, came as near to blushing as she had ever seen him and hotly denied it, but admitted that he found Philippa very attractive. However, when they had all said 'good night' and he had reached his room he was conscious of a definite thrill on finding a letter from her propped up on his dressing-table. Opening it, he saw that it was quite a long screed and he ran his eyes swiftly over the neat lines of round, firm writing. It ran:

'Dear Simon,
    'Firstly I want to thank you for all your sweetness to me during our journey. The others have all been charming, but for natural, unforced sympathy and thoughtfulness in a thousand little ways you have excelled anything I could ever have thought possible in a man.

'I'm used to men being attentive to me, and before the bomb I suppose I rather took it for granted that they should be; but since I've lost my tongue I have noticed that sort of thing much more. Not to be able to talk—when one used to be quite an amusing person—is a pretty ghastly handicap. Most people are awfully anxious to be kind, but since I left the nursing-home I've found that nearly all my men-friends seem to get tongue-tied themselves when they're with me and, it has seemed to me—but perhaps I'm being unjust to them—a little bored with a wretched girl who has to write out every remark she makes. So you'll understand how very grateful I am to you for these last few days.

'Now for the second and really more important point of this letter. You've all been terribly close about the reason for your trip to Haiti, but I'm not altogether a fool, and within a few hours of having got to know you all I became convinced that five people who feel as you do would never be running away from our dear England while there's a war on, unless they had some definite object in doing so; and even if they were, *why* in God's name choose a benighted spot like Haiti?

'Quite definitely you're going there on some secret mission or other—even a child could guess that. And the fact that none of you understand Creole is going to prove a most frightful hindrance to your plans.

'I lived in Jamaica for five years before the war, and during that time I travelled a lot in the West Indies with my uncle, visiting nearly all the islands. His hobby was the study of the natives and I used to help him with his notes, so before the bomb I could speak Creole fluently, and I learnt quite a lot about these queer, unhappy "high yallers" who are a mixture of the aboriginal Caribs, Negro and European.

'The Haitians are a far from pleasant race. Why they should differ from the others, who are mostly a simple, happy-go-lucky people, I can't say—but they do. Perhaps it's lack of example from the better type of White, but every Haitian seems to be a born thief and liar, and their cruelty both to their animals and to each other is almost unbelievable.

'As the Duke suggested, you can hire an interpreter, of course, but it's quite certain that he'll cheat you and let you down in a score of different ways. So why not take me?

'Although I can't speak, I can listen to what the natives say, write it down for you and write the reply that you are to make. Honestly, I shall be able to look after you and get you what you want better than a dozen paid interpreters. Besides, I should be utterly miserable living on my aunt's plantation in Jamaica. I can easily cable her that I am staying with friends and shall not be joining her, at all events for the present. Do be a dear and talk this suggestion over with the others.

> Yours very gratefully,
> Philippa Ricardi.'

167

Having finished the letter Simon hurried along with it to the Duke's room.

'What d'you think about her offer?' he asked when de Richleau had finished reading it.

'It's certainly not one to turn down lightly. She's right, of course, about the fact that she could be much more useful to us than some Mulatto hireling who speaks French. All the same, I don't like the idea of involving her in the risks we shall have to run.'

Simon nodded. He was torn between a strong desire to press for acceptance, purely on the selfish grounds of keeping Philippa in their party so that he should see more of her, and reluctance to bring her into danger.

'We could put it up to her,' he hedged, 'but perhaps we ought to decide ourselves. It would be difficult to make her understand the risks in one short talk, and we must settle this thing tonight.'

'Let's consult the others,' said the Duke, and, collecting Rex on the way, they walked along to Marie Lou's room.

When the situation had been explained, Marie Lou said at once: 'Of course we'll take her. Why not? The poor girl is only too anxious to have a chance of doing something for her country, and it would be a shame to refuse her.'

'Yes,' added the practical Richard; 'and if these Haitians are as untrustworthy as she says, before we're through we may be thundering glad to have someone with us who understands their lingo.'

'Sure,' Rex agreed. 'On a job like this we'd be plumb crazy to turn down such an offer.'

'All three of you are for it, then,' said the Duke slowly, 'and I admit that you're all talking sound common sense. I don't know why I'm reluctant to take the girl myself, but somehow I have a feeling that if we do she'll run into some grave trouble from which we shall be unable to protect her.'

'If you have a premonition of that kind we'd better leave her behind,' said Marie Lou with a sigh. 'But it does seem rather silly unless you feel very strongly about it.'

'No,' said the Duke; 'it's not really a premonition. I think perhaps I'm influenced by the fact that she lacks the power to call for help in an emergency; but between us we ought to be able to look after her.'

168

Simon grinned. 'If she does come I'll never let her out of my sight.'

'I thought that was the way the wind was blowing,' smiled the Duke. 'All right, then. Marie Lou had better go along and talk to her. The really awful things that can happen to an unprotected spirit on the astral should be stressed as heavily as possible. If she shows the least sign of levity I won't take her, but if she evinces serious understanding and is still willing to take the risk she can come.'

Marie Lou was away for a good hour while the others sat smoking and talking together. When she returned, she said: 'It's all fixed up. I gave Philippa as clear an outline as I could of what we're up against, and she's read so many books on folklore and theosophy that she has already managed to piece together some sort of muddled version of the Old Wisdom on her own account. She's obviously ready to receive knowledge, and I think she's been sent to us for that reason. In any case, all I told her has made her more anxious to come than ever, and she has promised faithfully to obey, without argument, all orders, however fantastic they may seem to her.'

Next morning they drove inland to the airport, where Rex did a quick run over the hired plane, and by half past nine they were off.

He had not flown since he had been wounded and forced to bale out, but he soon found that although his injured leg was not capable of the instant reactions on the rudder-bar essential to a fighter-pilot it was perfectly good for ordinary flying.

Passing out over the Florida cays they flew for an hour above the more western of the thousand islands sprinkled in the blue tropic sea which make up the Bahamas; leaving behind them by twenty minutes to eleven the southernmost tip of Andros, the largest of the widely-scattered group. For a further hour and a half they sighted no land until the easternmost point of Cuba loomed up on the horizon. Crossing it, they flew on and by one o'clock they were approaching Haiti from midway between the two capes that enclose the great bay of Gonave, at the innermost indentation of which lies Port-au-Prince.

As they peered down de Richleau and Marie Lou recognised the queer lobster-claw formation of the coast which they had seen in their astral bodies on the night that they had harried the Black Magician to his home.

Not once on their long journey from England had any of them sensed the presence of Evil, and they felt confident that their enemy could have no knowledge of the fact that they were about to carry the war into his camp. Yet now, when they were flying high over the middle of the vast bay, with both headlands remote points in the far distance, de Richleau felt a sudden presentiment of coming trouble.

He had hardly turned to speak of it to Rex, beside whom he was sitting, when the plane entered an air-pocket and dropped like a stone, several hundred feet.

Rex gave a gasp of surprise. No pilot expects to meet air-pockets over calm, open sea, as they are caused by inequalities of the earth's surface. The instant they shot out of the air-pocket the plane was pitched sideways by a violent wind, and the amazed Rex had great difficulty in preventing it from turning over. Below them the blue sea sparkled tranquilly in the sunlight. There was no trace of any storm, yet it seemed as though they had been caught up in a hurricane..

De Richleau knew, and the others guessed, that this was no natural phenomenon. Somehow their enemy had learnt of their approach and was exerting all his strange powers to wreck the plane. It was flung from side to side, turned up on end and dashed seaward as though a giant invisible hand was striking at it. Shouting, gasping, they were thrown about until they were bruised, breathless and shaken.

In vain Rex strove and battled at the controls. No brain or nerve could counter that ghastly, unnatural attack. The plane rapidly lost height, rushed into a falling-leaf spin and streaked headlong towards the waters. By a superhuman effort Rex wrenches it out of the spin, but the strain proved too great. One of the wings tore, flapped and crumpled. The plane fell again, sideways this time. There was a frightful moment as they hurtled downward, and it seemed that the water was rushing up to meet them.

Next instant the wrecked plane struck the waves with a great smack and plunged right under. One of the front windows burst from the impact and with a hissing roar the waters came surging into the cabin. De Richleau's only emotion was one of bitter fury. The enemy outwitted him at the very start by lulling them into a false sense of security and now they were to be drowned like rats in a trap.

14

In Deadly Peril

The plane was up-ended, nose down, with its occupants a writhing heap of arms and legs struggling in the cockpit. Rex and the Duke were underneath; Richard and Marie Lou had pitched forward on to them. Simon and Philippa, who had been seated in the tail of the plane, were on top of the pile.

Down—down—down plunged the plane, so that it seemed to them in their terror that it would never stop until its engine became embedded in the ocean bottom. From the burst window in the front of the cockpit water was foaming and bubbling up between the tangled limbs of the six trapped passengers; yet while the plane continued its hideous dive they were powerless to move against the impulse that had flung them together in its nose.

The sea was crystal clear, and Marie Lou, who had been thrown forward so that her face was pressed against one of the side-windows, could see the under-water scene past which they were rushing as clearly as though she was staring into a plate-glass tank at an aquarium.

During her yachting holidays in peace-time she had often gone out in the glass-bottomed boats which are specially designed so that passengers can peer down at the beautiful submarine gardens which lie off the coasts of many islands in the Tropics. She had, too, spent hours swimming in warm seas, pushing along in front of her a glass-bottomed bucket through which she could study the lovely waving coral fans, the countless varieties of anemones, shrimps, prawns, sea-weed, lobsters and the multitudes of rainbow-hued fish

172

which darted in and out of the gently undulating under-water vegetation.

Now with very different emotions she saw some of those gaily-coloured denizens of the shallows. A shoal of tiny orange fish flitted by, a long barracuda, slowly opening its evil jaws, stared at her for a moment, a pair of blue-and-yellow-striped angel-fish passed so close that had it not been for the window she could have stretched out her hand and touched them; but she was no longer conscious of their beauty. One awful thought stifled all else in her mind. In a few moments those fish would be nosing their way into the submerged plane as it lay on the bottom, and very soon they would be eating her; nibbling her flesh from the bones of her drowned body.

After what seemed an interminable time, but actually was only a matter of seconds, the speed of the plane's downward plunge decreased. Simon grabbed the back of one of the middle seats and with a great effort heaved himself off the others. Seizing Philippa's arm he pulled her towards him. Richard and Marie Lou struggled up after them towards the tail of the still descending plane. Now that the weight of the others had been taken off Rex and the Duke they too were able to regain a semi-upright position. Both were half-submerged in the water which continued to bubble in through the broken window. With extraordinary presence of mind, instead of trying to fight his way upward with the rest, Rex sat down in the gaping hole, thereby partially blocking it; but, sitting there, the water was up to his chest and was still spurting up in a fountain from between his legs.

Slowly, almost imperceptibly, the plane stopped moving; then reversed as the buoyancy of the air inside it began to carry it upwards. Its speed increased and a moment later with a loud plop its tail shot out of the water.

'Get up into the tail, all of you—get up into the tail!' yelled Rex. 'Your weight will right her.'

Barking their knees and shins on the seat-backs they climbed across them up into the tail of the plane. Suddenly, their weight having balanced that of the engine, it tilted and fell over on its belly. The water, which had risen to the level of Rex's neck, rushed forward the whole length of the cabin, momentarily submerging the others as it hit the walls of the tail with a resounding whack.

De Richleau stumbled to the middle of the cabin, now awash knee-deep. Reaching up, he pulled the ripcord of the emergency exit in the plane's roof and, getting one foot on a seat-back, heaved himself up through it. Richard staggered forward, clutching Marie Lou, and lifting her small body in his arms he thrust her up towards the Duke, who was kneeling there ready to draw them up after them. They then helped Philippa up and Richard, Simon and Rex followed. Five minutes—minutes that had seemed hours—after the plane had struck the water all six of them were crouching precariously upon its roof.

'That was a near thing!' gasped Richard.

'You're telling me!' panted Rex. 'What in Hades hit us?'

'An astral tornado,' said the Duke. 'It couldn't possibly have been an earthly one; the sea remained calm the whole time. Somehow the enemy must have got wind of the fact that we were approaching Haiti and exerted all his powers to wreck us. But the effort must have proved most exhausting so it's unlikely that we'll be subjected to any further attacks for the time being.'

Rex shrugged. 'Well, that's *some* comfort; but he's put us in one helluva spot. God knows how we're going to get ashore!'

When the astral storm had first struck them they had been right in the centre of the great blunt-ended, lobster-claw-shaped bay of Haiti, but the huge pincers were eighty miles apart, so they were as far from either as if they had been wrecked out in the North Sea half-way between Margate and Lowestoft. They had, however, penetrated a considerable way into the jaws of the pincers and Rex had been about to pass north of the Ile de la Gonave, which guards the approach to Port-au-Prince; and they knew that they were somewhere in the twenty-mile-wide channel of St. Marc, between the island and the northern portion of the claw.

At first they could see no land at all, but, on standing up, Rex, who was by far the tallest of them, said that each time the swell lifted the plane he could make out a smudge to southwards, which must be the Island of Gonave; though he reckoned that they were at least seven or eight miles distant from it. Turning, he scanned the horizon on every side. There was little steamer traffic between Port-au-Prince and the outer world, and they knew that their best hope of rescue lay in some native fishing-boat; but the sea was absolutely empty.

The Duke began to unlash the small collapsible rubber dinghy from the roof of the plane. 'At all events, the sea is smooth,' he said with a cheerfulness which he was far from feeling, 'and this will take two of you. With about three hours' hard paddling you ought to be able to make the shore and bring us help.'

None of them liked to voice the thoughts that were in their minds. Whom should they send? And how long would the plane remain afloat? Almost certainly it would become totally waterlogged and would sink long before the rubber dinghy could be paddled ashore and whoever was in it come out to their rescue in one of the island's boats.

At length de Richleau said: 'It's no good sending the two girls; they wouldn't be strong enough to paddle the distance alone, and the dinghy won't hold more than two.'

'Philippa must go,' said Madie Lou at once. 'She's the youngest of us, and it's entirely our fault that she's here.'

The dumb girl could not argue but she shook her head and pointed to Marie Lou and Richard.

'Yes,' said the Duke. 'Marie Lou is right. We've let you in for this, so we must get you out of it. Besides, you understand the language of the islanders so, through whoever goes with you, you'll be able to secure help for us with the least possible delay. The question is—who is to go with you? It had better be Rex, as he is the strongest of us.'

'Not on your life!' exclaimed Rex. 'I don't need any boat to get ashore. In this warm climate I could swim that distance with one hand tied behind my back.'

They knew his prowess as a swimmer and his giant strength and realised that whoever else might drown there, in that lovely tropic sea, Rex would almost certainly be able to save himself.

So Marie Lou said: 'Greyeyes had better go. We mustn't forget the reason that we're here at all, and it's infinitely more important that he should be saved than any of us.'

He smiled at her. 'Theoretically you may be right, Princess, but as leader of the party I regard myself as captain of

175

this ship. Nothing you can say or do would induce me to leave it before the rest of you.'

'It's simple, then,' said Simon. 'Richard is stronger than I am, and speed's important. He must go.'

But Richard shook his head. 'Can you see me leaving Marie Lou? Don't be silly, Simon. It's your job, and you're quite strong enough to paddle that distance in a smooth sea.'

'Ner,' Simon began to protest, but de Richleau cut him short.

'I agree with Richard. Don't waste time in arguing, please. It's going to be pretty hellish here, exposed as we are to this torrid sun, and every moment counts if you're going to get help before the plane sinks under us. Come on, now; off you go.'

Rex had been blowing up the rubber dinghy while they had been talking. Realising the urgency of the matter Simon argued no further but helped Philippa into the frail craft and got in behind her. After a good push-off they began to propel the little boat canoe-fashion towards the land which they could not yet see.

A chorus of farewell and shouts of good luck followed them and every ten yards or so Simon turned to look back. His weak eyes were full of unshed tears and he felt a physical pain right down in the pit of his stomach. He wondered desperately if he would ever see those dear friends of his again.

They had got out of so many tight corners, but somehow this was different, because there was nothing at all that they could do to help themselves. Rex's great strength, Richard's common sense, Marie Lou's feminine wisdom and even the Duke's subtle, cunning brain were all utterly useless to them in this extremity. Their only hope lay in clinging to the wreckage of the sinking plane as long as possible and then swimming for it, while praying that he might be able to bring them help in time.

They, too, were fully conscious of their dire extremity and wondered if ever again they would hear Simon's chuckle or see his kind, good-natured smile. Sadly they watched the bobbing rubber boat until it was hidden from them by the gently heaving swell.

De Richleau roused himself and glanced at his watch. It

had been just after one o'clock when they had crashed and it was now only a quarter past, but already they were beginning to feel the grilling effects of the tropical sun. It was a brazen ball of fire, almost directly above their heads, in a cloudless blue sky. Crouched as they were on the roof of the wrecked plane, not an inch of shade was available from its scorching rays, which had already dried their sodden outer garments. All of them had lost their hats during the mix-up in the plane and had instinctively knotted handkerchiefs, pirate-fashion, about their heads; but these were scant protection and de Richleau feared that they might get sunstroke unless they could rig up some form of cover by using the things inside the plane. He was also extremely anxious to get up their luggage.

He spoke to Rex, who pulled the ripcord of the emergency exit, which they had closed behind them to keep as much air in as possible. A wave of air gushed out as they scrambled back into the plane to see what they could salvage. They found that the cabin was now awash waist-high, but they pressed forward towards the cubby-hole in the tail where their luggage was stowed. To de Richleau's fury he found that the pressure of the water was so great that in spite of their united efforts they could not drag open the door of the cubby-hole, and there was no other way to get their luggage out.

Every moment that they spent inside the plane was a risk, because there was always the possibility that the engine and the load of water might become too heavy for the fuselage so that it suddenly plunged, carrying them down with it. All the same, they set about a methodical search of the cabin. Kicking round with their feet and stooping to reach under-water with their hands, they passed up to Richard such things as they could find, through the escape exit.

They secured a small satchel of Richard's which contained his gun, his passport and money, together with a flask of brandy, some chocolates and a tin of cigarettes; then they fished up a couple of sodden rugs, Rex's mackintosh and—the best prize of all—Marie Lou's dressing-case. Now that the air could flow out the water in the plane was again rising rapidly so abandoning further attempts at salvage they climbed out and reclosed the escape exit.

The cigarettes and many of the things in the dressing-case were soaked through, but feeling that some of them might come in useful later on, they laid them out on the baking-hot roof of the plane to dry. In the meantime Marie Lou's pots of face creams proved a gift from Heaven, as their foreheads, noses, ears, necks and the backs of their hands were already going red with sunburn, and all of them had sun-bathed in the pleasant places of the earth so often that they knew that lovely warm sensation meant agony later on. Without a moment's delay they set about covering all the exposed portions of their skin with the pleasantly-scented greases which she recommended as the most suit-able.

The wireless of the plane was now submerged and useless but its aerial ran from the plane's tail, a few feet above the fuselage, to a short staff near the cockpit, so they were able to drape the wet rugs over this, forming a rough tent under which they could get a little shelter from the blazing sun.

Almost at once the rugs began to steam as the heat rays drew off their moisture, but they crawled under them and lay down, with Rex at one end and de Richleau at the other to keep a lookout for any sail that might bring hopes of rescue.

By the time they had completed these arrangements it was getting on for two o'clock. For the next quarter of an hour they crouched in miserable silence under the scant cover of the tent, which was barely enough to shield them and soon became intolerably stuffy.

It was about twenty-past two when Rex gave a shout and stood up to wave frantically. In the distance he had spotted a large motor-boat which was coming towards them. The others all stumbled out of their shelter and joined him in shouting and waving. It seemed that the people in the boat could not possibly help seeing them and that they were already as good as saved.

Their disappointment was all the more bitter when the people in the boat made no response to their signals and, after having approached within quarter of a mile, it suddenly turned right round and headed away from them.

In angry disgust they sat down again, but after this sudden lifting of their hopes they positively could not keep still. Every few moments one or other of them stood up to peer in the direction in which the boat had gone. This constant emerging from their shelter exposed them to the sun and they knew that Marie Lou's face-creams were only a scant protection against it. They were getting badly sunburnt now, but took little notice of that lesser evil seeing that they were all in peril of their lives. Although none of them mentioned it, they were all conscious that the plane was gradually sinking; inch by inch the water was creeping up its sides.

It was de Richleau who suddenly said: 'The only chance of our being able to continue to use the plane as a raft until Simon gets back is for us to take our weight off it.'

Richard gave a half-hearted laugh. 'Go in for a swim, eh? Well, that's not a bad idea; at least it'll cool us off a bit.'

In consequence the men turned their backs on Marie Lou and they all undressed, then one by one they slid over the side. The cool of the water by comparison with the roasting roof of the plane was a blessed relief, as it eased their taut, parched skin and gave them new vitality. By hanging on to the side of the wreck they were, too, able to take advantage of a small patch of shadow, and each of them rested by turns in this way while the others swam about to take their weight off the waterlogged machine.

After they had been in the water for some twenty minutes Richard suggested that one of them ought to climb up on to the plane to see if there was any further sign of the motor-boat or other craft about, and Rex gave him a push up on to it. Shading his eyes with his hand he stared round, then suddenly cried that he could see the boat again; it was running sideways-on to them, about half a mile away.

He waved and shouted till he was hoarse, but apparently no one in the boat saw him so he gave up, having come to the conclusion, as the boat continued to patrol up and down, that its occupants were engrossed, to the exclusion of all else, in trolling for fish.

'Come down, darling!' called Marie Lou, 'or you'll get baked to a cinder,' and Richard suddenly realised that his silk pants had dried stiff on him while he had been standing there; so he dived in again and Rex clambered up to take his place. In doing so he cut his hand on a jagged strut of the plane where the wing had snapped off during the astral storm which had wrecked it. He thought nothing of it at the time, and stood for about ten minutes exasperatedly hail-ing the seemingly sightless people in the launch until de Richleau came up to relieve him.

The Duke in turn signalled without result but he knew that it was much easier for them to see the motor-boat than for the people in it to see them, because while the boat with its big cabin stood at least ten feet out of the water the plane was right down on the water level, so that if they saw him at all it would only be as a small figure standing apparently on the water and entirely hidden every other moment by the intervening swell-crests.

As he stood there he knew that if they were rescued they were all in for a ghastly time from the exposure which they had sustained. Sun-bathing is a thing which should be indulged in at not too infrequent intervals and little by little at each fresh start, and none of them had sun-bathed since the beginning of the war. In consequence their bodies were a tender pink-and-white without the least trace of pigmentation left behind from old sun-bathing holidays. All of them in the last hour or so had gradually turned a dull, pinkish red and the stinging of the burns was already perceptible.

It was just then that his thoughts were switched to a far graver menace. Rex was swimming some way away from the plane, and cutting through the wavelets no more than twenty feet from him was a sinister triangular fin.

'Shark!' yelled the Duke. 'Shark!'

For a moment Rex did not seem to hear, the menacing, sail-like fin cut the water in a streak towards him, but suddenly he turned and came racing for the submerged plane, his head under water, his arms flailing and his feet threshing in a powerful crawl stroke.

Richard had scrambled on board and was dragging Marie Lou up after him. As Rex shot forward, churning up the water, the Duke saw the fin, which was now only a few yards from Rex's feet, suddenly disappear and he knew that the shark had dived to turn upon its back and attack its victim. Desperately he looked round for some weapon with which he might fend off the brute while Rex climbed out of the water, but there was no pole, or anything at all, that he could use; only the rugs, their clothes and the oddments which they had salvaged from inside the plane.

Rex spluttered up within a foot of the fuselage and it now

looked as though the fact that the plane was almost submerged would serve him in good stead. It was so low in the water that he had only to fling himself on to it and draw his legs up after him. But at the very second that he grabbed the tail-end of the plane de Richleau saw the shark immediately beneath him. The brute, which was at least twelve feet in length, had turned upon its back and its white belly was so plain in the translucent water that the Duke could see the sea-lice upon it. Its great mouth, with its seven rows of saw-like, gleaming teeth, was gaping open and Rex's left foot dangled almost inside it.

Richard was just behind de Richleau and with frantic fingers he had been wrenching open his satchel. Next second he fired with his automatic, under the Duke's arm, sending three bullets into the belly of the shark.

The brute's tail whacked with a thud against the side of the wreck, rocking it so that de Richleau was thrown off his balance and fell to his knees. The great jaws snapped as the shark thrashed in its death agony; its teeth grazed Rex's heel but he had jerked up his leg just in time and lay, panting, at full-length along the tail of the plane.

For thirty seconds they all crouched there gasping, then Richard suddenly cried, 'Look' and pointed. Three more of the sail-like fins had appeared, moving swiftly towards them, and in another moment the three new-comers were fighting a desperate battle over the body of their dying comrade.

The water was no longer clear, but opaque and muddy with the shark's blood as it was torn in pieces by its cannibal shoal-mates. Marie Lou shivered and turned away, sick with nausea, so she did not see the end of the orgy, or that within a few minutes another dozen sharks had arrived upon the scene to join in the fray for any bits of fish-meat that might be left in the crimson, whirling water.

'It's the blood that attracts them,' said the Duke with a shudder; 'they've some sort of instinct by which they can scent it a mile away.'

Rex looked at the small wound in his hand which was still bleeding slightly. 'That's it,' he said. 'I ought to have realised. I cut myself climbing out of the water a little time back. It must have been my blood that the first brute scented.' He laughed, but it was a mirthless laugh, as he

181

added: 'My swimming powers won't win me a medal now when the old bus goes under. Those devils wouldn't let the strongest swimmer get ten yards before they pulled him down.'

The others did not reply. They were staring at the water. It was quite clear again now and not a trace of the first shark remained. But having finished their banquet the others had not gone away; they were basking there, quite patiently, the fins of fifteen of them all protruding above the water.

The four friends had done many thousand miles of ocean travel and they had seen sharks follow a ship for weeks, waiting for any garbage that might be thrown overboard. Night or day was all one to those ravenous brutes. They had no sense of time once they had scented their prey. They would not give up until they had secured the victims that they could see sitting there, half-naked, on the wrecked plane.

It was only three o'clock and Simon could not possibly yet have reached the coast, but the plane was now awash in all its length and might suddenly sink under them at any moment, leaving them to be torn limb from limb by the merciless brutes who lay in wait for them.

15

Strange Gods

For what seemed a long time they all sat staring at their patient enemies, who swam slowly backwards and forwards or lay basking and apparently comatose. But, roused again by the blistering heat of the sun, Rex grunted:

'We'd best get our clothes on, otherwise we'll be fried here.'

They were all terribly thirsty but had nothing with them to drink except Richard's flask of brandy, and the Duke said that to drink that would only make their thirst worse.

Painfully they drew their stiff garments on to their scorched limbs, then they spread themselves out on the surface of the wreck in the hope that by distributing their weight more evenly it would bear them a little longer. Rex crawled up on to the tail, which was cocked up a little but dipped almost to sea-level under him, de Richleau remained in the middle of the fuselage, while Richard and Marie Lou sat each side of the cockpit where the wings joined the body.

While they were moving they kept a wary eye upon their nearest enemies as a slip might have proved fatal, and having settled themselves again they clung on to their precarious holds, knowing that if they lost them nothing could prevent their being torn to pieces. The sea lapped gently at the sides of the plane with a little chuckling noise, but it was an evil chuckling, and the beauty of the summer seascape was entirely lost to them. They could think only of their roasting necks, their parching thirst and the red death that awaited them in the blue waters.

For over half an hour they had been so engrossed with the sharks that they had not looked in any other direction. The Duke then roused himself to concentrate sufficiently to slip out of his body in order to find out how Simon was faring. To his relief he saw that the rubber boat was beached upon a pebbly shore and that Simon and Philippa were hurrying along the beach about half a mile from it; but there was no human habitation in sight so it might be hours yet before they could get a boat and a rescue party. He was brought back to his body by a sudden commotion.

Unobserved by the castaways, a native fishing-smack had appeared on the scene and was now tacking towards them only two hundred yards away. When they heard a faint, distant hail behind them it came as a shock mingled with positively stunning relief.

Switching round they saw the boat and their excitement, which had brought the Duke back to his body, was so great that they nearly lost their balance as they stood up to shout and signal in reply. The smack was quite a small one, manned by three Negroes, one of whom was standing up in the bows waving to them.

They had hardly grasped their good fortune at this prospect of an eleventh-hour rescue when they noticed that the motor-boat was some way behind the fishing-smack; it had now turned and was also coming towards them. Evidently the people in it had only just seen the castaways, their attention having been attracted to them by the cries of the Negro fishermen.

There followed an acutely anxious five minutes as de Richleau's party wondered if the now totally submerged plane would bear them just that little extra time necessary for their rescue before plunging to the sea-bed; but during it he was able to cheer his friends with the news that Simon and Philippa had reached the coast in safety. As the motor-boat came nearer they saw that it was a powerful launch. Racing past the smack, it circled round, driving the sharks away; then, easing down its engine so as not to capsize the plane with its wash, it came right alongside.

Its occupants were a very tall, bespectacled Mulatto, with markedly negroid features but a pale skin, and a crew of four Negroes. The Mulatto wore a panama hat and was dressed in a suit of spotless white duck, so it looked as though he was a person of some standing.

As they were helped aboard the poor old plane bobbed up again a foot above the waterline, and seemed as if, now that it was relieved of their weight, it was good for another half-hour or so, although it had been in imminent danger of sinking when they were on it.

Gasping out their thanks to their rescuer they staggered into the blessed shade of the launch's cabin. They had spoken in English and the Mulatto replied to them in a garbled travesty of the same language.

'Me very happy make you safe,' he said courteously. 'You very bad ways. Them shark no good feller. Eat 'em up quick. Me Doctor Saturday, please. Very happy make you acquainted.'

'Thanks a thousand times,' muttered de Richleau hoarsely. *'Parlez-vous français, Monsieur le docteur?'*

'Ah, oui; certainement,' the tall Mulatto gave a quick smile which displayed two tombstone-like rows of very white teeth, and from that point the conversation was carried on in fluent French.

Realising that they would now soon be in Haiti, the Duke took the precaution of introducing himself and his friends under assumed names; then they told the Doctor that for the best part of two hours they had seen his launch and had been signalling to him. His distress at hearing this was evident and he was most profuse in his apologies, explaining that he and his crew had been engrossed in fishing for amber-jack. The first indication they had had of the wrecked plane was when they had heard the shouting of the Negro in the fishing-smack.

It had now come up with them, and Doctor Saturday threw the three grinning Negroes in it a handful of small change, which Richard supplemented with three twenty-dollar bills from his wallet as he felt that he and his friends really owed their lives to the fishermen—though that was obviously no fault of the Doctor's.

As the launch headed away on the Doctor's orders the fishermen, overwhelmed with the gift, which represented more than they could earn in a couple of months, babbled their thanks in their Creole dialect for as long as they could keep within shouting distance, grinning all over their shiny black faces.

The relief of the four castaways at their rescue was almost surpassed by their intense joy at being able to get out of the blistering sun, and as they sat down on the comfortable settees in the cabin they began tenderly to examine their burnt and blistered limbs.

Doctor Saturday looked at them gravely and said in his excellent French: 'You've had a terrible gruelling in this hot Haitian sun of ours, and I'm afraid your burns will pain you for some days to come, but I can at least ease them for you.'

As he spoke he went to a cupboard and produced some cotton-wool and a large bottle of milky-looking liquid which, when they dabbed it on the sore places, instantly relieved the pain.

'And next,' added the hospitable Doctor, 'I expect you would like a drink.'

A chorus of approval met this suggestion so he opened a small ice-chest and produced whisky, rum, lemonade, lime-juice and some bottles of home made soda-water, then got glasses for them. The iced drinks tasted perfectly heavenly and they were at last able to relax after their terrible ordeal.

'Where were you making for in your aeroplane?' asked the Doctor. 'Porto Rico or Guadeloup?'

'Neither,' replied Rex. 'We ran right into some electrical disturbance when we were no more than twenty minutes' flying-time from our destination—we were heading for Port-au-Prince.'

'Indeed!' Doctor Saturday raised the white eyebrows which stood out in such contrast to his yellow skin. 'You surprise me. We have few European visitors to Haiti. Do you know the island at all?'

De Richleau replied swiftly so that he could get in his own version of the reason for their visit before the others spoke. 'No. But I am a scientist whose subject is the study of native customs, and it has long been my wish to pay a short visit to Haiti to see what sort of a country the coloured peoples have made for themselves under a government of their own choosing.'

The Mulatto shook his head sadly. 'I fear you will be disappointed in us. I do not believe that the Negroes are naturally an idle race, because they work well in cooler

186

climates such as that of the northern United States and of South Africa. But it has been their misfortune that they have lived mainly in countries where the heat is not conducive to hard work and where life may be sustained very easily from swiftly-growing crops and an abundance of fruit which has only to be gathered from the trees. The people here are incurably lazy—perhaps as a result of their environment. In any case, far from advancing in culture and prosperity, they have tended to slip backwards during the hundred-and-forty-odd years since the slaves revolted and became their own masters. Port-au-Prince is a poor sort of capital to have to show visitors.'

'Do you live there, Doctor?' Marie Lou inquired.

'Yes, Madame; so at least I shall have the good fortune of being able to convey you to your destination. I told my boatman to head back there with all speed directly I picked you up, but it will be some hours before we get in. Your plane crashed a good sixty miles from Port-au-Prince.'

'That's a long way for you to have come on a fishing expedition,' remarked the Duke.

Doctor Saturday shrugged his high shoulders. 'The fishing is much better out here. The fruit of the sea in its abundance is another blessing which God gave to our islanders; great numbers of them in the coast-towns live almost entirely on fish, so some of the better kinds no longer frequent coastal waters.'

'Can you recommend a decent hotel in Port-au-Prince?' Richard asked, after a moment's silence.

'There is only one,' Doctor Saturday showed his white teeth in another friendly grin, 'and I would not like to be responsible for recommending it to people of quality like yourselves. The bar is quite good, and it forms an important social centre. Many of our leading politicians spend most of their time there, but the food in the restaurant is indifferent, and as its windows are on a level with the street some hungry fellow may, if you are not very careful, stretch his hand in and grab the food off your plate. That has often happened.'

'Dear me,' said the Duke. 'In that case I think we'd better take a house for ourselves.'

'I was hoping,' said the Doctor, 'that you would honour

187

me by being my guests during your stay. Cultured visitors are very rare in Haiti, and it would be a real pleasure to have you in my house; which is large, and even you, I think, would find it quite comfortable.'

'That is most kind,' said the Duke with a little bow. 'I'm sure we should be delighted to accept for a night or two while we make some arrangements for ourselves, but we would not dream of burdening you any longer.'

'I shall hope that you will reconsider that when you have been under my roof for those few days,' smiled the tall Mulatto. 'Also, you must let me arrange a few sight-seeing tours for you. Although our towns are poor places our scenery is very beautiful.'

'I wonder whether it would be possible for us to witness some Voodoo ceremonies?' remarked the Duke, with the idea that by leading the conversation in this direction he might learn the names of the principal practitioners of Voodoo in the island, one of whom was unquestionably the enemy that he had travelled all these thousands of miles to destroy.

The Doctor raised his white eyebrows. 'So you are interested in Voodoo, eh? But naturally, of course, since you are a student of native customs. Most educated people in Haiti would tell you that Voodoo is not practised here any more. Haitians are the greatest wishful thinkers in the world. They will tell you that they are poor only because the Americans robbed them of all their money, and if you say: "But were you not already bankrupt, and owing great sums to Germany and France, when the Americans came?" they will reply: "That is not true. The French and the Germans say that we owe them money; but we never had it—they tricked us into signing some sort of document that we did not understand." In fact they will tell you any story which enters their heads to make you think them hard done by and a more high-principled people than they are, and for the time being they themselves quite honestly believe these things. Of the practice of Voodoo they are heartily ashamed, because they know that Europeans regard the cult as a barbarous one, so they would flatly deny that the sacrifice of chickens and goats to the old African gods still takes place. But as I myself am something of a scientist I realise the stupidity of denying anything which actually

188

exists, and the truth is that Haiti is positively riddled with Voodoo to this very day.'

'Do tell us about it, Doctor,' urged Marie Lou.

As the boat sped on in the bright afternoon sunshine, the Doctor poured them a further round of drinks, passed them cigarettes and lit a long black cigar for himself.

'Voodoo,' he said, 'was brought over from Africa by the Mondongo natives when they were first imported here as slaves, nearly four hundred years ago. It is a form of serpent-worship, but in Voodoo there are two pantheons of Loa—as the gods are called—the Rada and the Petro.

'When I say two pantheons I should explain that the Voodoo Loa are almost as numerous as the pebbles on the beaches. Apart from the big gods, every village in Haiti has a dozen or more local deities of its own who reside in the rocks, waterfalls, rivers and great trees. But of the big gods whom all Voodoo-worshippers acknowledge, the Rada family, which came from Dahomey, are the good gods, and the Petro family, which came from the Congo, are the evil gods. The head of the Rada gods is Dambala, the God of Gods, and wherever there is an altar to him you will find a green serpent, which is his symbol. His principal supporters are Papa Legba, who is the God of the Gate and must always be propitiated before Dambala can be approached, and Papa Loco, the God of Wisdom and Medicine. The chief of the Petro gods is the dreaded Baron Cimeterre.'

'The Lord of the Cemetery?' de Richleau hazarded.

The Doctor nodded and went on: 'Many of the rites by which he is honoured are in connection with the dead, and his priests often interfere with the newly-made graves in the cemeteries to secure certain things which they use in their horrible rituals. There is, however, nothing evil in the worship of the Rada gods; they represent the oldest mystery of all: that of the source of life as represented by sex.

'To Europeans some of the ceremonies—such as the Dance of the Six Veils, which is analogous to the nuptial flight of the Queen Bee and in which the Mambo, or Priestess, exposes her sexual organs for the adoration of the worshippers—are crude; but regarded honestly and without false hypocrisy these rituals only express the joy of healthy passion.'

'That, after all,' conceded the Duke, 'is the one thing that

189

the Creator of Life has given without discrimination to every race, from the Tropics to the Arctic snows, and to everyone alike, however poor, ignorant or humble they may be; so it's hardly surprising that a people whose worldly possessions can, generally speaking, be tied up in a single blanket should regard as on object for worship this one pleasure which is within the reach of them all.'

'Exactly.' Their new friend bowed, evidently much gratified by de Richleau's sympathetic understanding. 'The Rada gods, as the deities of Health, Fertility and Sexual Virility, are therefore offered by their devotees such little luxuries as can be spared from their own meagre stores: perfumes, cornmeal, eggs, fruit, flowers, sweet liquors, cakes and olive-oil. To Dambala every offering must be made upon a white plate, and the sacrifice to him consists of a pair of white chickens—a hen and a cock.

'The Petro gods, on the other hand, are propitiated mainly through fear or because a person wishes to do some evil to his neighbour. The Houngan, or priest, is a figure of dread in each village and he blackmails the whole community. There is, perhaps, a quarrel, and one party will go to the priest to have a ceremony performed which will cause his enemy to become sick and die. When without apparent cause the second party becomes ill his relatives know what has happened, so they go to the priest and offer a sum for another ceremony to be performed which will remove the curse. The first party is informed of this and offers a larger sum for the curse to be continued; and so it goes on, with the evil priest taking bribes from both sides until one finally outbids the other and the poor wretch who has been afflicted either recovers or dies.'

'Have they really the power just to wish death on a man?' Richard asked.

'Oh, yes. There is not the least doubt obout that; but they also have a great knowledge of poisonous herbs, and often use these to bring about their fell design if the afflicted person seeks the protection of a rival Houngan.'

'The people are nominally Catholics, aren't they?' de Richleau said. 'So how do the Catholic priests view all this?'

Doctor Saturday spread out his long, slender hands. 'In Haiti it is impossible for the uninitiated to say where Roman Catholicism ends and Voodoo begins.'

'That's a pretty strong statement against the Roman Catholic Church,' remarked Rex.

'No, no,' protested the Doctor; 'I do not mean it that way. The good Fathers naturally abominate these practices and have been fighting them for centuries; but when you visit our towns and villages you will gain the impression that the whole population—even in the remotest hamlets—are most devout Catholics; whereas, in fact, this is not so at all.'

Marie Lou frowned. 'I'm afraid I don't quite understand.'

'It is this way. The Haitians are still very primitive; comparatively few of them as yet can even read or write. They have no written literature at all: only the oft-repeated folk-tales and ancient jests which they tell around their firesides; and they have no artists. In consequence, they have never yet produced anyone capable of drawing original pictures of the Voodoo gods which could be accepted as standard types, and long ago they devised the expedient of utilising pictures of Catholic saints as the representation of Voodoo Loa. For Dambala they adopted Saint Patrick, simply because there is always a snake in any picture of him. For Papa Legba they use a picture of John the Baptist, for Papa Loco a picture of Saint Joseph; and so on. The result is that all over the island you will see altars apparently devoted to the worship of the Catholic saints but actually used for a very different purpose.'

'Do they have only gods in Voodoo or are there goddesses as well?' Marie Lou inquired.

'I fear, Madame, that women still occupy a very low status among most Negro races,' replied the Doctor apologetically. 'They are the chattels of men, who consider their purposes in life are to be possessed at will when young and to be used as beasts of burden when old, so it would be unnatural in the Haitians to prostrate themselves before female deities. Yet all the gods have their women as a natural attribute of prosperity and power, and to these, who are little more than handmaidens to the Loa, there is one extraordinary exception. This is a lady called Erzulie Frieda, who is a goddess in her own right, and she probably has more power to affect the destiny of men than any female deity who is worshipped throughout the world today.'

'How terribly interesting,' murmured Marie Lou, and the Doctor went on:

'She is often represented by the picture of the Virgin Mary, but she has nothing whatever in common with the Mother of Jesus Christ. To explain her best, I must ask you to imagine a living Venus who has the power to turn herself into a mortal woman and enter the beds of thousands of her worshippers every Thursday and Saturday night. She is always described by her lovers as a supremely beautiful young Mulatto, scrupulously clean, intoxicatingly perfumed, with a slim yet ripe body breathing insatiable desire, to which is coupled the accumulated knowledge and expertness in the arts of love of all the women who have ever lived.'

The Doctor paused to draw their attention to a shoal of flying-fish which were skimming from wave-crest to wave-crest within twenty feet of the windows of the launch's cabin, then when the shoal had passed he continued:

'The cult of Erzulie is, I think, the most remarkable thing connected with Voodoo, because it is no question of an occasional ceremony or a devotion which can be taken up and dropped again at will. Every year thousands of young men in Haiti receive her call and they must answer it whether they will or no. At first they do not realise what has happened to them but fall sick and have troubled dreams. A youth glimpses rich female garments and smells lovely scents in his sleep, but there is nothing tangible that he can identify. Then either the Goddess appears more openly and excites his lust or he consults a priest, describing the symptoms of his illness, and the priest tells him that Erzulie has done him the honour to choose him as her lover.

'Sometimes the young man is intensely distressed, as he may be in love with a mortal woman or happily married; but there is no escape for him if Erzulie has cast the eye of desire upon him. All sorts of ills befall him until he surrenders; but in most cases he does so quite willingly. For the reception of the Goddess he sets aside in his house a room with a spotless white bed, offerings of sweets and wine and flowers, and, under the pain of unbelievably horrible penalties no other woman is allowed to enter that room. He then goes through a special ceremony in which he devotes himself to the Goddess and becomes her servitor for the rest of his life.'

'If he has a wife, that's very hard on her,' remarked Marie Lou.

'It is, indeed, Madame,' the Doctor agreed; 'since Erzulie is the enemy of all women and is capable of inflicting the most grievous misfortunes—even death—upon any person who seeks to draw one of her lovers away from her. The jealousy of Erzulie Frieda is a terrible thing, and not a woman in Haiti, however strongly she might resent the loss of her own lover or husband, would dare to cross the Goddess.'

For a long time they talked on about the strange customs and beliefs of the superstitious, Voodoo-ridden Haitians, then of many other things as the sun gradually sank in the western sky and the launch raced on towards Port-au-Prince. Doctor Saturday proved a positive mine of information about the island; its people, flora, fauna and even fish. His large and extraordinarily white teeth flashed into a smile with great frequency and he was obviously most anxious to please. Richard did not like the way that the native crew cringed at the Doctor's every order, yet leapt to obey without uttering a word, but assumed that probably even the nicest Mulattoes treated their Negro servants little better than slaves. Marie Lou wished that their new friend would not make quite such frequent use of the spittoon just outside the cabin door. But they all considered themselves extremely fortunate in having been picked up by a man of his qualities and decided that if he was a fair sample of the upper-class Haitians the race had been much maligned.

Dusk was falling when the launch at last entered port and nosed its way in among a ramshackle collection of shipping. The great heat of the day was now long past, but the cool of the evening did little to alleviate the pain in the limbs of the Duke and his friends. Frequent applications of the Doctor's liniment had taken the worst sting out of their burns during the three-and-a-half-hour trip in the motor-boat, but they now felt as though they were being slowly grilled in front of a red-hot fire.

As all of them had been sunburnt on one occasion or other before, they knew the tortures that awaited them that night, and perhaps, in view of the seriousness of their burns, for several days to come, so they endeavoured to regard their pain philosophically and take comfort from the fact that they were alive at all. But it was difficult for them to keep their minds off the burning glow which now suffused their scorched skin.

On the wharfside the Doctor summoned a rickety Ford to follow his own car, which was waiting for him. Piling into the two vehicles, they drove past the few pretentious brick buildings in the centre of the town, out through the marshy suburbs which surround it, where the only buildings were tumbledown shacks and squalid mud hovels, then for a couple of miles up into the hills until they reached a long, low house before the whole front of which ran a broad verandah. With an apology for preceding them Doctor Saturday led the way in and bade them welcome; while his black houseboys ran out to collect the fish which he had caught earlier in the day.

In the centre of the building there was one huge, lofty room which was open at both ends so that a current of air could move unimpeded right through it during the great midday heats. It was well but rather incongruously furnished in the ornate French style of the 1890's, but the books and radio-gramophone, together with its spotless tidiness, showed that the Doctor lived the life of a cultured European.

Pausing only to remove his panama, which revealed a fine head of curly, snow-white hair, he led them out, along the verandah, to a series of bedrooms; all of which were sparsely but neatly furnished, were equipped with Venetian blinds, and had fine-mesh wire frames over the windows to keep out the mosquitoes. He also showed them a shower-bath at the back of the house and a fitted basin with a geyser. Taking a pile of clean towels from a cupboard he said that he felt sure they would like to tidy themselves while he told his staff that he had guests who would be staying for some time and had extra places laid for dinner.

Immediately they were alone de Richleau called the others into his room. His face was exceptionally grave as he said:

'God knows, I never imagined for one second that we'd ever be landed in such a hellish mess.'

'Mess?' repeated Rex. 'I reckon we've had a grand break.

The old Doc. seems a decent sort. He couldn't have been kinder; and this place is the Ritz compared with anything we'd find in that lousy town. Dammit, we were lucky enough to be picked up at all; but to have been picked up by a civilised old crooner, who wants us all to stay with him for keeps, seems super-luck to me.'

'You fool!' snapped the Duke. 'Haven't you realised that the whole of my impedimenta for our protection went down in the plane? We're in Haiti and our enemy must know that by now. The moment we go to sleep tonight we shall be utterly at the mercy of the evil entity we came here to fight.'

16

The Evil Island

'Hell's bells!' exclaimed Richard. 'And I never gave the fact that you'd lost all your protective stuff a thought!'

'I did,' said Marie Lou. 'I've been worrying about it, on and off, the whole afternoon.'

Rex pulled a face. 'Seems, then, that we're in one helluva jam.'

De Richleau spoke again with incredible bitterness. 'Without the things to make a proper pentacle we shall be as defenceless as a group of naked people facing a battery of machine-guns.'

'I was hoping you'd be able to get fresh supplies of most of the things in Port-au-Prince,' murmured Marie Lou.

The Duke shook his head. 'Some of them, perhaps, but when we drove through it quarter of an hour ago you saw what a god-forsaken place it is. Only a herbalist or a first-class chemist could supply many of the items I require, and I doubt if there is either nearer than Kingston.'

'Jamaica's all of two hundred miles,' muttered Rex.

'You're thinking in terms of air travel. By water it must be nearer three hundred.'

Richard was calculating quickly. 'If, down at the port, we could get a motor-schooner or a sea-going launch that does fifteen knots, we could make it in twenty hours.'

'Sure,' agreed Rex. 'And we'll get a boat all right. Thank God my wallet was on me when we crashed! Good American dollars will buy anything in this place.'

'They would also buy a plane in Jamaica,' added the Duke.

'A plane?' repeated Marie Lou. 'What for?'

'The return journey,' he replied quietly. 'I mean to stay here and face the music while you others go to Kingston to get the things we need; but you must get back at the earliest possible moment, as I dare not sleep for an instant until you rejoin me.'

'Greyeyes, you can't!' Marie Lou protested. 'It would be absolute madness. Even if the rest of us succeeded in getting to Kingston in twenty hours we should need at least four or five hours there to buy the things and get a plane. Then there's the two-hours flight back. We couldn't possibly rejoin you much under thirty hours, and you've been awake about twelve hours today already. No. We must all leave here as quickly as we can and keep one another from falling asleep until we're able to erect a pentacle in Kingston.'

De Richleau gave a faint smile. 'I think you ought to be able to make better speed than that. There must be boats here which do eighteen knots. If so, you could be in Kingston by one o'clock tomorrow. Four hours should be enough to get the things and two hours for your flight back. Allowing an extra hour for a slip-up somewhere, you'd still be able to rejoin me within twenty-four hours. I'm sorry, Princess; and I know the risk I'm running in taking on those extra few hours before you can return; but I've got to stay.'

'In God's name *why*?' boomed Rex.

'Because our enemy cannot be in two places at once, even on the astral. As I'm by far the most powerful among you, it's certain that he will concentrate all his force against me. If I stay here you'll have a free run to Jamaica and back and be able to sleep on the way; but if I went with you we should all have to remain awake and sustain another attack from him during the coming night. As he proved powerful enough to wreck our plane this morning, what is there to stop his performing a new magic to churn up the waters and wreck any boat in which the four of us attempted to make the trip?'

'You're right,' admitted Richard. 'If we all go the chances are we'll all be sunk in one fell swoop, whereas, since you're the king-pin of the whole party, if you stay here it's a hundred to one that he won't have any time to spare for us.'

But God Almighty! We can't leave you here alone—it's unthinkable!'

De Richleau laid a hand on his arm. 'It's got to be, Richard, and I'll manage to hang out somehow.'

The others joined Richard in pleading with the Duke to let one of them remain with him, but he was adamant in his refusal and cut short their pleas by pointing out that the sooner they departed the better chance there would be of their getting back before he fell asleep on his feet from sheer exhaustion.

'Don't waste another moment arguing,' he urged, 'but start at once, and I'll think up some excuse to make to Doctor Saturday for your sudden disappearance.'

They had no baggage to pack, nothing to collect; only the things they stood up in, Marie Lou's dressing-case and Richard's satchel. All of them now realised the imperative necessity for not losing a single instant. The Duke swiftly scribbled a list of the eleven items that he required and handed it to Richard. Then, hiding their forebodings for their beloved leader as well as they could, they said good-bye to him and, leaving the room by the wire-gauze doors that gave on to the verandah, set off on their quarter of an hour's walk down to the town.

It was just on eight o'clock. Full night had come, and de Richleau stood there staring after them through the soft, velvety, tropical darkness. The tree-frogs had started their nightly chorus in the branches of a great banyan tree which stood before the house and fireflies were flitting through the bushes. There was not even a ripple of wind, and against the purple sky the black-etched palm-fronds hung in graceful tranquillity. The warm dusk was filled with the scent of the moonflowers which were opening in the garden and the stars were coming out in the heavens above the bay.

Below him in the distance the lights of Port-au-Prince twinkled, turning it from a squalid, evil-smelling dump into a fairy city. The night scene was one of calm, untroubled beauty, but de Richleau knew that it was fraught with deadly evil. Somewhere far away a drum was beating, swiftly, rhythmically, calling upon one of the cruel, lustful Voodoo gods in a ceremony that was as old as Time. The island seemed at peace but the Duke's sensitiveness to spiritual atmospheres told him that the whole dark vista positively reeked of evil emanations and primitive, sensual urges.

A slight shiver ran through him and, pulling himself together, he turned away, feeling that he would need every ounce of resolution that he could muster for the ordeal which he was called upon to face. He knew that as long as he could keep awake he was safe from all except physical attack, and he did not think it likely that his adversary would attempt to murder him, at all events for the time being. But thirty-seven hours was a long time to keep not only awake but alert. He had already been through an exceptionally tiring day, yet that had carried him over less than a third of the period. He would have to remain on the physical plane, conscious and ready to cope with any emergency, until eight o'clock the following night. Worse: he had glibly announced that it would be easy for Rex to hire a plane in Kingston for the return journey—but would it?

The Jamaican capital was linked by air-routes with the other principal islands of the West Indies and with the United States, but all Rex's dollars would not enable him to buy or hire any of the machines that were actually in service; and Kingston was not a very big place, where one could just drive up to the airport and charter a private plane at half an hour's notice. To get a plane at all, he would probably have to find a private owner who was willing to hire or sell. That would mean time spent in locating such a man and persuading him to do a deal.

If they failed to secure a plane by six o'clock, at the latest, they would not be able to get back to Haiti before dark, and there were no night-landing facilities at Port-au-Prince. That would necessitate the postponement of their return until they could land by the early-morning light, and for the Duke it would mean nearly forty-eight consecutive hours without sleep. He had known that risk when he had sent them, but it was a grim thought to contemplate afresh now that he was alone.

Then again, it was not altogether certain that the enemy would allow the others to accomplish their journey without interference. The Duke had had to risk that; he had felt that it was better that they should take a chance than that all of them should remain helpless in Haiti, to be overwhelmed; and he was reasonably confident that the enemy would continue to lie in wait hour after hour ready to pounce upon him the second that he dropped asleep. But there was no guarantee that this would be so, and his fears as to what might happen to his friends out there on the dark waters, should he prove wrong, gave him even greater concern than his own desperate situation.

However, one of de Richleau's greatest qualities was fortitude in adversity, and he tried to comfort himself with the thought that whatever ghastly trials might be in store for himself or his friends the Powers of Light are greater than the Powers of Darkness and that, therefore, if only they endured, without wavering, all that was sent to them, even though they lost their Earth lives in this grim, weaponless battle, their endeavours and defiance of Evil would be accounted to them in those true lives which they could not lose—because they are everlasting.

He would have given a lot to have been able to have a hot shower, both to cleanse himself from the dirt and dust of the day and to refresh himself mentally, but his burns were too bad for him to dare to do so; he knew from experience that nothing was better calculated to aggravate the pain of severe sunburn, so on going to the bathroom he had to content himself with washing his hands and gently dabbing at his red face.

When he returned to his room he paused in the doorway, in astonished consternation. Marie Lou was sitting on the edge of his bed.

His grey eyes bored into hers and he snapped in a tone which she had never before heard him use to her. 'Why have you come back?'

She shook her head a little helplessly. 'Don't be angry with me, Greyeyes dear; I had to.'

'Why have you come back?' he repeated.

She spread out her small hands. 'When one's already been awake for thirteen hours, another twenty-four is a very long time, and we both know that it may be much longer than that before the trip to Kingston and back can be accomplished. One person alone would be almost certain to fall asleep, but two people might manage to keep each other awake. By tomorrow afternoon you'll be feeling like death, and by the evening you would have been sitting on your own, hour after hour, in this room, absolutely aching to close your eyes; so—so I decided to come back and keep you company.'

'What did Richard say to that?' he asked sharply.

'Naturally he loathed the idea of my being separated from him at such a time, but he said that I was right—and I *am* right—you know it, Greyeyes. We always have worked as a team; and to go on that way is our only chance of pulling through. I couldn't be of the least help to the others; but I can be to you; and it's too late to try to pack me off after them, because by now they'll be preparing to leave the port. God knows what will happen to us, but whatever we have to face we'll see this thing through together.'

De Richleau's expression suddenly changed and his voice was very soft as he took her hand and kissed it. 'Bless you, Princess, for your splendid courage. I owe a great debt to Richard, too, for his marvellous unselfishness in letting you leave him. You're right, of course, about our being able to keep each other awake, and the very fact of my having you with me will redouble my determination not to give in.'

She stood up and kissed his cheek, then she said: 'I wonder what's happened to Simon and Philippa? I've been terribly worried about them all the afternoon.'

'I don't think we need worry overmuch,' the Duke replied. 'As I told you just before Doctor Saturday picked us up, I know that they reached the shore in safety. I don't suppose that big island is very highly populated, and they probably had to walk some miles along the beach before they came to a village where they could get a fishing-boat to come out and look for us. If that happened it would have been extremely difficult for them to find the plane again, even if it was still floating, by the time they got out there. In consequence they've got much more cause to worry about us and by now they probably think that all four of us are drowned.'

'D'you think the enemy is likely to attack them tonight, though?'

'No. For one thing, as he probably doesn't even know yet that they left our main party, he'd find it far from easy to locate them; and for another, it's pretty certain that he'll concentrate on us. Fortunately Philippa understands the language, so with her to write down what Simon has to say, the two of them ought to be able to secure food and shelter without much trouble. It may be some days before they hear that we were rescued, but they're sure to learn of that in due course and manage to join us somehow.'

He refrained from adding: 'If we are here to join,' but Marie Lou was quite as conscious of that eventuality as he was, so she promptly changed the subject and asked:

'What are we going to do about Doctor Saturday? He'll soon be coming along to find out what has happened to us. How're we going to explain the disappearance of Richard and Rex?'

'I was thinking about that while I was washing just now—which reminds me to tell you that you mustn't have a bath however much you may want one, as it would make the pain of your burns almost unendurable. Saturday seems a very decent sort of fellow, and as he's an educated man it's hardly likely that he indulges in the practice of Voodoo; but it's all Lombard Street to a China orange that most of his house-boys are devotees of the cult.

'Through one of them our enemy may already have been informed of our arrival here, and it's important that we should prevent his learning—via any such human source, at least—that Richard and Rex have left the island. Fortunately we didn't give the Doctor our right names or any particulars about ourselves so it didn't transpire that you and Richard are married; so this is what I propose to tell him:

'I shall say that although all four of us were travelling together, that was only a matter of convenience as actually we are two separate parties. We'll adopt what Philippa told us of her uncle and herself. I am a scientist interested in native customs, and you are my niece. About the other two we don't know very much, except that they're engaged in some form of activity to do with the war—in connection, we *think*, with preventing German submarines from occupying bases in the West Indian islands. In any case, they asked us to make their excuses to the Doctor because it was important that they should see the British Consul here with the least possible delay, so they've gone down to the town to find him.

'When they don't turn up again it will be assumed that they're spending the night with the Consul, and the fact that they're not doing so can't be checked up, because I noticed that there is no telephone here. When they fail to appear or to send a message it will look like very bad manners, but there won't be anything that the Doctor can do about it, and when they *do* return we can put them up to making the right sort of explanations and apologies.'

'Seeing how important it is that our enemy shouldn't learn through the house-boys that they've gone off in a boat and spend any of his time attempting to find and destroy it, I think that's an excellent story,' declared Marie Lou.

'Good.' The Duke raised a smile. 'Then my beautiful niece had better tidy herself up, and we'll go along and tell our host that the number of his guests has unexpectedly been halved.'

Many of the things in Marie Lou's dressing-case had been ruined by the salt water but others had dried stiff in the sunshine, so she was able to improve her appearance with them. All the same, she was sadly worried at the redness of her broad forehead and small nose, knowing that although she had done her utmost to protect them they had caught the sun to such an extent that they were certain to peel, and she would look a sight for at least a fortnight. Then she caught herself up and gave a grim little smile at her reflection in the mirror. If her true self was still connected with her present body in a fortnight's time it was virtually certain that they would have succeeded in their mission and would be on their way back to England, but at the moment it seemed as though all the odds were that when she next left her body she would never be allowed to return to it and that within forty-eight hours it would be a rapidly corrupting piece of rubbish.

Such a possibility was not at all a frightening one for her, as she had no fear of death. It was, she knew, only a waking-up to a far fuller and more vivid existence, but the thought that her present incarnation might be within a few hours of its close saddened her greatly. Blessings and happiness in it had fallen to her far beyond the lot of most young women. She had derived great joy from her beautiful little body and was exceedingly loath to part with it. But far beyond this, there was Fleur, who would be left motherless in England; and her adored Richard, whom the Fates might decree should live on alone and be separated from her, except for very occasional meetings on the astral—since it is written

203

that the departed shall not seek to occupy the minds of those who remain and that the bereaved shall not strive to call back those who have gone on.

Ten minutes later she rejoined de Richleau and together they went through to the big living-room. Doctor Saturday was waiting there for them and at once came forward to say that dinner would be ready at any moment. In the meantime he hoped that they would like the cocktail that he had just mixed.

As they accepted, the Duke explained the non-appearance of the other two. He was a superb liar and told his story with such artistry that the Doctor did not appear to doubt for an instant his account of what had happened. De Richleau added smoothly that the others would have gone to the British Consulate immediately on their arrival in the town, owing to the urgency of their work, had they not been so exhausted and half-bemused as a result of their terrible experience and narrow escape from death. It was only when they had recovered a little that they had realised the gravity of their responsibilities.

'And,' he concluded brazenly, 'they hunted for you everywhere to excuse themselves but failed to find you.'

Doctor Saturday expressed mild surprise but said that he must have been in his bath at the time and that if the others returned they would still be most welcome; but, in view of the hour and the fact that they had lost all their luggage, he thought it probable that the British Consul would insist on putting them up for the night.

A few moments later the head house-boy appeared. He did not announce dinner but merely bowed in the doorway and ushered them into the dining-room, which was on the far side of the big hall. As Doctor Saturday begged them to be seated he casually mentioned that all his servants were mutes whom he had taken on and trained out of pity. He then apologised for the fare about to be offered to them, saying that had he had more notice he would have procured something more suitable, but that for dinner that night he hoped they would not mind the local dishes.

The repast consisted largely of fruits and vegetables, with one course of stewed meat, the strong flavour of which de Richleau recognised as goat; but it was so tender, and the island fruits so delicious, that both he and Marie Lou, who, having had no lunch, found themselves ravenously hungry, thoroughly enjoyed the meal.

Afterwards they sat in the semi-darkness on the wide verandah outside the big lounge-room, and the Duke, wishing to keep Marie Lou's thoughts occupied as much as possible before they retired to their night-long vigil, encouraged the Doctor to tell them more about the island.

'Haiti is like nowhere else in the world,' said the Doctor, 'and although its history extends over only four hundred years I doubt if any other country could rival it for tales of bloodshed, treachery and massacre. I could talk to you about it for hours, but I fear to bore you.'

'No, no,' said Marie Lou. 'Do please tell us about some of the revolutions and other exciting things that have happened here.'

'Very well, then.' The Doctor's teeth flashed in a smile, and he began: 'It's almost as though there has been a curse on the island from the very beginning. Even when Columbus discovered it, the five separate tribes of Carib Indians who inhabited it were perpetually at war with each other. The Spaniards forced Christianity upon them at the point of the sword and endeavoured to enslave them, but the Carib is a strange creature and very different from the Negro. He is primitive but strongly independent and in most cases the Aborigines preferred to die rather than work under foreign masters. Consequently the Europeans were compelled to import great numbers of African slaves to work on their plantations.

'Haiti was the native name for the island—meaning mountainous—but Columbus rechristened it Hispaniola and later, under the French, it was changed again, to Saint Domingue; and the larger, western part of the island, as you doubtless know, is a separate Republic which is called Santo Domingo to this day. By the middle of the seventeenth century it had become a favourite haunt of the pirates who roamed the Spanish Main, particularly the small island of Tortuga, which lies off the northern cape, as that has many sandy beaches which served them well for laying up and careening their ships.

'For the best part of two hundred years the French were the masters here, and in the days when Louis XV and Louis XVI reigned in France many noble and wealthy families had great estates in the island; but the French Revolution put an end to that. L'Ouverture, Christophe, Dessalines and Petion, whom we regard as our national heroes, led a series of revolts and by 1804 the Europeans were finally driven out.

'But, unhappily, little good came to Haiti from having secured her independence. A new internal war developed between the Negroes and the Mulattoes. The Mulattoes were richer and much more intelligent so they were able to hold their own against the far greater number of Negroes, but the hatred between the coloured and the partially-coloured portions of the population still continues. This internal strife has been the downfall of our people. It meant that instead of working in amity together, and being able to enjoy the fine inheritance which the French had left us, we quarrelled and fought; so that nine-tenths of the culti-vated land went back to virgin forest, and even the fine houses of the rich French Colonials became crowded tene-ments which it was nobody's responsibility to keep in repair and therefore they gradually fell into decay.

'An even worse curse has been the lack of honesty among our self-chosen rulers. Hardly one of them has ever given a thought to the welfare of the people. They have schemed and murdered to gain power, solely for the purpose of get-ting their hands on the exchequer. As each has succeeded in doing so he has found it empty, so for a few months he has sought to hold his rivals at bay by killing and imprisoning them until the meagre taxes that can be extracted from the people have amounted to a good round sum. They have then decamped overnight to Jamaica, en route for Paris, since the boulevards, with their bright lights and white women, are the Mecca of all Haitians.'

'It's surprising that none of them tried to make anything out of the place,' remarked the Duke. 'The soil is so rich that it could produce a huge profit with very little labour, and I've always understood that there is great mineral wealth in the island if only it were properly exploited.'

'That is so,' agreed the Doctor. 'Gold, silver, copper, iron, antimony, tin, sulphur, coal, nickel, and many other things, are here for the taking, but such ventures require capital, and whenever a Haitian government has borrowed the money from one of the European Powers for such a purpose our Presidents have promptly decamped with it; leaving the unfortunate people that much worse off owing to the debt incurred.'

'Surely your Government could have sold a concession to one of the big European or American mining syndicates?' suggested the Duke.

The Doctor shook his head. 'No. That they refused to do —and, according to *their* lights, they were wise in their refusal. The granting of any such concession would have meant giving a permanent status to white engineers and business men in the island. If that had happened an end would have been put to the abuses of our coloured politicians long ago. The white business men would have made official reports to their Government that murder, graft and every form of licence were rife here, and a very good case could soon have been made for the Power concerned to send a battleship to take us over. Negroes and Mulattoes, rich and poor, were all determined that whatever else might happen they were not going to have that, and for many years white people were definitely barred from even landing in the island.'

'Yet in the end the Americans took possession,' commented the Duke. 'What led up to that?'

'That was in 1915, when Jean Vilbrun Guillaume Sam was President. General Bobo rose against him in the north that summer and marched upon the capital. According to convention, Sam should have emptied the Treasury and politely retired to Jamaica. No one would have attempted to stop him, because that had become the accepted end of all Presidents who escaped assassination. Perhaps there was not enough in the Treasury to satisfy his avarice—I do not know—but he refused to flee. When his army of Cacos— as they call the machete men—deserted to the enemy he sent his chief military officer, Charles Oscar Etienne, with the palace guard, to murder all his political rivals whom during his presidency he had been able to catch and throw into prison. It was the most revolting butchery that you can imagine; even worse than the famous massacres of September which are made so much of in the history of the French Revolution. The prisoners were shot and then gutted with knives as they huddled, chained, against the walls, until the street outside the prison was literally a river of blood. Only three out of nearly two hundred escaped alive.'

'How utterly horrible!' Marie Lou whispered. 'What happened then?'

'The whole city rose against President Sam and he took refuge in the French Consulate, but the mob dragged him from his hiding-place, cut off his hands and tore him to pieces. It was the news of this terrible massacre which caused the United States Government to send Admiral Caperton with his American marines to take control of the island.'

'Another of your Presidents blew up the palace with himself and all the people in it—did he not?' said the Duke.

Doctor Saturday inclined his snow-white head. 'Yes. That was only a few years earlier—in 1912. It is President Lecomte of whom you speak, and it's true that he is supposed to have been blown up; but I do not believe he was. There is considerable evidence to show that his successor, Tancred Auguste, lured him from his palace by a false message, and that he was murdered in his coach at night while crossing the Champ-de-Mars. But General Lecomte was a popular man and the conspirators feared the vengeance of his bosom friend, the Minister of the Interior, Sansarique. That was why, at the point of the pistol, they later that night compelled a young engineer to explode the great store of munitions which were kept in the cellars of the palace because no President of Haiti would trust the army—apart from his personal bodyguard—with live ammunition. The explosion rocked the whole city and as far as six miles away people were thrown out of their beds. Three hundred soldiers and officials were belched out by the terrific eruption, and very few of them survived.'

They were silent for a moment, then Doctor Saturday went on:

'But perhaps our most fantastic story is that in this, the twentieth century, we were for a time ruled by a goat.'

'How on earth did that happen?' laughed the Duke.

'It was in 1908 that General François Antoine Simon became President. He was a crude peasant soldier, and was engineered into office by dishonest politicians who wished to rule through him. There was, of course, the usual civil war before he succeeded to the presidency, and he was such a stupid man that I very much doubt if he would have defeated his opponent had it not been for his daughter, Celestina, and her goat, Simalo. She was a Mambo—that is, a Voodoo priestess—of exceptional powers and the goat was her familiar; she had actually been married to the animal in a formal Petro ceremony. But Celestina, whatever her dark deeds, was a woman of considerable courage and ability. The people termed her "Our Black Joan of Arc", since it was she who led the campaign for her brutish father, and the Cacos of the enemy fled in terror before Celestina and her goat.

'Simon, Celestina and Simalo then installed themselves in the palace, and the dishonest politicians found that they had got more than they bargained for, as without consulting Simalo General Simon would never do what they required of him; and Simalo's views were often very different from those of the politicians.

'Their regime frequently resulted in extraordinary and very horrible situations. Upstairs in the big apartments of the palace the leading families in the island and the Europeans from the Consulates had to attend state receptions as the guests of a President who ate with his fingers and got disgustingly drunk, while downstairs they knew quite well that in Simalo's apartments the most revolting Voodoo ceremonies were being practised. At the banquets they had to make a show of eating the rich foods that were placed before them but they never knew what filth might be concealed in the thick sauces, and it is said that in this way they were sometimes made to consume human blood.'

'How disgusting!' exclaimed Marie Lou.

'Yes. It is not a pretty story, but the father and daughter brought about their downfall by their own ambition. Having become President, it occurred to General Simon that he might marry Celestina off to a wealthy husband, so they actually went to the lengths of arranging a legal divorce for her from her goat. The story given out was that Simalo was so heartbroken at the loss of his wife that he died; but the probability is that by General Simon's order the beast was killed. In any case, it was buried with almost regal honours, and through a disgraceful piece of trickery they even succeeded in getting a Catholic priest to read the Christian burial service over it in the cathedral. They pre-

209

tended that the coffin contained the body of a man. But even the most despicable among the rich men of Haiti would not take Celestina for a wife afterwards. With the death of the goat the luck of the Simons changed, and people said it was because she had broken her oath before the Voodoo Loa that Celestina's power had deserted her. Soon afterwards General Lecomte led a revolt against President Simon, who fled to Jamaica; but Celestina is still living in the island to this very day, as an old woman whom nobody any longer fears or troubles about.'

For another hour or more Doctor Saturday entertained his guests with other strange stories of the long tale of rapine and murder that make up Haiti's troubled history. But he told them, too, that they must not form the impression that all Haitian politicians were murderous crooks or that the bulk of the population were ignorant, superstitious savages. Since the American occupation honest and enlightened Haitians had had a chance to better the lot of their countrymen and, though still in its initial stages, much good work was now being done. Health, agriculture, education, sanitation and welfare centres were all absorbing the energies of enthusiastic young coloured men, most of whom had been to universities in the United States. He remarked modestly that owing to his own absorption in the scientific study of the island's flora he was unable to give as much time as he would have liked to assisting the work of progress, but that as a small contribution he trained and found occupation for many dumb natives and had even succeeded in restoring to some their speech.

Soon after midnight, feeling that they could not reasonably keep him up any longer, the Duke suggested bed; upon which the Doctor saw them to their rooms, where clean white cotton pyjamas, and two bath-robes to serve as dressing-gowns, had been laid out for them.

When the Doctor had left them they undressed, finding it a great relief to get out of their clothes. In spite of their interest in their host's stories, their burns had caused them so much pain during the whole evening that they had found it difficult to concentrate; but now that they were able to apply some more of the liniment which he had given them this slightly eased the constant smarting.

Having got into her pyjamas and dressing-gown, Marie

Lou slipped out of her room along the verandah to the Duke's as it was there that they had arranged to pass the night together.

She found that he had already pushed the furniture up against the walls and was sweeping clean the bare boards of the floor with the end of one of the woven-grass mats, which he had rolled into a bundle.

'You're going to attempt to make some sort of pentacle, then?' she said in a whisper.

'Yes. Anything's better than nothing,' he remarked, holding up a carafe of fresh water which he had just drawn from the bathroom tap. 'I shall charge this, and providing that we remain awake it should prove sufficient to keep away from us any manifestation which may appear.'

They had no chalk but Marie Lou produced a gold pencil from her dressing-case, and using one side of a pillow-slip as a measure she made little marks on the floor until she had plotted a five-pointed star in which all the sides would be exactly the same length.

De Richleau meanwhile sat with the carafe of water before him and the first and second fingers of his right hand pointing at it from the level of his eye, while he drew down power which flowed invisibly from his mind, through his eye, along his fingers into the carafe. After a few moments he picked it up and, dipping his fingers into it, drew a broad, wet line from one to another of the small crosses that Marie Lou had marked on the floor.

As they put their pillows and clean bedding in the middle of the pentacle, he said: 'It would be best if we did not discuss this business or make any mention of the others, so that when the enemy arrives—as he almost certainly will do when he thinks that we've had time to fall asleep—he will not gain any information through our conversation. I've never been in such a tricky position before, but I believe our best defence will be to endeavour absolutely to ignore as far as we possibly can anything that may happen. We'll talk about the good old pre-war days, tell such amusing anecdotes as we can think of, and hold competitions like memory-tests to keep our minds occupied. The great thing is to keep on talking as though we're completely unconscious that the enemy is trying to get at us.'

They sat down, cross-legged and facing each other, on

the bedding, immediately under the hanging oil-lamp that lit the room. The house had now fallen silent and the only sound which disturbed the stillness was the croaking of the tree-frogs. The first serious stage of the long ordeal which they were called upon to sustain had begun.

17

Battle Against Sleep

'First of all,' said the Duke, 'while our minds are still fresh I think we'd better plot out our night, dividing it into hours in which we're going to talk about certain subjects or play various word-games; then with each hour that passes we shall have something new to occupy our thoughts and not suddenly find ourselves stuck for ideas when our vitality is at its lowest ebb.'

Accordingly they made out a short list. For the first hour they were to talk about their earliest memories. For the second, they would indulge in a battle of wits where each would write down a subject on a piece of paper, and without actually mentioning what they had written would see which of them could first lead the other into talking of the subject chosen. For the third, they were each to recount their recollections of their first love-affair; and so on, right up to six o'clock, soon after which dawn would come and release them from the pentacle.

During the first three-quarters of an hour nothing at all happened, but it was an eerie sensation to be sitting there with the knowledge that a third, invisible, person might also be in the room watching them with quiet malevolence and planning various schemes which might lead to their undoing.

Shortly ofter one the oil-lamp above their heads began to dim. The Duke rose to his feet and turned up the wick, but that made no difference; the light grew fainter and fainter, spluttered a little and went out.

The darkness seemed charged with sinister vibrations

and for the first few moments after the light had died it appeared very black, but as their eyes became accustomed to it the bright starlight outside gradually lit the room for them so that they could still just make out each other's features and the objects of furniture which had been pushed against the wall. They then noticed that the places where the boards had been damped with the charged water now showed as lines with a phosphorescent glow, which was a considerable comfort to them.

From their previous experience they had realised beforehand that they would almost certainly be robbed of light, so they went on talking, quite unperturbed, but each kept their eyes fixed on the other's face, both grimly determined not to be drawn into looking behind them.

After a little while Marie Lou saw a thickening of the shadows over the Duke's shoulder, just outside the pentacle. It slowly condensed into the form of a small black astral, like a dwarf with a very big head; but she knew that it was only a *little* 'black' and took no notice of it.

De Richleau, meanwhile, could see over her head, and beyond it, too, the shadows were moving. As he watched they writhed and twisted until they formed a giant smoky hand with fingers that flickered backwards and forwards in a clutching motion, as though to snatch Marie Lou bodily from inside the protective barrier.

Anyone with less knowledge than the Duke might have been scared into shouting a warning to her, but he knew that their only hope of safety lay in complete passivity and he was able to bring into his conversation a little joke which made her laugh, whereupon the big hand suddenly shivered and dissolved.

After that, many strange things came and went outside the limits of the pentacle, obviously sent to try to terrify them into leaving it; but, far from becoming anxious, the Duke was now much easier in his mind. It was apparent that the water charged with power, from which he had made their astral defence, was sufficient without the many other items that he had used at Cardinals Folly to keep the evil manifestations at bay—at least, as long as he and Marie Lou could keep awake. In order to maintain its force, ignoring anything that might be jibbering at them from beyond the barrier, at intervals of about an hour he made the circle of the star on his hands and knees, remoistening the lines, from the carafe, as he went.

At about half-past two the enemy appeared to realise that they could not be scared and the manifestations abruptly ceased. For nearly two hours nothing happened, and they talked on about a multitude of subjects, de Richleau having soon come to the conclusion that the reason for the evil forces having been withdrawn was because their initiator hoped that if they were not molested further they would grow tired of talking and go to sleep.

Actually, neither of them felt in the least like sleeping, as both were conscious of an ally upon which they had not counted. All the portions of their bodies which had been exposed to the full rays of the sun were glowing with heat, and at times they were tempted to tear off the sun-scorched skin in the hope of securing even momentary relief. The pain had been bad enough when they were sitting out on the verandah talking to Doctor Saturday, but it had eased a little while they were moving about after having come up to their rooms. Then, when they had settled down for the night, it had seemed to become infinitely worse, so they doubted if they could have managed to get any sleep even had they been out of all danger and in the most comfortable beds.

Shortly before half-past four it seemed that the enemy's patience was exhausted or that he had suddenly realised the fact that it was not their intention to go to sleep. In any case, he changed his tactics.

A strange, heady perfume began to filter into the room until the whole atmosphere was laden with it. There was nothing that they could see, nothing tangible at which they could throw their defiant wills; but for that very reason the new manifestation was all the more frightening. The strong scent seemed to dull their senses like a drug, so that their limbs grew heavy; it became difficult for them to hold their heads upright, and they felt an awful yearning to relax and let great waves of sleep pass over them.

De Richleau stretched out his hand and took Marie Lou's. They were speaking much more slowly now and it required a great effort to continue their talk of old memories and irrelevant things; but each time there fell a pause one of them dug his nails into the palm of the other until the pain

215

jerked back the one who was due to reply and some form of answer was forthcoming.

How long that continued neither of them could tell but it seemed as though they wrestled there for an endless time with the intangible, awful thing that was weighing down upon them, until at last the scent grew fainter and they knew that they had won through that ordeal.

There was another pause, during which they were able to rally their strength a little. Then came the next attack: an attempt to hypnotise them into sleep by sound and at the same time to destroy their power of speech.

Very softly at first, they heard the beating of the Voodoo drums. The drumming went on and on with a terrible monotony that frayed their nerves to ribbons, slowly increasing in volume until the drum-beats were thundering in their ears so loudly that they could barely catch each other's words.

As the sound increased, so they raised their voices, and soon they were shouting at each other with all the power of their lungs. Both felt that they must either be overcome or go mad.

In vain they stuffed their fingers in their ears. It made no difference. The awful, primitive rhythm seemed to stun them with its volume; yet they struggled on. As a counter to the sound the Duke burst into song, and Marie Lou followed his lead. Wildly, crazily, they sang snatches of choruses from old musical-comedy shows, patriotic airs, and marching-songs—anything that entered their heads— sometimes together but often in opposition. They made the night hideous but their tuneless caterwauling enabled them to keep their thoughts concentrated on their own efforts and free of the somnolent effects of the insistent, never-changing rhythm.

Suddenly the drumming ceased and by comparison the silence was overwhelming. Yet it was not complete silence. Faintly, in the distance, a cock was crowing, and the crowing of a cock has the power to break any night-cast spell.

De Richleau drew in a deep breath as he glanced at the window. The stars had paled, grey light now filled the oblongs. Dawn had come.

They stood up and stretched themselves, now free to move outside the makeshift pentacle, that had served them so well. With their relief a new tiredness had seized upon them; but this was a normal thing which they knew they could fight for hours to come. De Richleau relit the lamp and they smiled at each other.

'Well done, Princess,' he said. 'It was pretty ghastly, but we've come through all right. I doubt, though, if I could have done so alone. I could have stood the drums, but not that awful perfume, unless I'd had somebody with me to keep me from going under.'

'I wonder,' she said slowly, 'if I'm looking as grim as you.'

They both turned and stared into the dressing-table mirror. That awful night had taken it out of both of them. De Richleau's face was grey and lined, while it seemed that Marie Lou had aged ten years.

He put an arm about her shoulders and shook her gently. 'Don't worry about that now; it's only a temporary thing. within a few hours you'll have recovered all your beauty.'

As is always the case in the Tropics, the sun rose very quickly. Within quarter of an hour after their ordeal had ended daylight had come, so they decided to go out for a short walk to freshen themselves up. Their burns were still too angry to permit them to bath, but having washed themselves and dressed they went out into the garden and a little way down the road. They did not, however, walk far, as the wound in the Duke's foot had not fully healed and still pained him slightly. When they got back they went into the living-room and collected some magazines. These were all several months old but served to keep them occupied until eight o'clock, when they felt that they could decently go in search of breakfast.

Having found the head house-boy de Richleau went through a pantomime of pouring out and drinking, upon which the dumb Negro pointed to the dining-room, and ten minutes later they were eagerly giving their attention to hot coffee, buttered eggs and a selection of the island's luscious tropical fruit.

They were just finishing when Doctor Saturday joined them. After having wished them good morning, he remarked: 'You were up very early for people of leisure. I do hope that you didn't sleep badly?'

'On the contrary,' lied the Duke genially. 'We found your beds most comfortable; but both my niece and I are accustomed to getting up early, and your lovely garden tempted us into taking a short walk.'

'I fear my garden is a poor place by European standards,' the Doctor smiled. 'We cannot grow your beautiful lawns here, and the garden boys are incurably lazy; it is difficult to get them even to keep it tidy; but I have managed to collect quite a number of interesting flowers and plants. To have examples of as many varieties as possible helps me in my work, you know. Now, what would you like to do today? Please consider me entirely at your disposal.'

'That is most kind,' de Richleau bowed slightly. 'We should be delighted to leave ourselves in your hands.'

'Very well, then. This morning we might have a look round the town, and, since you are keen to learn about Voodoo, this afternoon I will take you to a Hounfort.'

'What is that?' Marie Lou asked.

'A Hounfort, Madame, is a Voodoo temple, or perhaps one could describe it more correctly as a place in which a Houngan lives with his family and retainers and carries out his Voodoo ceremonies.'

'That really would be most interesting,' said the Duke.

When the Doctor had finished his breakfast his car was brought round and in it they drove down to Port-au-Prince. On the previous evening they had been too concerned with other matters to pay much attention to what little of the town they had seen, and they now realised that it was a much larger place than they had at first supposed. The Doctor told them that it contained a hundred and twenty thousand inhabitants, being by far the largest and, in fact, the only considerable town in Haiti, as there were no others in which the population exceeded twenty thousand.

The main streets were wide but ragged. Few of the houses were of more than two storeys but outside their upper floors nearly all of them had verandahs—airy balconies supported on pillars—upon which their owners could sleep during the midday heat. There were a few miles of tramway, and here and there a lorry or a battered car bumped along the uneven way, but there was very little traffic apart from a certain number of ox-wagons and poor, mangy little donkeys saddled with panniers which were stuffed to the brim with goods.

They visited the cathedral, a twin-towered architectural

monstrosity of Victorian times, and the Senate House, in which the theoretical representatives of the people held their meetings and heard the decisions of the President, in whom all real power was vested. There were numerous markets: one very big, open one in a wide space in front of the cathedral, and another, a covered market, which was entered through a quadruple-towered arch—one of the most hideous structures that de Richleau had ever set eyes on. It had been erected, Doctor Saturday said, to the memory of General Hippolite, who had been President for seven years, from 1889 to 1896, a record term in the whole island's history for a continuous and peaceful reign.

The curious bits and pieces in the meat market did not bear close inspection for anyone with a delicate stomach but the many varieties of local fish were interesting and the wealth of fruit and vegetables was positively astounding, for tropical varieties flourished in the lowlands and those natural to the more temperate climate of Europe, which had originally been brought over by the French, were still grown in the higher lands of the interior.

The attire of the citizens of Haiti was diverse. Most of them wore the wide-brimmed, locally-made, straw hats to keep off the strong sun, and the Doctor bought two of these for his companions. But in every other detail of dress the Haitians showed the most varied tastes; particularly the women, whose striped, spotted and self-colour head-coverings and neckerchiefs were of every hue under the rainbow. Although it was only ten o'clock it was already very hot, and few of the men in the streets wore coats; only a white, and generally dirty, open-necked shirt.

When the Doctor took them to the one hotel they found that the Haitian upper classes showed a very different taste in dress. No women, except the serving girls, were present, which made Marie Lou feel a little awkward, but the Doctor was greeted with respect wherever he went, and they sat down at a little table near the entrance to the big bar. In it, and at the neighbouring tables, there were at least a hundred men, all dressed, despite the heat, in black frock-coats or some kind of uniform.

The frock-coated men, whose wide straw hats had been enamelled a shiny black, were, the Doctor told them, Haitian politicians; and the others, although their uniforms differed almost without exception, were generals. It appeared that in Haiti they had had exactly the same number of generals in their army as they had had privates—to be exact, 6,500 of each—that is, up to the date of the American occupation. Before evacuating the island the United States officers had reorganised Haiti's defence force on more usual lines, but there were still countless generals who had obtained their rank when quite young men and had very determinedly stuck to it.

They did not look very much like generals, but more like black footmen in rather badly-designed and shop-soiled liveries, for in nearly every case the uniforms had done many years—and often even generations—of service, having been handed down as treasured possessions from father to son. The tunics, trousers and cloaks were of all colours and the oddest fits; the only thing which they had in common being tarnished gold lace, wherever it could be tacked on, and a rakish cockade of colourful plumage stuck in each battered shako or cap. Some of the generals carried revolvers in the gaily-tasselled sashes about their waists, while others clattered rapiers and sabres, some of which had seen service at the time of the French Revolution or, even earlier, in the hands of the pirates on the Spanish main.

The whole crowd talked and gesticulated incessantly, and it was clear to the visitors that this was the true 'house of representatives'; where the real business of the island was conducted during each morning session throughout the year, whether the Senate was supposed to be sitting or not. While they rested there the Doctor and his guests enjoyed an excellent 'planter's punch' made from iced rum, the juice of fresh limes, sugar and various other ingredients, but so many curious glances were cast at them that Marie Lou was heartily glad when they got away.

By eleven o'clock the town was beginning to empty, as the broiling sun was already high overhead, and people were making their way home for the midday meal, after which they would indulge in a siesta until three o'clock, thereby virtually dividing their working-day into two widely-separated periods—early morning and late afternoon.

Back at the Doctor's house, they lunched at midday and directly afterwards the Doctor said that he felt sure they would like to rest during the great heat; so they thanked him and went through to the side of the house in which the row of guests' bedrooms was situated.

'Well,' asked the Duke immediately they were alone, 'how are you feeling?'

'Not too bad,' said Marie Lou in a voice that belied her words.

It was now twenty-seven hours since they had wakened in their comfortable rooms at the Pancoast Hotel, Miami, and during that period they had been through a greater strain than most people are called upon to undergo in an unusually hectic week; but they knew that they had many hours to endure yet before they could hope for the succour that Richard and Rex would bring.

'Don't you think,' she said after a moment, 'that it would be all right for us to sleep a little now it's the middle of the day? As our enemy was at us all last night, he must be awake himself, otherwise he won't be able to sleep and attack us again tonight.'

De Richleau shook his head. 'I'm sorry, Princess, but the probability is that, like everybody else in the island, he's just about to take his siesta; so we dare not risk it. Still, if you like to lie down and cat-nap, I don't think there would be any harm in that. I shall have to shake you gently every few minutes to prevent you from dropping right off, but a lie-down and doze would be better than nothing.'

Knowing what was ahead of her and that she must conserve every atom of resistance that she could, Marie Lou agreed to the suggestion and lay down on the Duke's bed. She had hardly relaxed before she fell asleep, but he woke her and after about a quarter of an hour they had to give up the experiment as the constant dragging back just as she was leaving her body proved more of a strain than a relief.

Somehow or other they got through the next two hours, until the chief house-boy came to knock on their doors. Then they had a wash to freshen themselves and joined the Doctor in the big living-room.

Their mouths were parched, their eyes sunk in their sockets; whereas he was looking spruce and fresh in a clean suit of white drill. They both felt that he could not possibly help noticing their miserable condition, but he did not seem at all conscious of it; which they put down to the fact that

the faces of both of them were now disfigured by sun-
blisters as well as acute fatigue.

In spite of the applications of the Doctor's liniment and
some soothing poultices that he had sent along to them by
one of the houseboys, their foreheads, noses, ears and necks
had now gone a dull red and were a mass of tiny, painful
blotches. Marie Lou had done her best to disguise the dis-
figuring effects but the Duke had told her that she must on
no account put any of her scented powder on the raw
places, for fear it might poison them, so she had been unable to do very much except hide her burnt forehead under
a clean white handkerchief which she had tied across it
pirate-fashion.

The Doctor drove them off in his car, up the hill this
time, for about a mile, until they entered a considerable
village and, passing through it, came to the Hounfort. It was
a big enclosure containing several one-storeyed buildings
and a number of open thatches of banana-palm fronds laid
one on top of the other in a network which was supported
by a few dozen poles of all sizes and leaning at all angles.

The Houngan, a bald-headed, bespectacled, intelligent-
looking Negro, dressed in a long, white, cotton garment,
welcomed the Doctor and his companions. He spoke a little
very bad French but enough for the Duke and Marie Lou to
converse with him in simple sentences.

In the town that morning ugly looks had been cast at the
two visitors and some of the men lounging about the markets had hissed after them, '*Blanc*', since Whites are not
popular in Port-au-Prince; but here their reception was
very different and seemed full of the kindness which goes
with the genuine Negro character. The men, women and
children of the Houngan's family—which numbered the
best part of a hundred—all crowded about them with wide-
mouthed grins, and Marie Lou would have liked to make a
fuss of some of the little black piccaninnies had they not
been so abominably dirty.

Soon after their arrival the people from the village began
to crowd in, as it was a Wednesday afternoon and the weekly
service to Dambala was just about to begin.

As they stood apart, so that the Priest could proceed with
his ritual, Doctor Saturday explained that Dambala, the
chief of the beneficent Rada gods, was thought by many

222

people to be Moses. Why the great Jewish prophet should have been deified by the Negroes of the West African coast no student of folklore had ever been able to explain, but the two definitely had much in common. For example, the green snake which was Dambala's symbol had also been that of Moses. It is recognised that certain African Witch Doctors have the power to hypnotise a snake into rigidity so that they can use it as a walking-stick, but at their will it wakes and becomes live again in the hand. It is more than probable that Moses's rod was a hypnotised snake of a special variety which by habit attacked and ate another variety of snake; so that when he threw down his rod before Pharaoh he knew that it would become alive and devour the snake-rods of the Egyptian priests which were of the second variety. The snake which they saw beside the pool, near the Voodoo altar, was, the Doctor said, regarded not as the actual god but only as his servant or handmaiden.

Actually there were a number of altars, each dedicated to one of the principal Voodoo gods, both Rada's and Petro's. All the altars had an extraordinarily heterogeneous collection of objects piled on them in a jumble: pictures and cheap plaster figures of the Catholic saints who were associated with the various gods, bottles of rum, little bells, and innumerable crude pottery dishes containing offerings of food and beads. Each altar was canopied with an elaborate arrangement of palm fronds, the leaves of which had been frayed out by hand, until they looked like huge green feathers, and in and out among them were woven hundreds of streamers of coloured paper. The whole effect was far from impressive as they looked more like a row of dirty junk-shops than anything else.

The Houngan took the centre of the stage, sitting down in a low chair, and the Mambo, or Priestess, a huge old Negress, stood behind him, while on either side, on cane-seated chairs, sat the Hounci, Voodoo adepts who had passed the first degree of initiation, and the Canzos, who had passed the second degree of initiation. Among them were the drummers, each of the great drums which they clasped between their knees being dedicated to a particular god. Also near the Houngan was the *Sabreur*, or sword-bearer, and the *Drapeaux* who held above their heads two gay silk flags embroidered and fringed with silver. But only the most rudimentary order was maintained, as the Priest's assistants jostled one another for places, laughed, argued and cracked jokes with each other. The congregation, too, moved freely about the great compound, which was like that of an African chieftain; sometimes appearing to pay attention to what was being done, and at others disputing among themselves or going up to talk to the Houngan and his entourage.

'There will be four ceremonies,' said the Doctor. 'The first to Papa Legba, the God of the Gate, who lives in that great great silk-cotton tree outside the gate there. He must be propitiated before the way is open to any of the other gods. Next they will make a sacrifice to Papa Loco, the God of Wisdom, lest he become jealous and afflict them with some ill. The third sacrifice will be for Mah-Lah-Sah, the Guardian of the Door Sill. And finally there will be the sacrifice to Dambala himself.'

Seated in his low chair before the altar the Houngan covered his head with a ceremonial handkerchief and began a monotonous litany to which the whole congregation made the responses. It was a longish business and the visitors would have found it extremely wearisome had it not been for the sweetness of the Negroes' singing.

After a time the chanting stopped and they crowded into a big room, where spread on a wide table were all sorts of foods and drinks which were being offered to the gods. The Priest came out again, drew on the ground a design in corn-meal and poured a little of each of the dedicated drinks upon it. He then took pieces of all the offered foods and piled them up in a small heap in the middle of the design.

Two speckled chickens were now handed to him. He elevated them to the east, to the west, to the north and to the south, calling upon the Grand Master, while his assistants knelt down and he waved the squirming chickens over their heads. He next presented the birds at the altar dedicated to Legba, took both birds in one hand and a firebrand in the other, with which he set off three heaps of gunpowder which had been placed round the cornmeal design. Kneeling, he kissed the earth three times and the whole congregation did likewise. Suddenly the drums began to beat and some of the adepts began to dance. The Priest broke the wings of one of the chickens, then its legs, holding the throat so that the bird could not cry out in its pain.

Marie Lou turned away from the sickening sight. When she looked again she saw that the second bird had suffered a similar mutilation and that both had been placed on the altar, where, in spite of their broken limbs, the poor brutes were fluttering and squirming.

The Priest kissed the ground again and wrung both the birds' necks, putting them out of their agony; after which the corpulent Mambo took them from him and roasted them over a slow fire. When they were done they were put in a sack and to the accompaniment of a great deal of drum beating, chanting and stamping of feet the sack was carried outside and tied to Legba's tree.

To the uninitiated visitors the ceremonies that followed differed little except that grey roosters were sacrificed to Papa Loco and a white cock and hen to Dambala, while in all cases but the first the heads of the birds were bent back and their throats cut so that when held by the feet the blood could be drained out into a crock. To Marie Lou's disgust, the Houngan each time drank deeply of the hot blood, allowed each of the drummers a taste, then flung the bowl as far from him as he could, whereupon the assistants raced after it and milled about it like a rugby-scrum, fighting to secure a finger-lick of the wonder-working blood.

As the ceremonies proceeded the Negroes became more and more excited. From time to time one of them appeared to become possessed and, foaming at the mouth, danced until he dropped. At intervals the leading dancers stopped and demanded rum. The Houngan make a pretence of refusing them but on each occasion went inside and fetched a bottle. After each tot of the fiery spirit the dancing became more frenzied than ever, but there was nothing mysterious or frightening about the services as they were being conducted in the strong afternoon sunlight.

Just before the sacrifice to Dambala there was one untoward episode. Two women in black had sneaked into the compound and were standing quite near the visitors. One of the Houncis spotted them and told the Priest; upon which he rushed at them and drove them away with threats and curses. When he had quietened down a little, seeing that everybody spoke to him quite freely in the middle of his rituals, de Richleau asked him what the women had done. He replied in his broken French that they were in mourning and therefore had no right to attend a Dambala ceremony, which was for the living. Their association with recent death caused them to carry with them, wherever they went, the presence of the dreaded Baron Samedi.

'Lord Saturday,' whispered Marie Lou to the Duke. 'What a queer name for a god!' But the Doctor caught what she had said and turned to smile at her.

'It is another name that they use for Baron Cimeterre. You see, his Holy Day is Saturday. And it is a sort of joke, of which the people never get tired, that my name, too, is Saturday.'

Had the scene not been so animated, and the rituals so interesting, in spite of their cruel and disgusting side, Marie Lou and the Duke would have found it almost impossible not to fall asleep where they sat, in the shade of a tall fence, and with their backs propped against it, but the beating drums and wild chanting acted as a tonic to their tired nerves.

Almost unperceived by them, dusk fell, and to light the compound the Priest's assistants ignited torches of freshly cut pinewood. The scene now savoured of an orgy, as although the rituals were still going on, with the Priest kissing the sword and the flags and waving aloft his *ascon*, the Voodoo symbol of power, which is a sacred gourd decorated with beads and snake vertebrae, the whole congregation had given themselves up to the wildest extravagances.

The rum had made most of the Houncis and Canzos three-parts drunk and the drums had completed their intoxication. The women 'cramped' and shook themselves before the 'shuckers' until they fell quivering upon the ground, but they were not allowed to lie there. The men grabbed them up to continue their insane whirling. Now and then one of the congregation became possessed, raved, foamed at the mouth and collapsed in a fit, but their faces were bathed in rum to revive them. Clothes were torn away until many of the dancers were stark naked. Hot, sweaty bodies collided and limbs became locked in rhythmical ecstasy. The dancing grew more and more abandoned until the Doctor whispered to the Duke that as they had Madame with them he thought that they had better go; so they went out to the car and returned, through the soft, velvety darkness, by the winding track that led down the hill.

It was just on eight when they reached the house and Marie Lou and de Richleau were both hoping desperately that they would find Richard and Rex waiting for them in the living-room. If the plane had got in by sundown they should have had ample time to come up to the house. But they were not there. With bitter disappointment the Duke realised that his worst forebodings had been fulfilled. The others had not been able to secure a plane in time to leave Kingston before five o'clock, so there was now no hope of their arriving before dawn. Another whole night of sleepless watching would have to be endured.

Dinner was served almost immediately they got in, but during it de Richleau and Marie Lou could hardly keep awake sufficiently to make intelligent conversation. They had spent nearly five hours watching the Voodoo rituals and although the sight had kept them awake through a bad period of the afternoon the noise and clamour had also added to their exhaustion. After the meal both felt that they would scream if they had to continue small-talk with their genial host so they pleaded extreme fatigue after their long day in the heat to which they were not accustomed, and excused themselves.

As soon as they were in the Duke's room they looked at each other in dismay. They had now been awake for some thirty-eight hours yet there was not the slightest prospect of help reaching them for another ten at least, and how they were to face the second night neither of them knew.

Grimly the Duke set about charging another carafe of fresh water. Just as he had finished, Marie Lou burst out in a hoarse whisper:

'I can't go on—I can't—I can't!'

'You must,' said the Duke firmly. 'Another few hours and we'll win through.'

'I can't!' she moaned, and suddenly gave way to a fit of heartrending sobbing.

He let her be for a few moments then put his hands on her head and, concentrating all his remaining strength, began to charge her. In his exhausted state it was now very difficult for him to call down power and he could do little more than pass on to her some portion of the resistance

227

which still animated his own consciousness. Yet this ancient ceremony of the laying-on of hands took effect. Her hysterical weeping ceased. She felt soothed and comforted. She was still unutterably weary but the danger of an immediate collapse had receded.

'I'm sorry,' she murmured, mopping her reddened, half-closed eyes. 'I'll manage somehow. But we haven't got to settle down in the pentacle yet—have we? It's only just after nine, and the shorter the period we have to remain sitting there the less strain it will be.'

'That's true,' the Duke agreed. 'We're now both so tired that it would prove fatal to relax, but I don't think that we shall actually need protective barriers for another hour or so.'

'Then let's go for a walk,' Marie Lou suggested. 'It's the sitting still for hour after hour which is such a ghastly strain.'

De Richleau had given her much of his own remaining strength. He was sitting, bowed and limp, on the end of the bed, and he shook his head. 'I'm afraid I'm not up to it at the moment, Princess. I must remain absolutely still for a while to conserve my energies against the coming ordeal, and if you don't mind we won't even talk for the next half-hour.'

'Would it be asking for trouble if I went for a stroll on my own?' she inquired. 'I must occupy myself somehow and I'm far too tired to read. If I stretch my legs now I'll be better able to endure our long session once we get down to it.'

He hesitated for a moment. 'It's unwise for us to separate for any length of time, but if you don't go far . . .'

She smiled. 'I'm much too weary to want to walk any distance. I only thought of taking a turn round the garden.'

'Very well,' muttered the Duke; 'as long as you remain within call. It would really be better if you took your stroll up and down the verandah, where there's a certain amount of light from the windows.'

She touched his cheek for a second with her finger-tips, as she said: 'I won't be long.' Then she walked out through the wire-gauzed swing door of the room into the stillness of the tropic night.

At first she strolled slowly up and down outside the row of guest-rooms; then she increased her beat until it took her as far as the big living-room in the centre of the low house. Its doors were open, the lights were still on, and the Doctor was sitting reading, with his back towards her, at the far end of the room. He did not turn at the sound of her soft footfalls, probably imagining it to be one of the house-boys who was passing.

She went a little further. The next room was the dining-room; then came the Doctor's bedroom. There was another big room beyond it; then the servants' quarters, which occupied the end of the house that was nearest the road to Port-au-Prince.

There was a single light burning in the room beyond the Doctor's bedroom and she paused to look through the window.

Evidently it was the Doctor's study. In it were many books, a longi horsehair couch, some rows of test-tubes in a rack along one wall, and a number of instruments. There was nothing there at all to differentiate it from the working-room of any man engaged in medical or scientific studies —with one exception—a huge map which covered the whole of one wall. It was a large-scale Admiralty chart of the North Atlantic.

Marie Lou stared at it, then she gently pushed open the wire swing door and tiptoed into the room. Her mind was working furiously. She was recalling a number of things that had occurred in the past two days and which had seemed quite natural at the time.

The Doctor had been out in his launch fishing when their plane had been wrecked. For hours he had not come to their assistance; yet he *must* have seen it crash. He had rescued them only when they had already been sighted and were about to be picked up by the native fishing-boat. Yet now, it seemed inconceivable that he had not been aware that they were there, less than half a mile away from him, in imminent danger of drowning.

Then his name—Doctor Saturday. Lord Saturday was one of the aliases of the dread Lord of the Cemetery, the chief of the evil Petro gods. Why was the Doctor, too, called Saturday? Many of the natives and Mulattoes in the island had a whole string of names which they had received when baptised by the Catholic Church to which they paid a purely nominal allegiance; but others bore only a single name, from having been dedicated to one of the Voodoo gods at birth. Perhaps the appellation had started as a nickname, given to him years ago when his fellow-islanders had realised that he was devoting himself to strange and horrid practices.

And now this large-scale chart of the North Atlantic. The fact that it had a number of little flags stuck in it, marking places right out in the open ocean, clinched the matter in her mind beyond all doubt. The Doctor had come out in his launch to make certain that they were all dead, but since his attack upon them had failed he had taken them to his home in order that he might have them under his physical eye and be ready to seize the first suitable opportunity to strike them down.

He had not commented upon their exhausted condition but he knew of it and was biding his time. Their genial host was none other than the enemy whom they had come so far to seek, and he was sitting only two rooms away from her now, like a spider in his web, waiting until sleep should overcome them.

With a sudden surge of terror she realised that he might come in at any moment and find her there. She must get out—at once—and warn the Duke. At the very instant she was about to turn she heard steps approaching and the wire door swing open behind her.

18

The Dead Who Do Return

Marie Lou stood there, rooted to the spot. Temporarily all memory of her tiredness had left her. She was held fixed by sheer terror. There was a prickling at the back of her scalp and the palms of her hands were wet.

The Doctor must have heard her pass the living-room after all, and since she had not re-passed it he had come out to see where she had got to. Now that he had found her there he would realise at once that she had learnt his secret. The cards would be on the table. From the beginning he had been fully aware of the reason for their visit to Haiti so it would be utterly useless for her to pretend that she did not appreciate the significance of the big map at which he had caught her staring. Facing it still, she wondered frantically what he would do. Dreading that he might strike her down from behind, she wanted to swing round; but she dared not, for fear that immediately she did so he would be able to hypnotise her.

She wanted to cry out, but her tongue clove to the roof of her mouth for what seemed an interminable interlude. Then, like a douche of cold water down her spine, Simon's voice came: natural, good-humoured, cheerful.

'Marie Lou! Thank goodness we've found you.'

The reaction was so great that she almost fainted with relief. A queer little noise came from her throat. She staggered, then turned right round. He was standing there in the doorway, with Philippa just behind him.

He suddenly spoke again, this time with quick anxiety.

'Good God! What's happened to you? You're looking simply ghastly.'

She swayed for a moment then ran towards him and grasped the lapels of his coat. 'Simon,' she whispered hoarsely, 'Simon! Oh God! You don't know. But we must get away from here—quick!—don't make a sound! I'll take you to Greyeyes. We must get away—we must get away!'

Simon put an arm round her shoulders and led her out on to the verandah. Seizing his hand, she pulled him down the nearest steps into the garden, and with Philippa following they made a long circuit through the shadowy patches until they came round to the house again and reached the Duke's room.

He was sitting just as Marie Lou had left him, hunched up and staring with dead eyes at the opposite wall. At the sound of their footsteps he roused himself and looked round.

'Simon!' he exclaimed, rising to his feet. 'My call for help is answered.'

A smile twitched Simon's wide mouth but his eyes were anxious. 'What on earth have you been up to? You look like a death's-head. And where are the others?'

De Richleau sighed. 'All my protective materials went down in the plane, and we dare not sleep until we can make ourselves a proper pentacle. Richard and Rex left for Jamaica yesterday evening to get new things, but they won't be back until morning. Marie Lou and I haven't slept since we left Miami—which is getting on for forty hours.'

Marie Lou broke in abruptly. 'Never mind that now. Greyeyes, I've made an awful discovery. Doctor Saturday *is* our enemy.'

'What! Are you certain?' De Richleau stared at her.

'Yes; absolutely.' In a spate of words Marie Lou told them about the map in the Doctor's room and recalled the way in which, although he had been on the spot, he had refrained from coming to their assistance until the fishermen had made their rescue certain.

'You're right,' the Duke said gravely. 'It's just possible that people fishing might have been so occupied with a bite on their line that they wouldn't have noticed the plane crash, because it was all over so quickly; but the chart of the North Atlantic proves that the Doctor *is* the Adversary.

Any Haitian occultist working for the Nazis would have to have such a chart to register the results of his astral journeys, if he was to convey exact practical information to another occultist in Germany, and it's impossible to believe that there are two such maps in a place like Haiti. Anyone might have a war map of Europe or Africa pinned up on his wall, but not a great chart of the Western Approaches with flags stuck in it.'

'We must leave—at once—this minute!' urged Marie Lou. 'We should be mad to stay here a moment longer.'

De Richleau shook his head. 'No, Princess. You're wrong there. In the first place, until we can make a proper pentacle, wherever we went we should be just as much at his mercy if we fell asleep. In the second, your discovery gives us an advantage. He's still under the impression that we believe him to be a cultured man who is not mixed up in any way with Voodoo. If we play our cards properly we ought to be able to use the fact that we've discovered his secret while he still believes us to be in ignorance of it. If we were to run away he'd immediately guess that somehow we'd found him out; whereas by staying on we may be able to trap him before he makes up his mind to strike at us.'

Simon nodded vigorously. 'Um. After all, we've come thousands of miles to find him, so now that he's taken you into his house it would be silly to clear out.'

Marie Lou passed a hand over her eyes. 'Perhaps you're right. I don't know. I'm so tired I can hardly think any longer, but you and Philippa look quite fresh apart from your sun-burns. You must have slept last night.'

'Um,' Simon nodded again. 'Can't say I had a good night; I was too worried about all of you. 'Fraid I'd never see any of you any more. But after it got too dark for us to look for you any longer out there in the bay, we found beds all right, in the house of a Roman Catholic missionary.'

De Richleau's face suddenly lit up and his grey eyes flashed with something of their old brilliance. 'I've got it!' he cried. 'You can give us details as to how you found us here, later. The fact that you slept last night is the one thing that matters at the moment. I'm now more certain than ever that you were sent to us in our extremity as the result of my call. Marie Lou and I are dead-beat. I doubt if we could have hung out till morning, but we'll be able to pull through if we can get even a short spell. This is what you're to do:

'You'll go out of the house again and enter it by the doors of the big living-room. If Doctor Saturday is still there— well and good; if not, you'll call out until one of the house-boys comes on the scene and gets him for you. You'll pre-sent yourselves to the Doctor as two people who were tra-velling with us in the wrecked plane but not actually in our party, and describe how you got ashore in the rubber-boat. You'll then say that having arrived in Port-au-Prince you heard that we were here and so came straight up to con-gratulate us on our escape. The Doctor will naturally send for us and we'll have a nice little formal reunion. You will intimate that you haven't arranged for any accommodation in the town and he'll offer you beds. Soon afterwards, Marie Lou and I will again excuse ourselves on account of the long day we've had, then it will be your job to keep the Doc-tor up for as long as you possibly can while we get a few hours' sleep.'

'Splendid,' sighed Marie Lou, 'oh, splendid!'

'Talk to the Doctor about Haiti and its customs,' the Duke went on. 'Get him on to Voodoo. Ask him about the *Cochon Gris*, cannibalism and Zombies. He enjoys talking about his pet subject so you ought to be able to keep him up until two or three o'clock in the morning, while we get a respite. You'll probably have to pull us out of bed to wake us when you do come to bed yourselves; but that doesn't matter. We'll have gained new vitality in the inter-val and be able to carry on until Richard and Rex turn up. By the by, I'm supposed to be a scientist who is interested in native customs, and Marie Lou is my niece who helps me with my notes. Rex and Richard are two British agents who, although they arrived here with us, had to leave almost at once because they had urgent business with the British Consul. The Doctor believes that they're staying with him. Is that all clear?'

'Um,' said Simon. 'I'll keep the swine up till three o'clock anyhow.'

Philippa had made no contribution to the swift discussion but she meekly followed Simon as he left the room by the window.

Marie Lou returned to her own bedroom, while de Rich-

leau waited in his, until some seven minutes later Doctor
Saturday came down the passage and called out to them
that two friends of theirs, who had been wrecked with them
in the plane, had just arrived.

In the interval the Duke had partially undressed, as though
he was just about to go to bed. Opening his door he put out
his head and showed himself as he expressed delight and
said that he would be along in a minute. As soon as he had
got his clothes on again, Marie Lou joined him and they
hurried to the big living-room, where the sinisterly hospitable Doctor had already installed Simon and Philippa in
comfortable chairs and was just mixing drinks for them.

Each party congratulated the other on its escape, and
after saying how pleased they were at meeting again they
began to tell each other what had happened to them since
they had been separated.

It transpired that the coast of Gonave had not been as
distant as Rex had imagined and that Philippa and Simon
had reached it in less than two hours, but only to find themselves on a desolate shore along which they had had to plod
under a blazing sun for an hour and a half until at last they
had come to a fishing-village. There, with Philippa's help,
Simon had raised among the natives a number of willing
volunteers who had put out to hunt for the wreck in three
fishing-boats, but although they had searched the channel
until darkness had put an end to their anxious scanning of
the waters they had been unable to find any trace of the
wrecked plane.

The boat with Simon and Philippa had put back into a
small port further along the coast, called Anse à Galets,
which proved to be the principal town of the island, and
the natives had taken them to the house of the Catholic
Priest, who was the only white man resident there.

The Priest had done his best to console them for the tragic
loss of their friends, as by that time they were quite convinced that the others had been drowned. All the same,
Simon had insisted on conducting another search of the
channel on the following morning and had not given up
until late that afternoon, when another boat had landed
them in Port-au-Prince. Feeling that there was still an outside chance that his friends had beeen picked up and taken
there, he had made inquiries at some of the little cafés along

235

the harbour front. At the third he had learnt, to his great joy, that all four of his fellow-passengers had come ashore with Doctor Saturday on the previous afternoon and had gone up to his house with him; so, having obtained directions, he and Philippa had set off up the hill to join them.

'You have not arranged for any accommodation in the town, then?' said the Doctor.

'Ner,' Simon shook his head. 'We only landed an hour ago and came straight here from the harbour. I do hope you don't mind our butting in on you like this?'

'Not in the least,' replied the Doctor suavely. 'It is a pleasure to receive you here, and I hope that you will not think of going down to the town again tonight. There are the two guest-rooms which your other friends were to have occupied, so you must please make use of them and stay as long as you like.'

'Thanks most awfully. That's terribly good of you.' Simon's geniality almost outmatched the Doctor's.

It then occurred to the Doctor that his two new guests might not yet have eaten, and upon inquiry that proved to be the case; so in spite of their protests he insisted on going off to get his house-boys out of bed to serve some cold food.

While the Doctor was absent, de Richleau whispered his congratulations on the way in which Simon had handled the situation and told him that he and Marie Lou would slip away as soon as they could, so as to get as long a sleep as possible.

When the Doctor returned the Duke stood up at once, and as he and Marie Lou had already pleaded fatigue, nearly an hour before, their host did not seek to detain them. Having said how much they would look forward to seeing the others again in the morning, the two of them went to their rooms. No sooner were they in them than with a sigh of thankfulness they dropped, clothed as they were, upon their beds and fell into the deep sleep of exhaustion.

When the cold meats, flanked by dishes of mangoes, custard-apples, grape-fruit, sliced pineapple, papaws, bananas and avocado pears, were served, Simon noted with satisfaction that Philippa's healthy appetite had not been impaired by finding herself in such sinister company but he could spare her no special attention at the moment as his fertile brain was already working overtime.

236

While he ate he made polite conversation with the Doctor, but secretly he was also busy assessing in his mind what the Doctor's reactions would be to this new set-up. If he suspected the trick that was being played upon him he certainly showed no indication of it, as he had not betrayed the slightest sign of annoyance when the Duke and Marie Lou had said that they were going to bed. Yet if Marie Lou was right, and Doctor Saturday was indeed the enemy, he must know much of their hopes and fears.

He would certainly not have swallowed the tale that the Duke was Marie Lou's uncle and that Rex and Richard were two British agents who had come to Haiti on urgent business with the British Consul; or that the three couples were separate parties who had only joined up to make the trip in the plane from Miami to Port-au-Prince. He must be perfectly well aware that all six of them had set out from England together and that with the exception of Philippa they were the group who had already begun operations against him from Cardinals Folly.

In that case he would certainly have guessed that Richard and Rex were not staying with the British Consul but had been sent off by the Duke for some special purpose. There had then to be faced the grim possibility that the Satanist knew where they had gone and why, and would strive to bring about their death by another attack before they could get back to the island. If that occurred the remainder of the party would be permanently stranded in Haiti with no hope of receiving new supplies of the things that would give them proper astral protection.

Simon wondered if that was the Doctor's game—to let them hope on for the help that would never come, until they all dropped asleep from utter exhaustion. He wondered, too, why it was that having had the Duke and Marie Lou, all unsuspecting, in his house for over twenty-four hours he had not taken the opportunity to poison them by inserting something in their food, but he thought that he knew the answer to that question.

Doctor Saturday would kill his antagonists only as a last extremity, because by poisoning them he could only cut short their present incarnation; whereas if he waited until he could get the better of them on the astral he might be able to capture their spirits and force them to work on his behalf.

Pondering such possibilities between swift, amiable snatches of conversation in which he gave a vague fake account of Philippa and himself, solely because he knew that he would be expected to do so, Simon could at first see no reason why the Doctor should not have drugged his guests in order swiftly and efficiently to overcome their resistance, but after a moment he thought that he knew the answer to that one too.

Nearly all Satanists are sadists who derive great enjoyment from inflicting both physical and mental torture. It was highly probable that the Doctor considered that he had the situation completely in hand. If so, he was doubtless deriving a devilish pleasure from the knowledge that Marie Lou and the Duke had been compelled to suffer such torments to keep awake so long, and during the day he had probably been thoroughly enjoying the spectacle of their becoming more and more exhausted.

But if that was the case would the present trick defeat him? It would certainly not do so if Rex and Richard failed to arrive within the next twenty-four hours, as four hours' sleep out of sixty-four would be totally inadequate to sustain de Richleau and Marie Lou, and by then Philippa and Simon himself would also be at the end of their tether.

That, Simon decided grimly, was the game. The Doctor meant to prevent the reappearance of Rex and Richard then quietly enjoy the agony endured by the rest of them as they tried to keep awake all through the next day. If he was right—and Simon now felt convinced that he was—they were in a more desperate situation than any that they had ever encountered; but he had a stout heart in his frail body and the common-sense belief in tackling each situation as it arose.

His job now was to keep the Doctor awake for as long as possible, and if the Satanist was aware of what was going on it might prove even easier to keep him talking till two or three, for he would know quite well that an hour or two's sleep for de Richleau and Marie Lou could not possibly prevent the total collapse of all four of his victims by the following evening.

When the supper things had been cleared away they

settled down in comfortable chairs and Simon, to test out the ground, said: 'D'you know, it's an extraordinary thing but I don't feel the least bit sleepy although I was up soon after dawn. As a matter of fact, I rarely go to bed before one or two in the morning, so, if you're not too tired, Doctor, I'd be awfully interested to hear something of this strange island.'

Doctor Saturday gave his courteous little bow. 'I should be delighted to talk for an hour or two. I myself require very little sleep, and when I'm alone I often work in my study until the small hours of the morning. Please don't dream of hurrying to bed before you wish to go, on my account.'

As the two of them smiled at each other Simon felt certain that he saw in the Mulatto's eyes a glint of cruel humour, which made him more convinced than ever that he was right. The Doctor was so confident of his victory that he was perfectly happy to let them think that they were fooling him, while mentally preening himself upon being the big cat who was playing a game with four wretched little mice which he could gobble up whenever he had a mind to do so.

For quite a time they talked of a number of things—Haiti's abundant fertility, its hidden wealth, crops, climate, history, present form of government, leading men—and it was already past one in the morning when Simon asked:

'Is it true that there's still cannibalism in Haiti and that some of the natives eat human flesh just as their ancestors did before they were brought over from Africa as slaves?'

The Doctor shrugged his bony shoulders. 'You must not think too badly of us. Admittedly the poorer Negroes, who make up the bulk of our population, are still in a very low state of evolution, but they are very far from being savages. In Haiti there are, too, quite a number of educated men who are striving to enlighten the ignorant masses and during the last twenty years have greatly improved conditions here. Their first chance came when they had the backing of the United States Government, which took over the country for a period of nineteen years and has only recently given us back our independence. Having once got a start, these good men have been able to carry on their work, and although

239

cannibalism was rife here in the old days such practices are now much frowned on.'

'How about the *Cochon Gris*?' Simon asked.

Doctor Saturday shot him a swift look from beneath his beetling white brows and replied with another question. 'How did you come to hear of that?'

'Priest who put us up in Anse à Galets mentioned it to me last night.'

The Doctor lowered his eyes as he said slowly: 'The *Cochon Gris* is a thing that we do not talk of here; it is dangerous to do so—except, of course, at a time like this, among a group of friends, when none of the servants are about. It is, as you are evidently aware, a secret society, and I do not seek to conceal from you that its members practise cannibalism. But you must understand that it is not just a matter of eating human flesh for its own sake; the practice is an ancient ritual connected with the worship of the Mondongo gods which was brought over from the Congo. All decent people—Voodoo worshippers as well as Christians —hold the society in horror, and some years ago the most enlightened men in Haiti formed a league for its suppression.'

'They haven't had much luck so far, from what the Catholic priest told me.'

'There are great difficulties,' the Doctor spread out his hands. 'During the period of the French occupation all the Negroes were enslaved, so they were able to carry on these horrible rites only with great difficulty, but after the slaves gained their freedom—which occurred in Napoleonic times —it became much easier for them to travel from place to place and so attend such ceremonies. Consequently the cult spread, and in the 1860's it had gained an alarming hold over the whole population. During the Revolution the Roman Catholic priests had been killed or driven out with the other Whites, and for many years no Europeans were allowed even to land in the island; but the Catholic Church is very clever and in the '80's they recruited a number of coloured Fathers from the French possessions in Africa, and sent them here. These—and later the white Fathers, when they were allowed to settle in Haiti again—fought the *Cochon Gris*—or the *Secte Rouge*, as many people call it— with the utmost determination; so that by the opening of the present century its power had waned and it was driven underground. Nevertheless it is generally admitted that it still exists, and it is even whispered that some of the wealthiest people in Haiti are members.'

'Can't the police do anything about it?' Simon suggested. 'Surely cannibalism implies murder?'

'The trouble is that no one knows who belongs to this dreaded society, and it is certain death for any member who recants or is even suspected of lukewarmness once he has been initiated into the mystery. An indiscreet word is enough for the Sect to decide on the execution of anyone who might become an informer. That is why everyone here is so frightened of even speaking of the *Cochon Gris* in public. These people are absolutely unscrupulous and most averse to any mention at all being made of their activities or even existence; so you will see the wisdom of any ordinary person denying all knowledge of the society, when the penalty of careless talk may be to be dragged out of one's house one night and murdered in a peculiarly horrible manner.'

'How?'

'Backsliders or suspects are taken out to sea in a boat. One of the adepts smashes their right ear with a blow from a large stone. Poison is then rubbed into the bleeding flesh and the victims are thrown overboard, so even if they were sufficiently strong swimmers to reach the shore they'd die an hour or so later from the effects of the poison. Why this particular method of ensuring their captives' death should be used, when they could quite well knife or strangle them, I do not know; but that, according to report, is the inevitable practice followed from long custom.'

'Have you—er—ever attended one of their meetings—as a scientist, I mean?' Simon inquired with considerable boldness.

'Unless I myself were a member of the *Secte Rouge*, had I done so I should certainly not have lived to tell the tale,' the Doctor replied. And Simon noted that although from the Doctor's tone and smile, the implication was that he obviously was not a member, he had in fact hedged rather cleverly, and the probability was that it amused him to turn his phrases thus skilfully instead of telling a direct lie.

'However,' the Doctor went on, with an unexpected honesty, 'I have means of screwing information out of the natives, which the police do not possess, and as a man of science I am interested in all their customs, so I can describe for you what takes place at one of these meetings.'

The night outside was very still. Even the cicadas had ceased their chirping and a brooding silence hung over the mysterious land. In it the Doctor's every word was clear as he began to describe these barbarous ancient rites which might even at that moment be reaching their revolting culmination, at a place no more than a few miles distant, out there in the darkness.

'The members have facilities, which few people understand, for travelling very swiftly and they come from all parts of the island. Each one carries with him a *sac paille* containing ceremonial raiment. They meet at the Hounfort of a Bocor—that is, a priest who specialises in devil-worship. Actually, as far as the ordinary people are concerned, there is no way in which they can tell if their local Houngan is also a Bocor or not, and a Houngan may practise the usual Voodoo rites for many years without any of his congregation suspecting that he is a Bocor. On the other hand, certain of them have definitely acquired that reputation though there is never any means of proving it.

'A little before midnight the members assemble in the Hounfort, which is a compound surrounded by a number of small thatched houses. To see them then one might imagine that they were just ordinary people getting ready for a Voodoo service, but at a given signal they all begin to robe themselves. The Bocor plays the part of the Emperor and his Mambo that of the Queen. Others of the principal adepts fill the roles of the President, the Minister, the Cuisiniers, the Officers and the Bourresouse, which is a special guard composed of men picked for their speed and strength. The ceremonial vestments are very rich and strange and they have the effect of giving the whole assembly the appearance of demons with tails and horns. Some of them appear as dogs, goats and cocks, but most of them as grey pigs—hence the name of the society.'

'Sounds like a Witches' Sabbath in Europe,' Simon commented, recalling, with a shudder that he strove to suppress, a Walpurgis Eve ceremony in which he had once participated on Salisbury Plain.

The Doctor nodded. 'From such books as I have read on Witchcraft, you are right. When everyone is robed the drums begin to beat, but they have not the deep singing quality of the Rada drums; it is a keen, high-pitched note. To the rhythm of the drums they begin to dance, working themselves up into a frenzy, then each lights a candle and chanting a liturgy of Hell they depart for the nearest crossroad, bearing a small coffin which has scores of candles on it and is the symbol of their Order.

'At the crossroads they set down the coffin and perform a ceremony to the Petro god, Baron Carrefour, asking him, as Lord of the Roads and Travel, to favour them by sending them many victims. Soon one of the adepts becomes possessed, which is a sign that Baron Carrefour is willing to grant their request.

'Then they dance and prance down the highway to the cemetery, where they call upon Baron Cimeterre to give them success in their undertakings. Each person with his or her hand on the hip of the person in front and with a lighted candle in the other they advance through the gates. The youngest adept is stretched upon a tomb and all the lighted candles are placed round him. A bowl made from half a calabash is set upon his navel, and, placing the palms of their hands together, they all dance and sing as they move round the tomb until each person has returned to the place in which he has set up his own candle.

'The congregation cover their eyes while the Queen leaves the cemetery. The youngest adept rises and follows her, after which the others come streaming out. They then take up their positions on some lonely stretch of highway between two towns, from one to another of which it is certain that travellers will be passing. The Bourresouse, or hunters, are sent out in different directions and each group often covers many miles, while the Bocor and his assistants wait on the highway to waylay anyone who may come along it. The hunters carry with them cords, which are made from the dried intestines of human beings. These pieces of gut are very strong, and with them they bind and finally strangle the unfortunate wretches whom they succeed in catching. In the early hours of the morning the hunters return with two, three or perhaps half a dozen victims. These are then taken to the Hounfort, where the Bocor performs the ceremony of changing them into cows, pigs, goats, etc., after which they are killed and their flesh is divided among the congregation.'

'Phew!' Simon whistled. 'What a party! I certainly shan't go walking about the roads alone at night while I'm in Haiti. But surely, with all this light and noise, it would be easy enough for the police to locate and break up the meetings if they really had a mind to it?'

The Doctor shook his head. 'One would think that it would be easy for the police to put down the racketeers in the United States, which is a highly civilised country, but even there the G-men have found great difficulty in stamping out the well-organised and powerful gangs. From that you may judge how infinitely more difficult it is for law-abiding people to do so in Haiti. Each man fears that he may call down upon himself the most unwelcome attention of the *Secte Rouge*—the Negro police themselves not less than others. So all but a very few brave ones fight shy of having anything to do with this horrible business.'

For over an hour the talk turned on racketeers and secret societies not only in the United States but all over the world. With considerable satisfaction Simon noted that it was close on three o'clock and the Doctor still showed no signs of weariness. Turning a little, he glanced at Philippa.

He was by now used to the perpetual silence which she was forced to observe, but she had had her handbag with her when she had scrambled out of the wrecked plane so she was still in possession of her tablet, and it occurred to him that she had not written anything upon it the whole evening, confining herself to nods whenever she had been addressed. She had been sitting there impassively for over four hours, her round eyes fixed on their sinister host. He wondered if she was very tired, but did not like to ask her in front of the Doctor so he laid his hand gently on her arm and said:

'You feeling all right?'

Her large eyes seemed quite blank as she turned towards him, but she nodded twice and, looking away, lit a cigarette. It was his job to keep Doctor Saturday up as long as possible, so he swiftly put Philippa out of his mind and brought the conversation back to Haiti.

'Pretty awful fate to be caught by those Grey Pig people but even worse to be turned into a Zombie.'

244

'So you know about Zombies also?' said the Doctor with a slightly amused glance.

'Um,' Simon nodded. 'Not much, but the Priest told me something about them. They're bodies without souls—sort of Vampires, aren't they?'

'Hardly that. But it is another subject that is normally taboo in Haiti, as we are ashamed to let the outer world know that such awful things still go on here.'

'What is the difference?' Simon's eyes flickered quickly over the Doctor's face. 'That is, if you don't mind talking about it in private?'

'The only resemblance between a Vampire and a Zombie is that both are dead and have been buried yet have left their graves after their mourning families have departed. A Vampire is said to live in its grave but leave it each night in search of human victims, and it keeps life in its body by sucking the blood from living people—like a human bat.

'A Zombie, on the other hand, is one who is called back from the dead, and once it has left its grave it never returns to it but continues as the bond slave of the sorcerer who holds its soul captive. A Zombie possesses the same physical strength as it had before it sickened and died, and it sustains its vitality with ordinary human food which it is given in the hovel in which it lies imprisoned during the daytime. I say "prison", but that is not really the right word, because no bolts and bars are needed to keep a Zombie captive. They cannot speak, they have no reasoning powers, and they cannot recognise even the people who were dearest to them when they were alive. For them there is no escape; and they do not seek it; they labour night after night, year in year out, in the banana plantations, or at any other task which is set them, like poor blind beasts.'

'How—how frightful!' muttered Simon.

The Doctor nodded his white head. 'And it is even more frightful for a family which respects that one of its members has been turned into a Zombie. Think of it. Someone you love very dearly—your wife or your sister, perhaps—and whom you have always cherished and surrounded with every comfort, suddenly, to your great sorrows, falls ill and dies. Even if you are poor you stint yourself to make the best funeral arrangements you can afford, and afterwards you try to assuage your sorrow

245

by thinking of that person sleeping peacefully in the grave, relieved of all earthly cares and worries. Then, a year or perhaps two years later, you hear a whisper that your loved one has been seen and recognised, covered with lice and dressed in filthy rags, bowed down with weariness, stumbling away from some plantation in a distant part of the island one morning in the grey light of dawn.

'Your whole being cries out to go there, to rescue them, even though you know that if you could find them they would stare at you without a trace of recognition in their blank eyes. But you dare not do so. You know that if you attempted to seek them out the Witch Doctor who has enslaved them would learn of it and that before long you, too, would sicken and die and he would make a Zombie out of you.'

Fascinated against his will by this macabre subject, Simon inquired: 'How are the victims selected? I mean, are there any special qualifications which the Witch Doctor seeks in a person whom he decides to turn into a Zombie?'

'None; except that the man or woman concerned should not be too old for the labour required of them—usually work in the fields. And there are a number of reasons for making Zombies. For an unscrupulous man it is a good way of acquiring labour, since Zombies do not have to be paid; they have only to be fed, and any sort of garbage will do, providing it contains enough goodness to support their strength. Again, if one hates a person sufficiently, what could be a more subtle and satisfactory form of revenge than to go to a Bocor and have one's enemy turned into a Zombie? Quite frequently, too, people are made Zombies as a result of a *ba Moun* ceremony.'

'What's that?'

'*Ba Moun* means "Give man", and there is a definite similarity in it to the medieval European practice of selling oneself to the Devil. A poor man who is very ambitious, but sees no hope whatever of improving his status by normal means, may decided to go to a Bocor and ask for the help of the evil gods. Under the altar in every Hounfort there are jars containing the spirits of one or more long-dead Houngans and the more powerful Bocors possess many such jars. These spirits are invoked, and when the right offerings have been made to them they begin to groan; then the inquirer knows that the evil gods are prepared to listen to his supplication. He signs a deed in his own blood and puts it with money into one of the jars. He is then given a little box. The priest tells him that this contains some small animals and that he must look after them and tend them each night as though they were a portion of himself.'

'There's a similarity between that part of the affair and the toads and lizards and cats and owls which Witches in Europe used to keep as their familiars,' Simon cut in, and with a nod of agreement the Doctor proceeded.

'A bargain is struck by which the evil gods will prosper the man's affairs for a certain time but he agrees to surrender himself to them at the end of that period, and he is warned that, if he fails to do so, upon the third night after the expiration of the pact the little animals will become huge, malignant beasts which will devour him. There is, however, one way in which he can escape payment, at least for a time, and this is by giving some other member of his family to become a Zombie instead of himself. The pact is then automatically renewed for a further period, but the person given must be someone whom he holds dear and thus a definite sacrifice made by him. People have been known to give their whole families in this way—sons, daughters, nieces, nephews, parents, until they have no one left—hoping each time that they will die a natural death before the next payment is due; and often they commit suicide rather than face payment of the debt themselves.'

'That's a pretty grim picture,' Simon commented, 'but I suppose it applies only to the most ignorant and superstitious of the Negroes?'

'Not at all.' Doctor Saturday's white teeth flashed in a grim smile. 'That they may one day be turned into a Zombie is the dread of every man and woman in Haiti, from the blackest Negro to the lightest-skinned Mulatto. It is a fear that is ever present in the minds of even the richest, because there are other uses to which Zombies can be put beside working in the fields. Not long ago one of the loveliest young Mulatto girls in Haiti died with mysterious suddenness, and eighteen months later she was found one night wandering in the streets of Port-au-Prince. Her mind

247

was blank, and she was dumb, so she could not tell her story, but it was a curious coincidence that a very rich Negro, who had wished to marry her when she was alive, but whom her parents had rejected for her with scorn, had died only the day before she was found. I have good reason to believe that as he could not get her by marriage he paid a powerful Bocor to turn her into a Zombie, received her back from the grave after her resurrection and took his pleasure with her whenever he wished, keeping her hidden in his house. Then, when he died, his wife, wanting to be rid of the girl, turned her adrift.'

'What happened to her?' asked Simon.

'Naturally her family was most anxious to hush the matter up, so the nuns took charge of her and she was smuggled away by night, in a ship that was leaving for France, to enter a convent. But the Bocor who made her a Zombie would still have the power to bring her back to Haiti if he wished, and if he were a very powerful occultist he would also have the power to animate her brain and put into it such thoughts as he wished to express, even at a very great distance; though it would not be possible for him to enable her to speak.'

Suddenly the Doctor's manner changed. He stood up abruptly. From veiled mockery his tone hardened to one of open enmity and contempt, as he said:

'I have amused myself by talking to you for long enough, Mr. Aron. I am now going to bed and to sleep. When you wake your friends and they renew their struggle to escape meeting me upon the astral they may gain a short respite from the interest which I'm sure they will feel if you repeat to them what I have told you about Zombies—particularly the story of the beautiful Haitian girl who was sent to France. I was the Bocor in that instance, and in order to keep a watch upon you all, through her, during your journey it suited me very well to bring her back to Haiti.'

For a moment Simon did not catch the full implication of what Doctor Saturday had said, then his heart stood still. He slowly turned his head and stared at Philippa.

19

The Living Corpse

The beautiful dumb girl was sitting there without a trace of expression on her face. If she had heard the Doctor's words she showed no sign of it whatever, and it suddenly came to Simon that apart from eating the food which had been set before her at supper she had not made a single self-initiated action since she had entered the Doctor's house.

Even as he struggled against the bewildering horror of the situation his swift brain was working again. If, as the Mulatto had said, she was indeed a Zombie whose brain he had power to animate and direct even at a distance, he could presumably also empty it and leave it blank at will. Every idea that Phillippa had expressed by writing on her tablet since they had first met her on Waterloo station, nearly a week before, had, therefore, been pure persiflage—just a meaningless froth of written words—not in anyway expressing the personality that she had been in her true self two years or more ago, but conventional phrases having just enough individuality to convey to her unwitting companions the sort of person whom the Doctor *wished* them to believe her to be.

They had it only from her that she had been struck dumb by a bomb which had fell on a hospital in which she was nursing, and evidently that was quite untrue; yet it was just the sort of story that their clever enemy would have caused the girl to tell, knowing it to be a certain winner in gaining their sympathy for her. That other business, too, about her having lived in Jamaica and having had an uncle who had taken her all over the West Indies, was also a fabrication of the Doctor's, put out through her solely to enable her to remain in their company so that she could continue to act as a focus for him to keep an easy watch upon them.

Kaleidoscopic pictures of himself and the girl together during the last few days flickered wildly before Simon's mental eyes. He had held her hand and danced with her, and had it not been for his terrible anxiety about his friends on the previous night, so that his mind was capable of thinking of nothing else during those frightful hours when he did not know if they were dead or alive, he would certainly have made love to her; yet she was a dead thing —a body without a soul—something that had come back out of the grave.

As he stared at her smooth, faintly dusky cheeks and rich red lips, that seemed impossible; and yet, now that he knew, he had a great feeling of revulsion. There was something rather repellent in her apparent full-blooded healthiness, and he felt that even to touch her would now fill him with nausea. At the same time he was conscious of an overwhelming pity for her—or rather ,for the person that she had been before she had been robbed of her soul.

The lovely thing at which he was staring was only a lump of 'human' clay, animated entirely by a tiny portion of another extraordinary powerful will. Somewhere the girl's spirit must be imprisoned, suffering all the tortures of one that was neither in incarnation nor out of it, that could neither enjoy that tranquil period after the completion of a life on Earth nor go forth as a free spirit to animate another human body; but must watch in an agony of misery the uses to which the body that she could no longer control should be put, until some fatal accident or disease of the flesh rendered that body no longer tenable for the alien entity which had taken possession of it.

Another thought struck Simon. As long as he had imagined that he had the dumb girl's companionship he had not been afraid of the Doctor, although he was perfectly well aware that she could have done little to protect him—just as a man walking through a jungle at night might be comforted by the presence of his dog, although that dog could not guard him from the bite of a snake or a panther's spring. The others were sleeping, and so deeply that he doubted if his loudest shout would wake them. Philippa was not even a friendly animal, but a puppet in human form animated by the will of his enemy, and he was utterly alone with the malignant Satanist.

All those thoughts had rushed through his brain like lightning. At the last of them he had felt a sudden impulse to spring from his chair and dash in terror from the house, but resisted it; and, by the law that all resistance to Evil brings added strength, a new thought leapt into his mind. 'You fool! Your case is no worse now than it has been the whole evening. You had made a plan, and Philippa had no part to play in it. Therefore this frightful disclosure of the Doctor's makes no difference. He told you about Philippa only to terrify you. Don't let him succeed. Carry on as you meant to; as though he had not mentioned it, but had just announced—as you expected him to do sooner or later— that he was going to bed.'

Simon's plan was a very simple one and he had hatched it hours before. He was quite capable of following and taking part in a discussion while at the same time thinking of someone completely different, and during the whole session the Doctor had done nine-tenths of the talking, so Simon had had ample opportunity to consider the situation from every angle.

He was now absolutely convinced that when the Doctor went to sleep he did not mean to bother about the enemies that he had lured into his house; he would go out to lie in wait for Rex and Richard. If he could prevent their return he would be able to deal with the others at his leisure and during the coming day would derive a sadistic delight from watching them show signs of ever-increasing fatigue until they finally succumbed. Simon had decided that the best service he could possibly render, and indeed, as far as he could see, the only one which offered any hope of saving them all, was to carry the war into the enemy's camp. At whatever risk to himself, he must endeavour to sabotage the Doctor's plan so that Richard and Rex could escape his attack and manage to rejoin them.

According to what de Richleau had said, since their two friends had failed to return before sundown, and there were no night-landing facilities at Port-au-Prince, there was now no hope of their arriving until dawn. Evidently the Doctor had taken that into his calculations—hence his willingness to stay up talking until the small hours. He knew that the other would not take off from Kingston airport until two hours before sunrise; so, providing he was asleep by five or even six o'clock he would still have ample time in which to attack them during the latter half of their journey. Simon had set himself the task of keeping the Doctor awake until well after sun-up and he had spent a considerable portion of the last few hours in thinking of methods which might best enable him to do so.

Had his gun not gone down with the plane he would have been extremely tempted to whip it out and shoot the Doctor where he stood, taking a chance that, de Richleau and Marie Lou being asleep, their astrals were in the immediate neighbourhood. They could then have seized upon the Evil spirit at the moment of black-out immediately following death and have imprisoned it, thus accomplishing in one daring stroke the victory that they had set out to gain. But if the astrals of his friends were not in the vicinity the Doctor's spirit would escape and, since they had no protection, would have *them* at his mercy. So the risk was great. But in any case he had no gun or other means of meting out swift death to the Satanist, so he was not called upon to gamble with the fate of them all.

The obvious course was to endeavour to wound the Doctor or to hurt him so much that he would be unable to sleep on account of the pain; but that was easier said than done. The Mulatto had the appearance of a man of about sixty but he was powerfully built, and Simon, who was very frail, felt certain that he would get the worst of any physical encounter. Only a surprise attack could inflict the requisite type of injury, and such an attack is not easy when one's opponent is fully aware of one's animosity, quick-witted and prepared for any eventuality.

Nevertheless Simon was a redoubtable opponent when he set his shrewd brain to work and he had taken considerable care to review every portion of the human body in relation both to the pain it can give when harmed and to its accessibility for swift attack.

In those desperate minutes after the Doctor's revelation about Philippa, Simon had kept his eyes cast down so that his enemy should not be able to read his thoughts. Suddenly he lifted his right foot knee-high and, with all the force he was capable brought the point of his heel crashing down upon the Satanist's left instep.

The Mulatto staggered back, his face contorted with agony. The sharp heel-edge had dug right down into the delicate tendons of his instep, just above his shoe-lace, and as Simon ground the hard edge home one of the small fragile bones which make up the arch of the foot snapped under the stab.

As the Doctor dragged free his foot he panted slightly and his eyes seemed to start out of his yellow face with the intensity of their malevolence. He made no move to strike at Simon, but lifting his injured foot he whispered: 'By Baron Cimeterre, I swear you shall pay for that.'

But Simon had only started. The infliction of the wound was less than half his plan. Seizing the large oil-lamp from the table, he picked it up and hurled it at the Doctor's head.

By ducking the Doctor escaped the dangerous missile but under the suddenness and violence of the attack he gave back and turned to stagger from the room. The lamp crashed in a far corner and the oil ran out in a sheet of flame which greedily leapt up the flimsy curtains. Next moment Simon had jumped upon a chair. There was another oil-lamp, swinging from a beam in the centre of the room. Wrenching this away from its sockets—holder and all—he hurled that, too, after his retreating enemy.

The second lamp also missed the Doctor, but as it burst, another great pool of flaming oil ran across the wooden floor, devouring the rush mats as it went. In a few moments the house would be on fire, just as Simon had deliberately planned that it should be.

'Now, damn you, sleep if you can!' Simon screamed, and, leaping from the chair, he rushed out of the room to rouse de Richleau and Marie Lou.

They were sleeping as they had fallen, fully dressed, upon their beds, and at first Simon thought that he would never be able to wake them. He shouted at Marie Lou and pulled her up into a sitting position, but she only flopped back again with a little groan. Desperate measures were necessary and he had to smack her face hard before an semblance of consciousness returned to her. The Duke proved equally difficult to rouse, and five precious minutes had fled before Simon had them both on their feet and they had taken in his garbled account of what had happenned.

Still half-asleep, the other two stumbled after him as he raced back to the living-room. During the whole of his brief, violent attack on the Doctor, Philippa had not moved a muscle; she had just remained sitting in her chair, staring blankly in front of her. The fire had taken a rapid hold upon the wooden buildings and as they entered the sitting-room they saw that it was now half-obscured by flames and smoke. Philippa's chair was empty, but suddenly she emerged from the centre of the smoke-screen. Evidently she had tried to follow the Doctor to his room but had been unable to do so.

As she lurched towards them they momentarily recoiled in horror. Her great eyes were staring, her mouth was wide open in a strangled scream, but no sound came from it. Her hair and her clothes were on fire and she seemed distraught with agony.

In a second, de Richleau had off his coat and flung it round her, while Marie Lou and Simon strove to beat out the flames from her burning skirt with their bare hands. Somehow they succeeded, just before she fainted and slid down among them to the floor.

The greater part of the room was now a glowing furnace and the only door as yet unattacked by the crackling flames was that leading to the guests' bedrooms. The Duke and Simon grabbed Philippa up and, pulling her through it, carried her out by way of the nearest room on to the verandah.

Further along it they could see the fire had already spread to the dining-room and that unless it was swiftly checked it would soon be devouring the Doctor's bedroom and study. They could hear him, somewhere on the other side of the pall of smoke and flying sparks, shouting to his house-boys, and the sound of heavy running feet. For one brief moment Simon allowed himself to savour his triumph as he exclaimed viciously:

'Not much chance of that swine getting to sleep tonight now.' Then he turned his attention back to the poor, soulless body that they knew as Philippa.

De Richleau was already examining her and he said despondently: 'The poor girl's got terrible burns on her head, arms and legs. We must get her down to the hospital as quickly as we possibly can.'

'She—she's not a girl at all—she's a Zombie,' Simon jerked out. 'Doctor Saturday told me—said so himself just before I went for him.'

'What's a Zombie?' asked Marie Lou in a puzzled voice.

De Richleau answered grimly. 'Zombies are bodies without souls—dead people who have been called back from the grave to serve the Witch Doctor who has captured their souls. How utterly frightful!'

In a few swift sentences Simon told them what the Doctor had said of Philippa's history.

The Duke nodded. 'I should think, then, all the house-boys are Zombies too. But although Zombies can't talk they can feel, so this wretched body that we call Philippa is suffering every bit as much as if the girl's spirit were in it. We must get her to the hospital just the same. Heave her up, Simon, over my shoulders. It's only about quarter of an hour's walk down to the edge of the town and with any luck we'll meet help on the way.'

They bundled Philippa's body across the Duke's back in a fireman's lift and bowed under her weight he staggered down the verandah steps with Marie Lou leading the way and Simon behind to protect the small party's rear. To carry the body was a considerable effort for the Duke, and every hundred yards or so he had to rest for a moment, but when they had covered half a mile they met an early market-cart which was coming down a forked road towards the town.

Although they could not speak Creole the great fat mammy who was driving grasped the situation and helped to arrange the unconscious form upon her bunches of vegetables. Whipping her miserable donkey into an ambling trot, she drove straight to the hospital, while the others ran and walked beside the little cart.

At the hospital they were relieved of her charge by a Mulatto nurse, who wao called a Negro house-surgeon.

After what they had heard of Haiti it was a pleasant surprise to find that the hospital at least would have rivalled
any European institution in a similar-sized town for its
cleanliness, its equipment and the evident efficiency of its
staff, all of whom spoke passably good French. Philippa's
charred garments were cut off her and under a light covering she was swiftly wheeled away on a trolley for her burns
to be treated. The others, meanwhile, were asked to sit
down and wait for the surgeon's report in a bare but not
uncomfortable room.

While they waited they discussed the happenings of the
night and de Richleau gave unstinted praise to Simon for
his well-planned, courageous and skilfully-delivered
attack on the enemy.

The Duke said that normally any *Black* as powerful as
the Doctor would be able to overcome his own pain and
throw himself into a self-induced trance, but that having
set fire to his house would almost certainly prevent him
from doing that. He would naturally be extremely anxious
to save the valuable magical impedimenta, which he doubtless kept somewhere in his study, and other possessions, so
the chances were that it would be at least a couple of hours
before he had salvaged what he could and found a room in
some neighbour's house in which to sleep.

Simon had started the fire at about twenty minutes past
three. It was now just on four. Another two hours would
bring them to six, and it would take the Satanist at least
a further hour to subdue the acute pain in his foot before
he could get to sleep; so there was very little likelihood of
his being able to leave his body before seven and the
probability was that he would not succeed in getting out
of it until considerably later. Owing, therefore, to the
skilfulness of Simon's stategy there was good reason to
hope that he would have no time in which to work upon
the astral before dawn, and they all felt confident that Rex
and Richard would set out from Kingston at the earliest
possible moment which would enable them to make a daylight landing at Port-au-Prince.

Half an hour later the Negro surgeon came down to tell
them that Philippa's burns were extremely severe and that
he would not be able to answer for her life, but that it
was difficult to tell yet if she would survive her injuries. He

was a kind and friendly man and, seeing their depressed state, insisted on one of the nurses bringing them some hot coffee laced with rum to put them into better heart. When they had drunk it, he suggested that they should come back in the course of a few hours, by which time he hoped to have further news for them.

It was half-past five when they went out into the street and they saw that the sky was already paling to a faint grey over the mountains to the east. Having walked out of the town and a little way back along the road up to the Doctor's house, they turned a corner, fringed by a great growth of dense vegetation, and suddenly had a full view of it. Any efforts to check the fire had clearly failed. The centre of the house had collapsed, dense smoke was billowing from the building, and its two ends were now a mass of flame, so there was no doubt at all that it must be totally consumed within another hour.

Comforted a little at having inflicted such a grievous blow upon the enemy, they turned back and slowly covered the two miles down to the harbour. Soon after they reached it dawn broke and the sky beyond the hills became a fantastic, fiery sea of vivid reds and golds.

The port was now waking to the coming day. Fishing-boats with worn and patched sails were putting out, the café-keepers were taking down the gimcrack shutters of the bars along the water-front, and a gang of Negroes were chanting melodiously in the distance as they heaved upon the hawsers of a tramp steamer that was just about to put to sea.

De Richleau and his friends stood scanning the sky towards the west, hoping that at any moment now they might discern the speck which would transpire to be Richard and Rex in a hired plane returning to them. For over an hour they waited there, staring out across the blue bay and the coast to either side of the harbour with its fringes of ragged palm trees, many of which had been truncated by a hurricane; but although the sun was up and full daylight flooded the scene, no longed-for speck appeared to gladden their eyes and fill their hearts with new hope.

Owing to Simon's stratagems Marie Lou and the Duke had managed to get in over five hours' sound sleep, so in

spite of the night's excitements they were feeling fairly re-
freshed, but it was now more than twenty-four hours since
Simon himself had slept and he in turn was beginning to
feel very worn and heavy-eyed.

Partly to rouse him up, at half-past seven de Richleau
sent him with Marie Lou back to the hospital to inquire
for Philippa, remaining on watch himself. By eight o'clock
they rejoined him with the news that the surgeon had said
that her injuries were too severe for her to recover and that
he thought she would die during the course of the morning.

'That may not sound good news on the face of it,'
grunted the Duke, 'but it is so, all the same. We ourselves
must see to it, though, that this time the poor thing is
really dead and that her body can never again be reanimated.'

'Could it be?' Marie Lou asked.

'Certainly. She hasn't an injury in any vital part, and
although her burns may have marred her beauty her
physical form is still young and strong. That fiend we're up
against might quite well take her from the grave once more,
this time to work as a slave in the plantations, unless we
take proper steps to prevent him.'

'How will you do that?' inquired Simon.

De Richleau shrugged. 'There are ways. But it is not a
pleasant subject. The main point is that directly the semblance of life departs we must claim her body for burial.
In the meantime let's try and think of more pleasant
things. Breakfast might help.'

None of then had thought of food during these trying
hours, but they now realised that they were all distinctly
hungry, so they went to the least grimy-looking of the small
restaurants on the water-front and did ample justice to
some excellent coffee and a very passable omelette.

It was nearly nine o'clock by the time they had finished
and they were now becoming acutely anxious as to what
had happened to Richard and Rex. Even if they had
waited until dawn to take off in a plane from the Kingston
airport, having been unable to do so before, they should certainly have arrived in Port-au-Prince by now, as even in an
out-of-date machine the journey could easily be accomplished in two hours.

Without any particular interest they all saw a long, low, sea-going launch enter the harbour just as they were finishing their omelette but none of them remarked upon it until Simon spotted that at its stern it was flying the Red Ensign.

No sooner had he pointed it out to the others than two figures came from the launch's cabin and jumped on to the harbour steps, where it was just being tied up. It was their friends. Hastily telling the Negro waiter that they would be back, their faces glowing with delight, they ran across the road to meet them.

Rex was carrying a large suit-case and he waved his free hand in greeting. 'We've got the goods! But Holy Snakes it's good to see you! We've been at our wits' end for hours past thinking we'd be too late.'

'Yes,' beamed Richard, hugging Marie Lou. 'Thank God you're still all right. We reached Kingston at one o'clock yesterday, but all the tea in China wouldn't have got us a plane. There just wasn't one to be had. Luckily we spotted this boat. She's much speedier than the one we went in, so we hired her, and after we'd bought the other things we set off back at once. We made the return trip in just over fifteen hours.'

'Well done!' de Richleau smiled. 'Well done! Marie Lou and I would have been for it last night if Simon hadn't played a magnificent lone hand; but he got us a breather and put an ugly spoke in the enemy's wheel into the bargain.'

'You've managed to identify the enemy, then?' said Richard.

'Good God, yes!' exclaimed the Duke. 'But of course, you don't know—it's that plausible Mulatto, Doctor Saturday. I expect you're both famished, though? Come and sit down and we'll tell you all about it.'

More coffee and eggs were ordered and while the new arrivals ate they were informed what had happened in their absence. All five of them then began to discuss their future plans.

'You had better retain that sea-going launch for the time being, Richard,' suggested the Duke, 'and we'll make her our temporary headquarters.'

'You couldn't possibly get a pentacle twenty-one feet in

259

diameter on her, for our protection tonight.' Richard objected; 'her beam can hardly be as much as that.'

'We could make several smaller ones,' suggested Marie Lou, but the Duke intervened.

'Now we're together again a large one to contain us all would be much more effective, and I doubt if we could get a room of sufficient size in the hotel. There would also be all sorts of other objections to going there. We could, of course, hire an empty house, but that means interviewing agents and going out to see places which may not be suitable; so for the time being it will save us a lot of trouble if we use the launch. When night comes we can run it up on some quite beach and make our pentacle there on the sand above the tide-line. In the meantime I may have another use for it, and it has the added advantage that its crew are Jamaica boys—not Haitians—so they're much less likely to be got at by the Doctor.'

Having paid their reckoning they went to the launch and deposited in it the suitcase which Rex had been carrying. Then the Duke said that they had better go up to the hospital again and wait there until the life which animated Philippa's burnt body left it.

Simon remarked that although he was in no danger of falling asleep he would much prefer to rest a little rather than walk any further, as it was now getting hot, and de Richleau agreed that it was a good idea that someone should stay in the launch to keep an eye on the treasured suitcase; so they left him there and set off through the town once more.

The hospital was only about ten minutes' walk from the harbour, and when they reached it a young coloured medical student told them that Philippa had passed away just before their arrival.

De Richleau said that in that case they would take charge of their friend's body right away if arrangements could be made for some conveyance to remove it. He added the glib lie that as the girl's parents lived in Jamaica they would naturally wish her to be buried there, and speed was important otherwise the body would begin to decompose in the heat before it could be shipped across.

The young internee was both sympathetic and affable and went off to find the surgeon, who, he said, would make out the death certificate and arrange for the ambulance to take the body down to the harbour.

They then waited for nearly twenty minutes, and when at last the surgeon appeared his face was very grave.

'I must apologise,' he began in excellent French, 'for appearing to doubt your right to claim the body of the young girl you brought here early this morning and whose name you gave us as Philippa Ricardi; but a very extraordinary and most disquieting thing has occurred. The girl's face was not badly burnt and one of the nurses felt certain that she recognised her. Our nurse swears that she is Marie Martineau, a girl who was born and brought up in Port-au-Prince and whose history from her nineteenth year is surrounded by considerable mystery. We naturally sent for *Monsieur* and *Madame* Martineau and they were at the girl's bedside before she died. They have definitely identified her as their missing daughter.'

'Did she regain consciousness before she died?' asked the Duke.

'Yes. And, as often in such cases, she had passed beyond the stage of feeling any pain, so her death was a peaceful one.'

'Did she recognise these people who say they are her parents?' de Richleau went on.

'No,' said the surgeon, after a slight hesitation; 'I cannot say that she did. But they are quite definite about her.'

'I think you had better take us to them,' said the Duke.

'Very well.' The surgeon turned and led the way through a passage, up some stairs and into a long, scrupulously clean ward with a wide verandah. At its end a screen had been placed, and behind it a man was standing with his had upon the shoulder of a woman who, giving way to heartbreaking tears, was kneeling at the foot of the bed in which the body lay.

As de Richleau's party rounded the screen they took in the fact that both the man and the woman were Mulattoes well advanced in years. The man was the darker of the two and had been very handsome, his features having a definite resemblance to those of Philippa; while the woman was a characterless bag of fat which appeared to have been poured into the good-quality silk dress that restrained her ample figure.

The surgeon muttered a semi-introduction. *'Monsieur et*

Madame Martineau—these are the people who brought your daughter to the hospital for treatment.'

The elderly Mulatto glared at them as though he would like to have cut their hearts out; while the fat woman suddenly sprang to her feet and screamed in bad French:

'You ghouls—you grave-robbers! Where did you get her? My Marie! Where is the good God that he does not strike you dead for this?'

Trembling with indignant fury she went on: 'We rescued her—she was safe with the good Sisters in Marseilles. Poor little one! They said that she seemed happy in the convent and we paid much money for her keep. May the curse of Hell rest upon you that you brought her back here to the place where she had already suffered so much!'

'Your pardon, *Madame*,' de Richleau said quietly. 'You are, I fear, under an entire misapprehension as the the sort of people we are, and also as to the identity of this dead girl. Her resemblance to your daughter may be very strong, but her name is Philippa Ricardi, and I assure you that you are mistaken in believing her to be the daughter whom you appear to have sent to a convent in Marseilles. I know this girl's father and mother intimately and I have known her since she was a child.'

The lies slipped off his tongue as firmly and readily as the rest of his words and the others could see that the surgeon at least was shaken in his belief that *Monsieur* and *Madame* Martineau were really the bereaved father and mother; but neither of the parents would give way an inch. The woman insisted that Philippa was her daughter and the man, though obviously scared of them, backed her up.

A horrible and degrading scene followed in which for twenty minutes they wrangled over the body of the dead girl, disputing as to who had the right to remove and bury it.

The Martineaus flatly refused to give in, but the Duke was equally adamant. He knew that if they had the girl buried they would probably give her a lavish funeral and the ceremony would be conducted by a Roman Catholoic priest. But that would be no protection against Doctor Saturday's calling her back from the grave twenty-four hours later. De Richleau doubted if anyone in Haiti, except himself, could give her proper protection, and he was absolutely determined to prevent the poor corpse from being made into a Zombie a second time.

Eventually the surgeon intervened. Quieting the Martineaus, he said that, greatly as he regretted the scandal which would result, this had now become a matter for the police. He would not allow either party to remove the body until all concerned had appeared before a magistrate and the court had given its decision as to which party's claim it would sustain.

The Duke now knew that he was up against it. In his own mind he had no doubt whatever that Philippa was the Martineaus' daughter, and that her real name was Marie. The nurse also had recognised her, and in the course of an hour or two the Martineaus would doubtless produce a score of other people who would be prepared to swear to her identity; whereas he could not produce the least tittle of evidence that the girl's parents really lived in Jamaica. A verdict in favour of the Martineaus was obviously a foregone conclusion.

There was only one thing that he could do. It was a desperate step; but in any course upon which he had once made up his mind he never allowed difficulties or dangers to deter him.

'Rex! Richard!' he said abruptly, and went on in English: 'We are about to return to the launch, carrying all before us. Princess, you go ahead!'

Marie Lou knew that tone in the Duke's voice. She had heard it before when he meant business; so had the others. Without a second's hesitation she turned and, bowing to the surgeon, walked quickly down the length of the ward, while Rex and Richard moved up beside de Richleau.

The Duke spoke again. 'Richard, your gun! Rex, get that body—quick!'

The other two had already tensed themselves and they acted as though animated by springs. Whipping out his automatic, Richard sprang back and held the Martineaus covered. Rex dived at the bed and in his strong arms grabbed up the still form under the sheet.

There was a piercing scream from *Madame* Martineau. The surgeon, ignoring Richard's pistol, leapt forward to intervene. De Richleau hated to have to do it, but he swung his fist and with all his force sent it crashing under the surgeon's ribs, driving the breath out of his body. He could only gasp and groan as he doubled up and collapsed upon the floor.

Rex had flung the sheeted corpse over his shoulder and was pounding down the ward. De Richleau followed and Richard brought up the rear, waving his gun. Shouts and yells broke from the black and coffee-coloured patients in the double line of beds between which they ran. One flung a medicine bottle which caught de Richleau on the ear; a nurse hastily tipped a chair over in Rex's path before she ran, screaming murder, from the room. He nearly tripped but just managed to pull up in time, and kicked the chair aside. With pandemonium broken loose behind them, they charged out of the ward and down the stairs.

In the hallway an astonished black Sister flattened herself against the wall and added to the din by piercing falsetto cries for help. A porter tried to bar their path, but de Richleau thrust him aside as they tumbled through the doorway in a bunch. But doctors and medical students, attracted by the commotion, were pouring out of the passages and pounding down the stairs in their rear; while above, the Martineaus had rushed out on to the verandah and from its corner were rousing the lethargic natives in the street against them.

'Ghouls! Grave-robbers!' shrieked *Madame* Martineau. 'They are carrying off the body of my child to make her a Zombie! Help! Help! Oh, Holy Virgin, save her!'

Instantly the cry was taken up in Creole and bastard French, many expressions in which they could catch and understand. 'Ghouls!' 'Grave-robbers!' 'They have a corpse! 'It is the *Cochon Gris*!' 'No, no, it is a White Bocor who makes Zombies.' 'Stop them!' 'Tear them to pieces!' 'Ghouls!' 'Fiends!' 'Evil ones from Hell!'

Marie Lou had only a very short start. She had begun to run immediately she had got clear of the hospital and they could see her heading for the harbour fifty yards in advance of them. But the whole street was now roused; everyone was coming out of the houses and shops. Before they had covered a hundred paces she was headed off; two big Negroes started forward from the pavement and ran towards her. She saw that she could not possibly hope to dodge them so she halted, darted back, then hesitated for a moment, staring wildly round her, until the others came racing up.

All five of them now ran on together, but from one end of the street to the other people were pouring out of buildings and alleyways. Fruit, vegetables and stones were being hurled at them from every direction and they all knew that their plight was desperate. A sea of angry black faces surged up in front of them and it seemed certain that before they reached the harbour they must be torn to pieces by the infuriated mob.

20

The Body-snatchers

Rex, whose old home was in Virginia, knew all about
lynchings in the Southern States. As a boy he had seen a
town roused to frenzy by a report that a Negro had raped
a white girl. Men and women had sallied out from their
homes at night, marched upon the local goal, broken into
it and dragged out the cowering Negro. They had kicked,
buffeted and clawed him like a pack of beasts until he was
half-dead, then soaked his body in petrol and set it on
fire. It had been a sickening spectacle and from time to
time such outbreaks still occurred. Sometimes the accu-
sation was entirely without foundation, but rumour and
arrest were enough; unless the police could spirit the accused away to another town his fate was sealed, and such
a fate was the dread of every Negro.

In the present instance the rôles were reversed and a
great crowd of coloured folk were under the impression
that they had ample justification for administering mob
law to four Whites whom they believed to be making away
with the body of a Mulatto girl to turn her into a Zombie.
There was no question of the case being fought before the
magistrate now. If they were once swept off their feet, within the next few awful moments a hundred hefty boots would
break their bones and crush their bodies until they were
left five bleeding masses of pulp.

With the body slung over his shoulder Rex was leading,
but he had only one hand free and the sudden exertion
was causing the wound in his leg to pain him badly. Marie
Lou had slipped into the group just behind him so that
266

Richard and de Richleau ran on either side of her. As the two Negroes came at them Rex sent one of them reeling with a sudden, violent push in the face with his free hand; the Duke tackled the other by a kick on the shin which caused him to yowl, spin round and go sprawling on the cobbles.

For a moment there was a clear space in front of them, but a hail of missiles whizzed at them as they ran. Marie Lou got a lemon in her right eye, which half-blinded her, and a stone tore the knuckles of de Richleau's left hand. A dozen other oddments bounced from their bodies after giving them as many painful buffets.

Behind, to each side and in front of them the crowd were giving tongue; a loud, angry roar filled the whole street. Twenty yards ahead there was a side-turning which was only thinly covered by half a dozen people who were running out of it towards them. Rex swung right and headed for it.

A great Negress with a meat-chopper lifted it to slash at him as he passed, but Rex had been a rugger-player in his Harvard days, and in spite of the handicap of his game leg he swerved with amazing speed just in time to escape the blow. Richard crashed full-tilt into another Negro, knocking him over. Then they were through into the side-turning. But it was much narrower than the street, and scores more people, roused by the shouting, were streaming into it from the teaming courts and alleys which lay behind the docks.

A thick-lipped, yellow-haired Mulatto clawed at de Richleau and managed to drag him back for a moment, but the Duke's fist crunched on the bone of the fellow's nose and he released his hold with a yelp of pain.

Almost blinded by the shower of missiles and deafened by the shouting, they covered another hundred yards and came out into a wider street. Keeping his head, Rex turned left along it, making once more for the harbour; but a great portion of the crowd appeared to have guessed their intention and had taken a short cut for the purpose of heading them off. Fifty yards in front of them, men, women and children were tumbling over one another as they charged helter-skelter out of an alleyway.

The Duke groaned and glanced swiftly back. Another hundred or more curly-headed, shiny-faced coloured people were following hard upon their heels. Escape seemed utterly impossible. Within a few moments they must be dragged down. Then, a little way ahead of them on the left side of the road, he caught sight of a small church. There seemed just a chance that they might succeed in obtaining sanctuary there if only they could reach it.

'The church!' he yelled above the din. 'Make for the church!' But the way was blocked by half a hundred black or yellow angry, glistening faces. Richard was still brandishing his automatic. He knew that now had come the time when he must use it.

Whipping up the pistol, he fired two shots above the heads of the crowd. With a shout of panic they cowered away and scattered. The little party of Whites raced on, reached the church and dashed up the steps to its porch.

At that very moment, attracted by the noise, a tall, sandy-haired Roman Catholic priest came hurrying out of the big arched door. He had had no time to discover what the tumult was about and saw only that the mob of blacks and half-castes was pursuing five Europeans, one of whom carried a large sheeted bundle.

Instantly he strode out on to steps and sternly raised his hand, forbidding the rabble to follow its prey further. De Richleau knew then that, temporarily at all events, the Powers of Light had intervened on behalf of himself and his friends by directing them to the church and sending the priest to their assistance at that critical moment.

Without pausing to see the outcome of this check to their pursuers de Richleau thrust the others through the door of the church and ran behind them down the nave. At its end they darted along a side-aisle to a curtained opening and through it into the vestry. There, bruised and breathless, they halted for a moment to get fresh wind.

'How long d'you think we'll be safe here?' panted Richard.

We daren't stay; even if the priest could hold off the mob,' replied de Richleau quickly. 'Directly he learns why they're after us he'll insist on our surrendering Philippa's body; and that I refuse to do.'

As he spoke he was already turning the knob of the door

of the vestry, which led into the street. He opened it a crack so that he could peer out.

'The coast is fairly clear,' he whispered. 'Come on— quick! We must make the most of the lead we've got, before some of the mob come round to this entrance.'

Slipping out of the door, they covered another hundred yards towards the water-front before they were spotted. A small boy began to yell after them in a piercing treble, and within two minutes the hunt was in full cry again. But now, at the end of the narrow alley down which they were running they could see the masts of the ships in the harbour, less than four hundred yards away.

It sounded as though a thousand feet were pounding upon the hot, shiny cobbles behind them, but the way ahead remained unblocked. Suddenly a man darted from a doorway and, thrusting out his leg, tripped de Richleau, who fell full-length on to a pile of stinking garbage in the gutter.

Richard swung round and hit the man a stinging body-blow, which made him gasp and choke. De Richleau stumbled to his feet; but their leading pursuers were now almost on top of them.

Lifting his automatic, Richard fired again, sending another shot over the heads of the packed mass of shouting men and women.

At the report of the pistol the eyes of the leaders started with terror and rolled in their black faces. Pulling up with a jerk, they tried to scramble away from the menace of the gun into the nearby doorways of the alley. But the charging crowd behind forced them on.

Nevertheless, the single shot had given the hunted one more brief respite. Rex, limping badly now, with Marie Lou beside him, had reached the open and they were running diagonally across the wharf to the steps beside which the launch was moored. De Richleau and Richard pelted after them with every ounce of speed that they could muster.

As they shot out of the end of the alleyway they saw that they still had two hundred paces to cover and that scores of men who had been lounging in the bars and cafes along the waterfront were now tumbling out of them as reinforcements for the mob; and ugly reinforcements, as most of them were sailors, all of whom had knives.

Rex and Marie Lou were both shouting to Simon and as de Richleau and Rex caught up with them Simon suddenly appeared from the cabin of the launch. In an instant he had grasped the situation and was giving swift orders to the three Jamaica boys who formed the crew to be ready to cast off. Then, seizing a hatchet, he jumped ashore to help his friends.

Five hundred superstition-maddened coloured folk were now half-filling the wharf and more were crowding on to it from every street and alley. The angry shouting was so loud that it was difficult to hear individual voices, but above the roar the hard-pressed Whites could catch the French equivalents of 'Ghouls!' 'Body-snatchers!' and 'Zombie! Zombie! Zombie!'

In those last few yards they were almost overcome. A thrown knife pierced the calf of Richard's leg and as he stopped for an instant to pull it out he was grabbed by two burly stevedores. De Richleau was seized by a third, and Marie Lou fell at Simon's feet. But having reached the wharf-edge Rex just pitched the body into the launch and swung round to their help. With those mighty fists, like ten-pound weights, he laid out right and left about him until he had cleared a little space and both Richard's and the Duke's attackers lay writhing on the ground from his hammer-blows.

Marie Lou wriggled up again and jumped on to the fore-deck of the launch, where one of the Jamaica boys had already untied the painter. Another was at the wheel and had the engine running. The third had gone to Simon's assistance and with a boathook was striking out at the mob. 'Theirs not to reason why . . .' They were British subjects and Jamaicans who despised the riff-raff of the Negro Republic, and they gave loyal service to their white employers.

Somehow the rest of the party freed themselves from the scores of hands that clutched at them and strove to drag them back. Still striking, kicking and struggling, they fumbled into the boat. The moment they were all on board the launch shot away. Three Haitians, who had leapt on to the deck at the last moment, were attacked simultaneously and heaved overboard into the water.

But the chase was not yet over. While the frustrated

crowd, a thousand strong, now lined the whole wharfside shrieking imprecations at them, hundreds more were piling into water craft of every description to continue the pursuit, and several boats, which were already manned in the harbour, altered course to try to head them off.

In the next few minutes the Jamacian boy at the wheel performed miracles of steersmanship as he dodged one craft after another, but at the mouth of the harbour it was only by Richard's firing two more shots from his automatic across her bows that they prevented a customs launch, officered by a Negro in an admiral's uniform which had already done fifty years' service, from ramming them.

At last they were out in the open sea, and although thirty or forty boats of varying sizes were strung out behind them they felt reasonably confident that their own powerful craft could outdistance the others. As they tended their most serious hurts they saw their pursuers gradually dropping behind, but de Richleau's face was still grave. The Haitian Republic possessed a small Navy, consisting of coastal-patrol gunboats. These were almost obsolete but they were armed after a fashion, and in view of the major riot which they had brought about it was quite on the cards that one of these might be sent after them.

When Rex had picked up Philippa's body and carried it into the cabin, the Duke said: 'We must lose no time in burying her. Marie Lou had better attend to that nasty wound in Richard's leg, on deck. They can keep watch and see that the Jamaica boys don't come down. You others can stay here and give me a hand in what I have to do.'

As Richard and Marie Lou left the cabin the rest of the party took the body, unwrapped it from the sheet and laid it out on the floor. De Richleau then went into the tiny gallery which formed the forepart of the cabin and returned with a skewer, a hammer and a long cook's-knife. Placing the skewer over Philippa's heart, he murmured some words that the others did not understand, and gave it two swift blows with the hammer, which drove it right through her chest.

'The next part of the business is rather horrible,' he said in a low voice, 'so you needn't look if you'd rather not.' But Simon and Rex were so fascinated by the macabre scene that they remained staring down at the blistered, un-resisting corpse.

De Richleau then took up the sharp cook's-knife and, murmuring more words in an ancient tongue, bore down on it with all his weight until it had severed Philippa's head from her trunk.

To Simon's horror, as the head was severed he saw the full lips draw back into a smile; then the eyes flickered open for a second, and he distinctly caught the whispered words: '*Merci, Monsieur*.'

The effect of that dead face smiling and the voice from beyond the grave was so utterly terrifying that he fainted.

Having set him up on one of the settees, with his head dangling between his knees, the other two rewrapped the girl's body and head in a sheet; then the Duke sent Rex to the flag locker. He could not find a Haitian or French flag so returned with an old Union Jack, which they wound round the corpse.

'Thank God that's over!' murmured the Duke. 'Fetch Marie Lou now. We must get her to sew up the shroud.'

But at that moment Marie Lou came into the cabin to report with an anxious face that although the other boats had nearly all given up the chase a small grey-painted steamer, which looked like a warship, had left the harbour.

Simon had just come-too and said that he must have air, so de Richleau told Marie Lou what he wanted done and, leaving Rex to help her, assisted his still groggy friend on deck.

Rex found a length of chain which he tied round the ankles of the corpse to weight it, and Marie Lou hunted about until she discovered some twine and a sailmaker's pad and needle in one of the lockers of the cabin. She then sewed up the edges of the Union Jack so that it formed a sack for the remains, and Rex went up to tell the Duke that the dead girl was ready for burial.

When Rex reached the deck he saw that the Haitian gun-boat, a sea-going tug, a small yacht and two small motor-boats, all having fair speeds, were bunched together about a mile and a half astern; and the Duke said that he feared that this smaller but more powerful armada, which had left the harbour some time after he and his friends had put to sea, was gradually gaining on them. The tug's hooter blared out an almost continious succession of short, piercing blasts, evidently intended as calls on them to stop, and now and again the gunboat joined in with a shrill whistle.

Ignoring these signals for the moment, the four men went down to the cabin and carried up Philippa's remains. They were well out at sea now, so de Richleau felt certain that there was no chance whatever of the weighted body being recovered. He said a short prayer of his own devising, that he considered appropriate to the occasion, then the flag-covered corpse was cast over the launch's side, disappearing with a loud splash into the water.

The Jamaica boys had only just realised that the sheeted bundle brought aboard by Rex had been a corpse. They were looking askance at their passengers and the three of them gathered in the stern to jabber excitedly in their own dialect. Apparently they supposed that murder had been committed and that their white employers had chosen this manner of disposing of the body of their victim. In consequence, they were now alarmed by the possibility that they might be accused of assisting a gang of murderers to escape from justice. Their obvious fear for themselves was considerably increased a few moments later—and with better reason. There came a bright flash on the foredeck of the gunboat followed almost instantly by a loud report, and a shell screamed overhead.

It exploded more than half a mile in advance of the launch, sending up a great column of water, so it appeared that the master gunner was not much of a marksman; unless his first shot was intended only as a warning and he meant to make quite certain that it fell nowhere near them.

The Jamaica boys suddenly began a chorus of protest to Rex, who had hired them. They hadn't done anything— they didn't want to get killed. The launch must stop and the white folk must give themselves up. Then the one who was at the wheel shut off the engine.

Richard felt intensely sorry for them, but all the same, he produced his automatic and, taking a few steps aft, drove them, still clamouring, out of the engine pit. Then Rex grabbed the wheel and switched on the power again.

A second shell from the gunboat splashed into the water four hundred yards away, but it proved to be a dud. The

273

pursuing armada had, however, gained a good quarter of a mile on them during that brief interval in which they had been slowed up by the temporary cutting-off of the engine. A third shell whistled over and sent up a column of foam only a hundred yards to starboard, and de Richlieu yelled to Rex:

'Head for the shore! We'll beach her and take to the forest—if we can get there in time.'

As Rex turned the wheel and the launch swung round, a fourth shell burst in the air some twenty feet behind them. A splinter ploughed up the deck within three inches of Simon's feet, another smashed one of the cabin windows, de Richleau and Marie Lou were thrown to their knees and one of the Jamaica boys was knocked overboard by the force of the blast.

However dire their own extremity they could not leave the poor fellow to drown or to be eaten by the sharks which they knew infested the channel; neither could they abandon him to the chance of being picked up by the Haitians and lynched as one of the pursued party. With a curse, Rex swung the wheel again and, turning in a wide circle, put back. In frantic haste they hauled the dripping Negro on board, but by the time they had done so the gunboat with its accompanying flotilla had decreased its distance to within half a mile of them, and the nearest point of the coast, upon which de Richleau had hoped to beach the launch, was well over a mile distant.

Just as they turned towards the shore again two more shells came in rapid succession; one was a wide miss, but the explosion of the other, under-water, gave the launch such a buffet that it nearly capsized. As it righted and raced on, with them now drenched to the skin from the flying spray and crouching flat on the deck, they saw that the tug had altered course to endeavour to head them off. It was nearer to them than any of the other vessels and now that they were in closer range it opened fire with a machine-gun.

Bullets spattered the water and the gun cracked again, its report echoing across the bay. They had now only half a mile to cover to reach the beach, but the machine-gun lifted and a spate of bullets from it thudded into the launch, holing and tearing its woodwork. Almost at the same moment the engine stopped as a shell splinter from another high burst struck a part of the machinery with a metallic clatter.

The game was up; and de Richleau knew it. Without power they could not possibly reach the shore, and he suddenly realised that the launch was sinking from unseen hits which had holed her below the water-line. To attempt to swim for it only meant the possibility of having to face the sharks or the additional indignity of being dragged from the water, as within a few minutes the pursuing flotilla was bound to come up with them. Rising to his feet, he pulled out his white handkerchief and waved it in token of surrender.

Five minutes later they were surrounded by the Haitian flotilla and a hundred angry, indignant coloured men were staring curiously at them. A Mulatto in a sky-blue uniform, with a sash and tassels of tarnished silver lace, shouted at them through a megaphone in French, from the gunboat, to catch the rope that would be thrown and haul themselves alongside with it.

The cabin was full of water and the launch now sinking under them, but they did as they were ordered. A rope-ladder was lowered and de Richleau's party, including the Jamaica boys, pulled themselves up it.

Immediately the Duke reached the gunboat's deck he addressed the officer in fluent French and with the arragance of a victor rather than a captive. In firm tones he stated that seven of his party were British subjects and the eighth an American; and that the British and United States Goverments would call the Haitian Government to account for having, without the slightest provocation, endangered the lives of the occupants of the launch by firing upon them.

The officer was so dumbfounded at this impudence that he hesitated before answering, but he said that although he himself knew nothing of the matter it had been reported that the Duke's party had assaulted a surgeon at the hospital and, under her parents' eyes had forcibly removed the body of a girl who had died there that morning.

'Have you a warrant for our arrest?' snapped the Duke. 'If so, will you kindly show it to me.'

No, the Haitian Captain admitted, he had not a warrant, but in such an emergency he had considered it his plain duty to put to sea in order to prevent such evil-doers from leaving the country.

'Very well, then,' said the Duke, 'You have obviously only acted in accordance with your understanding of the situation, if extremely rashly. We will answer any charges which may be brought against us; but immediately we get back to port I shall look to you to inform the British and America Consuls of what has occurred and ask them to meet us so that we can tell them our side of this affair without the least delay. I shall also hold you personally responsible for our safety.

The Captain appeared to agree to this, as he nodded before ordering some of his men to escort the three Jamaica boys forward and the White prisoners aft. Ugly looks were cast at them as they were hurried away and there was a considerable amount of hissing, spitting and fist-shaking among the excited crew, but a junior officer prevented any open attack from being made upon them, took them below and had them locked in a roomy cabin which appeared to be the wardroom of the vessel. They then had their first opportunity to examine properly the many hurts they had sustained an hour before, when they had so narrowly escaped being lynched; while the gunboat chugged back to port.

Soon after the ship had docked the Captain appeared, with several armed sailors behind him, to say that they were to be taken ashore. The news of the riot and its cause had now spread through the whole Haitian capital. Even people in the outlying suburbs who had not heard of it had been attracted by the unusual sound of gunfire and the sight of their warship pursuing a launch out in the bay so that, in spite of the mid-morning heat, the entire wharf-side was now crammed with a heterogeneous mass of people ranging in colour from boot-polish black to lemon yellow.

The prisoners had seen through the port-holes the great expectant multitude which was so inflamed against them and de Richlieu had already made up his mind that if he and his friends stepped ashore their lives would not be

276

worth a moment's purchase. He voiced the feelings of them all as he said to the Captain:

'No, thank you. We have no intention of leaving this ship until the crowds are dispersed. The people of Port-au-Prince have been told a completely wrong version of what has happened and think that they have excellent grounds for regarding us as worse than murderers. Before we got fifty yards they would overcome your sailors and pull us to pieces. If that occurred, His Brittanic Majesty and the President of the United States would both send warships here. As just retribution for our deaths I have no doubt at all that they would blow half the town to pieces and then take over the country. Unless you wish that to happen, and Haiti to lose her independence for good and all, you will leave us where we are and send your magistrates here, together with the British and American Consuls, as soon as you can so that this unfortunate business can be settled without bloodshed.'

As the one dread of every Haitian official is that his country may once more be taken over by the Whites—a calamity for which the Captain had no intention of being held responsible—he saw the sense of this, so agreeing to the Duke's suggestion, he locked them in again and left.

It was getting on for eleven and the sun, now high in the heavens, beat down upon the deck above. The cabin had the curious and unpleasant stink peculiar to Negroes who have achieved a semi-civilised state in which they never cleanse themselves by swimming and rarely wash, and with it was mingled the smell of stale tobacco-smoke and beer.

For a little while after the Captain's departure none of them said anything; they were too occupied in endeavouring to recoup themselves after the physical exertions and mental stresses that they had been through, and all of them were conscious that although they had won a great spiritual victory by giving proper burial to Philippa's body and at last bringing peace to her spirit, they had landed themselves in most desperate straits.

The fact that the body was no longer with them when they were caught would hardly stand them in much stead, for it would be assumed that, fearing to be captured with the evidence of their crime, they had thrown it overboard simply to be rid of it. No doubt the Haitian magistrates would know all about Zombies, but it remained a most speculative matter as to whether they would officially acknowledge such a belief in front of Europeans. The goodclass Haitians were most averse to it being known that such a horrible abuse of corpses still existed in their country, but out of a fear—a fear which they had imbibed with their mother's milk—for anyone even remotely connected with such practices, they might well condemn the White prisoners almost without a hearing. Besides, none of the prisoners saw what sort of a defence they could possibly put up, since they had not a shred of evidence to prove that Doctor Saturday was a Bocor from whom they had rescued the girl's body and they certainly could not prove—as they had avowed in the hospital—that she was not the daughter of *Monsieur* and *Madame* Martineau.

The full grimness of their situation was finally brought home to them when Simon, now dead-beat after his many hours of unbroken mental and physical activity, sighed wearily and said that he would give a thousand pounds for an hour's sleep.

De Richleau gave a bitter little laugh and reminded them that he had been compelled to leave the suitcase containing the new impedimenta, which Richard and Rex had gone to such trouble to fetch all the way from Jamaica, in the flooded cabin of the motor-launch; and by its sinking they had once more been robbed of the means of securing adequate astral protection. Like a force that is beleaguered by land and sea, they were now in physical peril from any fate which the Haitian authorities might decree for them, and should they fall asleep, they would be an easy prey for the merciless enemy who would assuredly await them on the other plane.

A little after midday a junior officer entered the cabin followed by a sailor and a slatternly-looking Negro steward, who dumped down a tray on which were five bowls of cornmeal-mush, a hand of bananas, some mugs and a large jug of water. De Richleau asked the officer if they could soon anticipate a visit from the British and American Consuls, but he shook his head and replied in bad French. He had no idea; all he had heard was that they were to be taken ashore for examination in the cool of the evening, provided that a good portion of the crowd had dispersed.

When he and his men had withdrawn, the prisoners half-heartedly set about the meal. None of them liked the look of the cornmeal-mush but they ate a few bananas and, the stuffy heat having made them all extremely thirsty, eagerly drank up most of the water.

While they were eating, they spoke in low voices of Philippa. Marie Lou said that she wondered how the girl could have been planted upon Sir Pellinore, and the Duke replied wearily:

'How can one say? It may have been managed in a dozen different ways. Evidently our adversary is much more powerful than I imagined. He must have found out that we intended to come to Haiti. Perhaps his astral plane was present and listening to our conversation on the day that Pellinore came down to lunch with us at Cardinals Folly. If it was, he'd have learnt in one brief session all our plans for our journey and have had ample time to make his own arrangements.'

'Still, it must have been pretty difficult for him to foist the girl on us at such short notice,' remarked Richard.

The Duke shrugged. 'Not necessarily. Through his astral he may be able to communicate with a number of occultists in Europe, and just because he is working for the Nazis it doesn't at all follow that they are all in Germany. He may have given instructions in a dream to some Fifth Column-ist in London who is under his orders. How Philippa reached England from Marseilles I don't pretend even to guess; but quite possibly she was brought over from her convent, with other refugees, at the time of the French collapse. Once he knew that the French were going out of the war, that fiend, Saturday, may have decided that she would be more useful to him in London and had her shipped over. If she was ready to hand you can see for yourselves that it wouldn't have been difficult for German agents in London to fix it with Ricardi—who is either one of them or under their thumb—that she should pose as his daughter and that he should get in touch with Pelli-nore, mention casually the problem of getting the girl to the West Indies and, when Pellinore said he had friends proceeding there, ask him to get us to take her.'

They sank into miserable silence again, not caring to talk of the unpleasant possibilities which lay ahead of them that evening and the coming night; but Simon was now so tired that after a time he said that he doubted if he could hang out without sleep much longer, and the rest of them were terribly somnolent from the heat of the stuffy, smelly cabin.

It was Marie Lou who suggested that since charged water had served to protect the Duke and herself when awake, through those long hours of darkness two nights before, surely it must be a strong enough barrier to protect them while asleep during the full bright light of day; therefore why should he not charge the remaining water in the jug and draw a pentacle on the floor of the cabin with it, so that they could snatch a few hours' blessed oblivion during the sultry afternoon?

He agreed that, although there might be some risk in doing so, their extremity was such that it should be taken, and he was just about to pick up the jug when the door opened again. Doctor Saturday stood on the threshold.

Simon roused himself sufficiently to notice with a vague satisfaction that the Doctor was bearing heavily upon a stick and limping badly. He came in, closed the door behind him and leaned against it.

'Well? So your little hour of freedom has ended,' he said, his white teeth flashing in a smile that was now full of cruel, unrestrained malevolence. 'I must congratulate *Monsieur* de Richleau upon his resource and courage as a body-snatcher. It is only by a miracle that you're not all lying in the local morgue; torn and bleeding victims of the frenzied mob. However, since you have survived, it will give me great pleasure to settle your business personally.'

He paused for a moment, then went on: 'You need not imagine that the British or American Consuls will come to your assistance. I have considerable powers in this country as well as on the astral, so I at once took steps to see to it that neither of those gentlemen will be informed officially or unofficially of the plight into which you have got yourselves. If you have any apprehensions as to what may happen to you when you are brought before a Haitian court I can relieve you of them. You will not appear before any court, because you will all be dead before this evening.'

280

'Aw, go to hell! Get to blazes out of here!' snarled Rex. But the Doctor continued, quite unperturbed.

'In the war that is being waged across the water Britain will be defeated, and the British race will be for ever broken. Some of you may have heard what the Nazis have done in Poland: how they have transported the Polish men by the thousands in cattle-trucks to work in chain-gangs in their mines: how they have injected the whole of the virile population so as to make them incapable of producing children: how they have sent the Polish women by the thousands into brothels for the amusement of the German soldiery.

'Well—that is nothing compared with what Hitler intends to do to the British people in the hour of his victory. They will be enslaved in the fullest meaning of the word, and the arrogant British upper-class will be set to the meanest labours. The Nazis understand that there can be no permanent mastery of the world for them until the British race has ceased to exist. There is never to be another generation. Your men will be made eunuchs and your women rendered sterile. The old and useless will be slaughtered like cattle, then the British Isles will be depopulated by wholesome shipments of her remaining men and women to toil as beasts of burden for their masters on the Continent until death brings them release.'

'First catch your hare, then cook it,' Richard sneered. 'Every man and woman of British blood would rather die than surrender, and we'll paste blue hell out of those Nazi swine before we're much older.'

'You and your friends are already in the net,' the Doctor replied smoothly, 'and by your own folly you have all brought upon themselves an even worse fate than which will befall your countrymen. I have told you what the Nazis will do to them. And now I will tell you why I am giving Germany my aid; so that you, as representatives of your race, may for once understand the hatred it has inspired by its greed and arrogance.

'My father was an Englishman, my mother was a Mulatto girl of good parentage; but he did not think her good enough to marry, so her family, feeling that she had disgraced them, turned her out into the streets. Having taken his pleasure with her he had no more use for her at

281

all, and returned to his own country leaving her destitute. She was just another "coloured girl" who had served to amuse him during his travels. My youth was hard, but I had brains and a strong will. When I was eighteen I worked my way to England, and although I could speak very little of the language, I sought out my father. He not only refused to acknowledge me because a coloured bastard would have shamed him before his friends, but he drove me from his house; and when I persisted he had me prosecuted for creating a nuisance. Then the English police deported me as an undesirable alien.'

'Judging by what we know of your more recent history, they were probably right,' said de Richleau acidly.

The Doctor's face became a mask of fury. 'So you persist in your defiance!' he almost screamed. 'But I will break your pride—and break your will—even more thoroughly than the Nazis will break the spirit of the British people. You thought you were so clever today when you robbed me of that girl whom I had made into a Zombie. But a life for a life is not enough, and there is no escape for you from this place. The seed of death has already been planted in you. It is my will that all of you shall die within the next two hours, and out of you I will make five Zombies for the one that you have taken from me.'

Without another word he turned on his heel and, slamming the door behind him, relocked it.

'Temper, temper!' said Richard, trying to make light of what they all felt to be no empty threat but one with real and deadly purpose behind it.

'What did he mean when he said that he had already planted the seed of death in us?' asked Marie Lou.

'I've no idea,' replied the Duke; 'unless he arranged to have some subtle poison inserted into the food we were given for our midday meal. His authority here seems to be absolute. The Haitians evidently know that he's a powerful Bocor and consequently are scared stiff of him. But in any case he can't make Zombies out of us until we're actually dead.

'If he did have poison put in the food,' said Rex, 'it's a hundred bucks to a pea-nut that it was mixed up in the cornmeal-mush, and none of us ate any of that. We'd surely have noticed if the bananas had been tampered with, and we drank only plain water.'

It comforted them considerably to think that if the Doctor *had* put poison in their food they had escaped once more. But the cabin was like an oven, and apart from their anxious, gloomy thoughts they had nothing at all to occupy them. They were all literally drooping with fatigue, and Simon, who had been awake far longer than any of the others, could hardly keep his eyes open, so the project of making a pentacle with charged water was revivied.

De Richleau set the earthenware jugs before him, and, pointing at it with the first and second fingers of his right hand, on a level with his right eye, began to call down power, which passed in an invisible stream through him and into the jug.

To his surprise and extreme perturbation, the clear, tepid water suddenly began to bubble, and with a bitter grimace he lowered his hand.

'What's the matter?' asked Marie Lou.

He sighed as he looked round at the anxious faces of his friends. 'I'm afraid we're up against it. The water cannot be charged, because it is not pure. That spawn of Hell has got the better of us—he mixed some tasteless and colourless poison with the water, and we all drank a mug or more of it over an hour ago. It's too late now for us to make ourselves sick, as the poison must already be working in our veins. That's what he meant when he said that the seed of death was already in us.'

21

Coffins for Five

The minutes that followed seemed like an eternity as they sat contemplating the terrible fate with which their enemy had threatened them, and now that they knew they had been poisoned they almost at once began to believe that they could feel the symptoms of the noxious drug.

The intense heat from the tropical sun beating down on the deck above their heads and the stale smell of the airless cabin were calculated to induce drowsiness in anyone, but Richard and Rex had slept long and well returning from Jamaica in the launch the previous night, and both felt that the extreme torpidity which afflicted them must be partially attributable to some cause other than their surroundings.

Marie Lou had been sitting for a long time in one position and when she moved her leg she found that she had pins-and-needles in her foot, which with a sudden feeling of panic she put down to the first effects of the poison.

Simon was now conscious that in addition to his utter weariness he had a splitting headache; and this he could not help regarding, with a slight quickening of the heart, as a first sign of his approaching death.

The instinct of all of them was to *do* something—to get up and try to break their way out of the cabin—but they knew that, even if they succeeded, that would not save them.

The Negro guards outside were armed, so could kill them or force them back. In spite of the gruelling heat,

284

on the dock beyond the side of the ship a considerable crowd was still mustered, patiently waiting to learn what was to be done with the body-snatchers. They might perhaps bribe the guards, but if they attempted to leave the ship they would only be pulled to pieces, as at the first sight of them another wave of furious animosity would be certain to surge through the mob. Even if by some miracle they could escape from their guards and avoid a lynching, they had not the least idea what kind of toxin had been used to poison them, so they had no means of knowing what antidote they ought to take, quite apart from the fact that it might be exceedingly difficult to procure.

There was nothing that they could do but await events, and when they felt death creeping over them commend their spirits to the Lords of Light in the hope that those Timeless Ones might afford some protection in their extremity when they reached the astral.

Yet even that seemed a slender hope, because all of them knew sufficient of the Law to realise that any human who elects to wage war upon the Powers of Darkness does so at his own peril. In the great accounting he will receive due credit for the effort, but failure to emerge triumphant from such a conflict brings penalties which must be borne without complaint, so great suffering may have to be endured before the account is balanced and, in the end, the due reward obtained.

They had also learnt quite enough about Zombies in the last few hours to know that when they died their spirits would not be free to pass on until their bodies had ceased to be animated by the power that held them enslaved, and that those spirits would feel all the tribulations which might be inflicted upon their earthly clay.

De Richleau knew that there was one way out. Richard's pistol had not been taken from him and he still had about two dozen rounds of ammunition for it. If they used the pistol to kill one another, and the last to survive among them committed suicide, they might escape—providing that the killing was done in such a manner as to render their bodies useless. A shot apiece through the back of the neck, breaking the spinal cord where it joins the skull, would serve, since there would be no way of repairing the

285

blasted bone after death, and no corpse with a shattered spine could labour in the fields as a Zombie.

But that was a way out which he would not even contemplate. To kill the others, except by surprise, would mean obtaining their consent; as it was obviously impossible for him to borrow Richard's pistol and catch even one of them napping, without running the risk of bungling the job. If they agreed to let him kill them that would be tantamount to suicide; and afterwards he would have to commit suicide himself.

To do so was unthinkable; for it is written that no spirit is ever sent a greater load of suffering than by exerting its whole will it can bear. To commit suicide, as a means of escaping any other form of death, is, therefore, to interfere with one's kama. All suffering is the result of past debts which have been piled up in previous lives, and these must be worked off sooner or later. In consequence suicide is no escape—only a postponement—and for those who are weak enough to take it there is the additional penalty to be borne: for a greater or lesser time, according to the cowardice of the case, the spirit is not free to continue the great journey but remains tied, and must go through the last few awful moments of the self inflicted act again and again and again, until at last it is released.

'If only we hadn't lost the second lot of impedimenta,' said Richard, after a long silence, 'we could have made a pentacle in which to die. It might at least have served to protect us for those few minutes in which one blacks out at the end of every incar, and given us a sporting chance to fight afterwards.'

The Duke did not reply, but it was those words which caused a great light to dawn suddenly in his mind. He had always known that in his magical operations he was not quite White, but just a little Grey. He had not used his powers for self-advancement or personal aims, but almost unwittingly he still allowed his own deep-rooted passions and convictions to influence him. For example, he did not regard the Nazis from an entirely detached point of view, as a menace to the welfare of mankind; he *hated* them, with all the hatred of which his virile personality was capable; and that was wrong.

Perhaps it was because of that slight uncertainty of his own powers that in his magical operations he had always followed the rituals of the text-books and utilised such things as garlic, as a foetida grass, curcifixes, horseshoes and many other symbols. These things in themselves were, he knew, only focuses to attract power; they had not an atom of power in themselves, but were just bundles of herbs or pieces of wood and iron. A pure White Magician, confident in his own strength, would have despised them and relied entirely upon his own will.

Without any of these things, or pentacles, or mumbled phrases from ancient mysteries, he would have gone out, fearless and alone from his body on to the astral to give battle. In that strange moment all things were at last made clear to the Duke. He had been a coward. He had shirked the conflict when he should have gone out to fight, relying alone upon the intrinsic fact that Light is more powerful than Darkness.

As he sat there he thought that he could feel a slight stiffening of his limbs. On moving them a little he was sure of it. The poison had now really begun to work on him. But it was not too late. If he did not wait there to die, but threw himself into a self-induced trance and voluntarily left his body before it was taken from him, there was still a chance that he might defeat the enemy.

Suddenly he spoke. 'Listen, all of you; I'm going to leave you now. Whatever may happen in the next few hours, don't despair. I shall be with you though you will not be able to see me. You will, I know, support with courage all that may be sent to you. But I am going ahead because by doing so there is just a possibility that I may yet be able to avert the awful fate with which we are all threatened. If I fail we must all suffer—perhaps for many years to come; but remember that to merit such suffering we must all have done something very evil in the past for which we shall now be paying. We have all loved each other very dearly, therefore nothing can separate us permanently. Either we shall meet again as victors in our earthly bodies, before many hours are gone, or when we have paid our debt we shall meet in those higher, happier spheres which you all know.'

Stretching out his hands towards them, his grey eyes filled with a new and brilliant light, he added: 'May the blessing and protection of the Timeless Ones be upon you all in your hour of trial.'

Such was the awe with which his now radiant face filled them that none of them sought to dissuade him from his intention. His words had been too grave for any response other than a murmur of encouragement in the attempt that he was about to make.

When he had performed the rite of sealing the nine openings of his body and had commended it to the protection of the Powers, Marie Lou kissed his cheek tenderly; then they all sent out their thoughts to strengthen him as he settled himself in a corner of one of the settees and closed his eyes. For a few moments he concentrated his will, then his body gradually went limp and they knew that he had left it.

Directly he was free of his earthly form he cast a long last look upon the loved faces of his friends, then gathering his strength he soared up through the deck and out above the town. He could not give battle unless the Black Magician was also out of his body, but as it was not yet two o'clock he hoped to be able to catch him asleep during the midday siesta—in fact, much depended upon his doing so, as otherwise he would be deprived of any chance to save his friends from the first terrible trials which they would be called upon to endure after the semblance of life had left them. His immediate and very urgent problem, therefore, was to find the Satanist.

In a flash he was over the house on the hillside, but, as he expected, he found it a burnt-out ruin. There were some out-buildings about a hundred yards away from that end of the house which had been the servants' quarters, and in them had been stacked a certain amount of furniture which had been salvaged from the fire. But the Doctor was not there.

It seemed to de Richleau that there was quite a possibility that the enemy had taken up his quarters in some neighbour's house, so he visited a number of dwellings in the immediate vicinity—but without success. Swift as thought he sped back to Port-au-Prince.

The midday quiet still held the town. The streets were almost bare of traffic and there were very few pedestrians about. Even the considerably reduced crowd on the wharf-side had either congregated in the bars and cafés or had taken advantage of such patches of shade as could be found behind sheds and stacks of merchandise to sprawl upon the ground and doze.

In three thousand seconds the Duke traversed three thousand rooms in various buildings, but Doctor Saturday was not in any of them, and the task of finding him was, de Richleau realised, like looking for a needle in a haystack. The hour in which the Duke had hoped to accomplish so much was already up. It was three o'clock, and everywhere in the sun-scorched town people were waking and rising from beds, sofas, rocking-chairs and straw palliasses to set about the second half of their daily occupations.

Very reluctantly de Richleau decided that it would be waste of effort to search further. He had keyed himself up to give instant battle at any moment, but it was virtually certain that the Doctor—wherever he was—would by now have woken, and it would be many hours before he slept again. During those hours the prisoners on the gunboat must suffer all that was sent to them and the Duke knew to his sorrow that he would be unable to give them even comfort—let alone more material aid. He could only wait, praying that his courage would not ebb in the long interval that must now elapse before he could enter on his own ordeal.

Knowing that the sorcerer must sooner or later take possession of the bodies of his friends, he returned to the ship and found that there was already a marked change in their condition. At the moment he arrived Rex, with faltering tongue and laboured breathing, was complaining of the stiffness in his muscles and was endeavouring to flex them. But Simon roused himself to mutter that he felt just the same and that it would probably only prolong the mental strain if he fought against it. Richard was sitting with Marie Lou on his lap; her arms were about his neck and her cheek was pressed against his. The eyes of both were closed and it looked as though they were asleep; but the Duke knew that they were not.

For half an hour he remained there, watching the poison do its work and comforting himself a little with the thought that at least it did not appear to be causing them any great physical agony; although they were obviously suffering mentally as they felt their limbs gradually stiffening and going dead.

It is not an easy thing to surrender quietly and philosophically without any attempt to fight against a creeping paralysis which one knows must end in death, and from time to time they appeared to struggle a little against it. Simon was the first to go; he just seemed to drop asleep. Soon afterwards Marie Lou gave a little shudder and lay still. Richard, his face contorted, clutched her small body and strove to jerk himself up, but the effort proved too much and he fell back with his eyes still open but fixed and staring. Rex was the last to go; with a Herculean effort he staggered to his feet and drew himself up to his full, magnificent height, then he pitched forward across Simon, his great limbs completely rigid.

Although they all now had the appearance of death their spirits did not emerge from their bodies, and de Richleau knew that they were chained there, unable to free themselves yet equally unable any more to animate their frames through their own wills.

For some time nothing happened and it was nearly four o'clock when the officer in the sky-blue uniform entered the cabin with some papers in his hand. He gave one glance at the five still forms, uttered a shriek of terror and fled.

De Richleau was in no mood to be amused at anything, otherwise, having followed the Captain up on deck, he would have derived a considerable amount of fun from the scene that ensued. A number of Haitian notables had evidently been about to enter the cabin behind the officer, and in his panic-stricken flight he knocked several of them over. Without waiting to ascertain the cause of his terror they picked themselves up and came tumbling up the hatchway after him, to find that he had continued his flight by leaping for the gangway and dashing across it to the wharf.

In response to their shouts a squad of the *Gardes d'Haiti*

which was standing at ease on the quay, headed him off and half-led, half-pushed, him on board again, where for some moments he stood on the quarterdeck, his eyes rolling and his knees knocking together from excess of fear, quite unable to speak.

At last they managed to reassure him sufficiently for him to stammer out that all five of the prisoners had died from some unknown cause; and that, since they had been most evil people, he was terrified lest their Duppies, or spirits, which must still be lurking there, would get him.

This news filled the deputies and generals with obvious consternation and they hastily withdrew from the companionway, many of them even leaving the ship altogether to view further events from the safer distance of the quay. As the news spread among the crowd many of the superstitious Negroes and Negresses who were rubbernecking there evidently considered discretion the better part of valour and swiftly disappeared into the side-streets and alleys. For the spirits of five powerful Bocors to be loose was to them very far from being a joke.

The notables, too, would obviously have liked to leave such a dangerous vicinity, but apparently felt that their prestige would suffer if they took to flight; so the frockcoated politicians and 'musical-comedy' officers remained talking excitedly on either side of the gangway; but although each urged the other none of them could be persuaded to venture near the companion-way again.

De Richleau wished for a moment that he and his friends were all back in their bodies and had the use of them, as if they had walked up on deck at that moment there was no doubt that they would have been regarded with such dread that no one would have dared to lay a hand upon them. Soldiers, sailors, deputies and the common people would all have bolted like so many rabbits while the prisoners selected at their leisure another motor-boat and made their escape to sea.

However, the bodies of his four friends were now, for all practical purposes, no more than corpses, and had he endeavoured to return to his own he would only, he knew, have found it rigid and uninhabitable from the poison which had flowed through his blood-stream; so he continued to listen to the excited conversation of the Haitians, which in his astral he could follow perfectly easily although they were talking in Creole.

At length several of them reached a decision and set off at a quick walk towards the town. A quarter of an hour later they returned, accompanied by the Catholic priest in whose church the Duke and his friends had taken refuge that morning.

With no trace of fear the gaunt, sandy-haired priest walked straight down the companion-way, holding a small crucifix in front of him. Reaching the cabin, he pronounced a long Latin exorcism to drive away evil spirits. At its conclusion he turned in a matter-of-fact way to the crowd of half-castes who were gathered as anxious spectators behind him and told them that there was nothing more to fear—they could now proceed to remove the bodies.

At the orders of one of the more couragous Haitian politicians, who had remained throughout on the deck, the sailors produced some stretchers from the sick bay of the gunboat, placed the bodies upon them and covered each with a blanket. They were then taken ashore, the priest leading the procession.

When they reached the wharf there ensued a short discussion. The priest wished to take the bodies to the hospital in order that a doctor might certify them as dead, but the Haitians were very much against this and insisted that the five Duppies were doubtless still hovering somewhere in the neighbourhood, only waiting the opportunity to create the most frightful mischief, and that the priest must therefore take the corpses straight to the church; otherwise the evil Duppies might get into some of the sick people in the hospital and possess them.

A compromise was reached, by which the priest agreed that the bodies should be taken to the vestry of his church provided that a doctor came to certify them there.

This having been arranged the squad of *Gardes d'Haiti* fell in, the procession set off once more and the stretcher-bearers carried their burdens to the vestry from which de Richleau's party had made their escape earlier in the day. Soon afterwards the Negro surgeon arrived with two companions from the hospital. After a brief examination of each corpse they reached the unanimous opinion that there was no life in any of them and wrote out the death certificates.

The vestry was then locked up while the priest went away, but a quarter of an hour later he returned with two old Negresses, who set about performing the last rites. Each body was stripped, man-handled—somewhat to the watching Duke's repugnance—and washed; then, instead of being wrapped in a shroud, it was dressed again in its clothes as is the Negro custom. In due course some men arrived with five cheap wooden coffins. The bodies were put into them and—grim sound to the Duke's ears—the lids were hammered down.

On the priest's instructions the coffins were carried into the church and laid out in a row in the chancel. Having lighted a single candle for each and set these on the heads of the coffins, he said a short prayer for the departed and left the church.

In view of the rapid decomposition of corpses in the Tropics de Richleau knew that the burial would not be long delayed and would certainly take place that night. So far there had been no sign of Doctor Saturday, but the Duke did not doubt that the Satanist had means of ascertaining exactly what was going on and would put in an appearance in due course.

He felt very bitterly about having failed to locate the Doctor during the latter part of the day's siesta as had he done so he would either have triumphed or have known the worst; and in the former case he would have been able to spare his friends the horror that each of them must now be suffering. Although they had been certified as dead he knew that consciousness had never left them. As far as they were concerned, they were in the process of being buried alive, and the terrifying rites which had been carried out in the last hour must have been infinitely more frightening for them than for himself.

At five-thirty the priest returned. With him be brought the two women who had washed the bodies and the men who had delivered the coffins, to form a small, frightened congregation, which had evidently attended only because its members feared the priest more than the Duppies of the dead. A short service was held and the coffins were carried out to a waiting cart.

The street was packed with people from end to end, as most of the inhabitants of Port-au-Prince had turned out in half-morbid, half-fearful curiosity, to witness the last stages of this strange affair which had caused such excitement throughout the whole town.

The cart moved off, its driver having great difficulty in forcing the two mangy-looking donkeys that drew it through the press; and the priest followed in an ancient, rickety barouche. They drove for some two miles outside the town, to a large cemetery the vast crowd trailing after them in complete and awe-struck silence.

Inside the cemetery five shallow graves had been prepared in a row and the coffins were lowered into them. Only the boldest of the crowd would venture through the cemetery gates to witness the final stages of the service, and de Richleau, who had hovered above the cortège, suddenly saw that Doctor Saturday was among these.

The Satanist did not approach the graves but stood on the fringe of the little group and appeared to be watching the ceremony only out of the corner of his eye; yet as the priest read the last rites de Richleau felt certain that he could see a satisfied smile twitching the corners of the Doctor's mouth.

Immediately the service was concluded the grave-diggers hurriedly shovelled in the earth, which rattled with a hollow sound upon the coffins. The priest got into his barouche again, the crowd at the gates began to melt like magic, and with anxious glances at the setting sun those who had been in the cemetery hurried away from it, including the Doctor; who evidently had no intention of claiming his victims as yet.

There followed for the Duke a long and trying wait, during which he found it impossible to keep his thoughts from the tortures which his friends must be suffering down there under the earth. In vain he strove to reach them and to bring them comfort, but he very much doubted if they were even conscious of his astral presence, and their own spirits now had no means whatever of expressing themselves.

Darkness enveloped the sea, the coast, the groups of

graceful palm-trees, the poorly-kept little fields of maize, coffee and cotton, the scattered dwellings, the dense tropical jungle further inland and the ragged mountains beyond. The land became again what de Richleau had felt it to be two nights before, when he had gazed out from the Doctor's verandah; a place reeking with primitive sexual urges and saturated in stealthy, creeping evil.

One by one the lights in the houses went out. Then, at about eleven o'clock, somewhere in the distance he heard the sharp staccato note of the Petro drums as they began to beat at the opening of a Voodoo ceremony.

The drums went on and on, gradually increasing the pace of their rhythm until it felt as though the whole dark scene was pulsing to them. With his astral sight de Richleau, still hovering above the newly-made graves, could see the long road that led from the cemetery to the town. There was not a movement upon it, and he knew that after the happenings of the day not a soul in Port-au-Prince, with the possible exception of a Catholic priest, would dare to venture within a mile of that place while the darkness lasted; and the priest, who had buried the five bodies with the firm conviction that the dead do *not* return, would certainly not come out again to the cemetery that night.

In the opposite direction the road wound up along a rising cliff to a high place overlooking the sea and about quarter of an hour before midnight the Duke's attention was caught by a long snake of light gradually emerging from the blackness of the distant hillside. A few moments later it disappeared, only to reappear nearer and brighter, and the process was repeated. It was, as he knew, following the bends of the road that led down to the cemetery, and whenever it blacked out it was passing behind a mass of thick, tropical vegetation.

As the snake wound nearer the note of the drums grew louder and a dirge-like chant welled up into the still, sultry air. At the same time the snake gradually dissolved into a hundred separate points of gleaming light, and the Duke saw that it was a long procession in which each person was carrying a lighted pinewood torch. The head of what had been the "snake" reached the gates of the cemetery at exactly midnight.

The chant was abruptly broken off, the drums ceased to beat and a great shouting went up from the men and women who had formed the "snake". Then their leader advanced and, as a sudden silence fell, called aloud upon Baron Cimeterre, the Lord of the Cemetery, to give them entrance. De Richleau had no knowledge of how the thing was done, but silently and smoothly, without the touch of a human hand, the iron gates swung open.

The new graves were some distance from the gates but by focussing his sight the Duke could quite clearly see the head of the procession, which was now entering them. The leading figure was one to inspire terror into the most courageous heart. It was that of a tall man, decked out in the hideous panoply of an African Witch Doctor.

His body and arms were smeared with various-coloured paints, forming whirls, stars and circles. Above his short, full, grass skirt—like that of a ballet girl—there dangled from his belt a row of human skulls; a dozen long neck-laces of sharks' teeth and barracuda jaws hung from his neck and clattered on his breast. In his hand he shook a great *ascon*, a gourd dressed in sacred beads and snake vertebrae, the rattle of which is believed by Voodooists to be the voice of the gods whispering to their priests. Upon his head was a fantastic erection, from which emerged a pair of pointed horns, and his face was covered by a devil-ish mask. But de Richleau could see through the hideous trappings and knew that it was Doctor Saturday.

Behind him, each with a hand placed on the hip of the person in front, snaked the long procession, advancing slowly in a curious jog-trot dance of three steps forward and two steps back. As they came onward they began to chant in praise of the grim Lord of that fearsome place. At last they reached the graves and, one by one, sticking their torches upright in the earth before them, formed a sway-ing circle round the patch of newly-turned earth. Then there began the most macabre scene that de Richleau had ever witnessed.

At the signal from the Doctor a score of assistant devil-priests, all clad in weird garments and hideously painted, flung themselves upon the graves and with their bare hands tore the earth away until the five coffins were exposed. When this had been done a libation of rum was poured into the grave and little bowls of corn and fruit were offered. At another signal some of the associates wrenched the lid from one of the coffins. Rex was inside it. Grabbing at his arms, they dragged his body up into a sitting position.

The Doctor went down into the grave to face it and, amidst deathly silence, called aloud: 'Rex Van Ryn, I command you to rise and answer me.'

De Richleau knew that by the enchantments which the Satanist had performed Rex *must* answer. His head suddenly began to roll upon his shoulders, horribly grotesque, and from his still stiff lips there came a whisper: 'Here I am.'

The Priest of Evil lifted his ascon and beat Rex upon the head with it, to awaken him further. As Rex jerked himself backwards to escape the blows his limbs began to twitch spasmodically with the animation that was returning to his body. The associates then dragged him up out of the coffin and hustled him up the little slope at the edge of the grave.

As further coffins were opened de Richleau three times more witnessed this profanity inflicted upon his friends. Simon, Marie Lou and Richard in turn were wakened from their deathly sleep, reanimated and dragged, captive, from the tomb. Purely by chance the ghouls wrenched the lid off the Duke's coffin last. He then looked down upon his own corpse and heard the Satanist call him, too, by name. For the first time in many hours he felt a little glow of warmth enter his cold, tired heart. There was no answer—there could not be—because his spirit was still free.

There was an utter silence for a moment, then the Black Magician called him by name again. Still there was no answer.

Threats, imprecations and blasphemies followed, streaming from the thick lips of the devil's priest. He stooped and struck the corpse in the face, again and again, in a furious endeavour to drag forth a response. But there was none.

After ten minutes of unceasing effort he gave up the struggle, ordering some of his assistants to pick up de Richleau's still inanimate body and carry it away.

A thanksgiving ceremony to the Lord of the Cemetery was performed, then the devil-worshippers prepared to depart. They did not recede in Indian file as they had come, but, still holding their torches aloft, in one great crowd, in the middle of which Rex, Richard, Simon and Marie Lou, on their own feet but bemused and only semi-conscious, were hustled along.

The drums and the chanting began again; no longer a dirge but a paean of triumph at Evil having overcome Good. Stamping, gesticulating and dancing, the crowd of weirdly-dressed figures made its way up the hill for the best part of three miles, until it came to a great Hounfort, on the high place above the sea.

De Richleau's body was laid out in front of the altar to Baron Cimeterre and the other four victims were thrust forward until they stood in a row beside the Duke's body, upright on their feet but their heads and arms hanging loosely. A brazier was brought and on its fire the Witch Doctor heated some liquid in a small ladle. When it was warm he shook into it a little powder from one of the skulls at his girdle; then the four victims were held while he forced a drop of it between the lips of each.

At the Satanist's command the four were hustled away and thrown into a filthy shack, when they collapsed, half-conscious, upon the ground. It was lit by a single candle so that they could see faintly, but the Duke, who had passed into the shack and was hovering above their heads, felt his heart wrung at the blank stare which each regarded his companions. They did not know one another.

Outside a further ceremony was in progress, but the Duke could see that the evil priest was hurrying through it; and he guessed the reason. All was not yet done in this fell night's work. One of the five had failed to respond to the Doctor's summons and he was anxious to get to work upon the recalcitrant spirit which still defied him.

Immediately the ritual was concluded the Satanist had the Duke's body carried into a sanctum behind the altar, and as soon as his senior assistants were out of earshot of the crowd they began to question him anxiously as to what had gone wrong; but he at once assured them that there was no cause at all for alarm. He said that he had means with which he could force the corpse to answer and that he meant to apply them all in good time.

Reassured that there was no likelihood of the Duke's

Duppy suddenly appearing on the scene to revenge itself and his friends, the assistants went out and joined in the wild scene of depravity to which the lesser brethren of the Order had already given way. A hundred or more men and women, all of whom had participated in the ghoulish rites, were now executing an obscene dance in the compound. To the furious beating of the high-pitched drums they whirled, cavorted and leapt high into the air, and many of them seemed to have been seized upon by something more evil and more powerful than their own spirits, for here and there a number of them were frothing at the mouth as though about to be struck with a fit of epilepsy.

The Doctor came out and watched them for a moment, then he strode to the foul hovel which contained the four prisoners. Snatching a low cowhide whip from the wall, he laid about them with it. Unable to cry out, robbed of all their individuality and courage, they cowered away from him like four tortured animals, tears streaming from their semi-sightless eyes as he struck again and again at their shoulders, faces and legs.

'Zombies!' he panted with horrible exultation, suddenly flinging the whip aside. 'You are Zombies now! You will work fiendishly and tirelessly in my fields or at any degrading task that I may set you. For you there is no escape and no respite for many years to come. You are my slaves; and, as such, you shall labour like brute-beasts until accident or old age releases you. You have no wits, no understanding, and only a misty memory of the past: too little to recognise your fifth companion when he comes to join you. I go now, in the full knowledge of my power, to force his spirit and compel him to acknowledge that I am his master.'

De Richleau knew that there was nothing that he could do to help his friends and that his own body lay entirely at the Satanist's mercy. It was impossible for him even to begin the battle—that battle which meant so much—until the Doctor slept; and what powers the Satanist might be able to exert in the meantime was a matter which the Duke had no means of guessing. Perhaps he was already too late. Perhaps by his former cowardice he had robbed himself of all chance of being able to meet his enemy in battle on the astral.

Dismissing that awful thought which sapped his courage, he summoned all his fortitude to endure in patience the new ceremony of compulsion which his adversary was about to exercise upon his corpse, while he could only remain a helpless spectator.

22

The Great God Pan

Having returned to the sanctuary behind the altar, Doctor
Saturday stood looking down at the Duke's body while de
Richleau took up a position just above and behind his own
head.

He had never practised necromancy but he had read a
considerable amount about it so he was perfectly well
aware that his unfortunate corpse might now be subject
to all kinds of abominable treatment.

His only consolation was that he had sealed the nine
openings of his body early that afternoon so he felt
reasonably confident that the Doctor could not cause an
elemental to enter and take possession of it. But should all
the Satanist's efforts to reanimate it fail, it was quite on
the cards that in a fit of fury he would smash or sever some
vital part, thereby rendering it unfit for further service.

If he bashed in or cut off the head, or drove a knife
through the heart, stomach or liver, the effect would be
exactly the same as if his victim had blown out his own
brains before leaving for the astral, the Duke would still be
in a position to challenge the Doctor on the astral, but, even
if he had defeated the Mulatto, he would never again be
able to return to his own body.

He knew that, if only he could triumph over the Satanist,
it was really of very little moment whether he was able
to get back to his own body afterwards or not. It might
well be that his incarnation as Monseigneur le Duc de
Richleau, Knight of the Most Exalted Order of the Golden
Fleece, was now over.

It is written that each of us is allotted a certain span for every Earth life, and that no one has the power to prolong his time here for a single second; although, having free will, we may at our peril terminate our lives by suicide or, to our detriment in future lives, shorten our present existence by abuse of the body through over-indulgence in alcohol or other excesses.

If the sands of his recent incarnation *had* run out it would at least be a mighty consolation to know that by his last act of free will he had rescued his friends from their state as Zombies, even if he was unable to rejoin them; but that depended upon the outcome of the battle which he had yet to wage.

A thought which perturbed him far more than the possibility of a mortal wound being inflicted on his body was that his enemy might mutilate it. The Duke was completely powerless to lift a finger in defence of his own corpse, and there was nothing whatever to prevent the Doctor's emasculating it with a knife, cutting off the ears and the nose and putting out the eyes. If that happened, de Richleau, even if he won his astral battle afterwards, would still be compelled to return to the hideous wreck of a carcase that remained and to live on, perhaps for years, as a repulsive, shattered invalid. And that, he feared, was just the very thing that the Doctor *would* do when he had again called upon the recalcitrant spirit and it had still refused to answer.

The tall Mulatto removed his terrifying mask and great horned head-dress, then he spoke to the corpse very quietly. 'It is useless for you to continue to defy me. If you are still in your physical frame you will save yourself a very great deal of pain by sitting up at once. If you are not in your body you must be lurking not very far away and you will return to it immediately. De Richleau, I order you to answer me.'

He waited for a moment and, as no reply was forthcoming, went on: 'Very well, then; we'll soon see whether or not your spirit is in your body.'

With his long, bony fingers he untied the Duke's right shoe and removed both it and the sock. He then took a long taper of black wax from the drawer of an old carved chest at the side of the room and, lighting it, applied the flame to the sole of the bare foot.

De Richleau felt no pain whatever but he viewed the operation with considerable distress, since he knew that if he did ever return to his body he was going to find himself with an extremely nasty burn.

For a good three minutes the Mulatto held the flame under the arch of the Duke's instep, until the flesh blackened and gave off a sickly smell. Suddenly he lifted the taper and blew it out. Having replaced it in the drawer, he remarked:

'Now at least we know that it isn't that you escaped the full effects of the drug which I put in the water you drank at midday. You were clever enough to get out of your body before rigor mortis set in. However, I have no doubt whatsoever that you are close at hand listening to me, and the sooner you surrender the better it will be for you. I command you to return to your body.'

Once again he waited for a moment. When there was no response, he added: 'Since you still refuse, I must drag you back by force.'

Turning to the chest, he took from another drawer a little snakeskin bag. Opening its neck, he poured the contents on to a six-sided table and de Richleau saw that they were a collection of small bones.

The Doctor arranged the bones in a certain pattern and began to chant over them in a low voice. Almost instantly the Duke felt his astral jerk forward and downward towards the head of the corpse.

Metaphorically, de Richleau "dug his heels in" and resisted the pull, with all the strength of his will. For minutes on end the it seemed as though the back of his astral was breaking under the strain; everything went black before his astral sight and the monotonous chanting beat like thunder against his mind so that it excluded all else from his astral hearing; but somehow he managed to resist the terrific pull upon him. At last the Satanist ceased chanting and the tug on the Duke's astral stopped.

Making a gesture of annoyance, the Mulatto scooped the bones back into the bag and threw it into the chest.

For several moments he remained staring down at the body, a puzzled frown creasing his forehead. Then he said: 'I think I know why the bones failed to exert the necessary pressure on you just now. As a European you would

303

naturally not be subject to Negro magic to the same extent as if you were a coloured man. However, as I have both White and Black blood in my veins, you need not flatter yourself that you can elude me. The Ancient European magic will certainly break down your resistance. I don't think you will face for long the terror inspired by the Great God Pan.'

Going to the chest again, he selected a great variety of items and with some of them carefully erected a pentacle for his own protection. When the defence was completed he placed in its centre a small cauldron, under which he piled wood of three kinds and, with the aid of a pair of bellows, swiftly got the fire going. He then poured seven different liquids into the iron pot and waited patiently while they heated up. As soon as the mixture was brought to the boil he began to mutter an invocation, and every few minutes, after bowing to the North, to the East, to the South and to the West he cast into the bubbling froth one of the horrid things which he had taken from the chest.

As the ceremony proceeded the Duke became conscious of a terrible coldness that was now affecting him upon the astral plane, and he knew that one of the great evil entities of the Outer Circle was approaching. Very faintly at first, gradually growing lounder, he heard the sound of a flute; then quite suddenly the horned god appeared beside him.

De Richleau closed his astral eyes; he dared not look upon that face, for the sight of it in its evil beauty is said to drive men mad and to poison their spirits.

He felt his hand taken in an icy clasp and there was a gentle whispering in his ear. In vain he tried to shut his mind against it; in spite of all his efforts he felt himself being led away and carried swiftly to another sphere.

The cold decreased, the temperature became pleasantly warm again and, for some reason that he could not explain, he suddenly lost all sense of fear. Opening his eyes, he saw that he was in a woodland glade and that seated beside him on a tussock of grass was a good-looking young man with humorous, kindly eyes.

The young man smiled and said: 'You were terribly frightened, weren't you? But I'm not surprised. People have the most extraordinary ideas about me which aren't true at all. They think of Pan as the most terrifying person;

but you can see for yourself that I'm nothing of the kind. Of course, I can understand their fear of me in a way; it's entirely owing to all the slanderous lies which have been told about me by the priests of the Christian God. He's a dreary fellow, and it always amazes me that in recent centuries so many people should have chosen to follow him instead of me.'

De Richleau sat there, spellbound and quite fascinated, as the young man went on: 'It was an extraordinary piece of luck for you that the Mulatto decided to call on me. He's no mean antagonist, mind you, but he made a fatal mistake in thinking that his powers extended outside such help as he can secure from his own Voodoo gods. Naturally, as a European deity, I'm on your side—not his; so you needn't worry any more—everything's going to be quite all right.'

In spite of his first fears and suspicions de Richleau could not help feeling himself warm towards this candid and sympathetic young man. After all, when one thought about it a little it was perfectly clear that Doctor Saturday had indeed committed a most stupid blunder. The Duke, although nominally a Christian, was—apart from his unshakable belief in the Old Wisdom which teaches that each man carries God within himself—a pagan at heart. Pan was, therefore, the last entity that a Voodoo Witch Doctor should have called upon to assist him in coercing a cultured European who admired and respected the civilisation of the ancient Greeks.

'I'm so glad you're beginning to see things again in their proper perspective,' Pan remarked, evidently reading the Duke's thoughts. 'You've been through an extraordinarily wearing time with this Witch Doctor, but the fool has hoisted himself with his own petard now. You know quite a bit about sorcery yourself, so it's hardly necessary for me to remind you of the immutable law. If anyone summons an entity to do his bidding, and fails to control it, that entity is bound to turn upon the person who has called it up. I haven't the least intention of doing as the Mulatto demands and forcing you back into your body, though I could quite easily do so if I wished. Instead, I shall appear in one of my grimmer aspects to Doctor Saturday and settle his business for good and all. You will then have nothing more to fear, and when you wake up in your body you'll find the Doctor is dead.'

'What about my friends?' asked the Duke slowly.

'Oh, you needn't worry yourself about them,' replied the young-old god. 'On the Doctor's death their spirits will automatically be released.'

De Richleau sighed. 'If you really mean that you will do this I shall owe you a great debt.'

'Consider it as already paid,' smiled Pan. 'After all, I owe you something for having been, at heart, one of my followers for many incarnations past. Then there's another side to it. I know the reasons for your visit to Haiti, and, although I have many other aspects which are far more ancient, on earth I'm best known as a Greek; so we're allies you see and I'm every bit as much for putting these trouble-making humourless Dictators in their places as you are.'

'Of course,' smiled de Richleau. 'I little thought when the night began that I'd find a Greek god for an ally; but naturally you must feel that way. You were always the patron of laughter and dancing and love-making—the very antithesis of war and the dreary regimentation of young and old for which the Totalitarian leaders stand.'

At last the Duke was able to relax and take in the full beauty of the Attic scene. Blissfully he let his eyes rove over the stunted oaks, mossy banks and clearings starred with crocuses and scillas. It was a fundamental tenet of his faith that in the end the Powers of Light always trap the powers of Darkness causing them to become undone through their own evil actions; and that was what had happened to his enemy.

The ordeal had, after all, been less terrible than he had anticipated, and help had been sent to him much earlier than he could have hoped. In what had seemed his darkest hour he had been called upon to face the great god Pan, but Pan had turned out to be a friend. Doctor Saturday's fate was now sealed and a splendid victory had been won by the Powers of Light.

'Come on, then,' said Pan; 'let's get back to Haiti and put an end to your unscrupulous enemy.' And in a flick of time they were both back in the sanctuary of the Houn-fort.

The Witch Doctor was still mumbling over his cauldron and he could neither see nor hear Pan and the Duke as they arrived beside the corpse.

'Get back to your body,' Pan ordered, 'then I'll teach this impudent half-caste a lesson for daring to summon a European deity. When I appear to him he'll die of heart spasm—and that's a nasty, painful death.'

'Hadn't you better give him the heart attack first?' suggested the Duke.

'Oh no,' said Pan; 'that would never do. I should then appear to you as I appear to him, and you too would be utterly blasted with uncontrollable terror. It would affect your astral and cripple it for centuries to come; whereas if you're back in your physical body and keep your eyes shut, you won't be able to see me; so all will be well.'

De Richleau saw the incontestable sense of this, so he hesitated no longer. Thanking Pan, he slipped back into his body but remained utterly still, showing no signs of life.

Directly he had arrived he felt the stiff blood in his veins begin to uncongeal, giving him awful cramp pains; then, in spite of all his efforts to prevent it, his injured right foot twitched.

Next second he heard a silvery, derisive laugh. It did not come from the Doctor, but from Pan, and was cold, cruel, mocking. To his utter horror he realised that he had been tricked. He knew than that never for an instant should he have listened to Pan's subtle reasoning and fair promises. The deadly chill of the astral of the god's first approach should have been sufficient warning. Like a flash of light he slipped out of his body again.

Pan was still there. A frown darkened his handsome face. 'Why have you come out?' he snapped. 'Go back at once!'

De Richleau mentally shuddered, and cried: 'I refuse— I refuse!'

In a flick of time Pan's aspect changed. He had became great and terrible. The Duke strove to cover his astral sight, but could not. In desperate fear he called upon the Powers of Light to aid him.

In the instant preceding that at which de Richleau had slipped out of his body the Witch Doctor had seen the slight jerk of the foot. His face lighting up with evil triumph, he suddenly started forward. As he did so the empty eye-socket of one of the skulls dangling from his waist caught on a projection of the cauldron. The iron pot was not set quite evenly above the fire. Tipping up, it crashed over, spilling it contents upon the ground.

The Satanist gave a howl of rage. Before Pan's new aspect had reached its full degree of terror the form in which he was presenting himself suddenly quivered and disappeared. The spilling of the evil brew had broken the spell and de Richleau knew that his call for help had been answered.

For several moments the Doctor stamped, blasphemed and swore. At the very moment when victory was in his grasp his clumsiness had ruined the whole ceremony, and both he and the Duke were well aware that no man may summon Pan twice during the same night.

His astral still sweating with terror from his recent hair-breadth escape, de Richleau wondered what fresh ordeals he would have to undergo, but it seemed that for the time being the Satanist had exerted all the powers of which he was capable while still remaining on the physical plane.

When he had recovered his breath from cursing he addressed the Duke again. 'It was sheer luck that you escaped me that time. But you needn't think that you're going to get away. I have plenty of ways of subduing you directly I reach the astral.'

Having mopped up the spilt hell-broth he sprinkled some liquid upon the fire, which immediately caused it to go out, then sat down on a Witch Doctor's throne which occupied one end of the sanctuary. The back of the throne was formed from two large elephant-tusks, with their points up and curving inward, which had doubtless been imported from Africa; and the rest of it was constructed from other animal, reptile and human remains, mainly bones, teeth and skin. Two human skulls at the forward ends of the arms formed hand-rests, and although the Doctor was no longer wearing his mask and head-dress he looked a formidable figure seated there staring straight before him.

A first the Duke braced himself, believing that his enemy was about to throw himself into a trance and immediately launch an astral attack; but after a little he decided that for the time being no further call would have to be made on his powers of resistance. He was not sufficiently advanced to get right into the Satanist's mind and learn what he was thinking, but he could to some extent sense his enemy's mental condition and gradually he became aware of a thing that heartened him as nothing else had yet done —the Black Magician was worried.

Could it be, the Duke wondered, that the Satanist, knowing that all his spells had so far failed and that he must now give battle on the astral, was afraid? De Richleau hardly dared to hope that it might be so; yet what other reason could there be for his opponent's shirking an immediate settlement of the issue?

The minutes drifted by and still the Mulatto showed no sign whatever of attempting to throw himself into a self-induced trance. Instead, he presently stood up and began to walk uneasily up and down.

For over half an hour he padded back and forth like some caged animal. At last he sat down again, but only a few minutes. Then evidently having come to a decision, he put on his mask and head-dress, went outside and stood watching the wild dance of his followers which was still in progress.

Heartened still further, yet wary of some trap, de Richleau pondered upon the Doctor's actions and sought to fathom why he should apparently have abandoned the struggle, temporarily at least; but when there suddenly formed in the Duke's mind a theory that would explain his enemy's conduct it filled him with fresh perturbation.

In his present state he was definitely not dead. The fact that he had been able to enter his corpse and reanimate it, if only for a few seconds, proved that conclusively. Therefore, sooner or later the natural law would compel him to return to it whether he wanted to or not, and quite independently of the Black Magician's desire that he should do so.

His present situation was similiar to that which he had been on the last night on which he had gone out to keep watch on the Atlantic convoy. On that occasion, knowing that he could remain asleep only for a certain time, he had arranged for Simon and Marie Lou to relieve him. But now there could be no question of reliefs. When he had reached the uttermost limits of his power to remain asleep he must return; and not, this time, to a healthy body lying in the safety of a pentacle at Cardinals Folly but to the cataleptic corpse that lay below him in the sanctuary of the Voodoo Temple.

That, then, was the Satanist's new plan. He probably did not fear a conflict on the astral but simply preferred to avoid it. All he had to do was to stay awake longer than the Duke could remain in trance-sleep and the Duke would then *have* to answer the call which must result in his becoming a Zombie.

Swiftly and anxiously the Duke began to work out times. It comforted him immensely to be able to recall at once that from the moment he had left his bed in Miami he had slept no more than those bare six hours during which Simon had engaged the enemy. He had been awake for a stretch of thirty-nine hours previously to Simon's arrival, and again from half-past three the following morning until about two o'clock that afternoon—another ten and a half hours. It was now just after two a.m. so he had been in a state which must be counted as sleep for about twelve hours, but altogether he had had only some eighteen hours' sleep out of the total of sixty-seven.

Had he been called upon to face another long waking vigil his state would have been none too good, but the opposite applied now that his safety depended upon the length of time during which he could remain on the astral.

He then began to speculate upon his enemy's situation. If the Doctor had not slept since the night before the fire, he had already been awake continuously for forty-three hours. The Duke very much doubted if the Satanist had been able to get any sleep on the previous night, but the odds were that he had managed to snatch a short siesta that afternoon; yet such a respite could not have lasted more than three hours at the most. It looked as if the Doctor's position was considerably more serious than that of the Duke and that, however great his own powers as a magician, Nature could compel him to sleep before it forced the Duke back into his body.

Reassurred that the chances were at least even, de Richleau set himself to wait while he continued to watch his enemy's every move.

That night was still, warm and breathless. As a faint undertone to the Voodoo drums there came the beating of the surf on the coral strand below the nearby cliff. In the great compound, black, brown and coffee-coloured figures mingled in the ferocious dance, jerking their bodies obscenely and at times pairing to give way to unbridled licence.

The Satanist remained out there for over two hours; sometimes standing silent, sometimes urging his followers to new excesses. But by half-past three most of the devil-worshippers had satiated their lust and many, after having made obeisance to their leader, were departing to snatch a few hours' sleep before they would have to wake to face the labours of the day. By four o'clock the very last of them had gone, and the High Priest of Evil was left standing alone in the empty clearing.

For a few moments he walked to and fro, deep in thought; then he went in to stare again at the Duke's body. Having removed his mask he blinked his eyes once or twice and passed his hand over them in a weary gesture. On seeing those signs of tiredness de Richleau became still more confident that at the game they were now playing he could outlast his enemy; but his new elation was short-lived. With a sudden resolution the Satanist strode to his throne, sat down on it and again addressed him.

'You have defied my spells and by accident escaped the compulsion of Pan. If I had slept last night I would wait until Nature forced you back to obey my call; but why should I further weary myself here, when by passing to another plane I shall instantly be as fresh as a sleeper who wakes? Without the least conception of what you will be called upon to face you have asked for battle. Very well, then; you shall have it; I will come and get you.'

Throwing his head back, he raised his eyeballs until only the whites were showing, then closed his eyes. He remained like that for barely a minute, then a wisp of black smoke issued from his mouth.

De Richleau knew that for his enemy to be able to leave is body in such a manner, without his astral appearing in human form, he must be extremely powerful. Worse: the wisp of smoke had dissolved in a second so that the Duke, to his consternation, was left there without any trace of his antagonists and with no means of guessing what form the astral attack would take.

For what seemed a long time de Richleau waited, his every nerve keyed up to resist a sudden devastating assault. But nothing happened, and although he did not relax his vigilance his tension gradually eased. Then, gathering courage, he went out into the compound and called aloud:

'I am here, Saturday, ready to give battle. Why do you evade me? Is it that you are afraid?'

There was no answer to the challenge and the Duke's mind became troubled with a new anxiety. But his swift transference from the physical to the astral plane his enemy had given him the slip. In due course the Satanist would be compelled to return to his body, but that might not be for many hours, and long before he did so de Richleau would be forced to return to his. Once again it seemed that he would be undone unless he could find the Satanist and conquer him before that happened; and searching for an individual who was unwilling to meet one on the astral is like looking for a particular grain of sand on all the beaches of all the oceans of the world.

In the compound other astrals were now moving; those of some of the dwellers in the Hounfort and of other natives who were asleep in the vicinity. Most of them were 'Blacks' and shrank away at the sight of the Duke, knowing him to be their enemy and far more powerful than they; but some were merely almost blind creatures in a very low state of advancement. Presently there appeared from among those nebulous dusky shades a clear, distinct form and the Duke saw that it was the astral of his old friend with whom he had talked in China, when he had gone out to follow the Admiral.

'What are you doing here?' he exclaimed with eager interest, immensely cheered by the unexpected arrival of his powerful friend.

'I came to see how you were getting on,' replied the other. 'You're looking a bit worn, so I imagine you've been having a pretty hard time of it.'

De Richleau sighed and, rallying himself, swiftly related what had happened, then he described the critical situation in which he now found himself.

His friend immediately expressed sympathy and promised his aid. 'I'll tell you, though, what we ought to do,' he said. 'There's little to choose between us in the matter of spiritual strength, as we're both almost equally advanced upon the great journey. Either of us could, I feel certain, hold the adversary at bay for a few moments, and both of us together could overcome him. He may be able to remain in hiding away from his body for twenty hours, or even more, so the best way to arrange matters would be for me to watch while you rest. Sooner or later this Devil Doctor must appear; then I will immediately call you, and with our united strength we will defeat him.'

This plan seemed an excellent one to de Richleau, and on his friend asking how long he had been asleep, he replied:

'It was about two o'clock yesterday afternoon when I put myself into a self-induced trance, so I've done over fourteen hours.'

'That's a fair time,' mused his friend, 'so I think you'd better take a spell now and leave me to hold the fort until I can get your help should the enemy suddenly put in an appearance.'

It was now more than two hours since the Duke had been lured into returning to his body by Pan but the narrowness of his escape was still fresh in his mind. There was nothing unnatural in his friend's having come to look for him, as spirits that are linked by the bonds of love have little difficulty in ascertaining each other's whereabouts, yet the very suggestion that he should return again to his body put him instantly upon his guard. As he thought of it there formed in his mind a definite conviction that he *was not meant* to receive help from gods or men. It was *his* battle—and he must fight it unaided.

In turning to thank his friend but to tell him that he had decided to see the business through alone, he suddenly realised that the other was wearing the shovel hat of a priest, the brim of which cast a shadow over his eyes.

On an impulse which seemed to come from right outside himself, he grabbed the brim of the hat and tore it off. Then he knew that the thing he had suspected, only in that last second as his arm had shot out, was true. A powerful astral may assume the form of any human, perfecting its resemblance to the last hair and wrinkle; it can also copy a voice to the fraction of a tone; but it cannot change its eyes. The eyes of the astral before him were not those of his friend—they were those of Doctor Saturday.

Instantly the Doctor changed his appearance and be became the big Negro in which form the Duke had first seen him on that night when he and Marie Lou had hunted him back, over the Atlantic, to Haiti.

The Negro made no gesture of defence or attack. He only smiled and spoke through his spirit.

'Congratulations, my friend. You have passed every test. I am proud to have the honour to be selected as your opponent.'

De Richleau spoke sternly. 'You admit your defeat and are prepared to surrender to me?'

The other only laughed and said: 'There is no occasion for that, since I have done no more than play my part in a trial that was ordered to test your courage. You have come out of it with flying colours, and when you get back to Earth you will wake with all your friends, safe and sound in the launch, to find that your more recent experiences have been no more than a dream. The burial ceremony that you witnessed, the ghoulish rites and the happenings at the Hounfort occurred after you had left your body. They did not, in fact, take place at all—they were only scenes created in your mind by the Great Ones who have power, as you know, to make us Lesser Ones believe in the reality of anything which they care to present to us.'

Slowly de Richleau shook his head. 'That will not do. If such a trial as you suggest had been planned for me, and I had passed through it successfully, the Great Ones would not have sent the personality whom they had chosen to act as my adversary in the test to inform me of my victory.'

The Negro shrugged his big shoulders. 'I am only obeying orders and, personally, I'm not surprised that you're somewhat sceptical; but even caution can be overdone. It may be that this is yet another test. Of course, if you refuse to believe me, that is your affair; but I shall be extremely sorry for you, because the maintenance of such pig-headedness against an obvious acceptance of the known law will bring you into great peril.'

'Why?' asked the Duke in a hard voice.

'Because, my poor friend, although you don't appear to realise it, in your desperate endeavour to escape—as you thought—being turned into a Zombie you are at the moment in the process of committing suicide.'

'Your statement needs a little explanation,' said the Duke, but as he spoke he already had a vague and disquieting presentiment as to the other's meaning.

'Consider your situation for a moment,' the Negro went on quietly. 'Because you feared to die, by an act of your own will you threw yourself into a self-induced trance and left your body before the poison could affect you. There would be no harm in that if you intended to return to it; but apparently you refuse to do so; and if you fail to return your body must then obviously decompose until it is no longer fit for use as a human garment. You will then, arbitrarily and by your own act, have brought about the end of your recent incarnation. Can you deny that such a course would be suicide?'

'No,' the Duke admitted, and he saw at once that he was now between the devil and the deep sea. If for their own good reasons the Great Ones had indeed put him through a very severe test, it had obviously been their intention that he should become a Zombie and pay off some past debt in that form. But he had evaded that, and to do so he had virtually committed suicide: the worst sin against the spirit of which any individual can be guilty.

If, having been warned, he now failed to return to his body, for hundred of years he would suffer the penalty of living over and over again the awful hours through which he had passed since leaving the launch. Innumerable times he would again feel the same helplessness and misery as when he had seen his friends buried, and the same fear and horror that he had experienced while he had watched by his corpse in the sanctuary behind the altar. On the other hand, to go back now, whatever the astral who was talking to him might say—be it good or bad—seemed to him to be an act of surrender.

With a colossal effort he made up his mind, and said firmly: 'This test is beyond my judgment; but it is not beyond my will. Even if I suffer the penalties of suicide for countless years to come, I still refuse to re-enter my body.'

315

The Negro's eyes flickered and fell. In that instant the Duke knew that his decision had been right. Launching himself forward, he hurled himself upon his adversary at the second that the evil entity turned to flee. Suddenly he felt an enormous surge of new power rise up in him, and with a shout of triumph he streaked away in pursuit.

The Adversary climbed to the third plane; the Duke hurtled after him. Their progress slowed but they managed to stagger through the fourth and reached the fifth. This was the highest that de Richleau had ever achieved as a mortal man; the strain of remaining there was terrible for both of them. The Duke felt crushed, breathless, bewildered, blinded, but his enemy was in an even worse plight, and, gasping with fear, dropped like a plummet, straight down to Earth.

The Duke pursued him now with tireless vigour; as though filled with the very essence of Light from his recent nearness to the great Beatitudes. They were back in the compound of the Hounfort, the Satanist was crouching on the ground, whimpering like a stricken animal; while de Richleau towered above him, a brilliant, glowing being surrounded by a great aura of iridescent, pulsing flame.

'Mercy!' screamed the Priest of Evil. 'Mercy, mercy!' But de Richleau's heart was hard as agate and he drove the miserable wretch headlong into the sanctuary.

'Into your body!' ordered the Duke.

For a moment the Satanist made one last desperate effort, rising up again, black and formidable; but de Richleau struck him down by the power of his will. The astral wailed in utter fear and suddenly dissolved. As it did so the eyes of Doctor Saturday's mortal body flickered open.

'Well done!' said a silvery voice which the Duke recognised, yet without fear, as Pan's. 'That which I did before I was constrained to do by his enchantments; but now I will gladly do that which I promised; you have but to command me.'

'Appear to him!' cried de Richleau, in ringing tones.

Then, as the Duke hid his eyes under a glowing shield of light which now formed at his instant will, Pan materialised in all his awful glory.

With a screech that rang through the night the Witch Doctor leapt to his feet and dashed from the Voodoo temple; but de Richleau speed, like a Hound of Heaven, on his heeels.

Dawn was breaking as the Satanist, barefooted, raced across the compound and out on to the road beyond. His eyes were bulging in his head, his body was sweating with terror. As he fled he screamed wild imprecations and tore, with the gestures of a madman, at the heavy, ceremonial trappings which he was still adorned.

In a few moments he had wrenched off his necklaces, which seemed to choke him, and was tearing his body with his nails as he sought to snap the belt that held up his short, full skirt.

Suddenly it gave way, and as the skirt slid down to his knees he tripped and fell. Wriggling out of it, he sprang to his feet and raced on, now stark naked. Twenty yards further on he swerved, leapt on to a bank and began to run down its far side. It was very steep and ended in a cliff that dropped sheer a hundred fcct to the sea. Like the Gadarene swine, the Satanist plunged down the slope until he stumbled and fell again; then he rolled, pitching from tussock to tussock of the coarse grass until, a raving lunatic, he pitched over the cliff and hurtled downwards, his arms and legs whirling, to be dashed to pieces on the rocks below.

De Richleau hovered there until the spirit came forth from the mangled body. It was now quiet and submissive, with no more fight left in it. Since it had already been defeated on the astral, there was no need to take advantage of the momentary black-out which succeeds death to seize and chain it. Humbly it opened wide its arms and bowed its head in token of surrender. At the Duke's call two Guardians of the Light appeared and as they led the captive away a triumphant fanfare of trumpets filled the air.

■   ■   ■   ■   ■

When de Richleau got back to his own body he found it in poor shape. It was still suffering from the effect of the toxin which had passed into it with the water which they had drunk many hours before, but he forced it to obey him and crawled out of the sanctuary to the squalid hut into which his friends had been cast.

They, too, were still heavy and leaden from the drug that had thrown them into a cataleptic state, but by the law of the Timeless Ones, with the surrender of the Satanist the spirits of his captives had been released. Consciousness had just returned to them. They knew one another again, and when de Richleau appeared they knew that he had been victorious.

After·half an hour they had recovered sufficiently to leave the hut. Some of the natives in the compound were setting about their early-morning tasks, and when they saw the little party walk forth, with their sight and voices unimpaired, they fled in terror.

It was a sore, weary, crippled group that limped along the road until they came upon a Negro who agreed to give them a lift in his market-cart down to the British Consulate in Port-au-Prince. There, de Richleau felt, they would be safe from any unwelcome attentions which their reappearance in the town might cause, and, if necessary, cables could be sent to Sir Pellinore, who would use all the power and prestige of Britain to ensure them a safe conduct out of Haiti back to the United States.

It was Simon who remarked, as the cart jogged on in the early-morning light: 'I wonder if the Nazis will be able to find another Black·Magician powerful enough to carry on Doctor Saturday's work?'

'I doubt it,' replied the Duke; 'otherwise they would never, in the first place, have utilised an occultist who was living as far away as Haiti.'

'Then can we take it that we've broken the Nazi menace on the astral?' murmured Marie Lou.

De Richleau smiled but sadly shook his head. 'No, no, Princess. That will never cease until Totalitarianism in all its forms is destroyed root and branch. Whether or not Hitler and Mussolini themselves are great masters of Black Magic, nobody can possibly contest that it is through such ambitious and unscrupulous men, German, Italian *and* Japanese, that the Powers of Darkness are working and in recent years have acquired such a terrifying increase of strength upon our earth.

'The New World Order which they wish to bring about

is but another name for Hell. If through them Evil prevailed, every man and woman of every race and colour would finally be enslaved, from the cradle to the grave. They would be brought up to worship might instead of right and would be taught to condone, or even praise, murder, torture and the suppression of all liberty as "necessary" to the welfare of "the State".

'Incontestable proof of that has already been given us by the way in which the young Nazi-educated Germans have behaved in Poland, Czechoslovakia, Norway, Holland, Belgium and France. They butchered old men, women and children who did not even seek to oppose them. That was part of the Plan, and they obeyed the order to commit these murders in cold blood without a single recorded instance of any protest against them by officers or men. Seven years of the Totalitarian poison has been enough for the Evil to grip five million German youths and with it their hearts have gone cold and stony. If they triumph, within seventy years such words as justice, toleration, freedom and compassion will have ceased to have a place in the vocabularies of the races of mankind.

'In the New World Order all family life will be at an end, except for the conquerors, and only the worst elements, spiritually, will be allowed to procreate fresh generations to populate a world divided into masters and slaves. The right to homes and children of their own would be reserved to the Overlords; the rest would be herded into barracks and reduced to the level of robots without the right to read or speak or even think for themselves. There could be no revolt, because every officer, priest, deputy, editor, magistrate, writer and other leader of free thought and action in the conquered countries would already have been executed by the firing-squads; and leaderless herds cannot prevail against tanks, tear-gas, bombs and machine-guns.

'And unless men are free how can they progress upon the great spiritual journey which all must make?

'This war is not for territory or gain or glory, but that Armageddon which was prophesied of old. That is why all the Children of Light, wherever they may be, captive or free, must hold on to their spiritual integrity as never before and must stick at nothing, physically, in the fight, lest

319

the whole world fall under the domination of these puppets who are animated by the Powers of Darkness.'

As he ceased speaking they knew that although it would be many days before their burns, weals and wounds were healed there had come into their hearts a little glow of warmth. The Battle was still far from being over, but they had done the thing which they had set out to do. Their Victory was an episode—no more—in the Titanic struggle that was in progress, but the flame which animated their spirits was burning all the brighter for it, and they were returning to fight on for the England that they loved.

It seemed that the Duke guessed their thoughts, for he spoke again. 'As long as Britain stands the Powers of Darkness cannot prevail. On Earth the Anglo-Saxon race is the last Guardian of the Light, and I have an unshakable conviction that, come what may, our island will prove the Bulwark of the World.'

If you would like a complete list of Arrow books please send a postcard to
P.O. Box 29, Douglas, Isle of Man, Great Britain.